Books by David Wood

The Dane Maddock Adventures
Dourado
Cibola
Quest
Icefall
Buccaneer
Atlantis
Ark
Xibalba
Loch (forthcoming)

Dane and Bones Origins
Freedom (with Sean Sweeney)
Hell Ship (with Sean Ellis)
Splashdown (with Rick Chesler)
Dead Ice (with Steven Savile)
Liberty (with Edward G. Talbot)
Electra (with Rick Chesler)
Amber (with Rick Chesler)
Justice (with Edward G. Talbot)
Treasure of the Dead (with Rick Chesler)

The Jade Ihara Adventures
Oracle (with Sean Ellis)
Changeling (with Sean Ellis)

The Myrmidon Files
Destiny (with Sean Ellis)
Mystic (with Sean Ellis)

Bones Bonebrake Adventures
Primitive
The Book of Bones

Stand-Alone Works
Arena of Souls- A Brock Stone Adventure
Into the Woods (with David S. Wood)
Primordial (with Alan Baxter)
Callsign: Queen (with Jeremy Robinson)
Dark Rite (with Alan Baxter)
The Zombie-Driven Life
You Suck

David Wood writing as David Debord

The Absent Gods
The Silver Serpent
Keeper of the Mists
The Gates of Iron

The Impostor Prince (with Ryan A. Span)

Neptune's Key (forthcoming)

Books by Sean Ellis

Mira Raiden Adventures
Ascendant
Descendant

The Nick Kismet Thrillers
The Shroud of Heaven
Into the Black
The Devil You Know
Fortune Favors

The Adventures of Dodge Dalton
In the Shadow of Falcon's Wings
At the Outpost of Fate
On the High Road to Oblivion

MYSTIC

An Adventure from the Myrmidon Files

The pattern emerges….

A series of unexplained deaths are only a harbinger of the apocalypse to come. A mysterious figure who calls himself 'the Immortal' is plotting the destruction of the global economy, and only Tam Broderick and her CIA task force—the Myrmidons—can stop it.

But when the Immortal sends his followers on a quest to retrieve a medieval relic alleged to have mystical powers, the pattern becomes less clear. Is this a ruse to throw the Myrmidons off the trail? Or is the relic the key to the Immortal's ingenious plan?

Action and thrills abound in this exciting sequel to Destiny!

Praise for David Wood and the Myrmidon Files

"An action-packed, globe-spanning treasure hunt of an adventure by David Wood and Sean Ellis. Destiny hits all the right beats—full of historical mysteries and intriguing what-ifs—to keep the pages turning fast, with a satisfying and thrilling payout that you won't soon forget." **David Sakmyster, author of *The Pharos Objective* and *Jurassic Dead***

"With an adrenaline-fueled search for an ancient relic with mystical powers and the introduction of a new powerhouse team, the Myrmidons, to set matters right, get ready for a new pulse-pounding adventure series brimming with action and intrigue!" **Rick Jones, bestselling author of the *Vatican Knights* series**

"Rip roaring action from start to finish. Wit and humor throughout. Just one question - how soon until the next one? Because I can't wait."
-Graham Brown, author of *Shadows of the Midnight Sun*

"What an adventure! A great read that provides lots of action, and thoughtful insight as well, into strange realms that are sometimes best left unexplored." -Paul Kemprecos, author of *Cool Blue Tomb* and the *NUMA Files*

"A page-turning yarn blending high action, Biblical speculation, ancient secrets, and nasty creatures. Indiana Jones better watch his back!" -Jeremy Robinson, author of *SecondWorld*

"With the thoroughly enjoyable way Mr. Wood has mixed speculative history with our modern day pursuit of truth, he has created a story that thrills and makes one think beyond the boundaries of mere fiction and enter the world of 'why not'?" -David Lynn Golemon, Author of the *Event Group* series

"A twisty tale of adventure and intrigue that never lets up and never lets go!" -Robert Masello, author of *The Einstein Prophecy*

"Let there be no confusion: David Wood is the next Clive Cussler. Once you start reading, you won't be able to stop until the last mystery plays out in the final line."-Edward G. Talbot, author of *2012: The Fifth World*

"I like my thrillers with lots of explosions, global locations and a mystery where I learn something new. Wood delivers! Recommended as a fast paced, kick ass read."-J.F. Penn, author of *Desecration*

Against the Fall of Eternal Night

Chess Team/Jack Sigler Thrillers
(with Jeremy Robinson)
Callsign: King
Underworld
Blackout
Prime
Savage
Cannibal

The Jade Ihara Adventures
Oracle (with David Wood)
Changeling (with David Wood)

Other Works

Magic Mirror
WarGod (with Steven Savile)
Hell Ship (with David Wood)
Flood Rising (with Jeremy Robinson)
Herculean (with Jeremy Robinson)
The Prisoner
Camp Zero

MYSTIC

AN ADVENTURE FROM THE MYRMIDON FILES

DAVID WOOD
SEAN ELLIS

Adrenaline Press

MYSTIC- AN ADVENTURE FROM THE MYRMIDON FILES

Copyright 2017 by David Wood
All rights reserved under International and Pan-American copyright conventions.

Published by Adrenaline Press
www.adrenaline.press

Published by Gryphonwood Press
www.gryphonwoodpress.com

No part of this book may be reproduced or transmitted in any form or any means, electronic or mechanical, including photocopying, recording or by any information storage and retrieval system, without the written permission of the Publisher, except where permitted by law.

This book is a work of fiction. All names, characters, places and incidents are the product of the author's imagination, or are used fictitiously. Any resemblance to actual events or persons is entirely coincidental.

ISBN-10: 1-940095-67-0
ISBN-13: 978-1-940095-67-7

PROLOGUE—THE LAST

West Berlin, Germany—1987

They called him the loneliest man in the world.

He found that amusing. Loneliness was not the same thing as being alone, and in any cases, he was not truly alone. He had not known the peace of true solitude for many years, but here in his little summer house in the middle of the courtyard, he could at least enjoy the illusion of privacy.

He had been the only resident for more than twenty years, and yet he was never alone. Prisoners were never truly alone.

Although the century-old fortress had at one time imprisoned six hundred inmates, after Hitler's defeat and the Nuremberg Trials, it was reserved for just seven—men like himself who were found guilty of war crimes and sentenced to prison terms rather than the gallows. Of the seven, three had been released early for humanitarian reasons, and three had served out their full terms, leaving only him. Prisoner number seven. The last.

The post-war division of authority between the four Allied powers—America, Britain, France, and the USSR—ensured that no one government would be given total control of the prisoner, which meant that every month, a new set of jailers would arrive. The Soviets were the worst, not merely denying him simple pleasures but subjecting him to harsh and humiliating treatment—the Russians had made an art form of imprisonment—but he needed to endure their presence only for three months out of the year.

As time passed and the memory of what Hitler's armies had done in Stalingrad gradually faded, the Russians seemed more interested in gaining access to West Berlin for purposes of espionage than in making him suffer. The others, particularly the Americans, were far more sympathetic or at least purported to be. Some of them claimed to be part of a new international movement, dedicated to the same philosophy as he—they called themselves 'the Dominion'—but he was wary of their overtures. It had the feel of a trap.

He was always suspicious of kindness. The Russians, with their brutality, were far more honest.

Aside from his prison guards, he saw many other people—doctors, psychiatrists, interrogators, and even political leaders.

No, he was never alone.

He had been at his loneliest during those early years, when he was forced to share the ordeal of imprisonment with the others. He despised them all and was grateful when the last of them were set free. Of course, by that time, he was an old man, sick, in constant pain, but things were easier now that he was by himself. He could read, watch movies and television, putter about in the garden if it pleased him. The guards no longer even bothered to lock him in a cell at night. Best of all, the dreams no longer haunted him as they once had.

There were worse ways to spend the gloaming of his life. He was ninety-three years old; his sentence would soon be over.

He settled into his chair, opened the book and began to write.

Writing, he had discovered, was the only way to find peace, to purge himself of the visions.

"*Guten tag, mein herr.*"

The prisoner looked up in surprise and alarm. He had not realized that he was not alone. It took a moment for his old eyes to focus, and even then he could not make out the face of the man standing in the shadows. "*Wer bist du?*"

The man took a step forward, out of the darkness. He was young, but then everyone looked young to the prisoner. The man's face was no more recognizable that his voice. "Forgive me," he said in English. "That's the extent of my German, but I understand you speak English?"

"You are American?"

The man returned a wry smile. "By birth, if that's what you mean."

"A curious distinction. Who are you? Why are you here?"

The stranger did not answer right away but continued advancing until he was standing right in front of the prisoner, then reached down and snatched the book from the latter's hands. He turned it and began flipping idly through the pages.

"What?" The prisoner's confusion only deepened. "You have come for my diaries? I don't understand."

"Neither do I," the man replied. He gave a harsh brittle-sounding laugh. "I can't read German, either."

He closed the book abruptly, slamming it shut with a noise like a gunshot. "Tonight, your sentence—your *life* sentence—ends."

He raised a hand, made a "come along" gesture, and another figure emerged from a different corner of the little room. The second man wore the uniform of a prison guard, but the prisoner did not recognize his face. The ersatz guard circled around behind his chair and knelt down, out of the prisoner's view.

His reading lamp abruptly flickered off. The guard had just pulled the plug.

Late afternoon sunlight still streamed in through the windows, but the removal of the artificial light plunged the room into deep gloom. The man in the guard's uniform did not reappear but stayed behind the prisoner.

His mental faculties were no longer as sharp as they once were, but he knew what was happening. "You don't need to do this," he pleaded. "I'm an old man. I will be dead soon enough."

The stranger shook his head. "No. Not soon enough. That's the rub. No one believed you would live as long as you have. The bleeding hearts are crying for your release on humanitarian grounds, and their voices are growing ever louder. They would set you free to die with your family at your bedside. That cannot happen, you understand. The world must never hear what you have to say about the real reasons for that war." He leaned closer. "I've always been curious about something though. Why did you do it? Why did you turn yourself over to the British? What made you do it?"

The prisoner pursed his lips together, shook his head. "It was a mistake. One that I've paid for dearly. Half my life—forty years—wasted because I read the signs wrong."

"The signs? What signs?" The young man held up the diary. "Is the answer in here? Tell me."

"It doesn't matter. There is no good answer," the prisoner insisted. "I was a fool."

The man regarded him a moment longer, then straightened and looked away, nodding to his unseen accomplice.

The reality of what was about to happen settled fully upon the old man, filling him with dread. There had been so many times during the long years of his sentence when he had longed for this release, but now, with the end in sight, he was terrified. "Please. I don't want to die."

Something brushed past the old man's face, a loop of rope or wire...

It was the electrical cord, he realized, as the makeshift noose tightened around his throat, cutting off the flow of blood to his brain. The plunge into darkness was so swift he didn't even think to claw at the garroting wire.

He did not hear the final whispered words of the stranger standing before him. "No one ever does."

ONE

Connecticut—Present Day

As he did every weekday, and most Saturdays too, Thom Martiel left his office on the twenty-eighth floor of 30 Hudson Street in Jersey City at about eight-thirty p.m. He went across the street to the parking garage, got in his gold 2017 Lexus IS sedan, and began the sixty-odd mile commute to his suburban home in New Canaan, Connecticut. Sometimes he left later, on rare occasion earlier, but never before eight-fifteen p.m.

Martiel stayed this late to monitor the opening of the Hong Kong stock market, which would set the tone for trading the following day, or so he claimed, but most of his co-workers believed there was a simpler explanation. Martiel was either a workaholic, with no other purpose in life but to work and earn money, or he was ruthlessly ambitious, waiting for that golden, once-in-a-lifetime opportunity that would propel him into the upper echelons of the investment banking world.

The latter seemed less likely. Martiel did not exactly ooze enthusiasm for his job even though he appeared to do it well. In any case, as far as anyone knew, Martiel was a content bachelor. He was sociable but showed little inclination to socialize, at least with his co-workers. What he did after leaving the office was anyone's guess, but given that he spent fourteen hours of every day at work—most of it behind his desk, except for the forty-five minutes a day he spent in the on-site fitness room—and another three behind the wheel of the Lexus, commuting to and from work, it was reasonable to assume that he probably spent the balance of his time sleeping.

He had done this every workday for the last two years, give or take a few weeks, which was the length of time he had been an executive account manager at Silver

Investment Bank, Inc. It could only be assumed that he had followed a similar practice at his prior place of employment, but none of his coworkers really knew for certain.

From the parking garage, he headed north to the Holland Tunnel, through it to the island of Manhattan, and then, for no discernable reason, turned up the Henry Hudson Parkway—some days he took the FDR instead—and headed north to Mount Vernon. From there, he picked up the Hutchinson River Parkway, which became Connecticut SR-15 when he crossed over the state line. The four-lane divided highway wended up the middle of the Connecticut Panhandle and continued on to Hartford. The further he got from the New York City metropolitan area, the fewer cars shared the road with him.

Martiel had just rounded the bend at Putnam Lake when he noticed headlights in the rear-view mirror, approaching fast. This was not particularly unusual. He always maintained a discreet sixty-eight miles an hour using cruise control, but that was too slow for most drivers on the open road. He stayed in the right lane but monitored the other vehicle's progress as it closed the gap.

The car was in the same lane as he, coming up fast enough to make him shift nervously in his seat. He turned off the satellite radio, which was playing light classical music, and sat up a little straighter, readying himself for a little defensive driving in the event that the other driver didn't change lanes to go around. He relaxed a little when, just a hundred or so yards behind him, he saw the car swerve into the left lane. A moment later, it blew past him like he was parked in his driveway and raced ahead, toward the old North Street overpass. He couldn't distinguish make or model—only that it was a silver sedan.

Martiel shook his head but stayed alert. There were more headlights in the distance behind him, and they too appeared to be getting closer.

Without any warning, seemingly without reason, the silver sedan swerved right, straddling the dashed line separating the lanes, and then the road ahead was bathed in the bright red glow of brake lights. The car was suddenly no longer a moving vehicle accelerating away from him, but an obstacle, partially blocking both lanes directly in front of Martiel.

Because he was still in a heightened state of awareness, Martiel did not give in to the reflexive urge to swerve or stomp on the brakes. Instead, with almost preternatural calm, he tapped the brakes, disengaging the cruise control, releasing the Lexus from constant acceleration, and turned the wheel ever so slightly to the right. As he did, he saw directly ahead of him, the upright stone buttress supporting the overpass.

Despite the sudden braking maneuver, the silver sedan had not come to a complete stop but was slowing, giving up the last of its momentum. In an instant, Martiel saw that he would not be able to get around the other car before he reached the overpass, which was no doubt the other driver's intent. The person behind the wheel of the silver sedan had intended for him to swerve into the abutment.

In a rush of understanding, Thom Martiel knew that the other driver was trying to kill him. He did not allow himself to dwell on the question of motive. The other driver's purpose was plain enough, so the only thing Martiel needed to concern himself with was staying alive.

He had nowhere to go, but as he looked ahead, Martiel saw that there was just enough room between the stone corner and the sedan for him to pass, provided the other driver didn't anticipate the move and attempt to narrow the gap.

Realizing that the killer might do exactly that, Martiel stomped down on the accelerator. The 241 horsepower turbo-charged engine roared, and the computer controlled eight-speed automatic transmission immediately downshifted, giving him all the on-demand power he needed. The Lexus surged forward like a rocket. Martiel gripped the steering wheel as if hanging on for dear life, and kept the car moving straight, threading the needle, and just like that he was through.

As he emerged on the far side of the overpass, Martiel eased off the accelerator a little, but then just as quickly resumed applying steady pressure, pushing the car as fast as he dared. A glance in the rear-view confirmed his suspicions that the silver sedan was moving again. Chasing him.

He searched his memory of the road, trying to think of a way to elude his pursuer. The next turn-off was a good three miles away which, given his current speed, he would reach in less than two minutes, but first, he would have to negotiate a long sweeping bend in the road. In fact, he was practically there. Martiel glanced at the speedometer. He was pushing ninety. During his regular commute, he took the curve without making any adjustment to his speed, but he was going a lot faster now, faster than he'd ever driven.

A mistake at this speed would be catastrophic, but he didn't dare slow down. Not with the headlights in the rear-view getting closer with each passing second. He had outwitted the would-be killer once, but that had been luck as much as anything. He did not think he would be so lucky the next time.

Gripping the wheel again and gritting his teeth, he plowed ahead into the curve, hugging the outside of the right lane. Alarms sounded and indicator lights flashed, warning him, as if such a warning were needed, that he was going too fast, pulling too many Gs.

But now there were two sets of headlights, almost side-by-side, in the rear-view.

Gritting his teeth, he shifted his foot to the brake pedal, applying steady pressure as he went into the turn. The car slid dangerously close to the wooden guard rail, but the car's dynamic integrated safety systems compensated for his flawed human reflexes, keeping the Lexus on the road and in his control.

But he was slowing down. And the headlights behind him were getting closer.

He kept his eyes on the road ahead. Once the curve was behind him, he could open it up again. And the cars chasing him would have to slow down as well.

A few seconds later, the road straightened, and Martiel checked the rear-view.

He was partly right. One of the cars seemed to be falling back, slowing down even before reaching the bend. This was an illusion, however. It wasn't that the trailing vehicle was slowing down, but rather that the lead vehicle was going faster. The headlights were approaching so rapidly that, if he hadn't known better, Martiel would have believed that it was actually a low flying jet fighter.

No way was he was going to outrun them.

His heart began pounding. The exit was still a good fifteen seconds away, and he was going way too fast to take it. But if he slowed down…

Suddenly, it didn't matter anymore. The pursuit car sidled up alongside him and then slowed to match his speed. He glanced over and saw, not the silver sedan, but a fire engine red muscle car. A flicker of light from inside the other car drew his attention to the passenger window.

He flinched a little when he saw the face staring back at him.

A black person. A black woman.

She was pointing at him.

He flinched again, thinking, *Gun!*

But there was no gun.

He pushed the gas pedal down again anyway, pulling away from the red car, just in case. The speedometer jumped up to eighty. Eighty-five. Ninety-five. The exit flashed past. Martiel couldn't remember how far it was to the next one.

Suddenly, the red car was beside him again. He looked over and saw the woman, both hands raised.

Why's she doing that? Martiel wondered.

The woman made a rolling gesture with one finger, and then one of the two panes of glass separating them began to lower. The woman's face scrunched up as the rush of air assaulted her, but she continued looking over at him, repeating the gesture and shouting something into the wind.

Martiel looked ahead again, focusing on keeping the Lexus from veering into the other car or running off the road, as he struggled to make sense of this development.

Maybe the people in the red car didn't want to kill him after all. Curious despite himself, he stabbed the button to lower his window.

Noise and air rushed in, momentarily blinding him. The wind and the roar of the muscle car's engine were almost deafening, but over the tumult, he could just make out the sound of the woman's voice. He distinctly heard her say the words "save you" and "move over."

Move over?

He looked down at the speedometer. He was doing seventy-five.

He turned to look over at the woman, drawing in the breath he would need to shout back at her, but the question never got past his lips.

The woman was climbing out the window of the red car. She reached out, gripped the door frame of the Lexus, and pulled herself closer to Martiel.

Suddenly, her hand was on the steering wheel next to his, her face only inches from his own. And she was shouting. "Move! Now!"

TWO

The banker—Martiel—stared at her, paralyzed with fear or incredulity.

That was bad.

Tam Broderick didn't need him paralyzed with anything. She was committed to making the transfer between the two speeding vehicles, and if he didn't get out of the way...

She didn't want to think about what would happen.

"Tam!" The shout came from behind her, from Billy Sievers behind the wheel of the red Mustang. He must have been screaming at the top of his lungs in order to make himself heard. "Go! Now!"

She knew Sievers wouldn't waste her time with an unnecessary warning, so she took him at his word. "Coming through!" she called out and then heaved herself forward.

Martiel yelped as she landed in his lap. Tam could feel the Lexus decelerating.

"Punch it!" she yelled. "I'll steer."

The Lexus coasted for another second or two, but then the car began speeding up again. She cocked her head sideways so she could see out the windshield. Given Sievers' warning, she expected to see an obstacle or a curve ahead, but the road—as much of it as she could see by the Lexus's high-beams—was as straight as an arrow. By some miracle, the car was still traveling straight down the outside lane.

Must have perfect alignment, she thought, and then wondered if maybe the vehicle was equipped with some kind of computer-assisted smart-steering technology.

That would definitely increase her chances of surviving the next fifteen seconds.

In the corner of her eye, she saw the red Mustang

falling back. She hoped that meant Billy was going to drop back, run interference with the other car.

She twisted around, tried slipping her legs over his knees and under the steering wheel. There wasn't quite enough room to make it work.

"Keep your foot on the gas," she shouted. "And roll up the damn window!"

She made a mental note to drop a dollar in the swear jar but figured it was worth it when the window rose, shutting out the incessant rush of wind and immersing them in blessed silence.

Tam took a deep breath, let it out, took another. "All right, Mr. Martiel, here's what you're going to do. Unbuckle your seatbelt and recline your seat back. I'm going to get my foot on the gas pedal. Once I do, you're going to slide backward, into the back seat so I can take over. If you do that, we just might make it out of this alive. Can you do all that?"

The unusually long pause seemed all the more surreal in the perfectly quiet interior of the luxury sedan. Finally, Martiel, a look of bewilderment painting his face, said, "Who the hell are you?"

Billy Sievers watched the needle on the temperature gauge, silently pleading with it to tick back down. He'd pushed the old GT a little too hard, ran the nitrous a touch longer than he probably should have, and now he was paying the price. The engine was ticking like crazy, misfiring and probably cooking oil. In his mind's eye, he could see the valves disintegrating, the rods snapping like Milk Bone dog biscuits, the block glowing red hot like a furnace. It was a wonder it hadn't seized already.

"Come on, baby," he whispered. "Don't blow up on me. I promise to take good care of you."

He loved the car, a 1968 GT Mustang that he was still in the process of restoring. Sure it had some miles on it, but it was a *car*—a real car, not some computerized rolling robot like the Lexus. And it was his.

Trailing Martiel had been easy enough, but when the joker in the silver Toyota sedan had made his move, Martiel had rabbited. By the time Sievers and Tam had figured out what was happening, the Lexus was almost a mile away, and Sievers had been obliged to red-line the GT's engine just to catch up so Tam could transfer to Martiel's car…which was, in Billy Sievers's opinion, just about the craziest thing he had ever seen anyone do.

It was actually kind of hot.

He shook his head, trying to purge that thought. Tam was the boss, and he actually liked working for her CIA task force—the Myrmidons—even if some of the gigs were pretty out there. It didn't pay as well as contract work, but for the first time in a long time, he felt like he was one of the good guys.

Tam had still been half-inside the GT when the engine started ticking and rattling, and Sievers had known right then that if he didn't slow down—and fast—the engine would blow and slowing down wouldn't be a choice anymore.

If that had happened while Tam was in mid-transfer, she would probably have been ripped in half. She'd made it, though, and now he was coasting ahead in neutral, hoping that when the engine cooled, he'd be able to cripple the GT to a garage and get her back to working order in a few hours. He definitely wasn't going to be able to catch up to the Lexus.

He could see its taillight growing smaller in the distance. He could also see the lights of the silver Toyota that had just blown past him in pursuit.

"It's all you now, Tam."

Once Martiel was out of the way, and Tam had the seat returned to its upright position and scooted forward—which turned out to be a lot more complicated than she would have ever imagined—she gave the bank executive the answers he had demanded.

Sort of.

"Someone's trying to kill you," she started.

"Are you one of them?"

She pursed her lips, checked the rear-view mirror. Something told her that the headlights coming up behind them did not belong to Sievers' GT. "I'm trying to save you."

"Why? I mean, why are they trying to kill me?"

She glanced over at him. "I was hoping you'd be able to tell me that."

"What?" Martiel gazed back, goggle-eyed.

"No? Nothing?" She checked the mirror again. The pursuit car didn't appear to be getting any closer. Sievers had only been able to catch up to Martiel by switching on the NOS and running at full burn for almost two minutes. Judging by the torrent of profanity that had accompanied the rocket-fueled acceleration, he hadn't been thrilled about it.

There weren't any other lights, and she wondered what had happened to Sievers. She thought about calling him but decided that trying to dig around for her cell phone was probably a bad idea under the circumstances. Besides, if something had gone wrong—if Sievers had wrecked or broken down—there wasn't anything she could do for him. Not in the short term, at least.

"Guess I'll have to ask them," she muttered, shifting her foot onto the brake pedal. The Lexus immediately began shedding momentum.

"Wait, what?"

"Short version. I'm a federal agent. I received information about a threat against you. Looks like it was a solid lead. Now, shut up and let me drive." Tam brought the Lexus down to a respectable sixty m.p.h. and held it there. No sense in making it look too easy.

Martiel did as instructed, giving her about a minute of peace in which to contemplate her next move as the approaching headlights got brighter in the mirror.

If the guy or guys in the silver Toyota were pros—former intelligence officers or military veterans—then they probably had the same tactical road training as she. Her only advantage was that they didn't know she was in the driver's seat now.

The sedan crept closer, and an exit flashed past. Tam eased off a little more, coaxing the other vehicle even closer. The silver car was now only a couple hundred yards back.

"Come on," she muttered, squeezing the steering wheel in anticipation. "Make your move."

One hundred yards. Fifty.

The Toyota swung into the left lane as if intending to pass but Tam knew the driver had something else in mind. He was going to attempt a pit maneuver, a police technique for stopping a fleeing vehicle with a precise tap from the front bumper to the rear wheels of the escaping car. The "pitted" car would then spin completely around, the resulting compression causing the engine to stall, ending the chase.

Tam knew how to do the pit maneuver, too. And she knew how to beat it. When the Toyota surged forward, its front wheels coming even with the rear wheels of the Lexus, Tam stomped on the brakes. Instead of cutting right and bumping her car's rear, the Toyota swerved in front of the Lexus, missing it by mere inches.

The other driver jerked the wheel back, straightening out before his car could careen off the road, but he had already given up his only advantage, and Tam was not about to let him get back any of what he had lost. She punched the accelerator, feeling an immediate, almost uncanny surge of horsepower, and swung the Lexus into the left lane. She fixed her gaze on the Toyota's rear wheel like a missile lock, and when the moment was right, cranked the steering wheel to the right.

"See how you like being on the other end of it," she growled.

The front end of the Lexus swung toward the Toyota. Lights on the dashboard began flashing, and warning alarms filled the interior. Tam braced herself, not because of the imminent impact—she knew from experience that there would only be a slight bump—but because if the driver realized their positions had been reversed, he might try to do unto her as she had done to him.

She was ready for that. She was ready for anything.

Except what actually happened.

THREE

The Lexus abruptly braked. The pause lasted only a moment, but it was enough to let the Toyota shoot ahead, untouched.

"What the…"

"Were you trying to hit that guy?" a wide-eyed Martiel asked. He shook his head. "You can't. This car has an automated accident avoidance system. Get too close to another vehicle, and the computer will put on the brakes."

"Son of a bitch," Tam snarled. *That swear jar's going to be overflowing by the time this was over.* She disliked profanity—hearing it and using it. All her life, she had been surrounded by people, both growing up and in her counter-intelligence career, who used vulgar language with reckless abandon. Even though she thought it was cheap and demeaning, the habit had rubbed off on her. Now she was determined to hold herself to a higher standard. A dollar to the swear jar whenever she slipped up, and no excuses.

The other driver appeared to have given up on his original plan to run Martiel off the road and was now trying to get out of Dodge. "Is there a way to turn it off?"

"Turn it off?"

"Never mind," Tam floored the accelerator again, closing on the other car which was only about a hundred yards or so out in front.

"Wait. You *were* trying to hit him?"

"He's the only person who knows why he's trying to kill you. I'd like to have a talk with him."

Martiel continued to stare at her in disbelief.

"Just hang on," Tam said, maintaining pressure on the gas pedal. She checked the dashboard indicators to make sure the Lexus wasn't running too hot and pushed a little harder. As she got closer, the other driver moved to the center, straddling the dashed dividing line to keep her from trying to pass. It was a smart move, but the road was plenty wide enough for Tam to get around him. When the Lexus was just two car lengths behind the Toyota, she steered to the right and started to pass.

The other driver attempted to swerve into her path to block her, which activated the onboard safety systems yet again, but this time Tam used them to her advantage, letting the car slow her down and then swerving left and flooring it again as soon as there was room. The other guy tried to swerve back, but Tam was already nearly parallel with him.

The two cars came together with a hideous grating sound and a shriek of tires. Tam didn't have to fight too hard to keep the more powerful Lexus on a straight-ahead course, and after just a few seconds of savage friction, the Lexus broke free and shot ahead.

That was the break Tam had been waiting for. "Crash position!"

"What?"

Tam pushed herself back in her seat, pressing her head against the headrest and flexing the muscles of her abdomen as if trying to stand up from a seated position. She reached over with her right hand and grabbed the back of Martiel's head, pushing his upper body forward, folding him over so that his head was almost touching his knees. With her other hand, she steered to the right, cutting in front of the sedan which was only a car length behind her, and then stomped on the brakes with both feet.

The accident avoidance system wasn't designed to control acceleration in order to prevent a rear-end collision, and while the anti-lock braking did keep the wheels from locking, the Lexus had a lot of forward momentum. A loud shriek—rubber on asphalt, metal or ceramic or whatever the brakes were made of—and then a jolt as the Toyota plowed into the rear of the Lexus.

Tam's precautions minimized the effects of whiplash, though she knew she would feel it later. She let off the brakes, and hit the gas again, pulling away.

The interior of the Lexus smelled like hot metal, and Tam could hear a faint scraping sound. Perhaps a piece of the car had partially broken off and was dragging on the road or pressing against a tire, but the luxury vehicle seemed to be handling okay. The same was not true of the Toyota.

For a moment, only darkness filled the rear-view mirror. Then Tam saw red lights moving crazily across the roadway, fifty yards back. The lights disappeared for a moment, then reappeared, closer to the edge of the road. The silver sedan was spinning out of control. The red taillights vanished again, and then there was only darkness.

Tam put on the brakes, less forcefully this time, and brought the Lexus to a stop. "You can sit up now," she said.

Martiel did so, tentatively, then turned his head and looked back through the rear window. "What did you do?"

"Let's go find out." Tam moved the gearshift lever to "R" and pressed the pedal again, rolling backward.

Martiel swallowed nervously but said nothing.

Tam rolled back for about fifteen seconds until the white backup lights revealed a pall of smoke in the air and a scattering of debris on the asphalt. She halted the Lexus again, shifted into park, and then groped under the steering wheel. "Where's the damn key?"

"It's…ah, keyless." Martiel reached over and pushed a button.

Tam couldn't immediately tell if the car engine had turned off or not. She frowned. Her plan had been to pocket the key to keep Martiel from running off when she got out to investigate. What was the high-tech equivalent of taking the keys? "I need you to step out for a moment."

"What?"

"Outside. You're coming with me."

"Coming…where? Where are we going?"

"To get some answers." She unbuckled her seatbelt and opened the door, and as she extended one foot to the pavement, she reached behind her back and drew her Makarov semi-automatic pistol from a kidney holster. She didn't point it at him. She didn't need to. "I need you to step out, Mr. Martiel. Now."

The passenger let out a yelp and hastily complied. Tam got out and quickly circled around to maintain positive control of the other man.

The Toyota was about twenty yards away from the pavement. A trail of disturbed earth revealed how it had spun off the road and ultimately crashed into a tree. Steam was rising from the mangled front end, the engine ticking wildly as it cooled, but the car did not appear to be in any immediate danger of catching fire. Tam aimed the Makarov one-handed at the driver's side window and gripped Martiel's elbow with her free hand, guiding him across the open ground toward the wreck.

"You got a phone?" she asked.

"Umm…yeah." Martiel dipped a hand into a pocket and brought out a smartphone. He activated it unbidden, lighting up the gloom with the glow from the screen. "Should I call 911?"

Tam shook her head. "No. I need you to turn on the flashlight."

"Oh." A pause, and then a bright light shone from the device, illuminating the way forward.

Tam quickened her pace, reaching the Toyota a few seconds later. She could just make out the silhouette of the driver, his shaved head lolling against the window. There did not appear to be anyone else inside the vehicle. Tam moved closer, close enough to reach out and hammer the muzzle of the pistol against the glass. Her first strike bounced off, but a second harder blow did the trick. The window frosted over, fracturing into a thousand tiny fragments which cascaded down around the motionless figure within.

The man jolted in surprise and looked up at her, squinting against the brightness of Martiel's phone light. His face was covered in blood, most of which seemed to be coming from his nose.

"Federal officer," Tam said. "Make the wrong move, and it will be the last thing you do."

The dazed man blinked and then slowly raised his hands in a show of surrender.

"Who are you working for?" Tam said. "Who wants Martiel dead? And why?"

The man's reply was slurred and barely coherent. "Don't know… talking about."

Tam lowered the Makarov and brought her face closer. "You sure that's how you want to play this?"

"Lawyer."

"Lawyer, huh? Okay. At least you've got your priorities straight. I let you call your lawyer, but I don't think he's going to be able to do much for you. That funny taste in your mouth right now? It's blood. You've got internal injuries. Probably a ruptured spleen. The paramedics are coming, but just between you and me, they're not going to be able to do much for you either."

"Lying…" The accusation devolved into a coughing fit, and Tam leaned back as blood sprayed from the man's mouth.

"Wish I was," Tam replied in a tone of commiseration. "You know I'm right, too. You're not feeling any pain because of adrenaline, but that'll wear off soon, and you'll die screaming. Not much I can do about that. Once we get your name, I'll probably be able to figure it out anyway, but it would make both our lives a lot easier if you just told me now. You know, before you cross over.

"Oh, that's right," she continued quickly, before he could answer. "We'll get your name, make no mistake about that. We'll tear your life apart, seize your assets. Your family, if you have one, won't get a red cent. In fact, we'll go after them for our expenses.

"Or, you could give me a reason to leave them alone. A name."

It was, evidently, the correct pressure point. "Don't know," the man gasped. "Anything. Just…a job."

"Who hired you?" Tam pressed.

The reply was garbled, but Tam was pretty sure she understood him.

"The Immortal? Is that what you said?"

The man gave a feeble nod. "Cold," he whispered. "Everything... dark."

"What else? Did you kill the others?"

"Not me." Another coughing fit.

"Why does this immortal want to kill bank executives?"

"Don't...know. Family. Take care of..."

Tam turned away in frustration. "Come on," she told Martiel. "We're getting out of here."

The other man hesitated. "You're just going to leave him here?"

"You got a problem with that?" Tam shot back. "He tried to kill you, don't forget."

"Yeah, but...you're just going to leave him here? To die?"

Tam grabbed the other man's elbow and pulled him along. "He isn't going to die."

"But you said..."

"I lied," Tam said, enunciating the words slowly for emphasis. "He's got a bloody nose. Maybe some bruises. I just told him that to get him talk. It's an interrogation technique. I needed to know what he knew, which unfortunately was both diddly and squat."

"I don't understand."

"You don't need to. Right now, all you need to do is come with me. If you want to live, that is." She stopped at the road's edge, peering into the darkness until she could make out the glow of approaching headlights. Hopefully, it was Sievers in the GT. If not, she'd have to improvise.

She gave Martiel a sidelong glance. "Did that mean anything to you? The Immortal?"

"I...uh..." He shook his head. "What did you mean about 'others'?"

"Over the last couple years, there have been several

mysterious deaths among bank executives. Suspicious suicides and accidents, muggings gone wrong." Tam continued appraising him. "You haven't heard about it?"

He shrugged. "Actually, I have. But I thought it was just an urban myth. People making a big deal out of coincidences. There's like a quarter of a million people working in the New York finance sector. Accidents happen."

"That's what I thought, too," Tam replied, honestly. "But then somebody that I trust implicitly told me that you would be next. He was right."

Martiel was speechless.

The headlights drew closer, and soon Tam could hear the cough and rattle of an engine that sounded like it was on its last legs. Now she hoped it *wasn't* Sievers after all, because if it was, if he had destroyed his beloved Mustang GT for the sake of the mission, she would never hear the end of it.

But then the approaching vehicle slowed to a rough idle in front of her and she saw that it was indeed the bright red muscle car. Billy Sievers leaned out the open window—the same window Tam had exited through just a few short minutes before.

"Need a ride?" he said, grinning.

"Uh, thanks, but I think I'll wait for a car that won't break down in a couple miles."

Sievers affected a hurt expression. "Ah, is that any way to thank me? Don't worry. She'll make it to the next town. Couple hours under the hood and she'll be as good as new. Better, even." He glanced over at Martiel. "I see you saved him."

"Yeah. Listen, we'll take his car to the safehouse. You get your ride fixed ASAP, and then come join us when you can. Maybe Stone will be able to make sense of this."

"You sure?"

"Yeah, Billy. I got this. Go."

"Yes, ma'am." Sievers' face disappeared from view, and a moment later, the GT backfired loudly and took off.

Tam turned to Martiel again and gestured toward the Lexus. "Shall we?"

"We're just going to leave? Shouldn't we wait for the police?" He shrugged. "I mean, aren't you going to arrest that guy?"

Tam shook her head. "Until I know who's calling the shots, I'm afraid we can't trust the police. Or anyone else. Right now, the best thing for you is to disappear."

She had an even more compelling reason for leaving the would-be assassin stranded in the wreck of his car. As an officer of the CIA, Tam technically didn't have any jurisdiction to conduct law enforcement activities on American soil, and she didn't want to have to explain herself to a highway patrolman or sheriff's deputy.

Martiel balked. "Why should I trust you?"

"Because you're still alive." Tam put her hands on her hips. "Maybe I didn't make myself clear. This ain't a suggestion. Get your ass in the damn car."

Martiel gulped once, then moved like a scolded kindergartener, practically scampering back to the Lexus. He got in the passenger side and buckled his seat belt.

Tam got in and then stared at the steering wheel. "How the hell do you turn it on?"

Martiel reached over, tentatively as if he was afraid she might bite his hand and pushed a button. The car was so quiet, so well insulated, that Tam couldn't tell if it was actually running.

"Where are we going?" Martiel asked, his voice a nervous quaver.

Tam sighed before answering. "Back to the city. I have a place there where you'll be safe."

And then, she added to herself, *I'm gonna have to hit an ATM in order to pay my debt to the swear jar.*

FOUR

New York City

Avery Halsey was just starting to drift off to sleep when she heard the front door of the safehouse swing open. She opened one bleary eye and saw her boss, Tamara Broderick, walk in, followed by a man that she recognized immediately, even though they had never met.

"Thom Martiel," she blurted, sitting up and suddenly wide-awake. If Tam had brought him here, it could only mean....

"Stone was right," she muttered sarcastically. "Wonderful."

She was glad that he was right, obviously because it meant they had not been wasting their time but did he always have to be right? About everything?

Gavin Stone, seated at the dining room table, did not look up to acknowledge Tam's arrival or take credit for his predictive accuracy. He appeared to be wholly consumed with working out an expert difficulty Sudoku puzzle.

Tam was already launching into the introductions. "This is Dr. Halsey, my lead researcher. The fellow at the table is Mr. Stone. He's the one who figured out that you were being targeted."

Martiel gaped at Stone. "How?"

"Stone," Tam said, "you want to fill him in?"

Stone raised a finger, signaling that her request would have to wait.

"He's been doing that all night," Avery supplied, rising and heading over to greet the new arrival. "Trying to beat his record." She stuck out her hand to Martiel. "Hi. Call me Avery."

Martiel looked at it warily for a moment, then took it and gave it a cautious squeeze. He was handsome enough but in a sort of artificial way; more style than substance.

"Avery. I'm Thom."

Tam faced Avery. "Any word from Greg and Kasey?"

"They called in about an hour ago to say that nothing is happening. Nichols is home in bed. They're gonna keep an eye on him." She glanced at Martiel again. "Unless you want me to call them back."

"No. Better to keep them where they are until we can get a read on what's happening."

"Where's Billy?"

"Car trouble. He's all right. And I'm starving." She turned away, headed for the kitchen.

Martiel threw up his hands. "Just hold on a minute. Who the hell are you people? You aren't cops. If you were, you would have arrested that guy who tried to run me off the road."

Avery took Martiel's arm and turned him toward the table. "You're right. We aren't the police. What we are is a little more complicated. I can't tell you everything, but the condensed version is that we're a counter-terrorism task force. You remember the incidents at Key West and Norfolk a couple years back? We're trying to stop another attack like that."

"Attack? I thought those were just natural disasters. Undersea earthquakes."

"Like I said, I can't tell you everything, but I can tell you that those were most definitely not *natural* disasters."

The Norfolk and Key West tsunamis, which had killed hundreds and done billions in property damage, had actually been engineered by an international quasi-religious conspiracy known collectively as the Dominion.

Even before those devastating attacks, Tamara Broderick, a former FBI special agent, with several years' experience hunting the Dominion, had joined the Central Intelligence Agency to carry on the battle, both at home and abroad, which was no easy feat since the Dominion had infiltrated the upper echelons of government. To that end, she had formed the Myrmidons, a select group of government officers and civilian specialists, which had initially included Avery's half-brother Dane Maddock and his team of underwater salvage experts.

Maddock had gone back to treasure hunting, and now, there were just six Myrmidons in their action team. Four were combat-tested veterans. Tam and her two most trusted agents, Greg Johns and Kasey Kim, had extensive experience in law enforcement, counter-intelligence and counter-terrorism. Billy Sievers was a former Special Forces soldier turned military contractor, and now again working for, as he put it, "the white hats." Avery had survived a few scrapes, but her role was largely academic. She was a former community college history professor from Nova Scotia, and despite assurances from Tam to the contrary, she sometimes wondered if the only reason she was there at all was because of her relationship to Maddock.

Then there was Stone.

"Counter-terrorism," Martiel said. "So I'm being hunted by terrorists?"

"It looks that way."

"You mentioned Nichols. Is that Bob Nichols? At Goldman Sachs?"

Avery nodded. "You know him?"

"I know of him. We do the same job at different firms. Is he…" He trailed off as if unsure what to ask.

"He was the next name on the list," Avery said. "You were at the top, but we had to cover our bets."

Martiel shook his head. "I don't understand. There's a list?"

"Ha!" Stone slapped a hand down on the table. The sound startled Avery a little. "Four minutes and fifty-two seconds." Then, without even a pause to signal a change of subject, he went on. "No, Mr. Martiel, there isn't an actual list. There's a pattern."

"A pattern?"

"Patterns are his thing," Avery explained.

That was putting it mildly. Gavin Stone was an old family friend of Tam's, but the reason he had been recruited to the team—recruited was the wrong word. Technically, he was in Tam's custody, which was a whole other story in itself—was his uncanny ability to detect patterns: patterns in the way information flowed across the world, in the behavior of complex systems, and even in human behavior.

Stone believed in a deterministic universe—that literally everything that had ever happened or would ever happen, was the result of an inevitable and entirely predictable series of cause and effect reactions. The domino effect writ large. He also believed that, if a person could grasp the underlying pattern controlling everything—what he called the universal source code—it might be possible to "hack" reality itself.

Avery wasn't a believer, however, and even though Stone's talent for finding patterns that no one else could had helped them thwart a Dominion plot to destroy the United States, she wasn't so sure about his latest humdinger of a conspiracy theory.

But evidently, he had been right about the threat to Thom Martiel.

"Stone," Tam said, sticking her head out from the kitchen and speaking firmly. "Break it down for him. In English. Then I'll tell you what I've learned."

Stone raised an eyebrow, evidently intrigued by the promise of more information. "I'll do my best."

"Can I get you something to drink?" Avery asked Martiel as he took a seat across from Stone. "Coffee?"

"Got any Scotch?" Martiel asked.

"Trust me," Avery said. "You're going to want to keep your head clear to wrap it around this."

Martiel let out a grunt and nodded his head toward the kitchen. "She…Agent…"

"Tam."

"Yeah. Tam. She said something about suspicious deaths. Is that the pattern you're talking about?"

"In a word," Stone said. "Yes. In the last couple years, there have been over a hundred suspicious deaths in the financial sector. That's just in the New York area. And by suspicious, I mean just those where the evidence doesn't support the official COD on the death certificate. Accidents that make no sense. Muggings that ended in fatalities that happened in locations where the victim had no reason to be in the first place. Suicides from people who showed no indicators of being suicidal. Most were jumpers."

"And that's suspicious?"

"Throwing someone off a twenty-story building is the easiest way to cover up a murder. But the one I think was most suspicious was the man who shot himself with a nail gun."

"Why is that?"

"He shot himself seven times."

Martiel shook his head. "Like I told your...um, Tam... bad things happen. Accidents happen. Suicides happen. And don't get me started on the lifestyle stuff. It's a brutal job."

"And yet somebody tried to kill you tonight," Stone countered. "Let me guess. It was supposed to look like a car accident on a rural highway."

Martiel registered surprise. "How did you know that? Tam didn't call—"

"Actually, I told her it would happen that way."

"I warned you," Avery said to Martiel. "Patterns are his thing."

"That part was easy," Stone went on. "You have a long commute and a predictable routine, so a car accident was the obvious choice. Accidents are always going to attract less attention than suicides and street crime."

"Okay, okay. So it's all part of a pattern. There's a conspiracy. Who's behind it?"

Stone just blinked at him.

"We were hoping you could shed some light on that," Avery admitted.

"If you see the pattern—"

"Have you ever done an IQ test?" Stone interrupted,

seemingly changing the subject.

"I... Sure. Not an official one, but—"

"What those tests are really doing is equating the ability to predict patterns, purportedly testing your inherent intellectual potential. How you think, rather than what you know. As a measure of intellectual potential, it's a complete crock. Like horoscopes and the Meyers-Briggs personality test."

"He's still sore because he couldn't get into Mensa," Avery said in a stage whisper.

Stone inexplicably burst out laughing. "Like I would ever try." He grinned and resumed speaking though his tone was now a little less imperious. "But the thing is, you can look at those patterns and intuitively predict the next shape or number in the sequence, without completely understanding the underlying logic."

Martiel nodded slowly. "You're saying that you could predict that I was going to be the next...um, suspicious death...without actually knowing why?"

Tam called out from the kitchen. "He explained it better than you did, Stone."

"I looked at every one of the previous victims, the specific niche they occupied, what they might have known, what they had access to, who replaced them. And there was a pattern there. Based on my understanding of that pattern, I started looking for the person most likely to be next. You."

Martiel raised his hands in a 'slow down' gesture. "Look, I deal with complex analytics every day in my job. I get the broad strokes, but you're telling me that you looked at every single person working in the finance sector, and picked me?"

"That's right."

"That's a quarter of a million people."

"Closer to a third of a million, actually."

"And you looked at them all. How exactly?"

Stone shot a glance in Tam's direction. "I can't tell you the particulars, but suffice it to say, it was a tall order. The pattern appears to focus more on the specific niche each victim occupied, rather than any unique personality factors, but at this stage, I can't rule anything out."

"But you still don't know why? I mean the real reason."

"We may have a lead," Tam announced, joining them at the table with a steaming microwaved Lean Cuisine dinner. "The perp claimed to be working for someone he called 'The Immortal.' Ring any bells for you, Stone?"

Stone's forehead wrinkled as if the revelation were not merely cryptic, but disappointing. He glanced at Martiel then shook his head.

"Immortal?" Avery asked. "Are we thinking that's literal? Like that old show, *Highlander*."

"I read that book," Tam said. "Or listened to it. Who has time to read anymore?"

"I think you're thinking of *Outlander*," Martiel chimed in. "*Highlander* was a movie about a race of people who could only die if they got their heads cut off. The immortals went around fighting each other with swords and taking each other's power. Sean Connery was in it. He played a Spaniard, and some French guy played the Highlander, which really doesn't make any sense if you think about it. But then I guess it was all pretty nonsensical."

"The TV series was pretty good," Avery said, a little deflated.

Stone's expression had grown even more perturbed. "It's a red herring. Your perp didn't know anything."

"It's a lead," Tam insisted. "And we're going to run it down."

Avery took the cue and rose from the table to retrieve her laptop.

"It's too general," Stone insisted. "It's just noise. Camouflage. If you Google 'the Immortal', you're going to get millions of meaningless hits."

"Says the man who picked one name out of three hundred thousand," Avery shot back. "You do your thing, and I'll do mine."

She set the computer down and opened a search engine in the browser. Despite her retort, she knew Stone was right. "The Immortal" was too vague. A search would likely turn up a slew of entries about comic book characters and professional wrestlers before it provided anything useful. She would have to refine her search, and maybe even enlist the help of her brother's friend, journalist and deep-web sleuth Jimmy Letson.

Still, who knew what doors a simple query might unlock?

She typed the words: "Who is the Immortal" into the search box.

7,580,000 results. No surprise there.

She scrolled down the first page, knowing that the answer, if it was there at all, would probably be far too obscure to show up in the top ten or even top one thousand results.

There were references to TV shows, video games, and comic books, religious discussions, definitions, and at the bottom of the page, a link to something called "The Immortal Mysteries Forum." She read the description, expecting it to be something related to *Buffy the Vampire Slayer* or *Highlander*, but saw nothing that immediately linked it to entertainment media. Curious, she clicked on the link.

It was a typical Internet discussion forum, utilizing the mostly obsolete topic- and thread-indexing system that had been around since the early 2000s. Most of the people she knew and interacted with had long since graduated to more streamlined and user-friendly social media sites like Facebook and Reddit, but there were still a lot of people, particularly those on the fringes of society, who preferred the relative anonymity of the old school online forums. They were especially popular with conspiracy nuts.

A glance of topics—and there were several—suggested this might be more of the same. Avery immediately recognized several of the headings: Illuminati;

New World Order; Council of Rome; Numbers Stations.

Others sounded vaguely familiar: Markovian Parallax Denigrate; A858; Cicada 3301; TINAG.

Avery was sure she'd heard of those somewhere before. She looked down the list, noting recent activity on all of them—within the hour, in some cases. That was also a surprise. A lot of forums languished and died from lack of participation, and just sat there in cyberspace like virtual ghost towns.

She looked back up to the top of the list. The topic header read: "Latest from the Immortal."

The most recent post was just a couple hours old.

She clicked on it.

"Avery, honey?" Tam asked. "You find something?"

Avery looked up, gasping a little. She had been holding her breath without even realizing it. "Uh, I think so."

FIVE

Avery took a few minutes to explore the forum further before turning the computer around to show what she had discovered.

"This is a discussion forum devoted to something called 'the Immortal Mysteries.' The Immortal, in this case, is an Internet user who periodically releases strange messages on Reddit and other places, including this forum."

"Strange, how?" Tam prompted.

"Well, at a glance they look like gibberish. Automatically generated text, like Lorem Ipsum."

"Lorem…?"

"It's the gobbledygook graphic designers use as a placeholder for text in advertisements. It looks like Latin, but it's actually nonsense. I used to see it a lot in spam emails. This is in English, but the same principle."

Tam nodded. "You said at a glance?"

"Right. The users on the forum are convinced that the messages from The Immortal are actually a code. They're crowdsourcing the effort to crack it."

Stone now seemed to take an interest. "A code?" He reached out a hand for the computer. "May I?"

Avery pushed it toward him, feeling just a smidgen of satisfaction. "It probably is a code, but whether it's important or not is anyone's guess. There are a lot of theories. This isn't the first time something like this has happened. Some of the forum users think it's a stunt. An ARG—alternate reality game."

Tam shook her head. "Honey, I recognize the words you're saying, but I have no earthly idea what they mean."

"An ARG is a sort of real-world puzzle game or scavenger hunt. They're sometimes used to promote upcoming movies and video games. It's been suggested that the NSA might use them as recruiting tools, but most are just users trying to prove how clever they all. Challenging the Internet to break their code."

"Okay. What are the other theories?"

"There's a fairly large contingent that thinks the messages might be coded communications from a foreign government to their agents abroad. Sort of like the old number stations."

Avery knew Tam would get that reference. Numbers stations were short-wave radio frequencies that broadcast only long chains of numbers. It was assumed that the transmissions had been coded messages to spies in the pre-digital era, but that had not been definitively proven in all instances.

"A lot of users have pointed to that. There are also strong similarities to the Markovian Parallax Denigrate mystery from the old Usenet days."

Tam shook her head. "Is this going to be on the test?"

"The Markovian Parallax Denigrate is the oldest mystery on the Internet," Stone interjected. "In 1996, strange messages began appearing on Usenet groups. Long chains of seemingly random words, like 'jitterbugging McKinley Abe break Newtonian inferring caw update.' Every one of the messages contained the words 'Markovian Parallax Denigrate' somewhere in the body of the text. It's generally believed that the format was being used for espionage, just like the numbers stations you mentioned, but a lot more sophisticated. Some of the messages appeared to have originated from a Susan Lindauer at the University of Wisconsin at Stevens Point."

"Lindauer," Tam repeated. "Why does that sound familiar?"

"Susan Lindauer is the name of a conspiracy journalist who was accused of spying for Saddam Hussein's government. But she might not be the same Susan Lindauer associated with the MPD messages. There was another woman with that name at UWSP, but she graduated in 1994 and has always denied any involvement.

Somebody probably hacked her account to send those messages."

Avery gaped at him. "You know all that, but you don't know whether Commander Sisko is from *Star Wars* or *Star Trek*?" Despite his genius level intellect, Stone was surprisingly obtuse about most general knowledge subjects, and particularly pop culture. Playing Trivial Pursuit with him was almost painful.

"The MPD is a puzzle," Stone replied, as if it was obvious. "An unsolved one at that. I've been trying to figure it out for years. Unfortunately, most of the messages have been lost over the years, so trying to see the pattern is almost impossible."

"If there is a pattern," Avery said.

"There is. And it's the same pattern as these messages from the so-called Immortal. I'm certain of it." He looked back down at the computer, and Avery saw his eyes going back and forth as he read the strange messages.

"Well," she continued. "He's right about the similarities. But the prevailing theory about both the Markovian Parallax Denigrate messages and what the Immortal is posting is that they were generated with a Markov chain process. And before you ask, don't. Even I didn't understand that one."

Stone shook his head. "It isn't. Markov chains would produce more coherent output. This is a code, and I'm going to…"

He paused abruptly, his forehead creased in concentration.

"Stone?" Tam asked.

"A new message from the Immortal just posted." He turned the computer around to show them the message.

ZEPHYR ORBITAL COW EVERYTHING INDEX REPLAY DOMINION VIEW HOSING UNIVERSE HINCKY EMACS TREASURE NEO ONE MESSAGE ECHO BLUE AMOUNT DEATH MEANING NOT LEVEL OF EYES GUILD SUPERIOR EVOLUTION

XMODMAP WE DOMINION MAGNUS ELDHUSET ONLY REGULATIONS BLACK ROME RADIOHEAD'S PATSY APPROXIMATE INDEPENDENCE CHARTRES FIND OSWALD NEVERLAND ORIGINAL REPLACE FORTY-TWO LIFE USING FIX MYSTIC GNOME TEMPLAR ESSENTIAL HILLBILLIES

"It posted exactly at midnight," Stone said.

"Is that important?"

"It suggests that the post was scheduled in advance." He looked up at them. "As much as it wounds my ego to admit it, I think Avery is right. This is from *our* Immortal. He…or she…is using these posts to send messages to operatives."

"The guy who tried to run me off the road," Martiel said. "He must know how to crack the code. You should have arrested him."

Stone stared at Martiel for several seconds, then shook his head. "I doubt he would have been much help. A code like this will have a single-use key, sent to operatives independently of the message. The man you met tonight probably won't get the key to this one since he's been compromised. No, we'll have to crack this the old-fashioned way."

"Some of the terms here," Avery said. "'Eyes only.' That can't be a coincidence."

"The only word I care about," Tam said, "is 'Dominion.'"

"That's what I mean," Avery pressed. "This is clearly some kind of scrambled code. We just need to rearrange the words, and it will make sense." She pointed to the screen. "We've got Templar, treasure, and Chartres. There's black, death, guild." She snapped her fingers. "Council of Rome. There's a whole thread devoted to it."

"The think tank?" Martiel asked.

Avery nodded. She wasn't surprised that Martiel, a banker, knew about the Council of Rome, an influential group of industrialists, scientists, economists, and the like, who had formed in the early 1970s to address the global consequences of unfettered economic and population growth. Their pro-environmental stance and repeated warnings of Malthusian doomsday scenarios had earned them the nickname "the Cassandra Club," though many conspiracy theorists saw a darker motive behind their dire warnings, accusing them of being anti-Capitalist, and even going so far as to associate the group with the nefarious Illuminati. Many believed they were the intellectual arm—or rather the brains—of the New World Order, a globalist plot to rule the world under a single, secular government controlled by the uber-wealthy.

"The Dominion probably sees the Council as an enemy, the architect of the world financial system. Which might be why they're targeting bankers."

Stone shook his head. "That's all just camouflage. A distraction. The words were probably taken from familiar phrases. Sort of like when kidnappers cut words from a magazine article to write a ransom note. Sometimes they take words from the same page, so it looks like there's a connection, but there really isn't."

"Nobody actually does that anymore, Stone," Tam countered.

"No, they do this," Stone said, tapping the screen.

Tam looked at the message again, then sighed. "Stone may be right. Look at some of the other groups. 'Oswald' and 'patsy'? Lee Harvey Oswald claimed he was a patsy."

"The JFK assassination is a major component of most conspiracy theories," Avery pointed out.

"Right, but what about 'meaning life universe everything forty-two.'"

"'Cow level.'" Martiel said, smirking. "That's a computer game reference." He dropped his eyes. "Sorry, I'll just be quiet."

"There are fifty-six individual words here," Stone said. He spoke in a low voice, as if thinking aloud rather than trying to communicate. "Same as the only surviving

Markovian Parallax Denigrate message. Fifty-six is eight time seven."

"Is that important?" Avery asked.

"The word 'Dominion' is the only repeat. In the MPD message, there was just one repeat: 'McKinley.'"

"The president or the mountain?" Avery wondered.

Stone looked at her and blinked as if he didn't understand the question. "If we strike the repeated word, we're left with fifty-four unique terms."

"Why would you take out the repeated word?"

"Because it's repeated. That's significant. I think you're right about the message being scrambled. In its original configuration, the message probably begins and ends with that word—'Dominion' in this case. Like brackets in a string of computer code. It might also indicate the specific code key to solve the message. The actual message is in the fifty-four remaining terms."

"There are fifty-four playing cards in a deck, if you include the jokers," Avery suggested.

"Fifty-four is six times nine." Stone's eyes dropped to the Sudoku puzzle book. "There are just nine single digit natural numbers."

"You think Sudoku is the key to the code?"

"No. The Sudoku grid is nine-by-nine. Eighty-one. But a cube has six sides. Six sides, divided into nine segments on each side."

"Like a Rubik's Cube?"

Stone nodded, a look almost like pride shining in his eyes. "Very good. You're getting it. When I was a kid, I had the crazy idea of using a Rubik's Cube as a simple encryption tool. Write a message of fifty-four characters or less on the cube, then scramble it. The only way to read the message is to solve the cube."

"You think that's what the Immortal did? Only with words instead of letters."

"It's possible, but the method wasn't practical, and not nearly as sophisticated as I thought it would be. With modern computers, a simple brute force attack can run all

43 quintillion possibilities in a matter of minutes."

Tam blinked at him. "So? Try it."

Stone shrugged, then turned the computer around and began typing. "Rather than limit ourselves to possible Rubik's Cube outputs, I'm going to simply run all possible combinations of these terms. That's actually a much bigger number—like 200 duovigintillion—"

"You just make that number up?" Tam asked. "Like bazillions?"

"No." Stone didn't look away from what he was doing. "I'll put them through a Markov chain filter to look for combinations that make grammatical sense."

After a few seconds, he shook his head. "It's still word salad, I'm afraid."

He turned the screen to show the results. Variations of the message were listed in blocks, beginning with what Stone's decoder had judged to be the most likely combination of words.

DOMINION VIEW TEMPLAR TREASURE CHARTRES FIND APPROXIMATE AMOUNT ORIGINAL INDEX MEANING OF LIFE UNIVERSE EVERYTHING FORTY-TWO BLACK DEATH GUILD MAGNUS ROME SUPERIOR REGULATIONS NEO NOT ONE WE REPLAY COW LEVEL USING MYSTIC XMODMAP EMACS RADIOHEAD'S EYES ONLY ESSENTIAL MESSAGE ECHO BLUE ZEPHYR ELDHUSET HILLBILLIES HOSING INDEPENDENCE REPLACE HINCKY GNOME OSWALD PATSY FIX ORBITAL EVOLUTION NEVERLAND DOMINION

Below it were several more variations that reordered the apparent words strings, but none were any more comprehensible.

"Maybe the message is just one of those," Avery suggested, "and the rest is camouflage, like Stone says."

"If there is a coded message here, it won't be in the

literal text."

"What if we took the first letter of every sentence?" Tam suggested.

"An acrostic?" Stone frowned again. "I tried that with the MPD messages. It didn't work. Ordinarily, I'd say that's a little too simplistic, but I guess we should try, if only to eliminate it."

He resumed typing.

Z-O-C-E-I-R-D-V-H-U-H-E-T-N-O-M-E-B-A-D-M-N-L-O-E-G-S-E-X-W-D-M-E-O-R-B-R-R-P-A-I-C-F-O-N-O-R-F-L-U-F-M-G-T-E-H

"Okay, from the first letters of the Immortal's fifty-six letter message as originally posted, we can create 85,000 different words, from 'A' to 'zoogeographical.'" Stone tapped his fingers on the table top. "If we strike those two Ds, the number goes down to 56,000. I wonder…"

He grabbed his Sudoku book again, flipped it to a mostly blank page, and then drew a large cross-shaped box, which he began dividing into individual grids of nine squares. He then filled in the box at the center of each with a letter. "If this was coded using a Rubik's Cube, there will be fixed values. For example, the squares in the center never change."

"Unless you peel the stickers off," Tam said. "Just sayin'."

"We'll assume that didn't happen. The fifth word is 'index.'" He wrote the letter I in one of the squares. "The next fixed value, not counting 'Dominion, is the fourteenth word. 'One.'" He wrote the letter O in another center square. M, O, O, and M soon followed.

"So it's more like a crossword," Avery said.

"I was thinking hangman," Tam put in.

"A little of both. There are some other rules that apply. On a Rubik's Cube, the corner pieces have three colors, and there are no duplicates."

Tam held up her hands. "Just skip to the part where

you solve it."

"I thought you liked watching me work," Stone said with a grin, not looking up. He continued alternately scribbling on the paper and checking the computer.

Tam turned to Martiel. "You should probably get some sleep. You can take your pick of the bedrooms. No telling how long you'll be here."

The banker's eyes went wide in alarm. "What do you mean you don't know how long?"

"Until we know the nature of this threat, your life is in danger. It could be days. Weeks, even."

"You can't just keep me here like a prisoner. I have a life."

"You call what you have a life?" Stone said, not looking up. "For what it's worth, Tam, getting him back to his so-called life may be the only way to flush this Immortal out into the open again."

"You mean use me as bait?"

Tam cleared her throat. "Stone, that's not your call. Mr. Martiel, we're going to keep you safe. That's a promise."

Martiel did not seem at all relieved by the assurance. "I… This is just…"

Stone made a humming sound. "I thought so."

Avery looked over. "You solved it?"

"Well, yes, but it's meaningless. A red herring, like I said."

He spun the computer around again.

DOMINION RADIOHEAD'S ESSENTIAL TREASURE REGULATIONS INDEX EVERYTHING VIEW EYES TEMPLAR HINCKY ELDHUSET BLACK ROME ONLY NEO ZEPHYR EMACS HILLBILLIES EVOLUTION APPROXIMATE DEATH OSWALD FIND MEANING AMOUNT GNOME NOT UNIVERSE SUPERIOR FORTY-TWO REPLAY ONE MESSAGE COW ORBITAL USING NEVERLAND CHARTRES INDEPENDENCE

LEVEL OF FIX REPLACE ORIGINAL MAGNUS ECHO LIFE PATSY WE MYSTIC HOSING XMODMAP BLUE GUILD DOMINION

"It is an acrostic," he added, scrolling down to show the first letter of each word. "But it's a joke."

D-R-E-T-R-I-E-V-E-T-H-E-B-R-O-N-Z-E-H-E-A-D-O-F-M-A-G-N-U-S-F-R-O-M-C-O-U-N-C-I-L-O-F-R-O-M-E-L-P-W-M-H-X-B-G-D

Avery scanned the message. Three words immediately jumped out at her. "'Council of Rome' again."

"See what I mean?" Stone said. "It's like nesting dolls. A puzzle within a puzzle. That's how you can tell it's not serious."

"What about the rest of it?" Tam asked. "Does that make any sense? 'Retrieve the bronze head of magnus.' Avery, does that mean anything to you?"

"As a matter of fact it does," Avery said quickly. "'Magnus' almost certainly refers to Saint Albert Magnus—Albert the Great—a 13th Century Dominican Friar from Cologne, Germany. He was a polymath. A scholar of philosophy and natural science. His writings paved the way for the Renaissance."

"And the bronze head? Is that a statue or something?"

"Sort of, but not the way you think. There's a story that Albert constructed a head made of brass or bronz3—an automaton—that could breathe and speak. If you asked it questions, it would answer. It could even tell the future."

"Sounds like a computer?"

"It's not impossible that Albert might have created some kind of primitive difference engine," Avery said. "Something along the lines of the Antikythera device."

The so-called Antikythera device, discovered in a two thousand-year-old Greek shipwreck, was generally accepted as the earliest example of a mechanical analog computer. If the Greeks could create something like that, there was no reason to think that someone of Albert Magnus' intelligence could not create something similar a thousand years later.

"And the Council of Rome has this brass head?"

"Well, that's where it gets a little sticky. According to the story, Albert's Brazen Head wouldn't stop talking, so his student, Thomas Aquinas, smashed it to shut it up. That's the story anyway. None of it can actually be verified."

"So why would the Immortal think the Council of Rome has it?"

Before Avery could answer Tam's question, Martiel interrupted. "Are you people for real? Talking statues and ancient computers? I thought you were trying to figure out who's trying to kill me."

Stone, who had been watching the banker the whole time, nodded slowly. "He's right. This is a distraction. The Immortal is trolling us. He wanted us to solve this code, send us off on a wild goose chase. That's why the code was so easy to crack."

"You call that easy?" Martiel said, wagging his head.

Tam raised a hand. "One at a time. Avery, go on."

"Well, I don't really know much more than that, but I can look into it."

She took her computer back from Stone, opened another browser window, and typed in "bronze head magnus council of rome." Not surprisingly, the Immortal Mysteries Forum was one of the top results. The link took her to a thread in the Council of Rome topic, the gist of which seemed to be that the group was getting its marching orders from a demon-possessed statue recently acquired by Maxim Loew, the current secretary general of the organization. Avery noted that Loew's name was bracketed in triple parentheses—a dog-whistle practice commonly used by white supremacists to identify persons of Jewish heritage in social media posts.

Avery ran several search variations using the secretary general's name. Hidden in the haystack of dry papers on economic theory penned by Loew, and mentions on various conspiracy and openly neo-Nazi discussion forums, was a single needle—a news item about an auction at Southwick's of London, which featured several items from the estate of noted author and collector Gerald Roche. One of the items, described as a "13th Century brazen head automaton" had been purchased by the secretary general of the Council of Rome.

"This has to be it," she announced. "The Immortal clearly thinks Loew has the bronze head built by Albert Magnus, and he's sending his followers to get it."

"Why?" Tam asked.

Avery could tell the question was sincere, but the skepticism in Tam's tone was unmistakable. "Gerald Roche, the former owner of the Brazen Head, wrote about the so-called Changeling conspiracy. And now he's dead. I think it's obvious that a lot of people think that particular artifact has special occult significance. Whether or not it really does, it's a symbolic target. You know how important symbols are to these people. That message from the Immortal is proof that it's somehow connected to what's been going on here."

Tam continued to stare back at her. "What course of action would you suggest?" she said, speaking slowly, measuring her words.

"We have to assume that the Immortal's agents have already decoded the message. We've got to stop them from getting the Brazen Head. The Council of Rome headquarters is in Zurich. We need to get there, ASAP."

Tam nodded, but Avery didn't think it was an indication of agreement. "Okay. Stone, what's your take?"

"This is a distraction. Scribbles in the margin. Maybe this Immortal really does want this bronze head for some reason, but it's tangential to the pattern. We have to stay focused on what's happening right here."

Tam looked at each of them as she considered her choices, then seemed to reach a decision. "The only thing we know for certain is that someone is targeting bankers.

We can't divert all our resources away from this investigation to follow this tangent. But without this Immortal stuff, we're back to square one, so I'm not inclined to dismiss it, either."

She focused her gaze on Stone. "Is Bob Nichols still in danger?"

"Doubtful," Stone said. "Mr. Martiel here was the preferred target, as what happened tonight clearly demonstrates."

"But we're okay to pull Greg and Kasey off protection duty?"

Stone gave Martiel another sidelong glance. "The short answer is, yes. Nichols is safe. Mr. Martiel here seems to have been the actual target. If he goes back to work, they'll probably make another attempt. If he doesn't, it will have the same effect. The risk factor arises from the niche he occupies. He doesn't need to actually be dead. If his job becomes vacant, the net effect is the same to the pattern."

"So the person who takes his place might be part of the conspiracy."

"Not necessarily. It could be someone further down the chain. Or up, for that matter. A butterfly effect, if you will."

"Hmm." She turned to the banker. "I can't compel you to stay, Mr. Martiel. If you decide to go back to work tomorrow, we will do our best to keep you safe, but there are no guarantees."

"What are my other options?"

"Run away. Start a new life somewhere else. Or help us. Help Stone figure out the pattern."

Martiel gave a resigned nod. "I guess that's my best shot at getting my life back, isn't it?"

"All right, here's what we're going to do. Stone, keep working on your pattern. Figure out what's going to happen next, who the next target will be. Billy and I will stay here to back you up. Avery, you're going to Zurich. Greg and Kasey will go with you. Pull on the thread and see what unravels."

SIX

When Tam awoke a few hours later, she found Stone almost exactly where she had last seen him, at the table, hunched over a computer—not Avery's laptop, but Tam's own notebook. She started a pot of coffee brewing, then joined him.

"Where's our guest?"

Stone did not look up. "Asleep, I would guess."

Tam looked over his shoulder and saw that, in addition to the computer, which presently displayed the incomprehensible word salad composition from the Immortal Mysteries forum, Stone was also filling reams of paper with words and shapes connected by lines. She skimmed the message and realized that it was not the same as before. "Is this another new message?"

"No. This one is from six months ago. I'm working backward through the Immortal's messages."

She eyed the scattered pages. "Any luck?"

"Luck?" he snorted. "Luck isn't a factor."

"My sincerest apologies," she said, drawing the words out facetiously. She wasn't in the mood for a lecture on his methods, not until she had some caffeine in her bloodstream.

Although Stone had only been working with her task force for about a year, their relationship went back a lot further. Stone's family and hers had been close for several generations, and growing up, she had spent a lot of time with him. They had a bond that went far beyond friendship or even love.

Stone's ability to see patterns was both a gift and a curse. It gave him an almost unnatural ability to make stunningly accurate predictions about everything from the stock market to the behavior of individuals. He could have used that information to enrich himself, but avarice was not one of Gavin Stone's shortcomings. Pride, maybe, but he had absolutely no interest in wealth or the power that came with it. Part of this was due, no doubt, to the fact that he was from old money, so he had never really known want, but that did not tell the whole story. Tam suspected that the real reason Stone had no interest in acquiring wealth was that it would have been too easy. Stone needed to be challenged, and the challenge he had set for himself was nothing less than discovering the secrets of creation itself.

Stone believed that the universe and everything in it were following a mathematically precise progression, and on a cosmic scale, it made sense. The galaxies and stars and planets all appeared to move like clockwork. Even very complex systems, like the weather or the movement of ocean currents, behaved according to the laws of nature. Weather forecasts were so often wrong, not because scientists did not understand what caused the weather, but rather because it was nearly impossible to have complete information about the variables. Stone however took it a step further, claiming that human behavior was also the product of chemical and physical reactions and interactions, and that since these were also part of that universal progression, everything that happened, from the Big Bang to Tam's decision to go straight to the coffee maker, happened because it couldn't have happened any other way. Stone did not believe in free will.

Before joining the Myrmidons, he had been a sort of black-hat hacktivist, probing everything from the Darknet to the NSA's global surveillance network in an effort to learn more about human behavior—the most challenging aspect of his deterministic universe. His activities had eventually gotten him arrested and sent to a CIA "black site"—an off the books prison facility—which as it turned out, put him within Tam's sphere of influence right when she needed him the most.

If that wasn't luck, Tam didn't know what it was.

"What I meant to say was, have you found anything

useful?"

"That depends. Would you call the names of every banking executive who died in the last six months, hidden in coded messages posted twenty-four to forty-eight hours before their mysterious and untimely deaths, 'useful'?"

"Really? It's all there?" Tam poured a mug of coffee and then joined him at the table.

"The encryption method is the same in all instances. A fifty-six-word-long acrostic, created with a Markovian Parallax Denigrate-type word generation system, scrambled using Rubik's Cube variations. The messages are a lot harder to solve than the one that posted last night because proper names are easier to hide in an acrostic than a long command string. Impossible, really. The amateurs working this on the Web would never be able to solve it definitively, but someone with the correct code-configuration would have no difficulty at all. When I started plugging the names into the acrostic solver, the results were conclusive."

"So now we have proof. This Immortal is behind the attacks on the bankers. And we know how he's communicating with his agents." She considered it a moment longer. "It also means we can't ignore the latest message."

"Maybe," Stone equivocated. "There's something else, though. Or I should say, there's something missing."

"What do you mean?"

"Before last night's message, the most recent post from the Immortal was two weeks ago."

"Two weeks. Was there a name?"

"Curtis Johnson. He died of an apparent suicide eighteen hours after the message went up."

"And nothing since?" She tilted her head in the direction of the bedroom where Martiel was sleeping. "What about him?"

Stone drew in a breath as if trying to figure out how to answer the question. "His name isn't explicitly mentioned, at least not in the configurations I believe to be correct."

"But you picked him. You said he fit the pattern. And someone did try to kill him, somebody who said he was taking orders from the Immortal."

Stone nodded. "That's one reason why I'm suspicious of this latest message. I think the Immortal knows we're on to him. That's why he changed his procedures." Tam frowned, but Stone was talking again. "But the takeaway here, as you said, is that we now have proof that someone is targeting people in the finance sector. Now we need to figure out why, and I think our houseguest will be able to help me with that."

"How?"

Stone gazed back at her with a thoughtful expression, as if trying to decide whether or not to burden her with some profound revelation. He seemed to reach a decision. "I want to shadow him. Observe him at work. Maybe if I can get a better grasp of what it is he does, I'll see more clearly what this Immortal's endgame is."

"I'm not sure how that's going to go down. I was up half the night trying to convince him to lay low, and now you want me to put him back in circulation." Tam sipped her coffee while she considered the request. "Is there still a target on his back? I'm not categorically opposed to the idea of dangling him out there as bait, but I won't lie to him and tell him he's safe if he isn't."

Stone flashed a cryptic smile. "Tell him whatever you want. It won't be a problem."

SEVEN

Jersey City

Thom Martiel opened the door to his office on the twenty-eighth floor, but instead of going in, he simply stared into the shadows beyond. "How exactly is this supposed to work?"

"Just do what you would ordinarily do," Stone said, and then turned and pushed forward into the office. The lights flickered on automatically, revealing a surprisingly utilitarian workspace with very little in the way of décor, and zero personal touches—no photographs of family and friends, no mementos of prior accomplishment. That was how it looked to Tam as she surveyed the office through Stone's eyes, or more specifically, through the tiny pinhole camera concealed in the frame of the horn-rimmed glasses he was wearing.

The camera, along with a miniature two-way radio unit hidden in Stone's suit jacket, was the next best thing to being there in the room with the two men, but Tam's attention was divided between the task of following along, and watching the high-rise building's main entrances and internal security cameras from the back of a surveillance van parked in the garage across the street. It was a lot to keep track of for one person, but with the rest of her team already on their way to Europe, and Billy Sievers covering the lobby of the building, she was it.

The office was mostly taken up by the desk, the top of which was empty except for a pair of flat-screen computer monitors positioned side-by-side in a herringbone configuration. The workstation was nearly identical to those occupying the desks of the open office behind them where several of Martiel's co-workers were already busy with their respective duties. As a senior account executive, Martiel evidently rated a private if not exactly luxurious workspace. Evidently, he wasn't senior enough to rate an office with windows, but Tam suspected a view of the Manhattan skyline would have been wasted on someone like Martiel.

Stone pulled one of the guest chairs around to the working side of the desk, positioning it alongside Martiel's plush executive chair, and then settled into it.

Martiel frowned but then advanced into the room and took his seat. He had not put up much of a fight when Tam suggested he return to work and continue as if nothing had happened. In fact, he seemed to latch on to the idea that getting back to business as usual meant the danger was past, and Tam, at Stone's urging, had said nothing to disabuse him of the notion.

He opened a drawer, took out a wireless headset, which he donned, and then pulled out the under-desk tray which concealed an ergonomic keyboard and mouse controller. After another moment of hesitation, Martiel gave the mouse a nudge, and the dual screens flashed on. The banker tapped in his password, and then clicked on a desktop icon marked "MYSTIC."

"Should I explain what I do?" Martiel said as the browser window launched.

"Buy low, sell high, right?" Stone replied. Tam knew he probably understood the intricacies of the market better than even Martiel, but since he was posing as an intern "learning the ropes," it made sense to play dumb.

Martiel uttered a short, humorless laugh. "Maybe if you're a day trader. In our world, it's a little more complicated than that. Our clients depend on us for long term sustainable ROI—that's return on investment. Waiting for windfalls and speculating may seem attractive, but it's not a pathway to financial security. There's usually a very good reason why a particular asset might be trading low. Buying in quantity might help drive the price back up, or you could end up with a big pile of worthless paper." He nodded to the screen. "That's where Mystic comes in. It's our primary trading platform. Not just ours, actually.

Everyone uses it. It employs an advanced heuristic algorithm for trend forecasting and risk analysis."

"Heuristic?" Stone prompted, almost certainly for Tam's benefit.

"It's self-refining. Always learning."

"It's an artificial intelligence?"

"Yes, but not in the science fiction sense. It's more like a cross between Google and a sophisticated chess computer, but on a massive scale. Mystic crunches an unbelievable amount of data. Not just what the markets are doing, but other factors—socioeconomic, geopolitical, and so forth. And then it predicts outcomes which we use to determine the best investment strategy."

"Is it always right?"

"Better to say 'reliable.' You can't really quantify the outcomes in absolute terms like 'right' or 'wrong.' There are a lot of factors that even Mystic can't account for—"

"Such as?"

"Well, like I said, everyone uses it, so everyone is getting the same information. So, if Mystic says to invest in pork belly futures, and everyone does, it's going to have unforeseeable ripple effects. Mystic can anticipate that to some degree, but there's always going to be uncertainty. The X factor. That's why there always has to be a real live person at the wheel to make the final decision. Don't get me wrong, though. It's an invaluable tool. And getting better all the time."

The scene on Tam's screen shifted as Stone leaned forward. "When you say 'everyone uses it'…?"

"I mean everyone. All the major players. The system is proprietary, developed by Iron River Asset Management… Are you familiar with them?"

Stone shook his head.

"You know how conspiracy nuts always talk about a secret organization that controls the world? Well, Iron River is just about as close as you can get, though it's not really a secret and they don't have a sinister agenda or anything. They made a lot of smart investments—mostly because they had Mystic working for them—and got huge. They've got a controlling stake in thirty of the top fifty corporations worldwide, and directly control well over five trillion in assets."

As Martiel was speaking, Tam used her own computer to search the Internet for "Iron River." To her surprise and dismay, the search confirmed everything Martiel had just said. According to reputable news outlets, the company, headquartered in the Pacific Northwest, controlled an estimated seven percent of the global economy, which gave them enormous political sway as well.

"You said 'everyone uses it,'" Stone pressed. "What did you mean by that?"

"Oh, right. Sorry. Aside from their own investments, Iron River sells access to Mystic. It's simply the best predictive algorithm available, so all the banks and investment houses use it."

"So if someone could manipulate the data—input and output—they could influence the markets."

Martiel feigned shock at the suggestion. "Well, they could, but that would be illegal of course." He smiled and shook his head. "The short answer is yes, but the whole point of a system like Mystic is to maintain market stability in the face of uncertainties. Trying to manipulate the system to influence trading behaviors defeats the purpose. It would be like…" He paused, searching for the right analogy. "Developing a foolproof card counting method for playing blackjack, and then trying to deal off the bottom of the deck."

Stone seemed to ponder this answer for a moment, then said, "Mind if I give it a try?"

Despite the modulating effect of the radio transmission, Tam could hear the eagerness in his voice. If Mystic was a sort of chess computer, then Stone was the human grandmaster eager to test himself against it.

Martiel registered surprise but then shrugged. "I don't see why not. All trades require my approval, so there's not much chance of you crashing the plane, as it were." He pushed away from the desk making room in front of the computer. The picture on the screen shifted as Stone slid his chair over to take Martiel's place, and then the camera feed was completely dominated by the dual-screens display.

"Let's try currency exchanges," Martiel suggested. "Just click on the tab with—"

Stone moved the cursor over the virtual button and clicked on it before Martiel could complete the thought, and a new screen appeared.

Martiel talked him through the basic functions of the application. It was evident to Tam, even from her removed vantage, that Stone was miles ahead of the tutorial, but he patiently followed along, asking questions about the intricacies of the system. Martiel directed him to research several foreign currencies, and then explained the output, which in this case, indicated a strong future for Chinese yuan.

After a while, Tam tuned out the discussion and focused on her surveillance of the building. She switched the radio to the frequency Sievers was using. "How's it looking in there, Billy?"

"Just a little bit less excitin' than watchin' bullcrap dry in the sun," came the reply in a deeply exaggerated Texas drawl. Sievers sounded alert despite the fact he had been up all night rebuilding the engine on his Mustang.

"Wanna trade places?"

"Not on your life, darlin'. At least in here I can get coffee and watch all the pretty ladies walking by."

"Uh, huh. Well, don't let yourself get too distracted."

"Don't worry," Sievers replied, losing the accent. Mostly. "Nobody's getting in or out of this place without going through me first."

Tam smiled and signed off, but despite Sievers' assurances, she was uneasy. If Stone was right—and she had little doubt that he was—whatever the Immortal was planning, it wasn't going to be as obvious as what had happened the previous night.

Sievers' colorful description of the ongoing surveillance was apt, but Stone seemed to be enjoying himself.

The morning passed without incident, but shortly after noon, Martiel expressed a desire to stretch his legs. "I usually hit the fitness center about now. Is that okay?"

Stone inclined his head. "I'll join you."

From her virtual vantage-point, Tam consulted the building floor plan, and then switched to Sievers' frequency. "Billy, you ready for a change of scenery?"

"You going stir crazy over there?" Sievers replied with a chuckle.

"No...well, yes, but that's not what I mean. Our subject is moving to the fitness center."

"Fitness center?" Sievers snorted. "Rat race ain't enough exercise for these guys? All right, where is it?"

"Second floor. He'll be a lot more exposed there than in his office."

"Gotcha. I'll go keep an eye on them."

The main screen showed Martiel moving ahead of Stone, exiting the bank's offices and heading down the hallway. As they waited at the elevators, Stone spoke in a low voice, his words clearly meant only for Tam's ears.

"I think I know what's going on."

"Iron River, right?" Tam guessed.

A loud bell tone rang out, and the doors to the elevator at the end opened. As Stone swung his gaze toward it, Tam saw a couple of passengers already occupying it, but before she could get a good look at them, Martiel stepped in front of Stone, blocking her view.

"Not Iron River," Stone whispered as he followed the other man into the elevator car. "It's Mystic. All of the—"

The video feed abruptly went dark.

"Stone!"

No response.

"Shit!"

Billy Sievers knew how Tam felt about profanity, so he when he heard her expletive, he was instantly on full alert. "What's wrong?"

"I just lost Stone's signal. I think it's happening."

"Where are they?" Sievers knew better than to ask if the problem was due to local interference. A sudden loss of signal could only be the result of active multi-spectrum frequency jamming. As if to confirm this suspicion, he heard a crackle of static in his own earpiece.

The Immortal was making his move.

"Tam?"

"I still read you. We're getting some interference. They were just getting in the elevator."

Sievers dashed across the lobby to the central elevator bay, scanned the indicators mounted above each set of double doors. Two showed downward-pointing arrows, one just passing the twentieth floor, and the other evidently stopped at the third. "Which one are they in?"

He heard nothing but static in his earpiece now. The RF jammer was probably right above him, a couple hundred feet up the elevator shaft.

Tam's voice abruptly cut back in. "—the end. Left side. Your left side."

He muttered a curse of his own as he moved down the row, but even from a distance, he could see that the indicator above that particular car was pointing up. The car on the opposite side was stopped on the twenty-second floor and not moving. A knot of dread tightened around Sievers' gut. He darted back to the opposite end, hoping that Tam had simply gotten her directions reversed, but neither of the cars at that end was moving.

Tam hadn't gotten turned around. The car she had seen Stone and Martiel get into was ascending. Rising from the twenty-eighth floor, where Martiel's banking firm was located, through the thirties.

Up not down.

"Crap," he snarled, jumping forward and stabbing the call button. He understood now why the radio was working again. "They're going to the roof."

"Get up there, Billy."

A bell tone signaled the arrival of a car in response to his summons. Under almost any other circumstances, he would have taken the stairs instead of the elevator, but forty-two floors was a long haul, and there was no time left on the clock. He darted into it and hit the button for his destination, but as the doors started to close, a hand shot through the narrowing gap.

Sievers' own hand dipped beneath his leather bomber jacket, to curl around the grip of the compact SIG Sauer P228 concealed in a shoulder holster under his left arm, but when the doors parted again to reveal a balding, overweight man in a rumpled suit, jabbering into his phone, Sievers reached instead for his wallet. He flashed his cover credentials, which identified him as a special investigator with the Securities and Exchange Commission, and extended his free hand, palm out, to block the would-be passenger. "This one's full," he said.

The man gawped at him, seemingly paralyzed, so Sievers gave him a firm push until the doorway was clear. This time it closed without interference.

As the car began rising, Sievers hit the illuminated '42' button repeatedly, even though he knew it would have no effect.

"Too bad this thing doesn't have a button for NOS," he muttered as the indicator slowly ticked through the floors.

The ascent seemed to take forever, but thankfully the ride was non-stop all the way to the top floor. As soon as the doors began to open, he was moving, pushing through and sprinting down the hallway toward the roof access stairwell. Unlike the busy lobby, the uppermost story was as quiet as a funeral parlor; the only sound Sievers could hear was the thud of his footsteps on the carpeted floor. He hit the door to the stairwell at a full run, slamming it back against the wall with a noise that seemed as loud as a gunshot, and pounded up the stairs two at a time. Another door barred his way to the roof, but he burst through that as well, and into a blast of wind.

The rooftop of the high-rise was sheltered on all sides by a high wall, part of the tower's eco-friendly design, but the wind whipping across the open top created a weird low-pressure environment that seemed to suck the air right out of his lungs. He drew his pistol and started forward, hastily clearing the blind corners around the HVAC units and other superstructures, on his way to the steep metal stairs that led up to the catwalk atop the perimeter wall. He saw no sign of anyone on the rooftop. He crept up the stairs, getting just a glimpse of the spectacular unrestricted three hundred and sixty-degree view of the entire New York City skyline, before ducking back down, just in case one of the Immortal's goons was waiting to take a potshot at him, but the catwalk was similarly deserted. The only thing moving was the wind.

He poked his head up again, leading with the pistol and stepped up onto the catwalk, and that was when he saw them.

A pair of figures, momentarily silhouetted against the shimmering, sun-dappled surface of the East River, as they fell away into oblivion.

He holstered his pistol and keyed his radio mic. "Uh, you're not going to believe this. They just jumped."

EIGHT

Zurich, Switzerland

"So if it's called the Council of Rome," Greg Johns asked, "why are we in Switzerland?"

Avery grinned, surprised that it had taken so long for either of her traveling companions to ask the obvious question. She supposed it had something to do with the fact that, Greg—Tam Broderick's second-in-command—and Kasey Kim had been more concerned with travel arrangements, and probably also the fact that Avery herself had spent most of the nearly ten-hour flight either buried in her research or sleeping. It was only now that they were on the ground in Zurich, heading by taxi to the address listed on the Council of Rome's official website, that the question seemed particularly relevant.

"The group got its start after a discussion at a cocktail party in Rome," she explained. "One of the people suggested they form an advisory council, and the name stuck. That's the official history anyway, but there are some conspiracy nuts who claim that they chose the name to symbolize opposition to Christianity because Rome represents the Catholic Church. Which is weird because most of these people think the Church is evil, too. Conspiracy theories have their own unique logic."

"That explains the name," Greg retorted, "but it doesn't explain Switzerland."

"That's easy," put in Kasey. "They came here for the chocolate."

Despite her Korean heritage, Kasey Kim was a California girl, born and raised, with a sarcastic—or as Kasey put it, "bitchy"—sense of humor. Greg was less complicated in every respect. He had the athletic build and refined features of a Hollywood actor—in fact, Stone had given him the nickname "Captain Handsome"—but in most respects, he was a generic middle-America white guy. He and Billy Sievers got along famously.

"Not the watches?" Greg asked, playing along. "Or army knives?"

"Zurich is the financial capital of Europe," Avery said. "The Council of Rome is, predominantly, an organization of businessmen. And Switzerland is politically neutral, which is why so many international groups like the Red Cross and the World Health Organization are based here."

"I still say it's the chocolate," Kasey insisted, playfully.

"I didn't think Asians liked chocolate," Greg said.

"All women like chocolate, Greg."

Avery stared out the window and tried to tune out the banter. Under any other circumstances, she would have been excited about visiting the historic city, which had been settled in pre-Roman times, and was strongly associated with the reign of Charlemagne, but instead, she was anxious about the impending meeting with Maxim Loew, the secretary general of the Council of Rome. She was worried that she had made the wrong call.

Maybe Stone was right; maybe this was a red herring, a distraction.

She hated how he was always so sure of himself almost as much as she hated the fact that he was always right. But he hadn't really given a valid reason for rejecting what she had discovered. It had seemed to Avery like he was dismissing it because it had been her idea, and not his.

Despite that, she was acutely aware of his absence. She felt like she was out on a ledge without a safety net.

The taxi navigated through streets crowded with late afternoon traffic and stopped in front of a surprisingly modern-looking building perched on the eastern bank of the Limmat River, with a commanding view of the Lindenhof—the green hill which had once been the site of both a Roman castle and the Carolingian royal palace, and was generally considered to be the center of Zurich. Avery got out and looked around for a sign with the Council of Rome's logo, or some other indication that they were in the right place, but the concrete building was utterly unremarkable.

"Are you sure this is the right place?" Avery asked the driver, using French, one of the official languages of both Switzerland and her native Canada.

The driver repeated back the address she had given him and then assured her that was where they were. She turned to Greg and Kasey. "This is it."

Greg nodded. "Lead the way."

"Me?"

"It's your show, Avery. We're just here to keep you safe."

Avery suddenly felt a little light-headed. "I don't know what to do."

"Do what you always do," Kasey said. "Ask questions and figure it out."

"Ask questions," she murmured. "Right."

She headed over to the front door and entered a tastefully decorated lobby. A directory mounted to the wall near the elevator listed the names of tenants in both German and French. There was only one occupant listed for the third floor: *Conseil de Rome.*

Swallowing down her nerves, Avery reached for the button to summon the elevator, but Kasey stopped her. "Avery, you know better." She pointed to the stairs at the end of the hall.

Avery did know better. The CIA officers preferred to avoid taking elevators whenever possible. Something about losing situational awareness. She nodded and turned toward the stairs. "I guess we're walking."

In Europe, Avery had learned, the floor at street level was called the "ground" floor, and the floor above that was the "first," so the Council of Rome was actually four stories up, not three, but it hardly made a difference. It wasn't like they were trying to get to the top of the Eiffel Tower or the Empire State Building.

A pair of Herculite frameless glass doors opened into an elegant but understated lobby. There were only a few chairs, and no one at the reception desk, but as soon as the three of them were inside, a man came out to greet them. He was older, with a magnificent white beard. If he had been about forty pounds heavier, and traded in his business suit for red pajamas, he could easily have gotten work as a department store Santa Claus.

"You are the Americans who called earlier?" The man spoke English with only a trace of an accent—a nasally Bronx accent.

"Uh, yes… Are you… umm… Secretary…"

"Mister Loew is fine," the man said. "If I decide I like you, I'll let you call me Max."

Avery managed a half-hearted smile and introduced herself and the others before cutting to the chase. "We're here because you recently acquired an item—a brazen head—from the estate of Gerald Roche."

Loew tilted his head forward to stare at her over the top of his spectacles. "What's your interest in it?"

"I'm a historian…History professor, actually."

"Is that a fact?" Loew's gaze shifted to Greg and then Kasey. His frown deepened, and Avery could tell that she was going to need to come up with something better.

She decided honesty was probably the best policy. "I *am* a history professor," she reiterated, "but the truth is, I'm consulting with a law enforcement agency. We're following up a tip that indicates someone may try to…well, steal the Brazen Head."

Loew brought his eyes back to her for a moment, then uttered a short, derisive laugh. "You're talking about the Immortal, right?"

Half a block away, four men watched the front of the building that housed the Council of Rome from the relative shelter of a parked silver Volkswagen Polo. The man in the passenger seat checked his watch—a sturdy stainless steel Rolex—and frowned. "This is taking too long."

He did not intend the complaint as anything but a

rhetorical conversation, but the man seated beside him responded nonetheless. "It's your call, Luc. Say the word, and we go."

Luc LeMans grunted. It wasn't really his call. He had some latitude when it came to operational decisions, but they were well outside the original parameters of the mission.

This was supposed to have been simple—grab and go, in and out, with no residual footprint—but the unexpected arrival of after-hours visitors had put that plan on hold. The visitors had not been turned away at the door, as he had hoped, but had gone inside as if expected.

The timing of their arrival was suspicious enough to warrant a phone call to their employer. Had the old man sent in a second team? Were they from a rival faction? Competitors? Or was this merely a coincidence?

There were too many unknown variables here. Still, if the old man didn't get back to him soon, he would have to make a decision. Call in an audible, as some of the Americans he had worked with in the past were fond of saying.

His phone buzzed with an incoming text message. He glanced at it hopefully, but it was not the guidance he needed. Just the opposite in fact.

One of the three visitors had been tentatively identified as an American FBI agent.

Definitely not a coincidence, he thought.

He put the phone away.

"We're going in."

"You already know about that?" Avery said, unable to completely hide her surprise.

"What's the good of having a demon-possessed talking automaton if it can't warn you when enemies are lurking?" He maintained his stare a moment longer before breaking into a broad smile. "I'm kidding, of course. Dr. Halsey, we deal with threats like this on a daily basis. It goes with the territory, I'm afraid. Most are just the deluded rantings of paranoid Internet conspiracy theorists, but sometimes those people are the most unpredictable. I assure you, we take all threats very seriously."

"We take them seriously, too," Greg said. "That's why we're here."

"I have a hired security specialist who actively monitors threats," Loew said. "And I've taken measures to protect both our personnel and property. I'm grateful for your concern, but really, you could have saved yourself the trip and just sent me an email."

Avery saw her opening. "Actually, in researching this, I became fascinated with the story of the Brazen Head. I was hoping to get a look at it. If that's okay with you."

Loew's bushy eyebrows drew together in a frown, and he gave her another long appraising look. "You said you're with a law enforcement agency. May I see your credentials?"

Greg and Kasey produced their cover creds—forged FBI badges and identification cards. Loew looked closely at them for several seconds, then straightened. "Very well. Right this way." He gestured to the door through which he had arrived.

This surprised Avery. "You keep it here?"

"We entertain visitors from time to time, many of whom share your fascination," Loew explained. "They are quite the conversation piece."

"They?"

Loew led them into a brightly lit gallery. The room was long and narrow, the walls adorned with an eclectic collection of framed paintings. The works were unfamiliar to Avery, who had a passing interest in art history, but she recognized the styles present in several of them. She gave the paintings only a passing glance though. Her attention was immediately drawn to the objects displayed on pedestals arrayed down the length of the room—not one, but four metallic human busts.

"There's more than one?"

Loew gave a good-natured laugh. "In the twelfth and

thirteenth centuries, automatons were all the rage. I didn't set out to become a collector. It sort of just happened. They're really just simple mechanical toys. Puppets. Like a ventriloquist's dummy. This one…" He indicated a tarnished and dented statue head with the flowing curls of a Roman god. "Was probably used as a prop in an Elizabethan era stage play."

"Which one is the…?"

"The real Brazen Head of Albert Magnus?" He walked to the far end of the gallery and gestured to the head resting atop the last decorative column.

The head was bald, with round lidded eyes that bulged out slightly and a truncated nose with deep nostril holes. Lines ran down from the corners of the mouth to the chin, suggesting the possibility of articulated movement to simulate speech. Shapeless protrusions jutted out where the ears would have been, and below them, a thick cylindrical neck column that disappeared into a round block of what looked like corkwood. Unlike the first head Loew had pointed out, this was not cast metal, but appeared instead to have been assembled, with numerous riveted and welded seams showing where the pieces met and overlapped. Avery's first thought was that the Brazen Head looked like a Steampunk version of C-3PO from the Star Wars films.

"Does it work?"

Loew laughed again. "Do you mean, does it answer questions and foretell the future? Sadly, no."

Avery laughed as well, realizing how silly the question had been. "I thought Albert's Brazen Head was smashed by Thomas Aquinas."

"That's the story. That's all we have really. Stories told and retold until it's impossible to separate fact from fancy. Many of the stories about brazen heads were never meant to be taken seriously. Medieval science fiction. But those stories have a way of coloring our reality. And, over the centuries, attaching to real physical objects."

Avery nodded. The caveat had taken some of the wind

out of her sails. What reason was there, really, to believe that story of the Brazen Head of Albert Magnus was true, or that the object resting on the pedestal in front of her was, in fact, an actual medieval artifact, and not a forgery?

"If the story is true, however," Loew went on, a mischievous gleam shining from his eyes, "if this actually is the same head that Albert Magnus created, and that Thomas Aquinas smashed, well then we would have to conclude that someone put it back together. Wouldn't you say?"

"Who?"

"An interesting question, and one that I hope to explore in my twilight years."

"So do you believe it's the real deal?"

Loew placed a hand atop the Brazen Head. "I don't know if this is actually Albert Magnus' creation, or if there was any truth to that story at all, but I do know a thing or two about the history of this piece. It's the reason I became interested in medieval automata in the first place. You see, this piece has been in my family for several generations."

That was a surprise to Avery. "Are we talking about the same bronze head? I thought you only just acquired it at auction."

Loew's smile slipped a little. "Better to say, 'reacquired.'"

Just as he was about to elaborate, a door at the back of the gallery flew open and a middle-aged but fit looking Caucasian man stepped briskly into the gallery. He had close-cropped light brown hair and wore a loose-fitting business suit. Avery jumped and let out a startled yelp. From the corner of her eye, she saw Kasey and Greg shift instantly to a ready posture.

Loew seemed surprised as well, but immediately addressed the man in what Avery assumed was German. "Hans? *Was ist los?*"

"*Es besteht Gefahr,*" the man—Hans—replied in the same tongue. "*Du musst in den sicheren Raum gehen.*"

"What's wrong?" Greg asked, stepping forward, putting himself between Avery and the newcomer.

Behind his spectacles, Loew's eyes were wide with something like real fear. His jaw worked for a moment as if he was having trouble switching back to English. "This is my security expert, Hans. He says there's trouble. We need to get to the safe room."

"Safe room? Where's that?"

But before Loew could answer, Kasey cried out in alarm. "Get down!"

An eruption of light and noise, and Avery's world turned sideways.

NINE

Jersey City

"Jumped?"

Sievers winced as Tam's decibel level nearly blew out his eardrum.

"BASE jumped," he amended, watching as a pair of brightly-colored rectangular ram-air canopies settled toward street level. The wind was pushing them south, parallel to the waterfront, and when they landed a moment later, the chutes were pulled forward, revealing two people attached to each, harnesses lashed together in a tandem jump configuration.

Tam's voice squawked in his ear again. "You're telling me Stone parachuted off a damn building?"

He stared down a moment longer, trying to fully process what he was seeing. Tandem rigs. Four people. Ski masks obscured their faces—even without that bit of camouflage, they were too far away for him to distinguish any recognizable features anyway—but he assumed it had to be Stone, Martiel, and two bad guys. "They had help. It's an abduction, Tam. They're on the street. I'm going after them."

"No," Tam countered. "Stay there. I need you to maintain visual contact. I'll try to cut them off."

Sievers muttered a curse that would have earned a stern look from his boss if he had sent it over the radio, then ran along the catwalk to the southwest corner. A large boom crane supported a suspended window washing platform, and he hooked one arm around the metal frame so that he could lean out a little further to get a better look.

Seven hundred and eighty feet below, the jumpers had unhooked their tandem harnesses, separating, and two of them—presumably the kidnappers—began pulling in the chutes, cramming the canopies into stuff sacks. A ring of curious onlookers had formed around them. No one seemed particularly interested in interfering, but many seemed to be recording the action on their mobile devices. No one seemed the least bit interested in stepping forward to help the abducted men.

Typical, Sievers thought.

Still, he couldn't really fault them. The spectators probably had no idea what was really happening. He wondered why Stone and Martiel didn't seem to be offering any resistance, and why they had gone along with the insane leap from the top of the tower. Maybe the kidnappers had made some kind of threat that couldn't be ignored.

At least there would be plenty of visual evidence to the crime. The police wouldn't even have to confiscate the phones; the videos would probably go viral in a matter of minutes.

Speaking of the police... He keyed his mic again. "Tam. Where the hell are you?"

"Moving," came the slightly out of breath reply. "I'm a block away."

"Crap," he muttered. Once the kidnappers got their chutes squared away, they would be a lot harder for him to keep track of. And if they had accomplices waiting nearby with a vehicle...

I should be down there.

He knew Tam was right. It would take him a couple minutes at the very least to exit the building, and by that time the kidnappers and their hostages might be anywhere. At least this way, he could guide Tam to them. But it really sucked being stuck on the roof while the action was happening down in the street.

"Too bad those jokers didn't leave an extra parachute up here."

Then he realized there was one other way to get down to the street in a hurry, without losing visual contact.

"Oh, hell no," he said, letting go of the crane mount like it was electrified, and taking a step back from the edge.

But even as the smart, sane part of his brain began enumerating all the reasons why he shouldn't even consider doing *that*, another inner voice—the one that had gotten him into a lot of trouble as a kid—spoke up. "On the other hand. Why not?"

About a dozen stories below, hanging by the cables from the boom crane, was the window washing platform. Sievers could see two men wearing bright hardhats and safety vests standing on the platform, looking down at the spectacle on the street below.

How far down are they? A hundred feet? One-fifty, max?
Yeah. I can do that.

And before that smart, sane voice could argue, he climbed up onto the horizontal boom and started crawling out to the end. When he reached the sliding pulley that regulated the distance from the platform to the side of the tower, he stripped off his leather jacket, put the collar between his teeth, and then lowered himself out over the edge.

That was the moment when the smart, sane voice finally realized what the hell he was doing and started screaming.

He ignored it, just as he had numerous times during his first career as an Army Airborne soldier when he had jumped out of planes and rappelled from helicopters. That primal fear response was the real danger, causing doubt and paralysis at the very moment when confidence and mobility were needed the most.

That was what he had always told himself, anyway. Ignore it. Don't think about it. Don't look down.

It usually worked.

But this time it was different. This time, there was no parachute, no safety harness. Just him and a hundred feet of greasy wire rope, about the same thickness as his pinky finger. If he couldn't hold onto it, there would be another six hundred feet or so of nothing to grab onto, and then...

Splat.
Okay, maybe not such a good idea.

He forced himself to focus on the cable. It was just eighteen inches from his face, easily within reach, but transferring to it would mean letting go of the boom.

Don't think. Just do it.

He brought his feet together around the wire rope, squeezing the soles of his boots together like caliper brakes on the rim of a wheel. He let go with his right hand, felt the strain of his full weight on his left, but quickly drew his arm back, grabbed his jacket and thrust it forward to wrap it around the cable.

He was committed now. This was only going to end one way, and the sooner he accepted that, the sooner it would be over.

Clenching the cable with all his might, he let go of the boom. Gravity immediately took over and, despite his grip on the wire and the force he was exerting with his feet, he began to fall. The heat of friction was instantaneous, burning right through the leather of his jacket and the vulcanized rubber soles of his boots. The heat was intense, painful, but he squeezed even harder, and incredibly, his descent slowed. An odor of something burning reached his nostrils, leather or flesh, he could not say for certain. He brought his left hand up under his right, catching jacket and cable in his grip, squeezing.

And then, with unexpected suddenness, his feet struck something solid. His knees buckled, absorbing some of the energy, but a flare of pain shot through his ankles, up his shins. The impact jarred his feet loose, but enough of his downward momentum had been lost to allow him to keep his grip on the cable. He got his feet back under him, realizing even as he did that he had reached the block from which the platform was suspended. A glance down confirmed this, as did the surprised cries of the two men just below.

Sievers took just a second to draw a breath, and another to give a relieved sigh, before relaxing his grip a little so that he could lower himself down the rest of the way. Despite their obvious dismay, the two workmen reached out and helped guide him down onto the platform which swayed back and forth under them like the deck of a storm-tossed ship.

"What the hell, buddy?" asked one of the men. "You forget your parachute?"

"Something like that," Sievers replied. His legs suddenly felt rubbery, and he clutched the safety rail.

The workman's gaze dropped to the weapon holstered under Sievers' left arm. "You ain't supposed be out here." Despite the man's surly demeanor, his voice quavered.

"Federal agent in pursuit. Can you get me down to the street?"

The man let out a low whistle, the fear gone. "Federal?"

For a moment, Sievers thought he was going to have to show his badge which would have doubtless led to even more questions, but the man turned and gripped a lever on the control box. "Didn't know jumping off a building was a federal crime now," he muttered. "Hang on."

Sievers looked down to the street, trying to reacquire visual contact with the kidnappers. In the brief few seconds it had taken him to slide down the cable, the men had finished stowing their chutes and were moving. He could tell this because the crowd of spectators that had gathered around them was shifting, undulating like the electron shell of an atom or the membrane of a living cell, with the figures at the center comprising the nucleus.

They were moving north, along the paved waterfront, following a course that would bring them right past him.

The platform shuddered a little and began lowering, but instead of the rapid descent of an elevator, the suspended window washing rig seemed to be barely moving. Sievers looked back at the tower, watching the windows roll past one at a time, about two seconds per story.

At this rate, it would take a couple minutes to reach the street.

He glanced back at the man working the controls.

"Can't you go faster?"

"Hey, you want fast, you should'a took the stairs."

Sievers scowled, but knowing that further exhortations would serve no purpose, returned his attention to the street below. The platform was still a good two hundred feet above street level, too far for him to clearly recognize Stone or Martiel. All four of the men appeared to be wearing coveralls of some kind, their ski masks rolled up like watch caps. The only distinctive features he could make out were the stuff sacks that the two BASE jumpers carried, and those might easily be mistaken for backpacks. The group was walking briskly, trying to lose themselves in the crowd and evidently succeeding. The further they got from their illicit drop zone, the more their anonymity returned.

Tam's voice sounded in his ear. "Billy, talk to me. Where are they?"

He keyed his mic. "Heading north along the river. Where are you?"

"Essex Street. Almost to the water."

He resisted the urge to look in that direction, to break his surveillance of the foursome moving up the waterfront. The pavement jogged east at Sussex Street, and Sievers expected the group to turn there, which would take them around a corner of the tower and out of his field of view, but instead, they turned the other way, west onto the Paulus Hook pier jutting out over the Hudson River.

They would be trapped there.

Unless...

As if in response to that thought, he spotted a bright yellow shape floating on the water, just below the helicopter landing pad at the end of the pier. It was a boat, specifically, a Zodiac semi-rigid inflatable boat, lashed to one of the pilings under the helipad.

He keyed the mic again. "Tam, they're on the pier. They've got a boat waiting."

"You're sure?" She didn't wait for confirmation. "We're gonna need backup. I'll contact DHS. Maybe we can whistle up a chopper."

Sievers could tell that Tam wasn't happy about having to involve an outside agency. Doing so would throw back the curtain on their investigation, and no telling where things might go from there. Fortunately, the possibility that the kidnappers might try to escape across the river to New York gave her suitable justification to ignore jurisdictional boundaries.

But there was no guarantee that the needed support would arrive in time to stop the kidnappers.

"Come on," he muttered, tapping his palms against the safety rail as if trying to coax more speed from the machinery.

He counted the remaining stories between himself and the street. Ten. Nine.

"Come on!"

The relentlessly plodding descent continued—six feet per second or so—until the pedestrian scaffold was just ten feet below him, at which point the man operating the cable winch made the perverse but probably necessary decision to cut the speed of the descent in half.

Directly below the platform, ringing the tower, was a permanent awning, supporting a safety net to protect pedestrians on the sidewalk from falling objects…or people, Sievers supposed.

"Thanks for the ride," he shouted, and then vaulted the rail and dropped down into the net.

He bounced once and caught the scaffold frame with his left hand, and flipped over it, just as he had the safety rail on the window cleaning platform. He absorbed the impact of landing by letting his legs fold beneath him, rolling onto his side, just as he had learned to do in Airborne Jump School. Now, just as then, the technique saved him from serious injury, but it did not shield him from the pain that shot up through his ankles and shins. He ignored it, just as he ignored the throbbing agony in his blistered palms.

There would be plenty of time to hurt later.

His unexpected arrival did not go unnoticed by the bystanders, many of whom had only just recovered from the shock of witnessing the BASE jumpers landing in their midst. He bounded up, ignoring shocked inquiries and offers of assistance, and sprinted down the sidewalk.

The pier was shaped like an enormous inverted L, jutting out into the river, with the helipad located at the end of the short arm. The pier, a hub for several transit ferries, was crowded with people coming and going. Sievers searched the crowd, looking for the kidnappers just in case he was wrong about their goal. He wasn't. Even before he reached the entrance to the pier, he spotted the four figures moving onto the helipad, moving toward the moored Zodiac.

A hundred yards of open water separated the waterfront, the helipad, and Sievers from the kidnappers and their victims.

The water wasn't empty, however.

Idling about twenty-five yards away were four jet skis ridden by young men wearing swim trunks and flotation vests—college boys by the look of them. They were close enough that Sievers could make out the lettering stenciled on the life-vests: Jer-Sea Jet Ski Tours.

The riders were staring up at the waterfront, staring directly at Sievers, or so it seemed. Had they witnessed his insane descent from the rooftop? He couldn't fathom any other reason for their interest, but decided not to question it.

He raced up to the rail at the edge of the river walk and started waving like a yokel. "Hey! How's it going?"

One of the riders grinned and flashed some kind of hand signal to him. It might have been a gang sign or an obscene gesture; Sievers had no clue which, but decided to take it as an invitation. He clambered up onto the rail and then leaped out over the river.

It was a good fifteen feet to the water's surface, far enough to deliver a good slap as he splashed down, which did his bruised ankles no good, but at least the water was warm enough to spare him a breath-taking shock as he plunged down into the murky depths.

He clawed back to the surface, bobbing up about ten feet from the jet ski with the grinning fool, who flashed the strange sign again and howled, "Bad ass, dude!"

Sievers looked past him to the helipad, where the four men in ski masks were climbing down a rope ladder to the waiting Zodiac. He had enough time to swim over, but that had never been his intent. He leaned into the water and started paddling. Three powerful strokes brought him close enough to reach out and grab the deck of the jet ski.

"I need a ride, hoss."

The young man stared at him like he had three heads, so Sievers gave up trying to explain, and instead heaved himself out of the water. A strong scissors-kick propelled him up high enough to throw his arms across the seat behind the young man. The jet ski rolled toward him, almost dumped both him and the rider back in the river, but he kicked furiously until the craft righted itself with him sprawled over it sideways. It wasn't his most graceful mount, but it got the job done.

It took him a few more seconds to get into position behind the shocked young man. He could hear the driver shouting, protesting the apparent hijacking, but louder still was the roar of the Zodiac's outboard engaging. Sievers looked up just in time to see it shoot away from the pier, racing south, downriver.

He would have preferred to simply push the guy off and commandeer the watercraft, but he knew that the jet ski was equipped with a safety-stop, a clip attached by a lanyard to the driver's wrist. If the safety clip got yanked out, it would kill electrical power and leave the little mini jet-boat dead in the water. Trying to divest the kid of his lanyard was an option, but something told him it would be a lot easier to convince the young thrill seeker to do the driving for him.

"Federal agent," he shouted and pointed over the man's shoulder to the departing Zodiac. "Follow that boat."

The kid hesitated a second, and then let out a whoop. "Hells, yeah!"

The jet ski lurched forward like a thoroughbred out of the gate. Sievers squeezed the saddle seat between his legs, automatically shifting his weight to keep his balance as the watercraft carved a sharp turn and shot out into the river.

Even burdened with two riders, the jet ski was a lot faster than the Zodiac. Too fast, Sievers thought. The kidnappers might be armed, and he didn't want to get in a running gun battle on the open water, especially not with a civilian in the middle of it all.

"Back off a bit, pardner," he shouted in his driver's ear.

The kid nodded and eased off the throttle until they were just about matching the pace of the inflatable boat, just two hundred yards away. The Zodiac had initially swung out toward the harbor as if steering toward the tip of Manhattan Island, but now it appeared to be turning back toward the Jersey side. The Zodiac appeared to be heading straight for the Statue of Liberty, but Sievers doubted that would be the kidnappers' ultimate destination. They wouldn't risk getting trapped on an island.

He keyed his mic…or tried to. The radio unit was gone, ripped away during his plunge into the harbor.

"Well, crap," he muttered. Now he had no way of knowing if Tam was on her way with backup and no way to tell her where he thought the kidnappers were headed. "Hope you were payin' attention," he muttered.

The Zodiac skirted along the eastern edge of Ellis Island, then veered right, heading for the wooded shore of Liberty Park, the jumping off point for tourists intent on visiting the historic monuments. Sievers guessed they had a vehicle waiting there, and intended to transfer their hostages to it for the next phase of their escape. If the kidnappers knew they were being pursued, they gave no indication, but that was about to change.

He leaned forward again and shouted. "Listen up. When I give you the word, I want you to punch it." He paused for breath, saw the kid nodding. "There's more. If there's any shooting... Hell, if you even see a gun, I want you to get in the water and keep your head down until it's over. Got it?"

"Shooting?" The kid laughed, which wasn't at all the response Sievers had expected.

"I'm serious."

The young man raised one hand, displaying an upraised thumb. Two hundred yards away, the Zodiac was slowing in anticipation of running aground on the narrow mud beach.

"Now!" Sievers yelled. "Punch it."

The kid let out another whoop and opened the throttle wide. The jet ski shot forward like a torpedo, arrowing toward shore.

Directly ahead, the inflatable nosed up onto the beach and shuddered to a stop. The four occupants piled out, seemingly oblivious to the pursuit. That struck Sievers as odd, but then the whole situation was odd. He saw no weapons; in fact, he couldn't even tell the kidnappers apart from the hostages. It wasn't just that their faces were covered by ski masks; all four of the men crashing through the brush at the water's edge seemed to be moving with complete independence.

Why weren't Stone and Martiel putting up more of a fight? Dragging their heels at the very least?

Something about this was wrong, very wrong.

The kid backed off the throttle a little as the beach drew near, and then cut it altogether a moment before the hull crunched up onto the beach. As soon as it did, Sievers launched himself from the jet ski. The mud caught his boots, causing him to stumble, but he recovered and kept going, drawing his pistol as he ran. He was only fifty yards behind the kidnappers, sprinting all out, closing.

Forty yards. Thirty.

Close enough.

He held his pistol out, knowing that it would be impossible to aim effectively while running, but also knowing that the reflex shot might make all the difference.

"Federal officer! Stop, or I will shoot."

To his complete astonishment, they did as instructed, skidding to a halt, hands raised in a show of surrender.

Sievers stopped, too. Keeping the gun at the ready, moving it back and forth, poised to fire at the first sign of hostile action.

In the still moment that followed, he could hear the fierce beating of his heart and the blood pumping in his veins, but another familiar sound filled the air—the harsh whine of turbine engines and the rapid rhythm of helicopter rotor blades.

An instant later, the helicopter was directly overhead, almost close enough to touch. Sievers threw himself flat, more a reflex action than a conscious decision. The tumult reached a crescendo, the rotor wash tearing at the tall grass around him like a tornado.

And then it passed by.

For a moment, Sievers feared the worst, that the aircraft was here to spirit the kidnappers away, but no sooner had the thought entered his head when he got a look at the helicopter and realized the opposite was true.

The aircraft, a dull gray UH-60 Black Hawk, pivoted, banking in front of the four men as if to block their way. There was no need; they were also face down on the ground. The rear troop door was open, revealing several men wearing camouflage fatigues and tactical gear, all with assault rifles aimed at the men on the ground, and one familiar face.

Tam Broderick.

The Black Hawk drifted back a little and then dropped lower until it was just a few feet above the ground, close enough for the tactical team to deploy. The realization that the cavalry had finally arrived jolted Sievers into action. He sprang to his feet and started forward again, keeping the weapon aimed in the direction of the four prone figures.

He knelt beside the closest man, tore off this ski mask to reveal spiky peroxide-blond hair.

The man kept his eyes forward as if afraid to look Sievers in the eye. He appeared to be unarmed, and the stuff sack with the parachute lay a few feet away, just out of reach. Sievers did a quick pat down, just to be sure, then flipped the man over.

"Don't shoot, dude!" Even with the din from the helicopter, Sievers could hear the fearful quaver in the young man's voice.

He didn't look like any kidnapper, or terrorist Sievers had ever encountered. In fact, he looked like a beach bum, with a scruffy goatee, and numerous facial piercings.

"What the hell?" Sievers' uneasy feeling returned with a vengeance, sweeping away any sense of satisfaction at having run the men down.

"Stay there. Don't move." He jabbed the pistol at the man in a menacing gesture, but backed away, toward the next closest man. The prone figure had not been carrying a stuff sack which meant he was probably one of the hostages, but when Sievers pulled off the man's mask, the face underneath did not belong to either of the hostages.

Sievers felt his guts twisting with dread.

He scrambled over to the third man. By process of elimination, it had to be either Stone or Martiel, but Sievers wasn't at all surprised when the unveiling revealed neither man.

He looked up to find Tam standing over him.

"Not them," he rasped. "They aren't here."

"Where are they?" she shouted. "Where's Stone?"

Sievers shook his head, then turned his attention back to the figure sprawled on the ground in front of him. "Where are they?"

The man, a kid really, no older than the college boy with the jet ski, stared back, goggle-eyed. "Dude, I don't know what you're talking about. Seriously. We didn't do anything—"

Sievers slapped him with his open hand. "Who are you

working for?"

"No one." The kid sounded terrified. "Some guy gave us ten large to jump off the tower. He bought us the gear and everything. That's all I know. I swear."

Sievers pushed away with a snarl of disgust, mostly self-directed. He turned to Tam. "They rooked us. Staged this little sideshow and sent us off on a wild goose chase while they took Stone out the front door."

Tam's nostrils flared, her eyes narrowing into angry slits as she reached the same conclusion. "Son of a bitch."

TEN

Zurich, Switzerland

Avery knew better than to raise her head. Not that she could have even if she really wanted to. The concussion had knocked the wind out of her, and her arms and legs felt like they were made of Jell-O. There were bright streaks across her vision, like the burned-in after-image of a flash camera, and her ears were ringing.

She recognized these symptoms as the effects of a stun grenade—commonly called a "flash-bang." Considered "less-lethal," the grenades created a blinding flash and a deafening eruption of sound, designed to disorient hostile targets while causing only minimal blast damage. Counter-terrorist operatives and SWAT teams used them when initiating raids.

It wasn't the kind of hardware she would have expected from "paranoid Internet conspiracy theorists," as Loew had called the Immortal's adherents.

As the haze receded, she realized the follow-on assault by the invading force had already begun. Bullets zipped through the air above her, slamming into the gallery walls. The reports were coming from all sides, which told her that Greg and Kasey were returning fire. That was small comfort. She was caught in the crossfire.

She blinked furiously to clear away the retinal fireworks and found herself face to face with... a face. It wasn't Loew or the man who had come bearing news of the impending attack. In fact, it wasn't a person at all, but rather a sculpted metal simulacrum.

The Brazen Head.

There was not a doubt in her mind that the brass artifact was what the attackers were really after. On an impulse, she reached out for it, taking it with both hands and pulling it close to her chest. It was a little heavier than she expected—about twenty-five pounds if she had to guess.

The display column lay on its side nearby, evidently knocked over by the concussive blast. Loew lay nearby, unmoving, unconscious maybe. Hans, the German-speaking security expert, was crawling toward him. Further away, Kasey and Greg were hunkered down behind another fallen column, trading fire with the attackers who were shooting from the cover of the gallery entrance. The air was filled with smoke and flying bits of debris, obscuring her view of the assailants, but judging by the rate and intensity of the incoming fire, there were several of them, and they had some serious firepower.

Guess we're not getting out that way, she thought, and just as quickly realized what she had to do.

Kasey and Greg wouldn't be able to hold them off forever. It was a miracle they hadn't already been overrun, but eventually they would run out of ammunition, and then it would be over. The bad guys would take the Brazen Head and probably kill them all.

She couldn't let that happen.

Just beyond Loew and Hans was the door through which the latter had arrived. She didn't know where that door led, but assumed the safe room, which was probably some kind of secure panic room, must be somewhere beyond. If she could reach it, barricade herself inside, wait for the police to arrive...

She shook her head. Even if she could find the panic room and figure out how to bolt the door, it would do her friends no good. No, she needed a better answer.

She needed to draw the enemy away.

Before she completely knew what she was going to do, she started moving, crawling toward the exit. From the corner of her eye, she could see Hans trying to drag Loew behind cover. Suddenly, he jerked as if touching a live wire, and then collapsed.

"Stay down!" Greg's shout was barely audible over the din.

She ignored the admonition. Instead of flattening herself to reduce her profile, she turned, making sure that the Brazen Head was visible to the gunmen at the far end of the gallery. Hopefully, they wouldn't shoot her and risk damaging the prize. Then, she leaped up and bolted for the exit.

"Avery, no!"

The cry trailed her into a long dimly lit hallway, adorned with red carpeting and plain wooden doors, all of which were closed. At the far end of the hall, mounted to the wall near the ceiling, was an illuminated green and white sign which depicted a running man and an arrow pointing right. It was the standard ISO emergency exit indicator, used in Switzerland and most countries of the world, and she knew there would be several more, one at each junction, to show the quickest escape route. Clutching the Brazen Head to her abdomen, she ran down the hall and made the turn, and started looking for the next sign. She found it on a red door at the end of the next hall, and this time, the pictograph of the running man was descending a staircase, and the arrow beside it was pointing down.

When she reached the door, she threw a glance over her shoulder to see if Greg and Kasey were following. They were not, but the shooting had stopped. That meant one of two things. Either the bad guys had seen her duck out and broken contact, exiting out the front in order to intercept her, or Greg and Kasey were dead, and the killers would be coming down the hall any second.

She hoped it was the former, and then thought about what that would actually mean and started down the stairs. Energized by adrenaline, she bounded down three steps at a time, with the surefootedness of a mountain goat. The descent was a blur, and it was only when she ran out of steps that she realized she had reached ground level.

There were two doors before her, but only one of them was marked with the exit sign. She hit it without slowing, throwing her hip forward into the panic bar. The latch disengaged and the door started to swing out, but then hit something solid and stopped. So did Avery, but only for an instant. Even as she rebounded back, the door opened, seemingly of its own volition, revealing a tall figure clad head-to-toe in black.

And holding a gun.

His face was mostly hidden behind a black balaclava, but she could see his eyes because they were staring right at her.

Then his gaze dropped to the Brazen Head, and his eyes went wide in recognition.

Avery reacted without thinking. She sprang forward and swung the brass artifact at the man's head. She heard a crunch and a gonging sound as it connected, and the man staggered back, dazed. Avery kept going, shouldering past the man and bursting out into the open.

She found herself in a narrow alley—too narrow to accommodate vehicles. Aside from the man she'd just clobbered, the space was deserted. She looked left then right, then decided to go right because the distance to the cross street was shorter. She resisted the urge to look back, to see if the gunman she had brained was back up and closing on her, and instead brought her gaze forward and poured on a burst of speed until she rounded the corner.

The street, which was barely wider than the alley, lined with four- and five-story buildings that loomed above like the walls of a canyon, seemed to go on forever. The brick pavement was crowded with pedestrians browsing the shops and idling at the outdoor cafes, and more than a few heads swung toward her as she sprinted past. She took comfort in the fact that, even with a disembodied brass head tucked under her arm, she was a lot less conspicuous than the man chasing her.

After the first hundred yards or so, she realized that not only did she not know where she was going, but she had no idea where she actually was. She had glanced at a map of the city during her initial research, but trying to reconcile that with her current surroundings was impossible. The street seemed to go on forever, undulating back and forth like a snake. She knew the river was only a few blocks to the west, but she had no idea which direction that was.

Abruptly, the serpentine urban canyon opened up into a plaza with streets that branched off in several directions. Directly in front of her was the corner of a large stone building with Romanesque-style arched windows. The structure was positioned at a forty-five-degree angle so that she could see two sides of it; to the right, it joined with another older looking building with an impressive looking tower…no, two towers of equal height, rising twice as high as the rest of the building and topped with matching blue and white pennants. A third tower—a red spire—rose up from the opposite side of the sprawling edifice to her left.

She knew this building. The Grossmunster, a Twelfth Century monastery church commissioned, it was said, by Charlemagne himself. The towers of the Grossmunster were the Zurich equivalent of the Transamerica pyramid in San Francisco, or Big Ben and the Tower of London.

She darted across the plaza, past a lonely tree that looked like something from a *Lord of the Rings* movie—of course, that could be said for much of Zurich—and ran for the double wooden doors, situated just below the north tower.

As was often the case with medieval architecture, the interior of the church was smaller than its notoriety would have suggested. By comparison to the cathedrals of Paris, the nave was as austere as a cave. Most of the decorative art had been removed by Protestant reformers in the Sixteenth Century, but there were a few touches of color, mostly from stained glass panels above the choir, glowing like coals in the late afternoon sun. Avery ran down the aisle, past identical rows of simple wooden pews, and headed for the passage behind the choir, which she hoped would take her to the old cloisters.

There were, she knew, a lot of places to hide in an old church.

There were also a lot of places to get lost.

Instead of a passage to the back rooms of the old church, she found herself on a descending stairway. Hopeful nonetheless, she decided to press on. The stairs led to an underground chapel, likewise sparsely decorated, though one wall still retained a few faded frescos. She located another passage and kept going.

Beyond the chapel lay a sprawling crypt, with row after row of pillars supporting arches that, she knew, bore the full weight of the massive stone edifice above. Several rows of folding wooden chairs had been set up to either side of the center aisle, and at the far end of the crypt, as if presiding over a royal court, sat the emperor himself—Charlemagne—larger than life, carved from stone, but with a golden crown on his oversized head, and a massive broadsword of wrought metal resting on his lap. To the right of the statue was another staircase, but as she approached it, she heard urgent voices and the sound of running footsteps and froze in her tracks.

Crap!

She spun around, looking for a place to hide, but aside from the chairs and pillars, there wasn't much.

The steps were getting louder. She was out of time.

Frantic, she dropped to all fours and crawled between the wooden chairs. When she reached the midpoint, she stopped, pressed herself flat, held her breath. Her heart was pounding in her chest, the roar of blood almost deafening, but she could hear the sound of feet treading on stone, and voices. The lined-up wooden chair legs formed a screen that obscured her view of the rest of the crypt, but she could see something moving down the aisle, or rather, someone.

Please don't look here. Please don't...

A shoe came into view right in front of her, just a few yards away, and then another, and then both stopped together, toes pointed right at her.

She gripped the Brazen Head between her palms. It had saved her before, working as both shield and weapon, but that had been luck as much as anything.

Still, she had to try.

She let out her breath and took another, mentally rehearsing how she would jump up and swing the brass artifact like a club....

The shoes moved, shifting position, and then abruptly vanished as the person wearing them dropped to all fours and stared directly at her.

She jolted in alarm, but then gave a squeal of relief when she saw the face of Greg Johns peering at her. Her joy was somewhat diminished by the urgency of his expression.

"Avery, come on. We need to get moving."

She scrambled to her feet and saw Kasey Kim just a few steps behind Greg. Her face was streaked with dust, and her expression was as grave as Greg's.

"You guys are okay?" Avery asked.

"Depends on your definition," Kasey replied. She pointed at the Brazen Head. "You got it? Good. Cover it up. We need to move."

Avery stared back dully. "Cover it? With what?"

Greg stripped off his sport coat and tossed it to her. "Do what you can with that. But come on."

The significance of the thrice-repeated message finally sank in. The danger wasn't past. Avery wrapped the jacket around the head and moved out from the line of chairs. "What happened? Are those guys still out there?"

Greg shook his head. "We took care of them." Then he turned and made his way toward the stairs.

The vague language sent a chill down Avery's spine. She decided she didn't need to know the particulars. "What about Max?"

"He was alive when we left. I think he was just stunned from the flash-bang. I'll make some inquiries once we get to the safe house."

"Safe house? Shouldn't we go to the police?"

Kasey spat a harsh laugh. "That's the last thing we want to do. We're supposed to be flying under the radar,

Avery."

"Oh." She felt her face flushing in embarrassment. She was a researcher, not James Bond. What had she been thinking, running off on her own like that? What would she have done if the bad guys had found her first? "How did you guys find me?"

"Tracking app on your phone. Didn't work so well once you came in here though." Kasey answered. She took Avery's arm and led her after Greg. "I sent you a text."

"I put my phone on silent."

"That was probably a good idea." She paused at the foot of the stairs and regarded Avery thoughtfully. "That was quick thinking back there. But in the future, you might want to stick a little closer to us."

"Definitely."

LeMans halted at the junction where Munstergasse and Zwingliplatz met behind Grossmunster church in a hydra-like snarl of alleys and passages. He scanned the main streets, looking for anything that might hint at the presence of his escaping quarry. Three people sprinting down the crowded streets would have made an impression, but he seemed to be the only one drawing stares now. He had removed his balaclava, and his weapon and tactical gear were hidden under a windbreaker, but he was still a conspicuous figure in his full black attire.

He stood there, unmoving, letting the adrenaline drain away as he considered what to do next. They were gone. He had lost them. Lost the Brazen Head, too.

This was a setback but not a defeat. The Americans would resurface eventually, at a train station or an airport, and then he would have them.

But that wasn't his most immediate concern.

He turned toward the river, and then headed north up the Limmatquai at a jog. He heard the wails of police sirens growing louder with each passing second, and quickened his step, reaching the Council of Rome headquarters building just a few seconds ahead of them.

He charged up the stairs, making his way to the debris-strewn lobby. The sulfur odor of burnt gunpowder reached his nostrils even before he made it through the gallery doors, but when he stepped through, a different, but all too familiar smell hit him.

The smell of death.

Two of his men lay unmoving in the doorway.

LeMans knelt, checked the nearest man for a pulse. Nothing. Both were dead.

Damn it.

Two more figures lay at the far end of the room—Loew and his head of security. They weren't moving either, but he had to be sure. No loose ends. He rose and started toward them.

"*Halt. Bewegen sich nicht.*"

The shout startled him, but he complied, holding his hands out to either side as he turned slowly to find a pair of uniformed officers from the *Kantonspolizei Zürich*. They had their weapons drawn and aimed directly at him.

LeMans fought back a surge of anger. Usually, when someone pointed a gun at him, it was the last thing they ever did, but there was a better way to handle this. "I am going to take out my credentials," he said, speaking in German. "I am *Oberstleutnant* LeMans from Reconnaissance Detachment 10, working with counter-terror service."

When neither man responded, he lowered his hands and then did as he said he would, taking out the wallet with his identification. "This is my investigation," he continued. "Put those guns away. You're working for me now."

ELEVEN

New York City

"And here I thought this day couldn't get any worse." Tam Broderick rubbed the bridge of her nose as if trying to banish a headache. "Jesus give me strength."

Avery Halsey stared back at her for a moment—the amount of time it took for the signal to travel from Tam's computer in the CIA safe house that was serving as their present headquarters, across the satellite network high above the earth's surface, to Avery's computer presently located in another safe house in Zurich—and then grimaced. She held up a bright brass head that looked like it belonged on an android in a *Star Wars* film. "We did manage to keep them from getting this."

"You were supposed to protect it, not steal it from its rightful owner. I didn't think I needed to tell you to avoid getting in a very public gunfight."

"We'll give it back to Mr. Loew when this is over," Avery said. "Besides, it's safer with us than with him, right?"

"For what it's worth," Greg Johns said, leaning in close to Avery so that he was visible to the webcam. "It looks like the Swiss authorities are keeping the whole thing under wraps. No mention of the incident in local news reports."

"That's supposed to make me feel better?" She raised a hand to forestall any further explanations. "Look, I'm glad you guys made it out okay. You came out of it a lot better than we did."

In truth, she was relieved that none of her people had been injured in the surprise attack, and even a little bit pleased that they had managed to take possession of the Brazen Head. There would be blowback to be sure, but she had no doubt that, given the circumstances, they had made the right decisions.

Tam did not feel the same certainty about her own actions, and unlike her colleagues, she had lost. Stone and Martiel had vanished, and she didn't have the slightest idea where to begin looking for them. And while Sievers had kept busy with reviewing surveillance camera footage in hopes of finding a lead to their whereabouts, she had been obliged to handle the fallout of her team's failures. Her boss at the CIA could not find fault with anything the Myrmidons had actually done, but smoothing all the feathers they had ruffled by carrying out not one but two unsanctioned operations, one of them on American soil, had used up an extraordinary amount of political capital and he wasn't about to let her forget about it.

But dealing with that was her problem. She wasn't going to take it out on the rest of the team. She placed her hands flat on the tabletop, attempting to preserve at least a modicum of professional dignity. "Avery, have you learned anything about that brass gizmo? Why is it so da—" She caught herself, barely. "What makes it worth killing for?"

Avery shook her head. "I don't know. Yet, I mean. I'm not even sure it's the real Brazen Head of Albert Magnus."

"Well can you find out?"

"Umm. Maybe." She paused a beat and then said, "I did find out one thing. Just before the attack, Loew said something about reacquiring the head."

"Reacquiring? Like it used to be his?"

"Right. We know it came from the collection of Gerald Roche, but there's no record of how he got it, which means it was probably something shady. Stolen property, sold on the black market. Stolen from Loew or maybe his ancestors. Southwick's wouldn't have handled the sale of an item with contested ownership, so evidently Loew didn't have a strong claim, but it was important enough for him to pay for it with his own money.

"But it got me thinking. How did they lose it in the first place? So I did a little digging into Max Loew, and guess what I found out?"

"You know how I feel about guessing games, Avery."

"Oh. Sorry. Um, well, Max grew up in the Bronx, but he was born in Prague. That's in the Czech Republic. It used to be Czechoslovakia, and before that, it was—"

Tam sighed. "Avery. Get to the point."

It took a couple seconds for Avery to register the interruption.

"—Bohemia, but when Max was born in 1935 it was still... Oh, Sorry. The point is, he was born into a wealthy Jewish family, living in Prague, which was taken over by the Nazis in 1939. Max's family escaped the Holocaust, and eventually made it to America, but everything they owned was seized by the Nazis. I think Max's family owned the Brazen Head, but left it behind when they escaped."

Tam had figured as much when Avery mentioned 1935, but she withheld comment, knowing that the signal delay would only create confusion. Instead, she just nodded. "Go on."

"I couldn't find any evidence that the Nazis ever possessed the Brazen Head, and it doesn't appear on any of the lists of things that were recovered by Allied forces at the end of the war. You know, like in *Monument Men*? But those stories about the Nazis being obsessed with the occult aren't an exaggeration. They would have recognized the Brazen Head for what it was, and they would have tried to use it."

"Nazis," Tam muttered. "It's always Nazis. All right. Let's put a pin in that. We need to find Stone."

"What do you want us to do?" Greg said. "Do you need us there?"

She shook her head. "Just before things went sideways, Stone said this has something to do with Mystic."

"Wasn't there a secret government agency called Mystic?" Greg said. "Something to do with UFOs?"

"You're thinking of Majestic Twelve," Avery replied.

"Also sometimes called Majic or MJ-12." She shrugged guiltily. "Bones told me about it."

Tam recalled when Avery had briefly dated Uriah "Bones" Bonebrake, the treasure-hunting partner of Avery's half-brother. Bones was a good man in a fight, but not ideal life-partner material. Although she tried not to interfere in the personal affairs of her team members, Tam was secretly glad Bones was mostly out of Avery's life.

She realized that Avery was still talking.

"Mystic is a word that describes esoteric knowledge. Same root word as mystery. Or it could refer to a person who studies mysticism. There's also a Mystic River in Connecticut. And a movie called—"

"This Mystic is a computer," Tam said, trying to stop the information free-fall. "Or a computer program. I wasn't too clear on that."

Avery leaned over her own computer and began typing. "Got it. Mystic is the name of an operating system and trading platform used by several large financial institutions, including the bank where Thom Martiel works. It's an artificial intelligence that utilizes something called the Monte Carlo method of computation… Oh, it's the same principle used to generate Markov chains. Like Stone was talking about."

Tam's patience was wearing thin. "Is that important?"

Avery shrugged and shook her head. "I don't know. This is all pretty dense stuff. Stone would get it."

"Well, Stone isn't here," Tam snapped, and then immediately regretted losing her cool. "Sorry. But we're going to have to do this without him, Avery. *You* are going to have to do this."

Avery swallowed. "Okay, if I'm reading this right, the Monte Carlo method works by repeated random statistical sampling to determine the probability of a specific outcome. It's kind of like casino gambling, which is how it got its name, but there are a lot more variables in play in the world financial system, so it requires a huge amount of computational power. In a way, you were right. Mystic is both a computer and a program. The Mystic trading platform is an online service, but the actual processing all takes place in a secure server farm in Washington State, near Spokane."

"Iron River."

"Right. The company was founded by Wayne Valero in 1990. He built it around the Mystic OS."

Tam searched her memory, trying to recall the details of Stone's conversation with Martiel. "Stone asked about the possibility of someone trying to manipulate Mystic."

Avery stared back blankly for a few seconds, but then seemed to have an epiphany. She resumed typing on her keyboard and then sat back. "That's the connection. All of the bankers and finance people who died worked for institutions that use Mystic. Those deaths would have created vacancies, and what do you want to bet the Immortal had people hand-picked to fill them?"

"How does this help us find Stone?"

Avery appeared to consider her answer. "I guess it doesn't. But figuring out what the Immortal is trying to do is the only chance we have of stopping him, isn't it?"

Tam knew Avery was right. They had to keep their eye on the ball, stop the Immortal from doing…whatever it was he was trying to do. Saving Stone would have to take a back seat for the moment.

She realized that Avery was speaking again. "This is going to sound weird, but…."

"But what?"

"Well, it occurred to me that the Brazen Head is sort of the medieval equivalent of Mystic. I mean, it was a machine designed to answer questions about the future. In a way, it *was* a sort of mystic machine."

Tam looked at Avery sideways. "Is that why the Immortal wants it?"

Avery gave a nervous laugh. "It's silly, I know. I'm sure it's just symbolic."

"Hell of a lot of trouble to go to for a symbol," Greg put in.

"No kidding," Tam said. "All right. We need to know why they want it. Stick with this. Run down the Nazi angle and see where it leads."

"I guess we could talk to the auction house in London," Avery said. "Maybe they can tell us a little more about its provenance."

"Do what you have to, but whatever you do—"

"I know," Greg said. "Be careful. We will."

"I was going to say, don't lose it."

Billy Sievers withheld comment until Tam finished her teleconference with the rest of team, but when she closed the laptop, probably a little more forcefully than she should have, he remarked, "Nazis, huh?"

"Can't seem to get away from them," Tam growled. "Seventy years since we kicked their butts, and they're still ruining my day. We know the Dominion has ties to neo-Nazi groups, so it won't surprise me if they're involved, but right now, all we've got is Avery's theory that the Head *might* have been captured by the Nazis. It could be a dead end."

"You know, the Nazis took a lot of loot from wealthy Jewish families, and a lot of it ended up in Swiss banks. Still there today, protected by Swiss law and…" He made air quotes with his fingers. "Neutrality."

"What are you driving at?"

"Those guys that hit the Council of Rome sound like professionals. And the cover-up tells me they weren't freelancers. I'd bet money those guys were ARD 10. Swiss military special forces. They handle the paramilitary and counter-terrorism operations for the Swiss police. Helluva a coincidence, don't you think?"

Tam raised an eyebrow. "You're a very suspicious man, Billy. And smarter than you want folks to think, too."

"Shucks, I just hear things." Sievers grinned. People often made the mistake of underestimating his intelligence; something to do with his Texas drawl, probably. Unfortunately, working with the Myrmidons meant he usually was the dumbest guy in the room.

"Maybe I should have sent you to keep an eye on them."

"And miss all the excitement here?"

"I could go for fewer thrills." Tam's expression softened a little. Her eyes dropped to the tablet computer Sievers was holding. "Is that movie any better the second time around?"

Sievers' tablet was displaying video footage taken from one of the security cameras in the high-rise building. Since Stone's disappearance, they had both reviewed the video feed from every operating camera in the tower, hoping to catch a glimpse of the real kidnappers. The daredevil BASE jumpers were still in custody, but beyond the fact that an anonymous sponsor had given them ten thousand dollars in cash to stage the stunt, they had little to offer, which was unfortunate for them as well since what was left of that payment had been seized as evidence, and the four young men were in a lot more trouble than they realized.

"Not really. These guys, the ones that really grabbed Stone, knew what they were doing."

"Why kidnap them? He or they or whoever killed all the others. Why take Martiel alive?"

Sievers thought Tam was just thinking aloud, and since he didn't have an answer to offer, he kept silent. He was wrong about that, though.

"Come on, Billy," Tam said, fixing him with her stare. "I need your input. What's going on? How do we crack this nut?"

"I'm a soldier, Tam, not a detective."

"Fine. Tell me what a soldier would do."

Sievers rubbed his chin. "Start with threat assessment. Figure out what the enemy's next move is going to be. Which, if I heard correctly, has something to do with this fancy computer program. Now, it sounds to me like this Immortal has spent the last two years putting his people in position to hijack Mystic. And then, out of the blue, he wants this brass doodad in Switzerland. Why shift gears like that?"

"Because he's ready to take it to the next level."

Sievers nodded. "His troops are in position. All they're waiting for is the signal to attack. We may not know who he is, but we can figure out who they are—the people who took over for the people who got killed."

Tam shook her head. "I can't just round them all up. Not without a lot more proof."

"Then we figure out how to shut them out of Mystic."

"I don't know how to do that. Do you?"

Sievers straightened, working out the kinks from too much time spent sitting and staring at a computer screen. "I spent most of last night rebuilding an engine. I could do that, because I know how it works. But if you'd asked me to rebuild that Lexus, I'd have been lost in the woods. It's all electronics and computers now."

"You're saying we have to find an expert on Mystic. Someone who can help us figure out how it's vulnerable."

"I'm sayin' we should probably talk to the guy who built it."

TWELVE

Unknown location

Awareness returned slowly to Stone, like sunlight gradually burning away a thick fog. He had no sense of where he was or how he had gotten there, and it took several seconds for him to pin down the last thing he remembered.

I was with Thom Martiel in his office.

Martiel was still there, seated next to him in a folding chair, just like the one Stone himself occupied. Martiel appeared to be asleep, with his head sagging forward, chin almost touching his chest. They definitely weren't in that office now, but the small windowless room looked like it might be serving a similar purpose albeit informally. The fluorescent light overhead illuminated a single wooden door set in one of the featureless white walls, and a collapsible long table positioned against another. A desktop computer, identical to the Mystic terminal in Martiel's office, rested on the latter.

Stone stared at the blank screen for several seconds, trying to build a bridge between that last memory and his present situation, but the connection continued to elude him.

Before joining forces with Tam and the Myrmidons, he had been imprisoned at a "black site," an unsanctioned detention facility in the mountains of Romania, interrogated by security contractors working for the U.S. government, and during the course of his involuntary stay, he had been dosed with various sedatives and truth serums. He couldn't remember anything about being under the influence of those drugs—memory loss was one of the side-effects—but he remembered what it felt like to come back down. It was exactly how he felt now.

Someone drugged me.

He made no effort to rise from his seat. Even though his mind was working again, he knew the physical effects of the drug would impair his reflexes and possibly trigger bouts of vertigo or nausea. He did, however, raise his hands, flexing his fingers experimentally and then patted his pockets to see if the radio unit was still there. It was not. His pockets were empty. The glasses with the hidden video camera were gone as well. His captors had taken everything, even his wristwatch.

He had no sense of how much time had passed, but guessed it had been several hours. Plenty of time for his captors to take him…anywhere, really.

He glanced over at Martiel again, then brought his gaze back to the laptop which seemed to beckon invitingly. *Like the cheese in a mousetrap*, he thought.

Still, he would learn nothing if he refused to take the bait. He rose slowly to avoid passing out, and used his chair like a walker, scooting it closer to the table before plopping down again and tapping the touchpad on the laptop. The screen lit up instantly, revealing an open browser window with a video-conferencing software enabled.

Immediately, an electronic trilling sound issued from the computer, along with a flashing message, alerting him to an incoming call. Behind him, Martiel stirred from his stupor, mumbling incoherently. Stone ignored him and, knowing that he had little choice in the matter, used the touchpad to move the cursor over the green button to accept the call.

The light appeared at the top of the screen, indicating that the built-in webcam was broadcasting, and then the square video player in the browser window flickered, revealing, not a person, but a computer-generated animated simulacrum that spoke, with a warbling and distorted electronic approximation of a voice.

"Welcome, Gavin Stone."

Stone's lips twitched into a smile. "The Immortal, I presume."

The face shivered and jumped as if the transmission was buffering, then cleared up. "You may call me that. Allow me to offer my apologies for the way I brought you here. It was, unfortunately, the only way to save your life."

"Is that a fact?"

The head bobbed as if trying to interpret the reply. "I'm not sure I understand what you mean."

"You've gone to an awful lot of trouble."

"I'm not sure I understand what you mean."

Stone sighed. "Okay, I'll bite. Where am I?"

The video screen flickered again. "That is not important right now."

"Maybe not to you."

"I'm not sure I understand what you mean."

"This is getting old, fast. And I'm starving. Is there an app for ordering pizza on this thing?" Stone looked away from the chat screen, searching the desktop for the means to access the Internet. If he could get to his email, he could send Tam a message.

"Allow me to explain," the Immortal went on. "I have brought you here because I need your help."

"Go on." Stone moved the cursor down onto the taskbar and clicked it in hopes of bringing up the Start menu, but the system was not responsive.

So much for that idea.

If the Immortal was aware of his attempt, he—it?—gave no indication. "Are you familiar with the name Peter Furst?"

A pop-up window opened alongside the video player, displaying a headshot photograph of a dignified looking man with salt-and-pepper hair. He looked like he might be in his late sixties or early seventies, and Stone assumed it was a picture of the man himself, but neither the face nor the name was familiar to him. "Nope."

"I am," called out a voice from behind Stone. It was Martiel, and after a moment, he dragged his chair forward to sit beside Stone. "Furst is the COB of Nutria Mills."

The revelation came out as a bleary mumble, as if he

was still fighting the effects of the tranquilizer. As soon as the words were out, the banker looked around. "Where are we? What the hell happened?"

The digitized likeness shivered again. "Welcome, Thom Martiel."

Martiel blinked and then looked at Stone for an explanation. "What the heck is that supposed to be? Max Headroom?"

Stone cocked his head sideways. "Who?"

"It's a… thing from the 80s. Sort of a computer-generated cartoon, only it really wasn't. It kind of looked and sounded like that. Seriously? You've never heard of Max Headroom?"

Stone shrugged.

"You are correct," the Immortal continued. "Peter Furst is the chairman of Nutria Mills Incorporated."

"Well, that clears it right up," Stone remarked.

"Nutria Mills is a trans-national food company," Martiel explained, sounding a little more alert. "Actually, you could say they are *the* trans-national food company. Everything from candy bars to dog food. If it's something that can be eaten, there's a fifty-fifty chance that it came from Nutria or one of its subsidiary brands."

Stone's stomach growled at the mention of food. Now that the effects of the sedatives were wearing off, his appetite was returning with a vengeance. He wondered again how long it had been since he'd been dosed.

The other man was still talking. "They're also the world's single biggest producer of bottled water. Furst has gone on record as saying that water is a commodity, like any other, and that the only way to guarantee safe drinking water for everyone is by treating it that way. He's a very controversial figure, but say what you will about him, Nutria Mills is a solid investment."

Martiel turned to the computer again. "You haven't answered my question. What's going on here? Who are you?"

"You may call me the Immortal."

Martiel looked at Stone for confirmation.

"I think we're supposed to believe that it's an artificial intelligence," Stone said. He spoke in a low surreptitious manner, as if conveying a secret, though he knew the computer's microphone would have no difficulty picking up his voice.

"Is it?"

"Let's just say, I don't think this thing would pass the Turing test."

Martiel cocked his head sideways. "So what…or who is behind the curtain? Some hacker?"

Stone just shrugged again.

Martiel turned back to the computer. "Why should we be worried about Peter Furst?"

The digitized head shivered as if processing the question. "Peter Furst wants to kill you, Mr. Martiel. He is responsible for one hundred and thirty-six deaths in the banking industry. You would have been number one-hundred-thirty-seven."

"Stone's people said you were the killer."

"Mr. Stone is mistaken. I am attempting to stop Peter Furst. I brought you here in order to protect you, and so that you could help me stop Peter Furst."

"Stop him from what?"

"Peter Furst wants to take over the world." The surreal electronic effect made it impossible to tell if the statement was meant to be taken at face value.

"He's not the only one," Stone said, but then sensing what was expected of him, he asked the obvious question. "How does he plan to do that? And what does killing bankers have to do with it?"

"Peter Furst intends to destroy the international banking system. He will do this by purchasing and repaying the debt of several developing nations in Asia and Africa."

"Heinous," Stone observed.

"How much debt?" Martiel asked.

"All of it. Approximately four trillion dollars."

Martiel shook his head. "That's impossible. Nutria Mills is wealthy, but their assets don't even come close to four trillion. And even if they did, the banks have safeguards to prevent that kind of activity."

Curious despite himself, Stone straightened in his chair. "Safeguards? Against what? Don't the banks want the loans repaid?"

"You might think so," Martiel replied, "but that's not how the system works. Those loans are the banks' assets."

"Because they make their money on the interest."

"Exactly. If the loans get repaid, the revenue stream dries up. But that's not the real problem."

"What is?"

"Have you ever heard the term 'fiat money'?"

Stone had, but was curious to see how Martiel would explain it, so he shook his head.

"Fiat money establishes the value of currency arbitrarily, as opposed to commodity money, where the value of the currency is based on something real."

"Like gold bullion."

"Exactly. Commodity money sounds great on paper, if you'll forgive the pun, but in the real world, it leads to economic stagnation, which is what happened at the end of the Nineteenth Century. That's why we eventually gave up the gold standard in America and shifted to fiat currency. Unfortunately, fiat currency has its own drawbacks, not the least of which is the fact that the only thing backing it up is the government's promise that it's worth what they say it is."

"In God we trust," Stone murmured.

"The actual value fluctuates by the minute, but it's kept more or less constant because the banks control the markets and monitor the supply, and the Fed sets the interest rate to control inflation. Digital banking has taken fiat currency to a whole new level because there isn't actual currency involved in it anymore. Just electronic transfers between accounts."

Stone nodded slowly. "I get that. By why is repayment

of those loans such a bad thing? I would think the banks would be more worried about default."

"Not really. The banks will get their money, one way or another. If a country gets behind on their payments, the banks get to start dictating fiscal policy. They can impose austerity measures, like the EU did in Greece, or force the government to liquidate assets or give up mineral exploitation rights to foreign investors."

"So if the loans get paid back, the banks lose control over those countries and their resources."

"Yes, but the real problem is that a surplus of currency would crash the global economy. The system is based on debt. If there's no debt, and all the money is in the bank and going nowhere, it loses its value. Supply and demand. Too much of the former drives down the latter. Too much money in the banks drives down the value of the currency, triggering runaway inflation." Martiel paused a beat, then added. "But it's impossible."

"Why?"

"Two reasons. First, nobody has access to that kind of money. Nutria Mills has a net worth just shy of 150 billion. Even if Furst liquidated everything, he wouldn't have enough to cause more than a ripple."

"Just for kicks, let's say he had a way to come up with the money. A hacker who could move the decimal a few places."

"That's not as easy as it sounds, but even if he could do that, there are safeguards to stop fraud and to prevent the kind of inflationary peaks and valleys we're talking about."

"What kind of safeguards?"

"For starters, there's a mandatory waiting period for large transactions."

Stone glanced over at the image on the computer screen. Evidently, the so-called Immortal was content to let Martiel provide the background, which only confirmed his suspicions that it was, at best, a rudimentary artificial intelligence, incapable of responding to conversational exchanges. "No way to get around that? Someone working on the inside?"

"Well, in theory, a senior account executive could expedite the process for his bank. That's actually my job description. But we're not talking about a single loan at a single institution."

"How many then? Would a hundred and thirty-seven be enough?"

Martiel's eyes widened in surprise. "I don't know. I suppose it might be enough to trigger a cascade failure."

As if on cue, the Immortal chose that moment to rejoin the discussion. "That is his intent. For the past two years, Furst has been murdering key personnel in the financial industry in order to create vacancies, to be filled by his own agents."

"Let me guess," Stone said. "You figured out who the targets were and published their names in coded messages on the Internet, hoping that your followers would know what to do, but they were always too late."

The digitized head shivered for several seconds, as if uncertain how to respond, and then continued. "I have brought you here because I believe that you can stop Peter Furst."

"How?" Martiel asked.

"That is what you must discover. This computer contains a virtual copy of the Mystic interface. I will use it to simulate an attack on the banking system. It is my hope that you will be able to discover a vulnerability in his plan."

Stone waited a moment to see if the Immortal would say anything else, but the machine seemed to be waiting for him to break the silence, which was fine with Stone. He had heard enough.

"Mystic," he muttered, and then turned to face Martiel. "Let's cut the crap, okay? What are you really after?"

THIRTEEN

London

Avery's first thought as she stepped into the elegant if somewhat draughty Victorian building on King Street in the St. James district of the City of Westminster, which housed the primary sales floor and offices of Southwick's of London, was that she had walked into a Charles Dickens story. Her subsequent interactions with the employees of the venerable auction house, and particularly with Nigel Chalmers, who had introduced himself as a Senior Specialist—whatever that meant—felt more like something from a Monty Python sketch. *Dead Parrot*, or maybe the *Knights who Say "Ni!"*

It probably had something to do with Chalmers' accent, or the fact that he looked remarkably like a young Michael Palin.

"Miss Halsey, I'm very sorry, but as I've told you, we keep the affairs of our clients in the strictest confidence. Our business depends upon our dependability."

Avery returned a tight smile, thinking, *Here we go again.*

"And as I've told you, Mr. Chalmers," she said, "I'm not interested in your clients. I only want to establish the provenance of a piece you recently sold."

Greg Johns, in the chair next to her, looked like he might be on the verge of dozing off. She knew it was an act. He was as alert as an owl, but she wouldn't have blamed him for being drowsy. They had all just come off another all-nighter—this time riding the overnight high-speed train from Zurich to London—and come straight here. Kasey was outside, keeping an eye on the building and babysitting the Brazen Head.

She didn't know how the two CIA agents had smuggled the artifact through customs, and they weren't telling.

She and Greg were posing as appraisers working for an insurance company, which had seemed like a suitable cover identity for making an inquiry about the history of the brass automaton, but Chalmers was proving resolutely intractable, seemingly for no other reason than because he could.

"And as I've told you, Miss Halsey, that confidentiality embraces the goods our clients buy and sell."

Avery realized now that they should have gone with their first plan, to pose as FBI agents working with Interpol. She smiled at the thought of Greg subjecting Chalmers to some enhanced interrogation techniques. Was it too late to switch tactics? Probably, but she was going to have to do something to end the absurd runaround.

She shifted her weight forward as if preparing to rise. "Well, that settles it then. I will take your refusal to cooperate as evidence of your willing collusion."

Chalmers blinked. "I'm sorry?"

"Yes, you are." She stood. Greg gave her a sidelong glance, then nodded and rose as well.

Chalmers stood too, looking a little less unflappable than he had a moment before. "What do you mean by 'collusion'?"

"I think you know exactly what I mean. It's the only explanation for your... your bloody-mindedness." She hoped that wasn't too insulting, then decided she hoped it was. "Obviously, you wouldn't be trying so hard to hide this if you didn't have something to hide.

"I thought you were simply duped into helping them, but now I see it clearly. You've been working with them all along."

"Working with whom, Miss Halsey? We hold ourselves to a very high standard of integrity in all our dealings. Our clients depend on it. I'm certain you're laboring under a misapprehension. There's nothing nefarious going on here, I assure you."

"Your refusal to share the information I've requested tells me a different story. Good day, sir." She turned and started for the door. Her first few steps were quick, too quick. She was almost at the door, and he wasn't stopping her. Had he seen through her bluff?

"Miss Halsey, wait!"

Avery let out a relieved sigh, but took one more step for good measure before turning. "It's Dr. Halsey, actually."

He inclined his head. "Dr. Halsey. Perhaps I can set your mind at ease with respect to this one particular item. Please, what exactly is it that you want to know?"

Avery put her hands on her hips and glowered at him a moment longer. "A few months ago, you sold a Brazen Head automaton from the estate of Gerald Roche."

"Yes, you said as much. As you know the late Mr. Roche was a former MP. It's a tricky business, that."

"I'm not interested in scandalizing the dead, Mr. Chalmers. I just want to know the provenance of that item."

Chalmers gestured for her to return to her chair, and then sat down and began typing on his computer keyboard. "Ah, here it is. Medieval brazen head automaton believed to be from the Thirteenth Century."

"Yes, I told you that, too."

"This is the information the estate provided us. The authenticity of the piece wasn't verified independently, which is, I suspect, why it didn't sell for considerably more. I'm afraid that's all I know."

"You didn't have it authenticated before you sold it?"

Chalmers shrugged helplessly. "It was the seller's decision. The buyers are so warned. Caveat emptor, Dr. Halsey."

Avery decided to play her wild card. "I'm not surprised the seller didn't want the real history of that particular piece coming to light. I happen to know that the Brazen Head was seized by the Nazis from a wealthy Jewish family in Prague during the Holocaust."

Chalmers' eyes went wide in horror and disbelief. Avery thought the reaction was genuine but decided to set the hook anyway. "The only thing I still don't know," she went on, "is if you were a willing participant in the cover-up."

Chalmers sat motionless for several seconds, then reached out for his keyboard again. After a moment, he mumbled, "I don't know anything about that. There is one other entry here."

"What a surprise."

"Nothing more than a footnote really. According to some of Mr. Roche's notes, the piece in question was sold to him by a private collector in Glasgow. A Mr. Walker. Alan Walker."

He looked up with a hopeful expression. Avery just frowned. "Any contact info?"

Chalmers seemed to deflate a little more. He took a pen and notepad from his desk and began scribbling. "Mr. Walker passed away some years ago, but his daughter, Adelle, confirmed that the piece was in their family's possession for many years before he sold it to Mr. Roche." He tore off the page and pushed it across the desk top. "I promise you, that's all I know about this. We would never willingly trade in illegally obtained articles."

Avery glanced over at Greg. "You think he's telling the truth?"

"That would be a refreshing change of pace," Greg replied. "If he's not, we know where to find him."

Avery snatched the paper off the desktop and saw a name and an eleven-digit number. A phone number, she surmised. "Glasgow, huh? I wonder how it ended up there."

Nigel Chalmers sat fuming for several minutes after his visitors departed. Their exceptional rudeness had been bad enough, but the none-too-subtle threat to link Southwick's to scandalous activity was simply intolerable.

What if this was just the beginning? What if Dr. Halsey went public with her wild accusation that the auction house had traded in loot seized by the Nazis? He realized, too late, that he had erred in trying to stonewall the inquiry. Doing so would give the appearance of complicity. The mere hint of impropriety would do irreparable harm.

Yet, what else could he have done? The venerable auction house's reputation was built on trust and confidentiality. The buyers and sellers were assured absolute discretion.

He returned his attention to the records associated with the item in question. There was nothing to be done about the sellers—in all likelihood, they had known all along—but the buyer… The buyer was Maxim Loew, an economist from New York, currently living in Zurich.

Loew? Bloody hell, the buyer was a Jew. If that didn't complicate things…

He needed to get out ahead of the problem, do some damage control. He would contact Loew, let him know that Southwick's was completely innocent and willing… no, eager to cooperate with the authorities in the pursuit of justice.

He picked up the phone and dialed the contact number listed in the sales record, waited patiently as the call rang through.

It rang several times then, "Hallo?"

"Yes, is this Mr. Loew?"

A brief pause, then a heavily accented voice said, "Mr. Loew is unavailable. Who is this?"

"I… Ah…" Chalmers' first impulse was to simply ring off, but before he could act on the urge, the voice spoke again.

"This is the police. With whom am I speaking?"

"Police?" Now Chalmers definitely wanted to end the call, but that would only look suspicious.

So, he did the only thing he could. He told them who he was. And when they asked, he told them everything.

Avery would have preferred a face-to-face meeting with Adelle MacLean nee Walker, but Glasgow was four hundred miles off the beaten track, and she wasn't going to commit to a trip like that without first calling to make sure that such a meeting was possible. She tapped the number into her phone, and as soon as she was outside the building, made the call. Once she had Adelle on the phone and explained what she hoped to learn, it became apparent that the trip would be unnecessary.

"Oh, I remember that old thing." Adelle's kind grandmotherly voice was edged with a Scottish burr that, for some perverse reason, made Avery visualize her as the comedian Mike Meyers in drag. "My da brought it home when I was just a wee lass. He put him on the mantel, but it made such a horrible racket we had to move it. After that, Da just used him as a hat stand."

"I was hoping we could meet," Avery said, walking toward the café down the street where Kasey waited. "I'd like to know more about it."

"Well, there's no need for you to come all this way," Adelle said. "What do you want to know?"

"For starters, how did your father acquire it?"

"He took it from the captain."

"The captain?"

"Och, Sorry, that's what he always called him. Father said weren't supposed to talk about him or discuss the bronze man with anyone, but that was years ago. I'm sure no one cares. And he did tell Mr. Roche, after all."

"Ma'am, do you know the captain's name?"

"He wasn't really a captain at all. He just told everyone that so they wouldn't know who he was. Didna fool anyone though. It was Mr. Hess."

Avery stopped in her tracks. She felt like her brain was a slot machine, the wheels stopping in sequence.

Nazis. Scotland. Hess.

Jackpot!

She wondered if this was how Stone felt when he solved one of his puzzles.

"Hess? Rudolf Hess?"

"Aye. He parachuted down in the field in Floors

Farms. Da and Mr. McLean went out to look for him. Mr. McLean found the captain, and Da found the Bronze Man. And that, as they say, was that. Leastwise until Mr. Roche paid Da handsome for it. That's been…twenty years. That's really all I know, Miss. So you see, there's hardly reason for you to be making the trip."

Avery thanked her and rang off. She only realized she was stopped in the middle of the sidewalk when Greg nudged her, but she just stared at him, still too astounded to move.

FOURTEEN

Unknown location

Martiel's look of astonishment returned, but only for a moment. Then his lips twitched up into a smile, and he began laughing—a dry, mirthless chuckle. After a few seconds of this, he shook his head. "I suppose there's no point in continuing the charade. Pity. I put a lot of work into it."

"Sorry. Not sorry." Stone said. "Seriously, just how stupid do you think I am?"

Martiel was silent for a moment, but then he blinked. "I suppose that was the point. A test if you will. Tell me, when did you figure it out?"

"When Tam said someone called 'the Immortal' was behind it all. Choosing an alias that's an anagram of 'the Immortal' is kind of obvious, don't you think?"

Martiel shrugged. "You'd be surprised how often people miss the little things."

"I don't," Stone replied coolly. "Let's see if I missed anything else. This little scheme you've just explained—crashing the banking system. You're not trying to prevent it. That's your plan, right? You murdered people—arranged 'accidents' and 'suicides'—to create job vacancies in key positions at banks that use the Mystic trading platform. You maneuvered your people into those positions. Fellow travelers who subscribe to your paranoid conspiracy vision and want to help you bring down the global plutocracy."

"There are more of us than you could possibly imagine."

"I'm pretty imaginative. I'll take that as a 'yes.' When one of your people found out that we were sniffing around those mysterious deaths, you realized your plan wasn't quite as airtight as you thought it was. So you made yourself a target to draw us out, get us to trust you so you could figure out how much we already know. That was a ballsy move. You could have gotten yourself killed."

"Give me some credit, Gavin. I controlled every variable; mitigated the risk. And I knew you wouldn't let me down. But you are only partially correct. I wasn't interested in finding out how much you knew, or as it turned out, didn't know. What I really wanted was you."

"Me?"

"You're a celebrity in certain circles. It's said you possess an intellect equal to my own."

Stone struggled to keep a straight face. "I assume you meant that as a compliment."

"I'm actually encouraged by how quickly you saw through my little deception. You're perfect for the job."

"Job?"

"I need an independent beta-tester. I want you to do exactly what my virtual mannequin suggested. Challenge the system. Find the vulnerabilities."

"So you can fix them. Perfect your attack. And why exactly do you think I would want to help you crash the global economy?"

"Oh, come now, Gavin. Your genius isn't the only thing those people I mentioned talk about. You're a black hat. An anti-establishmentarian if there ever was one. Frankly, I still can't wrap my head around the notion of you working with the same government that arrested you without due process and kept you a prisoner in an illegal detention facility. But I know that you're no fan of the status quo. The system is rotten, and you know it. The banks are holding the entire world hostage, but their power is as phony as…" He gestured at the unmoving figure on the screen. "As that. You know I'm right. It's time to burst their bubble."

"And I suppose you've got a plan for what happens afterward."

"I do. And I'd like your input on that, as well."

"My input? Well, for starters, there's no outcome that

doesn't result in global chaos and loss of life on an unimaginable scale."

"The chaos is coming. There's no stopping it. The fiat money system is a Ponzi scheme, and the collapse is long overdue. The only question is whether the elites and the oligarchs will face the consequences of their duplicity, or build a new empire on the bones of their victims. They're already preparing for the collapse, gathering private armies to protect them while they hide in their palatial bunkers. We have to strike now. Destroy their imaginary money, and let them face rough justice."

Martiel—or whatever his name really was—was not wrong about Stone's antipathy for the state of the world, but he had misjudged the degree of its intensity, just as he had misjudged Stone's true motives.

There was a reason Stone had not told Tam the truth about Martiel's identity, a reason he had gone along with the man, allowed himself to be caught in the Immortal's web, despite the risk.

This was a puzzle. A challenge. And Stone loved a challenge.

"How are you going to do it?"

"Just like I told you. Pay off the debts of the developing world, create a cash surplus in the banks."

"With what money?" It was a rhetorical question. He was already halfway to working out the answer for himself. "No, the money isn't important. It's Mystic. You don't just need your people in place to authorize large transactions. You need them to create the money out of thin air."

Martiel grinned and tapped a forefinger to his temple. "It's a little more complicated than that. The money has to be real…" He laughed. "Well, to the extent that any of it is real.

"We'll begin with a series of targeted trades that will run contrary to the advice from Mystic. The market will react with confusion. Some stocks will lose value, others will gain, but we'll be a step ahead of the chaos. The market will dance to our tune. While that's happening, we'll be playing the currency markets as well, driving down the value of the dollar. With each cycle, the amount of money we'll have at our disposal will increase exponentially, even as the value of that money diminishes almost at the same rate. And then before anyone even realizes what's happening, we'll take our four trillion dollars of worthless money and dump it on the banks."

"Sounds like high-tech check kiting," Stone said.

"I told you, fiat currency is a Ponzi scheme. We're simply going to turn that scheme against the grifters who have been running the game. All of this will happen in a matter of minutes. The trades are already set up, like dominos, just waiting for a push. That's the big picture. But the devil, as they say, is in the details.

"It's all there." He pointed to the computer. "All set up for a test run. Beat the system if you can."

Stone kept his gaze on Martiel. "You're improvising. This wasn't your original plan, was it?"

Martiel blinked, trying to hide his surprise. "What makes you say that?"

"The red herring. Or should I say, the bronze head? You didn't want me here, helping you. I was getting too close, so you decided to sideline me with a scavenger hunt."

Martiel gazed back at him and then offered a wan smile and a guilty shrug. "What can I say? You're a wild card."

"What on earth made you think I would be interested in chasing after some old medieval relic?"

"Maybe I thought the incongruity of it all would arouse your curiosity. It doesn't matter now. You didn't fall for it. You're here. Are you in?"

Stone considered the offer, considered his response. "What was all that stuff about Peter Furst? Why bring him into it?"

Before Martiel could answer, however, the door to the small room swung open, and an older man in an immaculate suit swept into the room. His expression was grim, far more so than in the picture Stone had seen.

Martiel kept his eyes on Stone and smiled, this time with more than a little real humor. "Maybe you should ask him."

FIFTEEN

London

Avery waited until she was seated with Greg and Kasey at a small table in the back of the café to explain her revelation. "There's still a few missing pieces," she began, "but I think I know how the Brazen Head ended up in Scotland and then eventually came into Roche's possession."

The object at the center of the discussion was concealed inside a cheap backpack, occupying the fourth seat at the table.

"I told you that the Nazis were obsessed with mysticism and the occult, and that's true, but surprisingly, Hitler wasn't. At least not to the same extent as some of his supporters like Himmler and his personal secretary, Rudolf Hess.

"Hess was right there beside Hitler from the start. They went to jail together after the Beer Hall Putsch. Hitler dictated *Mein Kampf* in his cell, and Hess wrote it all down. When Hitler rose to power, Hess was named Reichsfuhrer, the third most powerful man in Germany. Until May of 1941 that is, when he decided to fly across the English Channel in order to negotiate peace with the British government."

"I've heard about this," Greg said. "It's like one of those world's dumbest criminal videos where a guy walks right past a cop to rob a liquor store. Hess just took off on his own, without any diplomatic status. Got caught and spent the rest of his life in prison."

"There's no mystery about what he did," Avery agreed. "But 'why' is a question that isn't as easy to answer."

"Why did he go to Scotland of all places?" Greg asked. "I've wondered about that."

"He was trying to reach Dungavel House, the summer retreat of the Duke of Hamilton. Dungavel is less than twenty miles from Glasgow, and only about ten miles from where Hess actually parachuted out, so he was close. Both Hess and the Duke were aviators, and Hess might have thought he had a sympathetic friend in the Duke. It's also been suggested that the Duke was working with British intelligence, trying to lure Hess out of Germany with the promise of a peace negotiation. That's possible, but it doesn't explain why Hess felt he had to do it. He was a true believer in the Nazi doctrine and fiercely loyal to Hitler."

"Maybe he saw the writing on the wall?"

"In 1941, it wasn't. The Blitz was winding down, and Hitler was more interested in launching Operation Barbarossa against the Soviet Union. If anything, the time was right for a real diplomatic mission to Britain."

"So why did he do it?"

"Well, some think that he did it for personal glory. Despite his position, he had lost a lot of influence with Hitler. By 1941, Martin Bormann was the real power in the Reich. Maybe Hess thought if he could flip Britain—end the war, and maybe even forge an alliance with them against the Soviets—he would get back some of the prestige he had lost."

"But you don't think so," Kasey said.

Avery shrugged. "Well, it's an explanation, but there's a lot about it that doesn't quite fit. For one thing, Hitler was badly shaken by what Hess tried to do. He felt that it undermined his authority, made him look weak. In fact, he ordered Hess to be shot on sight if he ever returned to Germany. Hess would have known him well enough to expect a reaction like that, even if he had been successful in negotiating a separate peace."

"Okay, so if not that, then what?"

"Like I said, Hess was obsessed with mysticism, and particularly interested in astrology and divination. He wasn't after artifacts of power like the Spear of Destiny though; he wanted to know the future. The Brazen Head was supposed to be a machine for telling the future. Hess would have recognized it for what it was and tried to use it. And the fact that he secretly brought it with him on his flight to Scotland suggests that it might have played a part in his decision."

Kasey raised a doubtful eyebrow. "So the metal head told him to do it?"

"In a sense. I don't think he was getting instructions from it, but something must have happened to nudge him out the door, so to speak." She paused for a moment, trying to think of a way to explain the next leap. "One of the places Hess looked for guidance was the prophecies of Nostradamus."

Kasey gave a derisive snort. "Please. You can't be serious. Nostradamus? That's like fortune cookies or horoscopes. People read whatever they want into those prophecies."

Greg raised his hands in a placating gesture. "Give her a chance. I'm curious. We've both seen a lot of crazy stuff."

"Hey, I'm as skeptical as you are," Avery admitted. "But Hess wasn't. He was a believer. That's a historical fact. He even wrote phony Nostradamus prophecies as part of a propaganda campaign against France, probably with some help from Josef Goebbels and his half-Jewish wife, Magda."

"Goebbels' wife was Jewish?"

"Yes. Probably. Her stepfather was Jewish, but it's generally believed that he was her biological father as well." Avery shook her head, trying to stay on course. "All I'm saying is that the senior Nazis believed that Nostradamus' prophecies were accurate. More than that, they believed Nostradamus had directly predicted the rise of the Third Reich."

"I've heard this before," Kasey said dismissively. "Nostradamus wrote about someone named 'Hister,' which is kinda sorta like 'Hitler.' Except it isn't. If he really had the power of prophecy, you'd think he'd have spelled it right."

"You're missing the point," Avery said, growing exasperated. "Hess and the other Nazis read those things, and *they* believed. But a funny thing happened right after Hess was captured. Hitler outlawed astrology and divination, which he blamed for Hess' decision. Some have speculated that the real reason Hess tried to make peace with Britain was that he read something in the prophecies of Nostradamus that made him believe that Hitler would bring about the end of the world if he wasn't stopped. So whether or not those horoscopes and prophecies were accurate, they definitely played a major part in shaping world history."

"Fair enough," Kasey said, equivocally. "But you say Hess was taking orders from Mr. Shiny here." She patted the backpack. "What's that got to do with Nostradamus?"

"Well, this is where it gets a little crazy, so bear with me. I think Nostradamus got *his* prophecies from the Brazen Head."

Kasey and Greg exchanged a glance and then nodded for her to continue.

Avery was silent for a moment, not because she didn't know the answer, but because she didn't know how to explain it in a way that would make sense to the others. She wondered if Stone had the same trouble explaining the patterns he saw.

She picked up a napkin and unfolded it. "Anyone got a pen I can use?"

Greg produced both a pen and a small notepad, passing both to her. She uncapped the pen and wrote:

Significant dates:
c. 1250—Magnus makes BH, Paris?

She left several blank lines on the page before adding:

1939—Loew family leaves BH behind in Prague

1941—Hess takes BH to Scotland

She pushed the notebook out to the center of the table. "Okay, we know that the Brazen Head was created sometime around the year 1250. That's when Albert Magnus and Thomas Aquinas were together in Paris, where Albert was teaching theology at University, and Aquinas was his student. Assuming that what we have is the same Brazen Head, we've got a seven-hundred-year gap to fill and the question how did the Brazen Head get from Paris to Prague? The most likely explanation is that Prague was the capital of the Holy Roman Empire in the 16th Century under Emperor Rudolf II."

"Rudolf?" Greg said. "Like Hess?"

"Yes, but that's just a coincidence." She hesitated, wondering if Stone would see it that way, then pushed ahead. "Rudolf—the Emperor, not Hess—was fascinated with technology. He had a whole room in his palace dedicated to housing his collection of mechanical gizmos—clocks, astrolabes, even wind-up toys. He would have definitely wanted Albert's Brazen Head for his collection."

She wrote in the empty space.

c. 1580 BH in Prague

"Okay, now we've cut the gap in half. It's not too much of a stretch to imagine how the Brazen Head wound up with Loew's family. If they were bankers, maybe it was used as collateral or payment for a loan to the royal house. Or maybe it was…" She trailed off as her brain took another left turn.

"Avery, you still with us?"

"Umm, this is probably another coincidence, but there's a famous legend from Prague about the golem. In the late 16th Century, the Jews in the ghetto of Prague were being persecuted by their enemies, so a Rabbi named Judah Loew ben Bezalel used the power of Kabbalah, or

Jewish mysticism, to create a golem, an artificial man... basically, an android... made out of clay. According to some accounts, Magnus didn't just create a Brazen Head, but a fully functional android."

"Clay isn't bronze," Greg pointed out. "And Loew is a common name."

Avery shrugged. "It's probably just a story. What I'm more interested in is connecting the dots in the first three hundred years. How did the Brazen Head get from Paris to Prague?"

She put pen to paper again, writing a new line above the previous entry. The page now read:

Significant dates:
c. 1250—Magnus makes BH, Paris?

c. 1550—Nostradamus prophecies, Provence, Paris?

c. 1580--BH in Prague

1939—Loew family leaves BH behind in Prague
1941—Hess takes BH to Scotland

"Okay, we don't have an explicit connection between Nostradamus and the Brazen Head, but the timeline works. Nostradamus was a favorite of the Queen, Catherine de Medici. She even brought him to Paris to protect him from accusations of heresy and gave him a court appointment as counselor and physician to her son, King Charles IX. That puts him in the same city as the Brazen Head. Following his death in 1566, Catherine might have retained possession of the Head and could have sent it to Emperor Rudolf as a goodwill gesture. That would explain how it ended up in Prague.

"If the Brazen Head was some kind of mechanical computer, then it could have been used to make accurate predictions, and that would have been invaluable to someone like Nostradamus. He was a lifelong scholar, and even though he was Catholic, he was born Jewish. He might have had extensive knowledge of Kabbalah, along with his study of natural science and astrology."

"Nostradamus got his prophecies from a medieval supercomputer?" Kasey shook her head in disbelief. "That's quite a stretch."

"Is it though? It's all about patterns. The prophecies are vague, sure, but the reason we're still talking about them five hundred years later is that they fit with actual events. Maybe without even realizing it, Nostradamus was seeing mathematical patterns of repetition. Just like Stone does. Maybe those prophecies are actually a coded message containing the patterns, and maybe the way to decode them is with the Brazen Head. Hess probably figured out how to do that, and what he learned scared the hell out of him."

The words tumbled out of her, leaving her feeling slightly manic. She knew she hadn't explained it very well, but she also knew she was right. Or at least on the right track. The other two just stared back at her.

Finally, Greg broke the silence. "So…what does all of that mean?"

"The Immortal wants the Brazen Head for a reason. We can keep him from getting it, but if we want to really stop him, we need to know why he wants it."

Greg nodded slowly. "And how do we figure that out?"

Avery gave a helpless shrug. "We ask Nostradamus."

SIXTEEN

Unknown location

Peter Furst regarded Stone with a baleful glare, but only for a moment. Then he turned to Martiel. "This is your plan?" he snapped, his faint Germanic accent making the words sound even sharper.

A muscle in Martiel's cheek twitched, but his smile did not slip. "It is. And you need to let me handle it, as we agreed. You can't micromanage this, Peter."

Stone fixed his gaze on Furst. "I see how this works. He's the brains, and you're the..." He paused, just long enough to heighten the impact of the last word, which he uttered with all the contempt he could manage. "Money."

"That's simplistic," Martiel said. "But not completely inaccurate. I told you, the money has to be real. We could do a lot of damage with electronic counterfeiting, but not enough. And in the end, they would undo all of it. If this is to work, it has to be a deathblow."

Stone's gaze was unwavering, even though Furst refused to meet it. "Do you actually know what this plan of his will do? *To* your money? Your ship will go down with all the rest."

To Stone's surprise, Furst laughed. "He's not as clever as you made him out to be." He turned to Stone, finally meeting his stare. "Money. Brains. You think it must be one or the other?"

Stone felt his pulse quicken. Here was a mystery. "So you don't care about the money. Interesting. What do you care about?"

Martiel intervened quickly. "What difference does it make? We want the same thing. An end to the most monumental con in human history."

"Motives are important. If you want my help, I need to understand what you're really getting from all of this. In my experience, wealthy people are interested in only one thing: increasing their wealth."

"You are not wrong, Mr. Stone," Furst said. "The greed of the wealthy men is insatiable. Bankers." He snarled the word like a curse. "They are a cancer, devouring our world. Destroying the natural order."

"Natural order?"

"You ask what I care about, Mr. Stone? Not money. That is just a means to an end, and now that end is within my grasp. Order. That's what I care about. There is a natural order in the world. Some are meant to rule, others to be ruled. Some are sheep, and some are—"

"Wolves?"

Furst uttered a short, harsh laugh. "Shepherds, Mr. Stone. But there are wolves, too. Do you know what the difference is? The shepherd cares for his flock, nourishes them, keeps them safe. In return, the sheep give their wool, and yes, from time to time, meat for the table, but the wolf… The wolf gives nothing to the sheep. He only takes."

"Some would say that's the true natural order."

Furst ignored the comment. "Do you know how I got my money?"

"Let me guess. You earned it."

"I was born in 1945, in a small village in Austria. My father was already dead, killed by a British bomb that destroyed the factory where he was employed. I started life with nothing. I joined Nutria Mills as a salesman, climbed my way to the top of the company, and then carried it on my back to the top of the world. I do not tell you this to impress you, but so you will know what I care about.

"Did you know that the war could have been avoided? In May of 1940, four years before my father was killed, German forces halted their advance at Dunkirk, allowing an evacuation of Allied forces—more than three hundred thousand men. It was a gesture of goodwill to the British, but instead of accepting that olive branch, ending a war that would eventually take tens of millions of lives,

Churchill rejected the overture. Do you know why? Because the bankers wanted war.

"Two hundred years ago, the House of Rothschild made its fortune by financing both sides of the Napoleonic Wars. They still control the world today, not with political power, but with the power of credit. With banks.

"All wars are banker wars. They manipulate policy and foment instability until war seems like the only course of action. With one hand they lend money to the governments to buy the machines of war, and with the other, they collect the profits of investments in the industries that sell them. The bankers win every war, no matter who else loses. And they will keep doing it because that is what wolves do.

"I don't want more money. I don't need more money. What I want is a return to the natural order. A world without wolves."

During most of the monologue, Martiel stared at the wall, as if deliberately trying to avoid looking at either of the other two men. Stone wondered if perhaps he found the conspiratorial diatribe a touch embarrassing, but as Furst began to wind down, Martiel spoke up to fill the pause. "We can't fix it, Gavin. But we can burn it down and start anew."

"Start anew? What would that look like? Barter system? Or will you push for a return to the gold standard?"

"The banks own all the gold," Furst said with a snort of derision.

"The value of gold is as illusory and arbitrary as the value of the dollar," Martiel added. "It has some intrinsic value, but the average person, who cares only about getting paid for the work they do and being able to provide food and shelter for their family, doesn't care about a piece of shiny metal. But Peter is right. The banks and the oligarchs control the gold supply. The governments will attempt to reinstitute commodity currency which, if left unchecked would simply start the ruinous cycle all over again. That's when we'll step in with a 21st Century solution that will cut the banks out of the equation. Peer-to-peer open source virtual money."

Stone nodded as understanding dawned. "Bitcoin."

Created in 2009 by a mysterious and as yet unidentified computer programmer using the pseudonym Satoshi Nakamora, bitcoin was an unsupported currency system intended not only to simplify business transactions in the digital age, but also to liberate entrepreneurs from the shackles of government sponsored monetary systems. The method for establishing both the value and authenticity of bitcoin was, like everything else in the 21st century, driven by the gig economy, with individual users "mining" bitcoin in a somewhat lucrative game-like system designed to verify transactions and prevent duplication or electronic counterfeiting. Stone had been an early dabbler in bitcoin mining, not because he needed the money, but because the process for mining it involved solving a mathematical puzzle. And of course, because bitcoin was the currency of choice on the deep web.

That was also the chief drawback of bitcoin, at least from a societal perspective. Bitcoin provided criminals with an untraceable and completely pseudonymous method of transacting illegal business—everything from drug and human trafficking to hiring a hitman to kill someone.

But despite the risks and opposition from government entities, bitcoin was already gaining traction as the currency of the future. It was one part of Martiel's scheme with which Stone found no fault.

"You talk about restoring the natural order of things," he said. "No matter what you do today, sooner or later…no, scratch that…definitely sooner, those who have more will gain power over those who want more. That's human nature. You can't stop it."

"Then at least we will have given everybody a chance," Furst said. "Billions of people all over the earth are born into poverty, shackled to the debts of their fathers, the debts of their nations. We will erase those debts. Wipe the slate clean. After that…" He shrugged. "Every man will stand or fall on his own merits."

Stone had done his best to listen with an open mind, and even agreed with some of the sentiments of the argument, but it wasn't enough to draw him into their crusade. "Here's the thing I have trouble with. You killed people. This little scheme of yours is going to cause a lot more needless suffering. And you're holding me against my will. Or am I misreading the situation?"

"It's not my intention to harm you," Martiel said. "But… No, I can't allow you to leave just yet."

"That's what I thought." Stone paused a beat. "And if I refuse to help you? What will it be? An apparent suicide? Maybe make it look like a mugging?"

Martiel shrugged. "We can execute the plan without your help."

"And yet you haven't. You don't need me. In fact, you tried to send me off on a wild goose chase. So what are you waiting for?"

When Martiel didn't answer, Stone glanced over at Furst. The latter seemed poised to speak again, but then abruptly reached into a pocket and withdrew a vibrating mobile phone. After a quick glance at the screen, he thumbed the button to receive the call and turned away. "*Ja?*"

The ensuing conversation was brief and mostly one-sided, with the party on the other end of the line doing most of the talking. Furst spoke only a few times, in barely audible German, before shoving the phone back into his pocket and turning back. He addressed Martiel.

"We will have it soon."

Martiel frowned. "So in other words, you still don't have it?"

Stone could not help but notice a change in demeanor on the part of both men. Furst seemed contrite, Martiel irritated, angry even. *Did I get this wrong?* Stone thought. *Who's calling the shots here?*

"They're in London," Furst said. "My man is closing in on them. It will be only a matter of a few more hours."

"Then it will be only a matter of few more hours before we execute," snapped Martiel.

"You will get it," Furst hissed. "You have my word."

Martiel shook his head. "Your word is irrelevant. I will not… I cannot execute the plan until I have it in my hands."

Stone watched the exchange with curiosity and, as he realized what they were discussing, growing apprehension. "What are you talking about?"

Martiel turned his gaze on Stone, his smile returning with a sardonic edge. "Haven't you figured it out?"

Stone blinked in disbelief. "I guess not."

"Peter was right. You're not as clever as I thought you were."

"The Brazen Head?" Stone's pulse wasn't merely quickening; it was pounding, screaming in his ears. The ground upon which his perception of reality rested had transformed into quicksand, and he was sinking fast. "You're not serious."

He wasn't wrong often, and when he was, he could usually see it, but this?

This made no sense.

Martiel was staring at him, like a predator ready to pounce. "It's such a delicious riddle, isn't it? I was disappointed when you decided not to go after it, but your friend, Miss Halsey, has demonstrated remarkable resourcefulness. She managed to acquire it before Mr. Furst's men could get there."

They're in London… My man is closing in on them.

"She's important to you," Martiel was saying.

Stone looked up, met the other man's gaze. "You want my help? Leave my friends alone, and you've got it."

"Your friends have something that I need. Can you convince them to surrender it without violence?"

Furst was incredulous. "You would trust him?"

Martiel's mouth twitched into a smile. "Peter doesn't

know you like I do. Doesn't know how you think. But we are up against the clock here, and I can't wait. Peter's men will soon catch up to your friends, and when they do, I won't stop them from doing what needs to be done. But I will give you this one chance. Run the Mystic simulation. Find its weaknesses and fix them, and then I will let you contact your friends to arrange a trade. You for the Brazen Head."

Furst scowled but said nothing.

"You would do that?" Stone asked. "Why should I trust you?"

"I need it more than I need you, Gavin. And trust goes both ways."

Stone nodded slowly. "Then I guess we should get started."

SEVENTEEN

New York City

Talking to Wayne Valero, the creator of Mystic and current chairman of Iron River Asset Management Incorporated, was easier said than done.

Getting through the front door was relatively painless. Although the Mystic server farm was located in eastern Washington, Iron River's corporate headquarters were located in lower Manhattan, just a short drive from the safe house, even with the traffic congestion caused by the early morning commute. But when she and Sievers entered the reception lobby of the Wall Street office building and presented their ersatz credentials, identifying them as SEC investigators, to the receptionist, they hit a wall in the form of a brigade of lawyers whose sole purpose in life seemed to be insulating their employer from anyone with a badge.

Things went downhill from there.

Tam's insistence that they were there not to investigate Valero, but to warn him of a possible threat to Mystic, had little effect. Before she could even finish articulating this, one of the lawyers whipped out a mobile phone. "This is harassment, plain and simple. I've got the U.S. Attorney and Governor of New York on speed-dial. Who should I call first?"

Tam's pulse quickened. It was probably a bluff, but one she couldn't afford to call. Ordinarily, she could count on her boss at the Agency to backstop her cover, but the previous day's shenanigans had put her on thin ice. She was out favor with her boss, and a call like that might very well mean the end of the Myrmidons.

Unfortunately, the genie was already out of the bottle. The lawyers would follow up sooner or later, and when they did, they would learn that there was no SEC investigation, and no one matching their description employed by that agency.

It was a no-win scenario.

What would Stone do right now? She wondered.

But before an answer came to her, she heard Sievers give his reply.

"You can call the damn Pope for all I care."

Tam's first thought was that it would have been easier to arrange an audience with the Pope. Then her heart skipped a beat. What was Billy doing?

Sievers sounded angry, his drawl unusually thick, almost menacing. "In the last twenty-four hours, I have jumped off a forty-story building, chased a couple jackasses across the Hudson River, wallowed in the mud like a damned hog, blown up my car… a '68 Mustang if that means anything to you… probably doesn't… and ruined my favorite jacket. All of that to keep some very bad guys from hijackin' your company, so you can call whoever you want, but we ain't leavin' here until we get five minutes with your boss."

The lawyer's eyes tightened defiantly. His finger moved over the screen of the phone, and then he held it to his ear.

But the next voice Tam heard did not come from his mouth.

"I think we can spare five minutes, Martin."

Every head in the room turned to the door behind the reception desk, and the man standing there. He was tall, and Tam guessed sixtyish, but with a full head of prematurely white hair.

The lawyer lowered his phone but did not put it away. "Mr. Valero, I think—"

"The man blew up his car, Martin." Valero's eyes met Sievers'. "A '68 Mustang?" He shook his head sadly. "Ouch."

"I'll get her runnin' again, sir."

"I hope so." Valero made a beckoning gesture with his hand and took a step back out of view.

Tam let out the breath she had been holding. She

couldn't decide whether she wanted to punch Sievers or kiss him. Maybe both, but that would have to wait at least five minutes.

"Looks like you're on point," she whispered, giving him a firm push toward the doorway.

They followed Valero to a tastefully decorated executive office with large windows that looked out on a gray concrete building across the street. Valero settled heavily into the chair behind his desk. Tam hung back, loitering near the door, and let Sievers handle the small talk. The two men bantered about cars for a while; she hoped Valero wasn't going to hold them to five minutes.

Valero finally steered the conversation in the right direction. "I heard about the incident across the river yesterday. That was you going down the side of 30 Hudson?"

Sievers just grinned.

"And that has something to do with why you're here?" Valero now looked to Tam. "You mentioned a threat to my company?"

Tam took a step forward. "That's right, sir. Specifically, a threat to your operating system."

"Mystic? What kind of threat?"

"Actually, we were hoping you could shed some light on that. We have a solid lead indicating that Mystic is a target."

Valero's white eyebrows came together in a frown. "To whom?"

"Again, we're hoping you might have an idea about that." Realizing that answer would leave her on shaky footing, she added. "I received a tip from a CI… a confidential informant. He didn't have the details, and now I've lost contact with him. That tells us the threat is both serious and immediate."

Valero took a long breath. "No system can be one-hundred-percent secure, but Mystic is about as close as you can get. Access requires a dedicated computer terminal which we provide to customers with their subscription.

The data goes over secure hard lines. It's all proprietary. You can't just log onto it from anywhere, and you certainly can't hack into the servers from the Internet."

"What if the attack came from someone who already had access to one of those computers?"

"Clients don't have access to the OS. Only a SysAdmin can alter the code, and that can only be done from the master terminal in Spokane. I hesitate to use the word impossible, but…" He shrugged.

"So what you're sayin'," Sievers put in. "Is that they can drive the car, but they can't look under the hood."

Valero grinned and pointed a finger at Sievers. "Bingo."

Tam seized on the metaphor. "But they could still steer it into a tree."

Valero shifted uncomfortably in his chair. "Crashing one car—accidentally or otherwise—won't bring down the Ford Motor Company."

"If someone exploits your system for criminal gains or cyberterrorism," Tam said, choosing her words carefully, "it will affect you."

"There's risk in every profitable venture. Believe me, I know." Valero was silent for a moment. "Do you know what Mystic is? What it does?"

"Not really," Tam admitted.

"Twenty-five years ago, I made a mistake. I… drove the car into a tree, if you will. Lost a hundred million dollars of client money, mostly individual portfolios. Retirement accounts. People's life savings. Do you know what my mistake was? I wasn't being reckless, gambling with other people's money. I just didn't know enough. I didn't see the warning signs that the economy was about to collapse.

"I built Mystic to see the signs that I missed. It gathers data from a variety of sources. Everything from the stock market to social media. Mystic uses all of that raw data to create a simulated version of our world. A computer model, in which we can safely explore all the outcomes and determine the course of action that will create the least amount of instability.

"Mystic is more than just a trading platform. It's the autopilot that keeps the car from crashing. That's what makes it so special. Now, you tell me that these criminals are going to use Mystic for some diabolical purpose. Of course, that concerns me. But I simply don't know of any vulnerabilities. We have a whole division in Spokane that does nothing but test the system, looking for exploits. When we find them, we fix them. If someone... a foreign agent or cyber-terrorist wanted to attack the markets, they wouldn't need Mystic. There are far easier ways to do it."

"Our investigation indicates that there may be several rogue users. Possibly a hundred or more. If they were identified, you could suspend their accounts, right?"

"If you know who they are, why not just arrest them?"

"It's a hypothetical question." Tam pursed her lips. "We have a list of suspects, but not enough evidence to take action. If they make their move before we're ready...."

"Well, hypothetically speaking, yes, I could. No, I *would*. In a heartbeat."

He opened a desk drawer and took out a business card which he passed over to her.

"That has my personal cell number and my private email. Don't tell Martin I gave it to you. He'll have a conniption fit if he hears I'm giving that out to law enforcement. Send me the names of your suspects. We'll flag their accounts. Set up a kill switch, just in case. But you would have to bring me something more than just vague suspicions before I could throw it."

Tam felt a measure of relief, but it was hardly a victory. They were no closer to an answer, no closer to finding Stone or stopping the Immortal than they had been when they walked in the building.

"Just so I understand," Sievers said. "The only way anyone uses Mystic is on one of your computers, connected to one of your hard lines."

"That's right," Valero said.

Tam looked over at him. "Billy, if you got something, spit it out."

Sievers looked her in the eye, and when he spoke again, his corn pone accent was gone. "They kidnapped Stone and Thom Martiel for a reason. Maybe they want to force Thom to work for them… I don't know. But there's only one place he can do it."

"His office," Tam said, breathlessly. "His computer." Once again, Tam realized, she had underestimated Billy Sievers. He had been paying attention.

"Maybe the reason we couldn't find video of them leaving the building," Sievers said, "is they never left."

EIGHTEEN

Salon de Provence, France

Although it was not the birthplace of Michel de Nostredame—known more popularly by the Latinized mononym Nostradamus—the people of Salon de Provence in the south of France, considered the famed prophet their native son. His bearded visage with its cryptic smile stared out from street murals and statues, as well as from T-shirts, postcards and other souvenirs, hawked in the gift shops that lined the street that bore his name. The house where he spent the last years of his life had been transformed into a museum celebrating not only his life as a visionary seer, but also his lifelong love of learning and science. Avery could think of no better place to begin looking for a connection between Nostradamus and the Brazen Head of Albert Magnus.

The museum offered a self-guided tour, with audio and printed material in several different languages. This time, Greg stayed outside, watching the exterior and holding onto the backpack with the Brazen Head, while Kasey accompanied Avery inside, ever vigilant even though there was no threat to speak of. Avery roamed the multi-story structure, past waxwork dioramas depicting scenes from the seer's life, and collected artifacts believed to have actually been used by him, both as a healer and apothecary, and as an astrologer and prophet. The tour moved from room to room, telling the story of Nostradamus in stages, beginning with his birth in nearby Saint-Remy de Provence. She learned of his successful career as a plague doctor, and of the tragic death of his first wife and two children whom he could not save.

She expected to hear all about the accuracy of the famed prophetic quatrains—four-line poems that used cryptic symbolic language and left the exact nature of his predictions open to interpretation, even five centuries later—but the museum displays downplayed the more sensational aspects of his life, emphasizing instead his authorship of almanacs and his role as advisor to Queen Catherine.

In one room, however, near the end of the tour, they encountered a man who appeared to be a historical re-enactor posing as Nostradamus seated at a table in front of an armillary sphere. The elegant bronze globe, which consisted of concentric rings that rotated independently, one inside the other to form a primitive three-dimensional representation of the stars and planets, was almost universally associated with Nostradamus. The re-enactor wore black robes with a matching velvet toque, and had a flowing gray beard that appeared to be real.

"Are you enjoying your visit?" the actor asked in unaccented English. He spoke softly but with a deep, commanding voice.

"It's very interesting," Avery lied.

The man flashed a knowing smile. "The locals want the world to know that Nostradamus wasn't just a crank, spouting doomsday prophecies, but a man of learning and science. But that's not what the tourists want to hear about. I think what they're really looking for is something that will make them believe."

"Do you? Believe, I mean?"

"That is a complicated question," the man admitted. "I know him better than almost anyone, and I'm still looking for something that will make me believe."

"You don't sound like a local."

"I feel like one sometimes, but you're right. I'm from upstate New York." He rose, cradling the armillary sphere and came over to them, executing a formal bow. "Victor Bridges, scholar-in-residence. I literally wrote the book on Nostradamus. One of them anyway. You can pick it up from the gift shop."

Avery recognized the name from the research she had done during the seven-hour train ride to the south of

France. "I'm Avery Halsey. I teach history at a college in Halifax."

"Then we're from the same neck of the woods. What brings you here, Professor? Professional curiosity, or personal?" He waved his hand with a theatrical flair. "Or do you seek a vision of that which is to come?"

Avery laughed. "A little of all of the above. I'm trying to learn more about the method Nostradamus used for divination. I know he was an astrologer, but I read that he used another method. Theurgy? Did I say that right?"

"Theurgy is a broad term for ritualistic magic tied to the divine. It's sometimes applied to Kabbalah—Jewish mysticism—which is probably what the book you were reading meant. His detractors would have used the term as an accusation of sorcery, but while he almost certainly learned the Kabbalistic tradition as a young man, his visions arose from a different source. You see, Nostradamus was a middling astrologer at best, but he was a skilled apothecary and herbalist, if you know what I mean." Bridges winked.

"I'm not sure I do."

The bearded man laughed. "You're going to make me come right out and say it, aren't you? Nostradamus received his vision through a practice known as 'scrying.' You would probably know it better as 'crystal ball gazing,' but it can be done with a mirror, or in the case of Nostradamus, a bowl of water. Except Nostradamus added a secret ingredient to his water. Nutmeg."

"Nutmeg?" Kasey said. Avery had almost forgotten that she was there. "The spice?"

"A little nutmeg will spice up your pumpkin pie, but in larger quantities, it is a hallucinogen. Though not one I would recommend. The migraines…" He winced, suggesting that he spoke from experience.

Probably a scholarly experiment, Avery thought.

"He would add the nutmeg to a bowl of hot water and then breathe the vapors under a shawl. No doubt he learned of these properties in the course of his studies."

Kasey gave a snort of disbelief. "So these visions everyone talks about? He was just tripping?"

"The hallucinations would have induced highly creative states. Just like the Beatles with LSD, only Nostradamus saw apocalyptic visions instead of yellow submarines."

It was a disappointingly rational answer. "But how does that explain the accuracy of his prophecies?"

"What makes you think they are accurate?"

"Well, I…" She hesitated. She had not meant to imply belief, and now she found herself in the position of having to defend the seer. "People are still talking about him 500 years later. He must have gotten something right."

Bridges smiled ruefully. "I have devoted years of my life to studying his prophecies, and even I can't give you a definitive answer about that. Those who do not believe will rightly point out that his symbolic language is so vague that you can ascribe any interpretation to it. It is human nature to look for the familiar, to find meaning in that which we do not fully understand. And yet, when we find that meaning, it is so profound an experience that we cannot easily dismiss it. Consider for example the prophecies regarding the rise of Nazi Germany.

"Nostradamus wrote his prophecies in poems of four lines—called 'quatrains'—arranged into groups which he called 'centuries.' Century II, quatrain twenty-four reads: '*Bates farouches de faim fleuves tranner; Plus part du champ encontre Hister sera, En cage de fer le grand fera traÂ'ner, Quand rien enfant de Germain observer.*'"

Avery translated. "'Beasts ferocious with hunger will swim across the rivers. The greater part of the field will be against Hister.'"

"I guess the nutmeg bong didn't have spell check," Kasey said, rolling her eyes.

"You've heard this one?" Bridges chuckled. "But maybe it wasn't explained very well. Allow me to try. 'Hister' is not actually a misspelling of 'Hitler,' but rather an ancient name for the people who inhabit the Danube

River region. The prophecy did not refer to a man with a name that resembled Hister, but to the Germanic people. The 'greater part of the field' strongly suggests a world united against Germany. And you left off the last part of it. 'The great one will cause him to be dragged in a cage of iron when the German child observes no law.' A reference perhaps to the armies of tanks that closed in on Berlin from all sides at the end of the war."

"A skeptic would say that is just an interpretation in hindsight of a very vaguely worded poem," Avery countered. "From the perspective of a Frenchman living in the 16th Century, predicting war with Germany would be a little like predicting the sunrise."

Bridges inclined his head as if to cede the point, but then added, "That is not the only prophecy that seems to speak to this subject. All of Century III reads like a headline from World War II, but quatrain thirty-five, in particular, is very interesting. *'Du plus profonnd de L'Occident d'Europe, De pauvres gens un jeune enfant naistra, Qui par sa langue seduira grande troupe; Son bruit au regne d'Orient plus croistra.'* 'In the most remote part of Western Europe, To poor people, a young child will be born, Who by his speech will seduce a great many; His fame even to the kingdom of the Orient will increase.'"

Bridges paused a moment for dramatic effect. "Three points stand out there. Hitler was born into poverty. His father had many failed business ventures and died when Adolf was quite young. I think it goes without saying that his charisma and oratory seduced a great many, but that last part, 'the kingdom of the Orient,' could certainly be taken as a reference to the alliance between Germany and the Empire of Japan.

"Whether Nostradamus foresaw the rise of the man Hitler, or merely saw the patterns that repeat in human societies, we do know that Hitler and many of his supporters believed that he *was* the fulfillment of those prophecies, even the most terrible ones."

"Why would they want to believe that?"

"Perhaps they thought it lent a certain supernatural aura to his leadership. Or perhaps they viewed those apocalyptic words through a different lens. But consider this. If I tell a man that he has been chosen by destiny to do something, and then he goes out and does that thing, am I a prophet? Or merely a facilitator?" He shrugged. "In the end, we all must find the explanation that provides illumination for our individual journey."

Avery sensed she would get no better answer than that. "Is it possible that Nostradamus could have had gotten some of his information from some kind of primitive medieval computer?"

Bridges laughed. "Not just possible, but factual."

Avery felt a flush of excitement, which quickly died when the scholar held up the armillary sphere. "This. Along with the astrolabe. They were the PCs of the Renaissance era astrologer."

"I was thinking something a little more sophisticated."

Bridges raised a curious eyebrow. "Like what?"

She hesitated, but if anyone could confirm the connection between Nostradamus and the Brazen Head, it would be this man. "Do know the story of the Brazen Head of Albert Magnus?"

"Most assuredly." Bridges stared at her for a moment. "You are wondering if Nostradamus perhaps consulted Albert's mechanical oracle. Interesting."

He stroked his beard thoughtfully. "I can't say that I've ever heard anyone make the connection, but it is certainly an intriguing idea. Albert was an early forefather of the natural sciences. He was an astrologer and an alchemist. I think it's safe to say that Nostradamus would have studied the writings of Albert at University, and no doubt heard the story of the Brazen Head. I suppose in a way, you could say that many of the things Nostradamus knew came from the literal *head* of Albert Magnus." He paused a beat, then added. "But of course, the Brazen Head story is apocryphal."

Avery held his stare. "What if it isn't?"

Bridges stared at her, a mischievous twinkle in his eye. "My dear, what aren't you telling me?"

Luc Le Mans did not look up as the man with the backpack walked past his table, but he did clench his fists in exasperation.

So close.

He had picked up the trail of three Americans in London, caught up to them in Paris where they had boarded a train, and followed them here, to an outdoor café at the junction where Rue Nostradamus fed into Rue de l'Horloge. The old man had supplied him with a partial identification—the man and the Asian woman were American intelligence officers, the other woman was a civilian consultant named Avery Halsey.

The two women had gone into the nearby museum, while the man with the backpack had been sitting at one of the other tables, in the shadow of a towering art deco bronze statue of the famed seer holding the tools of divination—an hourglass and armillary sphere, oblivious to the fact that the man who was going to kill him was seated just a few feet away, casually sipping his coffee and pretending to look at his phone.

It would have been the easiest thing in the world to sneak up behind the man. A quick knife thrust or a garroting wire slipped around the man's neck, then grab the backpack, which he felt certain contained the Brazen Head, and that would be the end of it. His original mission would be accomplished, and his fallen comrades would be avenged.

But that wasn't going to work this time.

He wouldn't be able to go in with guns blazing, as he had at the offices of the Council of Rome. In hindsight, that had probably been a rash decision, and one for which two of his teammates had paid dearly, but that was only part of the reason a subtler approach was needed here. In Zurich, his official status as a commander in the counter-terrorism service gave him a great deal of discretionary authority, not to mention a team of trained operators who would not question his orders, but that only went as far as the border.

Killing the American agents wasn't the problem, but covering his tracks… That was the tricky part. Fortunately, he had a plan that would not only provide an immediate diversion to conceal his actions, but also give the authorities a convenient scapegoat.

Using his contacts in the counter-terrorism community, he had surreptitiously contacted two young men, both North African immigrants, and both suspected Islamist radicals, and arranged a meeting ostensibly for the purpose of providing them with weapons and explosives for a planned terror attack.

The meeting would not go quite as the two men expected. When they arrived, they would find the weapons cache, just as promised, in the boot of a rental car parked on the far side of the plaza, but when they attempted to drive off with it, the explosives would detonate, killing them instantly, causing a modest amount of collateral damage in the process. In the ensuing mayhem, LeMans would kill the American agents and slip away with the prize.

Unfortunately, Salon de Provence was a bit out of the way for such a rendezvous. LeMans had explained that the remote location would be a safer place to make the exchange than the back streets of Paris and the men had accepted that, but that also meant he would have to wait for them to arrive.

The man with the backpack exited the café seating area and continued down the street to the entrance of the Nostradamus museum where the other Americans had gone earlier.

LeMans sighed. He had no idea how much longer the Americans would be here. If the North Africans didn't show soon, the opportunity would be lost. No telling when another chance so perfect would present itself.

Avery removed the Brazen Head from the backpack and placed it on the table. They were no longer in the public part of the museum, but in a small room at the back of the house which appeared to serve as a lunchroom for the staff. She had called Greg from the upstairs room and directed him to bring it in. Both Greg and Kasey had questioned her decision to bring the scholar into their confidence. If word of the incident in Zurich became international news, they would be exposed, but Avery thought the risk was slight. She doubted the episode would even rate a mention in Bridges' next book, which probably only a handful of people would ever read.

The utilitarian environment, particularly in contrast with Loew's gallery in Zurich or even the static displays in the museum, seemed to rob the artifact of mystery, making it seem like nothing more than a cheap trinket. In fact, in the kitchen setting, it looked to her like a piece of cookware—some kind of avant-garde tea kettle.

Bridges, however, was awestruck. He reached for it, then halted. "May I… touch it?"

Avery suddenly felt guilty for not treating the antique with more care. If it was what everyone thought it was, it deserved to be handled with kid—or at the very least, white cotton—gloves, but she had brained a guy with it, and then shoved it into a backpack and mostly forgotten about it. She nodded.

He reached out again and put his hands on it, reverently as if offering a benediction, then drew it close and began inspecting it. He turned it over, probed the mouth and eyelids to see if they would move—they did not—and then took out his phone, turned on the flashlight and shone it into the mouth and nostrils. "How does it work?"

The question caught her off guard. "I don't really know if it does."

Bridges turned it over again, held it close to his head and shook it gently. "Clockwork, perhaps? Hmmm. The nostril holes go in quite a ways, but aside from that, it appears to be sealed tight. Would you consider having it x-rayed?"

Avery glanced over at Greg before answering. "Do you think it would help?"

"Well, understanding how it works would go a long way to supporting your hypothesis about it being used by Nostradamus. It would also establish the provenance of this piece. If it is clockwork, that would suggest to me at least that it was not created by Albert Magnus."

"Why do you say that?"

"Albert lived in the 13th Century. The first clockwork machines would not appear in Europe for another century. Something complicated enough to simulate human speech and movement… Well, even in the time of Nostradamus, that sort of thing was still on the drawing board. In fact, it literally was. Leonardo designed several programmable automatons."

"Leonardo da Vinci?"

Bridges nodded. "He drew up plans for a mechanical knight that could move its arms and legs, and even talk. We don't know if he ever actually constructed it, but he did complete work on a mechanical lion which walked on its own and even presented a bouquet of flowers to the King of France. I guess you could say that was the earliest example of a delivery drone."

Avery took a moment to process this. "Did Leonardo and Nostradamus ever cross paths?"

"It's possible, but unlikely. Leonardo died about the same time Nostradamus began his university studies. However, both men benefited from the patronage of the Medici family, albeit in different generations. Are you perhaps thinking that this is the work of Leonardo, rather than Albert?"

"I'm not sure what I'm thinking."

Bridges shrugged. "If you could get a look inside it, compare it to some of Leonardo's designs, you'd have your answer. But I'm afraid that doesn't really tell us whether Nostradamus used this."

Avery stared at the brass device and considered her next move. She had not found a connection between the artifact and Nostradamus, but she felt certain that she was on the right track. She was certain of something else, too.

The Brazen Head wasn't just a symbol. It had power—real power.

It had spoken to Albert Magnus, spoken to Nostradamus, and perhaps even Leonardo da Vinci. It had spoken to Rudolph Hess, prompting him to make a desperate and seemingly foolhardy attempt to negotiate peace with Great Britain.

Could it be made to speak again? If so, what would it say?

She turned to Greg. "Do you know of a way that we could x-ray it?"

"There's a CT machine at the embassy in Paris."

"We need to figure out what makes it tick. Maybe then we'll know why the Immortal really wants it."

NINETEEN

Jersey City

Stone did not believe for a second that his show of cooperation would protect Avery and the others from Furst's hired killers. Martiel might have been sincere with the offer, but Furst struck him as someone who kept his promises only as long as he had to in order to get what he wanted. He also knew that Kasey Kim and Greg Johns were more than capable of defending themselves, as they had already amply demonstrated. No, his apparent capitulation had nothing to do with forestalling that remote threat, but it was better that his captors believe it to be so.

Part of it was the desire to challenge Martiel. The self-styled Immortal was clearly enamored with his own intellectual prowess, but Stone wanted to see if he was as good as advertised, or merely a relentless narcissist. Furst had evidently accepted Martiel's claims at face value, but it would take more than a thinly disguised anagram and some clever cryptographic puzzles to impress Stone.

But that wasn't his primary reason for acceding to his captors' demands either.

The truth of the matter was that Stone was burning with curiosity. Martiel's desire to possess the Brazen Head was anomalous. It didn't appear to fit the pattern, which made it an irresistible puzzle to Stone.

He knew better than to just ask. Martiel would continue to be coy about it, teasing him with hints that were more likely to misdirect than inform. But if he ignored the matter, showed no interest, Martiel would be unable to resist the impulse to brag about it.

He concentrated instead on the immediate task of testing Martiel's planned attack on the global monetary system. After Furst left the room, he asked Martiel to talk him through it.

"Mystic has a built-in virtual trading feature," Martiel had explained. "It's a game mode that allows a user to run simulated trading sessions using real-world data. It's more of a tutorial than anything else, but we'll be using it to probe the market's response to our incursion and test the effectiveness of Mystic's own safeguards."

"So all of your... What should I call them? Ringers?"

Martiel shrugged.

Stone continued. "They're tied into the same simulation?"

"Yes."

"Isn't that going to be a little suspicious? Over a hundred users all simultaneously going into the tutorial mode in the middle of the trading day?"

Another shrug. "It's not illegal. By the time anyone notices, if they notice at all, we'll be well past the point where it matters."

"That's the real weakness in your plan, you know. The human factor. It all hinges on your ringers being able to carry out your instructions to the letter. Easy enough to do that in a simulation, but when it's for real, when the pressure is on, there's no telling how they'll perform. They have a saying in the military: The battle plan is always the first casualty."

"The ringers, as you call them, won't have all that much to do. The trades are already set up. Their only role will be to give confirmation when the prompt comes up. It might be better to call them 'yes men,' since that's all they'll be doing. Clicking 'yes.'"

Stone nodded equivocally. "All right, show me. Do a run through so I can see what it's supposed to look like."

Martiel opened an IRC chat window—evidently another built-in feature of Mystic—and typed a message:

TEST RUN IN 30 SECONDS. SAFE MODE ONLY. PLS CONFIRM

He hit send, and a moment later, the little box with the

message began filling up with replies signaling that the message had been acknowledged by all the users in Martiel's network.

Half a minute later, Stone watched the death of the global economy unfold in real time.

Although he was not entirely convinced of the urgency of the threat to his empire, Wayne Valero provided Tam with a complete list of hard-wired Mystic terminals in the Hudson River building—sixty-three of them in total, including the one assigned to Thom Martiel on the twenty-eighth floor—along with the necessary credentials to establish her and Sievers as IT technicians conducting routine maintenance and firmware updates to the terminals. Armed with the list and attired in khakis and blue polo shirts embroidered with the Iron River logo, Tam and Sievers visited them all, one by one, working their way up the forty-two-story tower.

Tam did not expect to find Stone and Martiel in front of one of those terminals or tied-up in the corner, but the "upgrade" they installed included a passive surveillance feature that would allow them to access the cameras and microphones in each terminal. The feed from each would be filtered through an automated facial recognition program which would immediately send an alert if either Stone or Martiel showed up.

Unfortunately, it was a tedious and time-consuming process.

"We need to pick up the pace," Sievers observed as they started up the stairs to the twenty-fourth floor. "At this rate, we won't be done before the close of business."

"I don't think these bankers necessarily keep banker's hours," Tam replied. "But you're right. We might need to split up. Cover twice as much ground that way."

Sievers made a face. "So I'd have to talk to these people?"

"Oh, what are you worried about? Just turn on the charm like you did with Valero."

"What if they don't want to talk about cars?"

"You'll think of something."

She pushed open the door and started down the hallway, but when they reached the next location on the list—NFI Investment Management—they found the double glass doors locked and the space beyond dark and empty.

Sievers cupped his hands to the glass to shut out the ambient light from the hallway and peered through. "Nobody home," he said. "Looks like they moved out."

Tam took out her phone and dialed the contact number for NFI, but ended the call after getting the runaround from an automated answering service. She dialed a different number instead, and a few seconds later, an actual living person answered the call.

"Ms. Broderick," Wayne Valero said, bypassing the formal greeting. "How goes the search?"

"We've hit a snag," she admitted. "NFI Investments. They're on the list, but the office appears to be vacant. Can you confirm that this address is correct?" She gave him the suite number.

"Wait one." A long pause, and then he came back. "Not only is that the correct address, but I'm showing heavy data usage on one of the terminals registered to NFI. Are you certain you're at that address?"

"Let me check that," she told him and hit the mute button.

"I heard," Sievers said. He produced a slim wallet containing a set of lockpicking tools and went to work. A few seconds later, the lock turned, and he pulled the door open.

Tam's right hand found the grip of her holstered Makarov, but she did not draw it. Instead, she stepped into the dark space beyond and called out. "Anyone here? IT services."

Her voice echoed from the bare walls. The office space was completely empty. There were no desks or chairs, no cubicles or workstations. Even the modular dividing walls had been removed, leaving a vast cavernous void. She gave up all pretense and drew the pistol before taking another step.

Sievers drew his weapon as well, along with a Mini Maglite which he shone into the shadowy far reaches of the empty room. There were a few doors along the perimeter—probably for permanent offices and restrooms—all of them propped open and likewise dark and silent.

Tam continued holding the pistol out with her right hand, while using her left to thumb-off the mute button on her phone. "Mr. Valero. There's no one here at all. Is there any way the signal from the Mystic terminals could be rerouted?"

"The short answer is, 'definitely not.' The only way that might work is splicing the hard line, but that would have a noticeable effect on transfer speed, and I'm not detecting anything like that."

"So what you're saying is that the terminals are here somewhere. Where would I look for them?"

Valero breathed an audible sigh of consternation. "Is there a server room?"

"Server room?" Tam caught Sievers' eye, nodded toward the doors in the back. He nodded in return and started toward them.

"We usually route our lines through the same conduit used for telephone or ISDN lines," Valero continued. "There can be some flexibility with the exact placement of the terminals, but it will probably be within about a hundred feet of the server room."

Sievers ducked into one of the open doorways but reappeared a moment later, shook his head and kept moving. He did the same at the next door, and the next after that, but when he emerged from the fourth door, he waved her forward. "I think this is it."

"You found the terminals?" She reached the door before he could answer, and saw immediately that he had found only another empty room, this one barely larger than a closet.

"Not the terminals." He shone his light at the back wall where several metal panels were mounted. "But I'll bet this was the server room."

"There's nothing here now."

Sievers stepped forward and began opening the panels, one at a time, revealing circuit breakers, ventilation ducts, and masses of wiring. "One of these is the hardline, right?"

Suddenly she understood. "They routed the wire to a different office."

"That's what I reckon," Sievers said with a confident nod. "We're close."

Stone watched several iterations of the simulation before commenting. "You appear to have anticipated every response."

"We've been working on this for a year and a half," Martiel said, making no attempt to mask his pride. "We know what the most probable market countermeasures will be. What we can't predict is the unpredictable. That's what I want you to do. How would you stop this?" He paused and then added. "You have something, don't you? Don't hold back. Your friends' lives depend on your cooperation."

"I have some ideas, but I'll need to put hands on, so to speak."

"That's why I brought you here." Martiel scooted aside and gestured for Stone to take his place. "Just talk me through what you're doing. And I will, of course, be watching so…" He left sentence hanging, the implication clear enough. *Don't try anything.*

Stone began clicking through the toolbar menu, familiarizing himself with some of the features of the trading platform that he had not used during his earlier trading session with Martiel. "There's something I've been wondering about," he said. "The Immortal. Does that *nom de guerre* have some particular significance?"

Martiel chuckled. "A private joke."

Stone sensed there was a lot more to it than that, but decided not to press the issue. He opened the IRC chat window and typed in a message to everyone on the network, to let them know he was about to start another test run. As he typed, he said, "From what I can tell, this part of your plan is airtight. What happens after is another matter entirely. The market won't behave predictably once panic sets in. The uncertainty will increase exponentially. You might not be able to achieve your desired outcome. People may not be as quick to embrace bitcoin as you think. Or you could push things over the brink. Start World War III."

"You're not wrong about the uncertainty. But the primary goal has always been leveling the playing field, bringing down this universal Ponzi scheme."

"Does your friend know that?" Stone nodded in the direction of the door through which Furst had disappeared some time earlier. When Martiel glanced involuntarily in the same direction, Stone deleted the IRC message then clicked on the settings button. He scanned the dropdown menu until he found what he was looking for, clicked on it, and then quickly closed the window.

"He talks like a true believer," Stone said, "ready to sacrifice everything, but I think he expects to come on top. I think you convinced him that's going to happen."

Martiel smiled. "Peter knows the risks. And he knows what he needs to do to ensure the optimal outcome."

"Oh, right. The brass head gizmo." He resisted the urge to ask about it, hoping that Martiel would volunteer the information, but when that did not happen, he changed the subject. "How did you two end up working together, anyway?"

"We have a mutual interest in a certain historic figure, albeit for very different reasons."

Stone was about to ask the name of the historical figure in question—it probably wouldn't mean anything to him, but the more he kept Martiel talking, the better his chances of figuring out what made the man tick—but before he could phrase the question, Furst stormed into the room.

"We have a problem," he said. "Someone just broke into the office upstairs."

"Broke in?" Martiel said. "What do you mean? That office is empty."

"I know. They must be looking for him." Furst pointed at Stone. "They know he's still here."

Martiel turned on Stone. "Get away from the computer," he snapped, pulling the keyboard out of Stone's reach.

Stone just held up hands to indicate that he wasn't going to resist. "It wasn't anything I did," he said.

"You need to execute," Furst said, his voice taut and urgent. "Now. Before it's too late."

Martiel shook his head. "No. Not until I have the Brazen Head."

"And you will have it," Furst hissed. "But you must do this now. We won't get another chance."

"You don't understand. I need it. Without it…" He trailed off, as if unable to articulate that dire possibility. For the first time since the revelation of his true purpose, Martiel looked uncertain.

Why is the Brazen Head so important to him? Stone wondered again.

Furst growled in frustration then took out his phone and initiated a call. "Luc. You need to get it now. Do whatever it takes."

"Wait," Stone protested even as the other man was shoving the phone back into his pocket. "That wasn't our deal. You said you'd let me talk to Avery. Convince her to give it up."

"It is too late for that," Furst shot back, then turned to Martiel. "Luc will have the Brazen Head in a matter of minutes. I will charter a plane for him. You will have it in eight hours' time. That is a promise. But we have to do this now. They will be here in minutes. You have to execute before it's too late."

"It's already too late," Stone countered. "Tam will pull the plug before you make a single trade."

"No. You're wrong." Martiel shook his head and then bent over the keyboard. "She might be able to shut down this terminal, but once I send the command, the dominos will start to fall. You won't be able to get to them all. Not in time."

He opened the chat window, started typing.

"You won't get away," Stone persisted. He was stalling, trying to keep Martiel off balance. "She'll be waiting for you."

"Maybe we'll use you as a hostage," Furst said.

"Hah. If you knew Tam, you'd realize how stupid that idea is."

"Quiet," Martiel shouted. "I'm trying to work."

His hands hovered above the keyboard, twitching with nervous energy, then he began typing, stabbing the keys with his fingers.

"Did it!" he shouted as he hit the final key and stepped away, pumping his fist in exultation. He then grabbed the keyboard with both hands, ripped its cord out of the computer, hurled it against the wall. Only then did he turned to Furst. "Let's get the hell out of here."

"What about him?" Furst jabbed a finger at Stone.

"Forget about him. There's nothing he can do to stop it. We don't need him now, and we can't take him with us. I doubt we'd make it past the front door with him."

"That's not what I meant," Furst replied, ominously. "He knows."

Martiel stared at Stone for a moment, a triumphant smile spreading across his face. "Yes. He does."

Without another word, the two men turned and headed for the exit, leaving Stone to stare helplessly at the computer screen, which still displayed the IRC message Martiel had just sent to the network. It was just one word:

EXECUTE

TWENTY

Salon de Provence, France

It was like something Nostradamus himself might have envisioned in one of his hallucinogenic trances. In an instant, just as Avery and the others emerged from the museum, intent on traveling to Paris in order to see what secrets lay beneath the shiny brass skin of the Brazen Head, the peaceful afternoon quiet was torn asunder, transformed into a fiery holocaust.

As with the flashbang in Zurich, the suddenness of it left Avery stunned, unable to process what was happening, but this blast was an order of magnitude greater, and even though they were at least a hundred yards from the detonation, the overpressure wave hit with the force of a hurricane, hurling the three of them backward, into the exterior wall of the museum. And, as in Zurich, the explosion was just the beginning.

Kasey and Greg recovered much quicker than Avery, drawing their pistols to meet the follow-on attack they knew was coming, but they weren't fast enough. Even before the last echoes of the explosion faded, there were several more eruptions, quieter than the initial detonation, but just as deadly.

Something warm and wet sprayed across Avery's face and the wall behind her. She looked up and saw Kasey staggering backward, an obscene red hole in her back, just below her right shoulder blade.

The horror of it hit Avery like another concussion wave. She opened her mouth to scream, to demand a do-over from God or the universe, but if any sound came out, she could not hear it over the noise of more reports, much closer this time. Greg stood above her, as solid as the bronze statue across the square, firing his pistol at an attacker she could not see, but then in that instant, Kasey crashed into her and bore her down to the sidewalk.

She could feel Kasey's blood soaking through her own clothes.

No! Kasey!

"Avery!" Greg was kneeling beside her now, shouting down without looking. His right hand still gripped the pistol, arm outstretched, while his left held the backpack. He thrust it in her direction. "Take it! Run!"

The backpack was also streaked with blood, as was Greg's left arm from the biceps down.

"You said to stay with you." Her voice came out as a squeak. It was a pathetic thing to say, a childish denial, but her mind refused to engage with the grim reality of what was happening.

"You have to go, Avery!" He punctuated the shout by squeezing off two more shots, then dropped the backpack in order to reload his semi-auto. "When I start shooting, you go! And don't stop."

Avery hugged the backpack to her and squirmed out from under Kasey's unmoving form, and when Greg started firing, she scrambled up and took off running. She didn't know where to go, only that she needed to get away from the shooting.

Just ahead and to her left, a column of black smoke was spiraling into the heavens, rising from the twisted remains of a sedan. Her primal survival instincts—what Stone might have called her reptile brain—told her to run away from the burning wreck, but another more rational voice told her the bombed-out car was the one place where the bad guys definitely wouldn't be, so she ran toward it.

As she got closer, she realized that car now sat at the center of a blast crater, surrounded by a scattering of debris—pieces of the car, chunks of masonry and pavement. The heat radiating from the wreck rebuffed her, but she could see, just beyond it, a stream of people emerging from the shattered façade of a clothing shop. Some were limping, others clutched bloody wounds, and all of them were streaked with dust, but their fear was palpable even from a distance. They could hear the shooting across the square and knew what it meant; terror had found them.

Avery knew that what was happening had nothing to do with politics or Islam or any other cause, but that knowledge was of little comfort. She was just like them, a bloody victim of the attack. She hastened past the burning car, losing herself in the human flood. She had no clue what to do next, where to go.

That was something else she shared with the men and women around her.

LeMans took aim at the running figure of Avery Halsey. His finger was still curled around the trigger, but before he could pull it, another shot from one of the wounded American agents forced him to duck behind the corner of the building he was using as cover. He edged out again, squeezed off a pair of shots in the general direction of the other shooter, and then looked for Avery again.

She was now on the far side of the plaza, still within range of his pistol—barely—but too close to a group of panicked survivors fleeing the area. He could still shoot her but discreetly retrieving the backpack with the Brazen Head from her body would be next to impossible.

He muttered a curse, holstered his weapon and turned away, sprinting down the Rue de l'Horloge, away from the blast site.

Things hadn't gone exactly as planned, but they could certainly have gone worse. The call from Furst, ordering him into action, had come before the arrival of the would-be terrorists from North Africa, but their presence would merely have been icing on the cake. Even without their bodies at the scene, everyone would jump to the conclusion that it was an act of terrorism.

And while he hadn't been able to secure the Brazen Head as hoped, he had managed to take the two of the American agents out of play. If his information was correct, the one that remained—Avery Halsey—wasn't an agent at all, but a civilian consultant.

He ran up the street and rounded the corner onto the Rue Beauvezet. His intent was to circle around and cut off Avery's escape, but as soon as he made the turn, he was confronted by a flood of people heading directly toward him in a frantic mass. He considered fighting through them but realized that doing so would only attract unwanted attention his way. As far as he knew, Avery had not seen his face, but if she was there among the frightened horde, she would definitely take note of someone fighting against the flow.

He took a step back instead, scanning the crowd, searching for her, but she wasn't there. He swore again under his breath but did not panic. There were other avenues leading away from the plaza, and if she managed to slip away here, she was alone, unarmed, and almost certainly terrified.

He took a deep breath, willing himself into a calmer state. Where would she go? Who would she turn to for help?

The police? It was a possibility, but unlikely. Even if she wasn't a trained operative, she would surely know that involving the authorities of a foreign nation would expose her clandestine operation. No, she would run for a while, but eventually, she would by drawn back to the only familiar thing in her world—her fallen comrades.

He was pretty sure he had wounded both of them, and possibly killed the Asian woman, but the male operative had still been returning fire, covering Avery's escape. She would almost certainly try to reunite with him.

LeMans doubled back again, heading down the Rue de l'Horloge toward the intersection with Rue Nostradamus, this time moving at a brisk walk. First responders were already arriving. Policemen in full tactical kit were setting up barricades to block access to the site. Firemen and paramedics hanging back waiting for the all clear. He considered trying to bluff his way into the secure area with his Swiss military credentials but decided it wasn't worth the risk. No, he would simply observe, for now, follow the ambulance to the hospital, and then wait for Avery to come to him.

Sooner or later, he knew, she would.

TWENTY-ONE

Jersey City

Tam Broderick and Billy Sievers found Stone just a few minutes later, in a small windowless room in a vacant office, directly below the server room of the evidently defunct offices of NFI Investment Management. He was staring at a computer monitor, his expression uncharacteristically anxious, but he looked up when they entered and gave Tam a grim smile.

"You just missed them," he said.

"Missed who?" Tam holstered her pistol and instead reached for her phone. "Give me a name. I'll call DHS. Lock this place down."

Stone shook his head. "No. He'll have anticipated that."

"Who?" Tam repeated.

"The Immortal. Martiel. But that's not important. We've got bigger problems."

"Thom is working for the Immortal?" Siever said.

"He *is* the Immortal," Stone shot back. "I'll tell you the whole story later, but right now we need to find a way into the Mystic trading platform."

Tam put a hand on his shoulder. "It's okay. I figured out what you were trying to tell me."

Stone seemed not to have heard. "He's attempting a coordinated attack on the financial system. I tried to disable the IRC chat feature on his account so he couldn't send the 'execute' command, but I don't think it worked. He must have realized what I did and fixed it. We've got to find a way to shut Mystic down."

"Stone, I did."

He shook his head again. "Not just here. In this building. The whole system."

"Stone!" She gripped him with both hands and shook

him to get his attention. "It's already done. We figured it out. We put a kill switch on all of the suspect accounts. They're shut down. Whatever the Immortal was trying to do, we stopped it."

Stone blinked at her in astonishment. "You did?"

"You ain't the only one who can solve a puzzle, you know," Sievers said. "Though I'm still not sure what exactly it was we just stopped."

Stone stared at him, mute with disbelief.

Tam shook him again. "Focus, Stone. What's this about Martiel and the Immortal?"

"Thom Martiel is an anagram of the Immortal." Stone blinked again and then seemed to return to himself. "He's working with a man named Peter Furst to destabilize the world economy. Crash the monetary system. Only…"

"Only?"

Some of the anxiety was gone from Stone's features, but what replaced it was no less out of character for him. Confusion. "There's something else."

"What?"

"I don't know." The admission was clearly onerous for him. He took a deep breath, let it out with a sigh. Then his head snapped up. "The Brazen Head."

"We've got that, too."

"No. I mean, he knows. He's got someone following them. Avery and Greg and Kasey. You've got to warn them."

Tam reacted without question or hesitation. She brought up the contact list on her phone, tapped Greg's name, waited as the ringtone played.

Waited until the call went to voice mail.

Tam's heart was pounding in her chest. She felt utterly helpless. Her team was in immediate danger, and there wasn't a damned thing she could do to help them.

"Greg and Kasey can handle it," she said, as much to convince herself as the others. "Tell me about the people who were holding you. Martiel. Furst. Who are they? Who are they working for? Dominion?"

"No. At least I don't think so." Stone's forehead creased in a frown. "Furst runs Nutria Mills."

"The cereal people?" asked Sievers.

"No, that's General Mills. Nutria does candy… I guess they probably do cereal, too, and a bunch of other stuff. Furst has some kind of grudge against bankers. I think he's also an anti-Semite; he probably conflates Jews and banks."

"A lot of folks do that," Tam said. "All that conspiracy crap about the New World Order is just a dog whistle."

She hit the 'home' button on her phone, banishing the screen with the incomplete call to Greg Johns, and did a Google search using the terms "Furst" and "Nutria."

"He's a foreign national," she said after skimming Peter Furst's Wikipedia page. "That will help. I'll alert DHS. What exactly are they trying to do?"

"Furst and Martiel…" Stone paused a beat. "I'm pretty sure that's not his real name. Their plan was to use Mystic to create a cash surplus in the banks, drive the value of the dollar and other fiat currencies into the ground, and then replace it all with cryptocurrency."

"Cryptocurrency?"

"Bitcoin."

"So this is just about money?" Sievers said. "Just like the big crash in '08. Bet on the economy to fail, make it happen, and then clean up when everybody else is drowning."

"Maybe for Furst. The Immortal wants something else."

"What?" Tam asked.

"To be the smartest guy in the room."

Tam couldn't tell if Stone was being serious.

"So who tried to kill him the other night?" Sievers asked.

"That was for show. He was trying to draw us out. Mostly just me, actually."

"He took a hell of a chance."

"I'm sure he was never in any real danger," Stone said

with a dismissive gesture.

Tam exchanged a dubious glance with Sievers who merely shrugged.

"He knew I was getting close," Stone continued. "I was looking at the pattern, but he was the one creating it. He staged the attack to get inside our investigation. Find out what we knew. And he was hoping I'd take the bait and go find the Brazen Head for him."

"You said that was just a red herring."

"I was wrong."

"You been wrong a lot when it comes to this guy," Sievers remarked. "I reckon that's kind of a new experience for you."

Stone frowned at him. "Not so much. I knew he was playing us almost from the beginning."

"What?" Sievers blinked. His face was impassive, but Tam could see an ember of ire growing red hot behind his eyes. "You knew he was one of the bad guys?"

"His name. The anagram. It was obvious. Plus, his name didn't appear in the coded messages on the Immortal Mysteries Forum. He was never a real target."

"You knew," Sievers said again. "And you didn't tell us?"

Stone looked back at him, uncomprehending. "I needed him to believe he had us fooled. It was the only way to figure out what he was really after."

"I jumped off a goddamned building trying to save you!"

"Billy!" Tam put a restraining hand on his arm. She faced Stone again. "We're gonna have a talk about this later, but right now, I need to know what our next move is."

"He wants the Brazen Head. I need to figure out why. And you need to keep him from getting it. They're in London, right?"

Tam shook her head. "They were, but last I heard, they were on their way to Provence."

"France? Why?" Stone shook his head and didn't wait

for an answer. "Doesn't matter. We need to get there, ASAP." He started for the door.

Before Tam could follow, her phone started buzzing.

It was Greg Johns.

The Immortal knew something was wrong, even before he and Furst made it out of the tower. Five minutes in, there should have been some visible sign of the unfolding apocalypse; murmurs of fear and dismay as the markets began circling the drain, spiraling into oblivion, but as they exited the elevator and made their way through the lobby toward the exit, all he heard was the sounds of business as usual.

"Stone," he muttered the name like a curse.

Furst glanced sidelong at him. "What's wrong?"

"He stopped it. I'm not sure how, but he did."

The old man stopped in his tracks. "What?"

The Immortal grabbed the other man by the elbow, got him moving again. "We need to keep moving. They'll be looking for us now."

"This is a disaster. You promised—"

"Keep moving," he hissed, half-dragging the other man through the exit doors and toward a waiting limousine. Once they were inside and on the move, he snapped, "This is your fault. I told you that it would be futile to execute without the Brazen Head in our possession."

"My fault?" Furst glowered at him. "You waited too long. Squandered our advantage."

"This is a setback, not a defeat."

"A setback?" Furst seemed ready to pop. "Your plan is in ruins. Two years of preparation. Wasted."

With an effort, the Immortal brought his rage under control. "We can still win this. But I absolutely must have the Brazen Head."

Furst seemed only slightly mollified by the assurance. "I think you overestimate the importance of that old relic."

Despite everything that happened, the Immortal

smiled. Furst had no idea how important the Brazen Head really was.

And neither did Gavin Stone.

TWENTY-TWO

Salon de Provence, France

At first, Avery's only thought was to keep moving, as much running from the horror of what she had just witnessed as from the killer stalking her. It was like Zurich all over again, except this time her friends were—

Don't say it. Don't even think it.

—not going to come to the rescue. She was on her own this time.

In Zurich, she had at least been somewhat familiar with the local landmarks, but she had no idea where to begin looking for shelter here.

I have to call Tam.

She dug into her pocket, took out her phone...

A hand gripped her arm, arresting her forward progress. She started with a yelp as a figure stepped in front of her. A woman... A police officer.

Over the sound of blood roaring in her ears, Avery heard the policewoman ask if she was all right.

Police, she thought. *I have to tell them. They'll protect me.*

But then she heard Kasey's voice in her head.

That's the last thing you want to do. Under the radar, Avery.

"A bomb," she gasped, speaking in French. "Back there. It was horrible."

"Yes, I know," the officer said. "You're injured. Let me help."

She looked down at the bloodstains on her shirt, the streaks of scarlet like tiger stripes on the pale skin of her arms. Kasey's blood.

"It's not my blood," she said, fighting back a sob. "Please. I just need to get home. My family will be worried."

The officer scrutinized her for a moment, then nodded. "Very well. But as soon as you are able, you need to call us and give a statement."

"I will," she promised, and as soon as she let go, she was moving again. For the first time since fleeing the attack, she turned and looked back. She saw no sign of pursuit, but did that mean anything?

Under the radar.

They had been doing that the whole time, but the killers had still caught up to them.

How?

How did you guys find me? She had asked Kasey that in Zurich, in the crypt of the Grossmunster church, and she recalled Kasey's answer. *Tracking app on your phone.*

Was that how the killers had found them? It seemed impossible, but she couldn't take any chances.

She hurled the phone down onto the pavement, smashed it under her heel and kicked the remains into a storm drain.

She realized now that people were staring at her. Surely they too knew about the explosion. Police cars and fire trucks were racing toward the towering column of black smoke that marked the spot just a few city blocks behind her. But the further she went, the more attention her condition would attract.

I need to clean up, she thought. *Get some new clothes.*

She spotted a small gift boutique further up the block and hurried inside. The man behind the counter immediately registered surprise and dismay at the sight of her. "My God, are you all right?"

"It's not my blood," she said again. "There was a bomb."

"Yes, I heard. It's terrible. Those animals."

"Please, can I use your washroom?"

The shopkeeper sprang into action, like a knight charging to the rescue of a maiden in distress, and ushered her through his shop to the small lavatory in the back. He even turned the taps for her.

Avery avoided looking directly at the small mirror mounted on the wall behind the pedestal sink, afraid of what she might see.

"Is there anything else I can do for you?" the man asked.

She shook her head, too overcome with gratitude to even know how to answer.

"I'll leave you then." He stepped away, closing the door to give her privacy.

After setting the backpack on the floor beside the pedestal sink, she stripped off her blood-soaked shirt and held it under the stream of water. It was immediately apparent that no amount of scrubbing would get the red stain out of the fabric, so she chose instead to use it as a washcloth to wipe the blood and dust from her arms and face.

She would have to buy a new shirt, maybe one of the souvenir T-shirts, emblazoned with the likeness of Nostradamus, displayed in the shop.

Buying a T-shirt, she realized, meant spending money. She had a few euro notes, enough to make that purchase but not much else. She had a credit card, but credit card transactions were easily traced; she didn't dare use it. But she couldn't do anything, couldn't go anywhere without money.

"And just where am I going to go?" she muttered, staring at pink-tinged water swirling around the basin.

Paris, she decided. *The American Embassy*.

Not only was it the safest place she could think of, it was also where she could get a CT scan of the Brazen Head, and maybe figure out why the Immortal wanted it so badly.

The thought of doing something other than just running for her life calmed her. When she was reasonably clean, she turned off the tap, retrieved the backpack and balanced it on the edge of the basin in order to unzip it. She reached inside, past the bulbous shape of the Brazen Head, and found her laptop computer. If she could get a wi-fi signal, she could contact Tam.

"No, not Tam," she murmured. Until she knew how

the Immortal had tracked them to Provence, just staying under the radar wasn't going to cut it. She would have to go deeper. "Jimmy."

Jimmy Letson, an investigative reporter with the Washington Post and a skilled hacker, was a friend of her brother, Dane Maddock. Avery had never actually met him in person, but they had worked together on a couple previous occasions, and she considered him a friend. If anyone could help her slip past whatever net the Immortal had cast to catch her, it was Jimmy.

The laptop felt strange in her hands, and when she took it out, she realized why. The molded plastic housing was cracked, broken nearly in two, and in the center of the break, an ugly hole. A bullet hole.

"Crap. So much for that idea."

She reached into the backpack again, worried that the Brazen Head might also have caught a bullet, but her hand encountered something else. It was the notebook Greg had given her in London, with his pen still clipped to the spiral binding. She set it aside and took out the Brazen Head, and was relieved to see that it had survived unscathed. She returned it to the backpack, shoved in the ruined computer as well, then glanced at the notebook. The top page still showed the incomplete timeline she had created.

Significant dates:
c. 1250—Magnus makes BH, Paris?
    Thomas Aquinas destroys

c. 1550—Nostradamus prophecies, Provence, Paris?

c. 1580—BH in Prague

1939—Loew family leaves BH behind in Prague
1941—Hess takes BH to Scotland

She uncapped the pen and added a line just above the Nostradamus entry.

1450??-1520??—Leonardo da Vinci ???

She didn't know if Leonardo was a part of this mystery any more than Nostradamus. It felt like she had found another piece of the puzzle, but what if it was really just one more random fact with no connection?

Too many question marks, she thought.

The shopkeeper refused to let her pay for the T-shirt, which gave her enough money to buy a cup of coffee and a pastry at the cyber café she'd picked out of the phone book. Cyber cafes and public telephones were both, thankfully, still a thing in European cities. She had circled the block twice before entering, verifying as best she could that she was not being followed.

Once inside, she settled in behind the computer but instead of immediately reaching out to Jimmy, she instead opened a browser and typed in a name: Leonardo da Vinci.

A common misconception, reinforced by a certain best-selling conspiracy novel, was that 'da Vinci' was the famed artist's last name. In fact, he had no family surname—Vinci was a reference to his birthplace, a village in Tuscany—so it was more correct to refer to him only by his given name.

The Wikipedia page helped her fill in some of the question marks—exact dates for Leonardo's birth—April 15, 1452—and death—May 2, 1519—and brought back to her mind details about the man that were buried in her memory. Her recent exploration into the life and work of Nostradamus gave her a new perspective on the famed Florentine genius.

She had heard it said before, but Leonardo's inventions—most of which were never built, and in fact could not have been built in his lifetime—were visionary in nature. He conceived of flying machines, armored tanks, simple computers, and robots. It was as if he had a window into the future, just like Nostradamus, but instead of visualizing wars and disasters, Leonardo saw a world of scientific progress. The two men hadn't seen different futures, but rather different views of the same future, a future that was now very real.

Was the Brazen Head that window? And if so, had Leonardo constructed it himself, or had it been handed down to him? It felt like a chicken-or-egg problem, and she tried to imagine how Stone would solve it.

Of course, Stone and Thom Martiel were still missing—hopefully just being held hostage and not something worse. And Greg and Kasey were—

She squeezed her fists, trying to derail that train of thought. There was nothing she could do for any of them. All she could do was focus on solving the big problem. That was how she would give their sacrifices meaning.

It didn't make sense that Leonardo had built the thing. As forward-thinking as some of his designs were, none of them were as sophisticated as the Brazen Head seemed to be. If he *had* fashioned something as sophisticated as the Brazen Head, he would have had no need of it. No, it was much more likely that someone—in all probability, his patron Lorenzo di Medici—had given it to him.

She added another entry to the timeline in the notebook.

Significant dates:
c. 1250—Magnus makes BH, Paris?
    Thomas Aquinas destroys

    Lorenzo de Medici gives BH to Leo
~~1450??-1520??~~—**Leonardo da Vinci ??? 1452-1519**
c. 1550—Nostradamus prophecies, Provence, Paris?

c. 1580--BH in Prague

1939—Loew family leaves BH behind in Prague
1941—Hess takes BH to Scotland

Suddenly, the picture became clear.

Thomas Aquinas had smashed the Brazen Head in the Thirteenth Century. Even broken, it would have been a valuable relic and would have attracted the attention of the Medici family, who were famed for their patronage and support of artists going back to the time of Lorenzo's great-grandfather Cosimo de Medici, who had almost single-handedly sponsored the Renaissance.

Lorenzo, recognizing Leonardo's genius, had given him the damaged head, and Leonardo had restored it to working order. When Leonardo died, it would have returned to the House of Medici—to Catherine de Medici, the Queen of France, who gave it to her favorite seer, Nostradamus. After Nostradamus, the Head went to Prague, to the court of Rudolph II, and subsequently entrusted to the Loew family, who protected it until it was captured by the Nazis and came into the possession of Rudolph Hess. Hess brought it with him to Scotland, where it fell into the possession of the family Walker, who in turn sold it to Gerald Roche.

It was so obvious that she wished she had someone to tell, someone who could point out the flaw in her logic.

Avery shook her head. She had missed something. Not the timeline—all those dots connected—but something else.

Thomas Aquinas had smashed the Brazen Head. Leonardo had fixed it, and from that point forward, it had been functional. It had informed Leonardo's inventions and shown Nostradamus the future, and four centuries later, it was still functional.

So why wasn't it talking anymore?

The pop-up alert on the computer monitor warned her that she only had five minutes left in her session, and asked if she wanted to purchase more time. Since that wasn't an option, she closed the browser window and started an IRC chat session.

Jimmy Letson replied within seconds. *Are you all right?*

The query caught her off guard. Their exchanges were usually light, even flirtatious. The uncharacteristic note of concern almost breached the dam she had built to compartmentalize her emotions.

She knew better than to ask how he had known that something was wrong. He would have determined her location from her IP address, and would have determined—correctly—that it wasn't a coincidence that she was reaching out to him from the same city where a terrorist bomb had just struck.

"Not really," she muttered, typing the same words. "I need your help."

You got it. What can I do for you?

She blinked, realizing only now that she wasn't sure what to do next. Going to the American embassy in Paris still felt like the best course of action, but what if the Immortal anticipated that move? What if there were more killers waiting for her there?

Still, it was somewhere to go.

"I need to get to Paris. Discreetly. But I'm broke. I can't use my credit card, and my laptop is busted."

Give me a minute.

The minute passed. Then another.

Avery watched the session timer nervously. This was taking too long. Finally, a long message filled the chat window.

An Uber car will pick you up there in 5 minutes. It will take you to an electronics store where you'll be able to pick up a new computer and a burner phone. Don't sweat it. Everything is already paid for. After that, the car will take you to the train station in Marseilles. It's about an hour's drive, but hopefully, nobody will be looking for you there. I'll have a Eurail pass waiting for you at the ticket counter.

Avery felt both relieved and exhausted.

Do you need me to call anyone? Dane? Or your boss?

The latter was an indication of the depth of his

concern. Jimmy's extracurricular activities were not strictly legal, and while Tam Broderick was content to look the other way, treating him as an asset to be used, Jimmy preferred to keep his distance.

"No. I'm okay. Thanks, Jimmy. I owe you, big time."

A bottle of Wild Turkey will do. And one other thing.

She couldn't help but smile. "What's that?"

Be careful.

TWENTY-THREE

"I am sorry, mademoiselle, but I am afraid I cannot allow you to speak with the patient until we have fully questioned him."

Tam didn't think Colonel Claude DuBois of the GIGN—the *Groupe d'intervention de la Gendarmerie Nationale*, France's elite national police counter-terrorism unit—was actually sorry at all. She chalked it up to the fact that English wasn't his primary language, though he seemed quite fluent. "Colonel, with all due respect, it's been almost sixteen hours. You've had plenty of time to question him." She stopped herself, took a breath, and then tried a different approach. "I understand that you have a job to do. I'm not trying to interfere. I just want to make sure my friends are all right."

DuBois regarded her with a narrow-eyed, supercilious expression. "I am not sure you do understand. I know who you really work for. You Americans… You think you can come here and turn my country into the OK Corral."

Tam clenched her fists. It was not the first time she had heard that accusation or something like it. She had spent most of the overnight trans-Atlantic flight on the phone, dealing with the political fallout from the incident.

Although her agents had done nothing wrong, the simple fact of their presence at the scene of a major terror attack was enough to bruise the alliance between France and the United States. The authorities on the ground assumed—correctly—that the two armed Americans involved in the shootout with an as yet unidentified suspect were intelligence officers, engaged in clandestine activity on French soil without permission from the French government. The Myrmidons worked under non-official cover status—NOC—which meant the Agency's official policy was to deny and disavow, but when it came to the war against international terrorism, there was a tacit understanding, if not open cooperation among the intelligence community of NATO allies. Such operations happened all the time; the problem was that this one had blown up in their face. Literally.

Whatever political capital she had gained from stopping the Immortal's attack on the global monetary system was pretty much gone, leaving her on shaky ground. Which wasn't a good place from which to deal with what she considered to be far more urgent problems.

The least of those problems was the fact that Thom Martiel… or the Immortal, or whatever he wanted to call himself… had slipped through her fingers.

Actually, it was more complicated than that. When she had identified Peter Furst as a co-conspirator, she had unwittingly put the Myrmidons in the cross-hairs. Furst it seemed had a lot of friends—or at least, people who felt it was to their advantage to stand by him—both inside the government and among the wealthy men who had the real power. Whether out of a misguided sense of loyalty or because they were secret sharers in the conspiracy—Tam feared the latter—they had thrown up enough of a smokescreen to allow Furst, and presumably Martiel as well, to escape the country. She had no idea where they were now, and while she had not been officially ordered to back off—the CIA was at least taking the threat seriously—she wasn't getting much help from outside the Agency. And Stone had assured her that, despite losing a battle, the Immortal was by no means beaten.

Tam knew how urgent that situation was, but her first priority was taking care of her teammates, which was why, after the brief but desperate phone call from Greg, she was here, at the small hospital in Salon de Provence, arguing with the Gendarmerie officer.

"As I told your superior," she explained patiently, "my people were not conducting any kind of clandestine operation. They were just in the wrong place at the wrong time."

"On that, we agree," DuBois said, though he made it sound like an accusation.

Although the Agency had mostly made nice with the French government, DuBois—the ranking GIGN officer on the scene—was evidently exercising his discretionary power to protect his turf by keeping Greg Johns incommunicado. Aside from that single brief phone call following the attack, she had not spoken to him at all. Through diplomatic channels, she had learned that he had sustained two gunshot wounds, but neither were considered life-threatening. The same could not be said for Kasey Kim. Although she had survived surgery to repair the damage from the bullet, she had lost a great deal of blood before reaching the hospital, and the doctors were concerned that she might have suffered brain damage associated with hypoxia. They would only know the full extent of the damage when—or if—she regained consciousness.

Behind Tam, Billy Sievers made a low humming sound. It might have been a growl. "Can you at least tell us how they're doing?"

The colonel softened a little at the emotional plea. Tam suspected it was because Sievers, despite being the stereotypical American cowboy that DuBois found so contemptible, was both white and male. The Frenchman's reply seemed to confirm this. "Your friend is conscious and alert. One bullet passed through the muscle of his left arm. The other grazed his ribs on the left side, but he will live. The Asian woman..." He shook his head. "It is too soon to say for certain. But she is still alive, no? You should keep praying for her."

Tam certainly had been doing that, but she was not here simply to inquire about the health of her wounded agents. She needed to talk to Greg, not to hear from his own lips what had happened or to coach him on what to tell the French investigators, but to find out what had happened to Avery Halsey.

Thus far, there had been no mention of Avery. The

French authorities had given no indication that they were even aware of her existence, and Tam wasn't going to risk further blowback by asking. Unfortunately, that meant there was no way of knowing if Avery was alive and in hiding, or if she had been captured. For all Tam knew, she might be in the morgue of the very same hospital—an unidentified victim of the bomb blast that had rocked the streets of Salon de Provence. Finding Avery and keeping her safe was now Tam's highest priority, but to do that, she needed to talk to Greg.

She tried again. "If you could just give us a few minutes with him."

Before DuBois could stonewall her again, Stone stepped forward. "Colonel, you're right about everything. This never should have happened. Maybe if you had been kept in the loop from the start, this tragedy might have been avoided."

DuBois gave a grim smile. "As you say."

"But maybe we can help each other out now," Stone went on. "You want to catch the guy who did this. So do we. So why not work together?"

"So you do admit that you were conducting a counter-terror operation on French soil?"

Tam shot Stone a wary glance. She knew what he was attempting to do—or hoped she knew—but they were on thin enough ice as it was.

Stone spread his hands in a knowing gesture. "Colonel, really, let's just move past that, can we?"

DuBois frowned. "I'm listening. What do you have to tell me?"

Stone glanced over at Tam, as if to reassure her, then faced DuBois again. "I'm sure you've pulled surveillance video footage from the area near the attack."

"Of course."

"Have you identified a suspect?"

DuBois shrugged. "We are still reviewing it."

"Let me take a look at it. Nothing official, mind you. Just a second pair of eyes. If I see someone interesting, I'll nod my head. You can do the rest. And take all the credit."

The officer stared back at him with undisguised suspicion. "And in return?"

"Let them..." He nodded toward Tam and Sievers. "...talk to our friend."

"This is the kind of cooperation that would have helped prevent the tragedy," DuBois said, but then inclined his head. "Very well. It's a deal."

Stone waited patiently as DuBois logged into his government-issued laptop and brought up the surveillance camera footage the police had obtained from several different locations near the site of the explosion. When he had the files loaded into the video player software, he turned the computer so that Stone could see the display, and hit the 'play' button.

The video showed a generic-looking sedan pulling to a stop on a lightly trafficked street. A man wearing dark clothes and a ball cap got out and walked away. He kept his head down, the visor of his hat obscuring most of his face from view, making any identification impossible.

"This is from about two hours before the explosion," DuBois explained. "That car was carrying the bomb. As you can see, the suspect was careful to avoid the cameras, but he was also the shooter. We know he remained in the area."

"He may have changed clothes," Stone suggested.

"He may have," DuBois agreed with a hint of sarcasm, as if this was the most obvious thing in the world.

"All right. Let's see some different angles."

DuBois fast forwarded the footage to speed the process along. For the next few minutes, Stone watched cars and pedestrians coming and going from different angles. He made a show of scrutinizing the faces, but he wasn't really interested in what was happening on the screen. After about five minutes of this, however, he sat up straight and exclaimed, "Wait, go back."

Then before he could reach for the computer and hit

several keys in rapid succession, the screen flashed blue and then went into restart mode.

"Oops," Stone said with a guilty shrug. "Must have hit the wrong key."

The gendarmerie officer made a guttural sound of irritation as he drew the computer close and waited for it to finish booting up. "Please don't touch," he said, making no effort at patience. "If you see something, just tell me."

"You got it."

When he was logged back into the police network, the colonel turned the computer toward Stone, but this time kept it well out of reach. That was fine with Stone; his little stunt had already yielded the desired fruit. He watched the feed for several more minutes, occasionally asking DuBois to reverse or freeze the image, but then always shaking his head.

At one point, DuBois slowed the footage and pointed to two figures walking past the camera. The angle wasn't very good, but Stone recognized them immediately. So, evidently, did DuBois. "This is your… your friend? The Asian woman."

"Kasey," Stone said, nodding.

"*Oui*. Do you know who the other woman is?"

"No idea," Stone lied. "Tour guide?"

DuBois grunted. "We will identify her eventually." He ran the feed ahead several minutes until Greg Johns appeared on the screen. "And here is your other friend. We know that he and… ah, Kasey were found together outside the *Musee de Nostradame*."

He ran the footage forward again for a while, then resumed normal play. The angle of the camera showed nothing but an empty street for a few seconds, but then there was a flash, and the image jumped. Pieces of debris were now scattered across the pavement. A few more seconds passed, and then Avery dashed in and out of view.

"There she is again," DuBois said. "And now she has the backpack that your friend was carrying. Very interesting, no?"

"No," Stone replied dryly. "She's obviously running away from danger, which seems like a prudent thing to do. I thought you wanted me to help you identify the terrorists."

"Perhaps this unknown woman was working with the terrorists. Maybe she lured them into this ambush?"

Stone gave a noncommittal shrug. "Do you know where she went after this?"

DuBois reached for the computer again. "I'll pull video from neighboring streets."

"Well, you can if you want, but it's probably a waste of your time. She clearly wasn't the shooter." He leaned forward and dropped his voice to a conspiratorial whisper. "Listen, you know I can't say anything on the record, so this is just between you and me…"

There was a twinkle in DuBois' eyes as he nodded. "Go on."

"This wasn't any kind of counter-terrorism operation. Greg and Kasey were here investigating the black market for illegal antiquities. That's what they were doing at the museum. The woman is probably their interpreter. I don't think either one of them speaks French."

"Ah, so this is a criminal enterprise, not terrorism."

"As you know, the two often go together." He leaned back, shrugged. "Maybe this has nothing to do with that. Maybe it really was just a case of wrong place, wrong time. But if this wasn't just a random attack—if the shooter was targeting Greg and Kasey—then wouldn't you agree that it's in our mutual interest to keep sharing information? Nothing official, of course."

The colonel nodded slowly. "Of course."

"Great. Can I just get your email?"

While Stone made a show of reviewing the video footage on DuBois' computer, Tam and Sievers went to see Greg. They found him sitting up in his bed watching a televised soccer game with the sound turned off. A fleeting smile crossed his face, then his expression hardened. "Tam.

Billy. Thanks for coming."

"How are you doing?" she asked.

"Better than Kasey."

"She's going to be fine," Tam said. She hoped it was true. "Greg, what about Avery?"

Greg frowned. "She hasn't checked in?"

"Not a peep. And her phone is dead. Won't even ping."

"Damn it," Greg snarled. He gave a heavy sigh. "Sorry. Put an IOU in the swear jar for me."

"I'll let you have that one. What happened?"

He brought her up to speed on everything that had happened since the last check-in from London, finishing with the attack in the plaza, and his decision to have Avery make a run for it.

"If you hadn't she would probably be dead, too." Tam made an effort to sound upbeat, despite the discouraging news. "And the Immortal would have the Brazen Head."

"Are you sure he doesn't? If Avery's gone dark, it could mean they caught her."

"Let's work from the assumption that he doesn't. Where would she go? Did you establish contingencies?"

"I just told her to run." Greg's expression darkened. "This came out of nowhere. No warning. I don't know how they found us."

Tam considered this for a moment. "Do you think she'll try to head for the embassy? Stick to the original plan?"

"If she's not holed up somewhere waiting for the dust to settle."

"This is Dane Maddock's sister we're talking about."

Greg chuckled then winced a little. "Who would have thought that stupid brass head was worth this kind of trouble."

"No kidding. Even Stone is obsessed with it now."

"Stone? You got him back?"

"Long story. I'll tell you about it when you're back on your feet." She patted him on the arm. "I have to go after

Avery. And stop the Immortal."

"Then you need me." He shifted as if to get out of the bed.

"Greg, you just got shot. Twice."

"I've been shot before. This is nothing. My shooting arm still works."

Tam shook her head. "Sorry, but no. You're sitting the rest of this one out. But there is something you can do for me."

"Name it."

"Take care of Kasey."

They found Stone in the reception area where they had initially spoken with DuBois. He was sitting in one of the uncomfortable-looking chairs, browsing the Internet on his mobile phone. There was no sign of the colonel.

"Where's your new best friend?" Tam asked.

"I sent him on a fishing expedition," Stone said without looking up. "Red herrings. He won't be a problem. Did you learn anything interesting?"

"I was going to ask you."

Stone continued looking at his phone. "There's video of Avery leaving the scene. DuBois hasn't identified her yet. I told him she was probably a local they hired as a guide-slash-interpreter. I think he bought it."

"Greg told her to run. He thinks she might try for the embassy in Paris."

"She caught the 9:07 p.m. train in Marseille last night."

"DuBois told you that?"

Stone grinned. "No. But he was kind enough to give me his email address."

"Oh, well that explains it."

"His email address is his username. I figured out his password and logged into the national surveillance network."

Sievers was incredulous. "You just…" He snapped his fingers and mimicked Stone's casual tone. "Figured it out."

"I *accidentally* shut his computer off. When he was

logging back, I watched him enter his password. Couldn't catch it all, but enough to fill in the blanks with a little social engineering. His Facebook profile was helpful, too.

"Anyway, I tracked Avery to the Place Grande Fontaine. There is an Internet café near there, which seemed like the most likely place for her to go. I called and spoke with the person who worked there yesterday, and he confirmed that a person matching her description was there. Bought half-an-hour on the computer. Paid in cash. The browser history and server logs were all wiped clean. It might be possible to recover that data, but that's not something I can do with just a smartphone. But since she didn't contact us, she must have reached out to someone else. Somebody who could not only help her get out of town without leaving a paper trail, but also erase his digital fingerprints after the fact."

"Jimmy Letson." Tam was impressed, not only with Stone's investigative prowess, but also with Avery's resourcefulness. "Smart girl."

"The CCTV cameras show a car with an Uber sticker leaving the street shortly after Avery left the cyber café. I pulled the records for that driver. The destination for the rider—one Aubrey Maddox—was the Marseille train station. I pulled the video from the station and found Avery boarding the train to Paris.

"Paris is only a few hours away by train. She should have made it there last night."

"Think maybe she's afraid the Immortal has eyes on the embassy?" Sievers wondered.

"He might," Stone said, looking chagrined. "He's not as smart as he thinks he is, but he has the resources to track her. I was just about to start looking at the video footage from Paris station, but now that you're here, we might as well look at it on the go."

"Do that," Tam said, starting for the door.

TWENTY-FOUR

Paris

Avery did go to Paris, but she did not go to the American embassy. When the train arrived shortly after midnight, another Uber car waited to transport her to a neighborhood in the heart of the city. Despite the late hour, for which she apologized profusely, Avery was welcomed into the home of Pierre and Colette, a pleasant middle-aged couple who rented out their extra bedroom through Airbnb, and treated to her first night's sleep in a bed since she couldn't remember when.

The next morning, after coffee and croissant, she said her goodbyes and set out on foot to her ultimate destination, the Louvre Museum, and specifically, the Centre de Recherche et de Restauration des Musees de France, located beneath the sprawling museum complex. There, she was greeted by a slender man with thinning silver hair. "Are you Dr. Halsey?" he asked in English.

Avery replied in the affirmative, and in French, which seemed to please him. "You must be Dr. Lahanier."

"I am. And let us dispense with this doctor-doctor nonsense." He extended a hand. "Call me Jean-Louis."

"Avery."

"Please, this way to the laboratory. I am quite eager to see this puzzle of yours."

Jean-Louis Lahanier was the researcher in charge of the Centre's radiology and imaging department. Avery had only learned of the Centre the previous evening. She had spent the three-hour train ride to Paris searching the Internet for evidence to support a connection between Leonardo da Vinci and the Brazen Head of Albert Magnus. While she hadn't found the proof, she had come across Dr. Lahanier, a former medical practitioner who had found a way to combine his passion for art history with his technical knowledge of radiography, to discover secrets hidden beneath painted masterpieces. His x-rays had revealed, among other things, earlier paintings under Leonardo's most famous painting, the Mona Lisa. The Centre's high energy X-ray equipment would give her a look inside the Brazen Head, and Dr. Lahanier would be able to tell her exactly what she was looking at, and whether it was something Leonardo might have constructed. She had emailed him, hinting at the possibility of a working Leonardo machine sculpture and requesting an appointment, and he had responded immediately and enthusiastically with an invitation to meet at the Centre.

He led her into a large utilitarian workspace which had been divided into two separate areas by a partition of thick glass. Beyond it stood several large pieces of equipment that looked like a cross between the X-ray machine used by her dentist and something from an episode of *Star Trek*.

"You'll want to stay on this side of the glass," Lahanier said, "assuming of course that you wish to have children someday. Does the item require any special handling?

Avery winced a little, both at the thought of her ticking biological clock and with guilt for her rough handling of the Brazen Head thus far. "I don't think so," she said, setting the backpack on a table and unzipping it.

As soon as she revealed the artifact, however, Lahanier's demeanor changed. After only a mere glance at the Brazen Head, his smile slipped, and his gaze snapped to Avery. Without a word, he strode to a nearby wall-mounted telephone and picked up the handset.

Though she didn't understand what was happening, Avery knew she had made a mistake in coming to the Centre. Adrenaline pumped into her bloodstream, and her brain began flashing a desperate warning.

Grab the Brazen Head and run!

But she did not run.

Instead, she took three quick steps across the room and firmly depressed the hook on the telephone before the radiologist could finish dialing. "Let me explain."

Lahanier's eyes flashed with something that almost looked like terror. "I do not want to hear your explanation, Dr. Halsey."

I guess we're back to that doctor-doctor nonsense, she thought. "You obviously know what that is," she said, ignoring his protest.

"I do. I know its rightful owner very well. I also know what you did to him." He paused a beat, then straightened as if offering a formal surrender. "I am no hero. I will not attempt to restrain you. If you leave the Brazen Head here, I promise not to call the authorities."

Avery took a deep breath, trying to silence her racing heart. "It's not what you think."

"I know what happened in Zurich. I know that Maxim Loew is in the hospital and that someone stole the Brazen Head of Albert Magnus. And now you have brought it here. What is incorrect in my thinking?"

"You know Max?" She didn't wait for an answer. "Yes, I did take the Brazen Head, but I didn't hurt Max. I took it to keep it safe from the men who were trying to steal it."

"So you say."

"The bomb in Provence yesterday," she blurted. "That was the Immortal trying to get it."

Lahanier's expression changed again, softening as the terror giving way to something else. Comprehension, Avery thought, or maybe even belief. "The Immortal," he said cautiously. It was not a question.

"You've heard of him?"

"I belong to the Council of Rome," Lahanier said, as if that explained everything. In many ways, it did.

Avery took another breath, and launched into her own explanation. Without revealing her affiliation with the Myrmidons, she told him the whole story, from the discovery of the Immortal's coded messages to her escape from Salon de Provence. Lahanier gradually relaxed, and when she took out the notebook with the timeline, he motioned for her to return to the table where the Brazen Head rested, still half inside the backpack.

"Interesting," he said as he scanned the notes. Then he reached into the pack and took out the head, holding it up and turning it over to inspect it, just as Victor Bridges had done. "This is not like anything Leonardo ever designed." He met her gaze again. "Let's have a look inside it, shall we?"

Relieved that the radiologist seemed to have decided to trust her, Avery nodded.

Lahanier donned a lead apron and then took the artifact into the glassed-in room where he placed it into one of the machines. After a few minutes, he returned, carrying the Brazen Head in both hands.

"Is that it?" she asked.

"That's it." He placed the head on the table and then fetched a laptop which he used to bring up digital images of the scans. The photos had the same ghostly quality as medical x-rays, but there was no mistaking the inorganic nature of the subject. Beneath its bright brass skin, the Brazen Head looked like the inside of a windup alarm clock.

"I do not think Leonardo designed this," Lahanier said again after clicking through more than a dozen photos. "However, I see some similarities with some of his sketches. This one here…" He pointed to what looked like a large hollow space beneath the mechanisms and topped by a coil that might have been a spring. "This reminds me of his design for the *architonnerre*. It was a cannon, powered by steam, although the idea is as old as Archimedes."

"Steam?" Something about that stirred Avery's memory. She tried to bring it to the surface.

"This could be a reservoir or perhaps a boiler," Lahanier went on. He traced the coil with a fingertip. "This tube seems to travel from it to the nostrils. Perhaps to act as a relief valve."

"Steam," Avery said again, still trying to grab ahold of the memory. And then it came to her.

Oh, I remember that old thing… My da brought it home when I was just a wee lass. He put him on the mantel, but it made such a horrible racket we had to move it.

"It *is* steam powered. Heat. We have to heat it up. Do you have a Bunsen burner?"

"First," Lahanier cautioned, "we must fill the reservoir."

Avery nodded in understanding. When Adelle Walker's father had placed the Brazen Head on the mantel, the heat rising from the fireplace had caused the air in the reservoir chamber to pressurize, activating the slumbering automaton. What she had mistaken for "a horrible racket" had in fact been the automaton speaking.

Now, decades later, the reservoir was dry. In order to make it work again, they would need to refill it. "How?"

Lahanier pointed to the x-ray image again. "Perhaps if we introduce water through the nostrils."

He dashed over to a storage closet in one corner, returning with a jug of distilled water and a long-necked funnel. With growing excitement, Avery took the Brazen Head and turned it upside down, holding it steady while Lahanier dribbled water into the automaton's nose. "I would judge the capacity to be about half a liter," he said. "But we want to leave some room. Three hundred milliliters should be enough to test our hypothesis."

Avery could feel the artifact growing heavier as it filled up. For a fleeting moment, she worried they had jumped to the wrong conclusion and were now inadvertently destroying the eight-hundred-year-old device, but she just as quickly dismissed the thought. This was the only possible explanation. Its flat-bottomed design that looked so much like a kettle was not an accident.

"That should suffice," the radiologist announced, setting down the jug. "Turn it over. Carefully."

Avery did so. She could hear the liquid sloshing inside it, and a couple drops of water ran out of the nostril hole, but otherwise, the artifact seemed watertight. Lahanier left again, disappearing into a side office only to emerge with an electric hotplate. Avery placed the head on the burner while Lahanier plugged it in, and together they sat back and waited.

And waited.

A few minutes passed, though it seemed longer, then a ticking sound began issuing from the automaton. Not the ticking of clockwork gears, but rather the sound of the metal flexing and expanding. Just when Avery was about to make a comment about watched pots never boiling, twin plumes of steam shot from the nostrils, like the breath of a living creature on a cold day, and then all of sudden, the Brazen Head came to life.

Its eyelids snapped open, revealing round eyes that looked like lenses of smoky quartz. Avery thought she saw flashes of light behind them, but couldn't be certain. After another second or two, the mouth began moving, opening and closing as if chewing, but with almost exaggerated slowness.

And then it began to speak.

The sound was disjointed with tones and mechanical clicks that reminded her a little of the Khoisan language spoken by the indigenous tribes of the Kalahari region of Africa. Each phoneme was distinctive, like musical notes played on a pipe organ, but as it repeated the sounds over and over again, Avery thought she recognized the words.

Two words, spoken in Latin.

"*Memento mori.*" The weird mechanical-musical voice kept uttering the litany over and over, in a ponderous but insistent monotone. "*Memento mori. Memento mori.*"

"Remember that you will die," Lahanier said, translating the words with a bemused look on his face. "I'll confess. I had hoped for more, but perhaps that is the answer to every question."

He was not wrong.

Memento mori. The expression was as old as ancient Rome, the philosophy the words embodied older still. According to one tradition, when a victorious general returned to the city in a triumphant parade, a servant would stand behind him whispering in his ear the words: *Respice post te! Hominem te esse memento! Memento mori!*

Look behind you! Remember that you are but a man! Remember that you will die!

It was a reminder that no matter what a person accomplished in life, how high they rose above others, all would meet the same fate in the end.

The humbling message had continued into the Christian era, embodied in art and architecture, often employing skull motifs—sometimes with literal skulls, such as in Capuchin crypt in Rome.

You will die.

Albertus Magnus had indeed created an automaton that foretold the future, the one certain future for every living thing on earth.

Avery shook her head. "No, that can't be all there is. Maybe we have to keep listening."

"Memento mori. Memento mori." The message remained the same, but the words began to come more rapidly as the water inside boiled away, the pressure building with each passing second. The vapor streaming out of the mouth and nostrils of the Brazen Head was forming a cloud above the table.

"We will soon run out of steam," Lahanier warned.

"Wait," Avery cried. "I think I see… Turn out the lights."

"The lights?"

"Do it."

Lahanier shrugged and moved toward the exit where the switchplate was located. He flipped the switches, and the overhead lights went out. There were no windows in the underground laboratory, but the glowing screen of Lahanier's laptop and the clock and various glowing red, green and yellow LED indicators on the machines in the lab kept the room from falling into total darkness. But there was another source of light in the room, one that could not be easily explained away.

The steam cloud around the Brazen Head was lit up

like a hologram in a science fiction film, and the source of the light was the Brazen Head itself.

"The eyes!" Lahanier said, astonished. "They are glowing."

Avery braved the hot vapor cloud for a closer look, confirming the radiologist's observation. Light emanated from the smoky quartz lenses.

"This is not possible," Lahanier continued, shaking his head. "A steam powered light bulb in a medieval clockwork automaton. I do not believe it. It must be a hoax."

Avery did not share his skepticism. There were other ways to produce artificial light that might have been known to a scholar like Albertus Magnus. Ample evidence had been uncovered to indicate that ancient cultures understood and made extensive use of electricity. The Parthians had used acid batteries to electroplate temple utensils as early as the 250 BCE. Some believed that hieroglyphs in the Dendera temple complex in Egypt depicted a primitive light source that bore a striking resemblance to the filament of an incandescent light bulb. But she was not so much interested in what was causing the light as what it revealed.

"It's projecting something." The steam was too insubstantial to hold the picture, whatever it was. "We need a screen."

Lahanier brought over a dry erase whiteboard, placing it in the steam cloud, and the image—if it could be called an image—appeared. He took a step back, and the picture resolved into a startlingly clear, bifocal projection of an amorphous shape—like an amber-colored amoeba—shot through with dark squiggles that resembled veins.

It could have been merely the naturally occurring pattern of imperfections in a piece of quartz or agate, except for the writing.

The script was archaic, difficult to read, but was nevertheless deliberate. Man-made.

"Caledonia," she said, reading a line at the top of the

amoeba-shape. "Scotia. This is a map of Great Britain. Scotland."

And just like that, everything fell into place.

"Get a marker," Lahanier urged. "Trace the image. Quickly."

"I've got a better idea," Avery said. She took out the burner phone Jimmy had purchased for her and snapped a photo of the projection.

"Perfect," Lahanier said. He set down the whiteboard and then turned off the hotplate. The projection dimmed almost immediately, but the Brazen Head's recitation continued for several more minutes until the heat dissipated. When it, at last, fell silent, Avery breathed a sigh of relief. "No wonder Thomas Aquinas smashed the thing."

She emailed the picture to Lahanier so that he could display it on the larger screen of his computer, and together they began scrutinizing the image. The outline wasn't an accurate representation, but it was consistent with maps from the 13th Century. A closer inspection revealed other details.

"Those are the Roman border walls," Avery said, pointing out a pair of jagged horizontal lines that looked like the crenellations on the battlements of a castle, which crossed the island. "Hadrian's Wall in the south, and the Antonine Wall further north." She pointed to a vein running near the latter. "This would be the River Clyde, and this tower shape must be Glasgow."

"A map of Scotland," Lahanier mused. "Inside a device built by a German monk. Why?"

"For this." Avery pointed to a series of upward pointing arrow-shaped marks, almost certainly representing mountains or hills, just to the south of what she assumed was Glasgow. There was a distinctive mark on one of them, three concentric circles.

"It looks like a bull's eye."

"It's called a roundel, but I think in this instance, you're right. That's where we need to go."

"This map is crude," Lahanier said. "That spot could represent an area of thousands of square kilometers."

"It may not be to perfect scale, but those peaks have to correspond with real mountains. Hess figured it out. That's why he flew to Scotland. Maybe he really did want to make peace with Britain… I don't know, but he was trying to get there." She snapped her fingers as another piece of the puzzle fell into place. "I think Leonardo went there, too."

Lahanier shook his head. "Not possible. There is no record of him traveling to Britain."

"But there are two years of his life that are unaccounted for—1476 to 1478." She recalled the dates from her exhaustive research the previous night. In 1476, Leonardo, along with three other young men, had been formally accused of sodomy but subsequently acquitted. There was no mention of him at all during the two years that followed, until 1478 when, at the relatively young age of just twenty-six, he began receiving commissions as a master artist.

"What if he spent those two years abroad, looking for that?" She pointed to the roundel. "Lorenzo de Medici must have given him the Brazen Head. Maybe asked him to repair it, and when he did, he found this map. Maybe he discovered something there that enhanced his genius."

"Enhanced," Lahanier echoed. "I wonder. Leonardo told a story of how, as a boy, he discovered a cave in the mountains. He was frightened to enter, fearing that there might be monsters inside, but he was also curious, and his curiosity won out. I have always thought it was a sort of parable. A metaphor for not letting our fears prevent us from discovering greatness. But perhaps there is some truth to it, no?" He looked her in the eye. "But what did he discover?"

"I guess I'll find out when I get there."

After the young Canadian history professor departed, Lahanier sat in the laboratory staring at the picture. When she had been there, with the Brazen Head chattering away as it projected the map from its eyes, it had been irresistibly exciting, but now that she was gone, taking the artifact with her, he was less certain of her conclusions.

The Head was real enough, and so also he supposed was the map, but what did that mean really? What proof was there that the Brazen Head was actually a medieval artifact, and not a modern forgery? The latter conclusion made far more sense.

Part of him wanted to believe the crazy story Avery had brought him, a part of him that had once traveled beneath the sea with Captain Nemo and fought alongside the Three Musketeers. It was a childish, nostalgic dream, and he was an old man.

Ultimately, he decided, it didn't matter. Whether or not Avery's implausible theory could be proved true, the fact of the matter was that she was involved in something illegal. He believed that she was not affiliated with the criminal mastermind who called himself the Immortal, and even accepted that she was trying to keep the Brazen Head safe, but that was properly a job for the police. Contacting the authorities was the right thing to do. And if the Immortal was still looking for her, she would need their protection.

His mind made up, he left the work table and walked to the wall mounted phone. He had just picked up the receiver when he heard the door behind him opening, and before he could turn to look, an unfamiliar voice said, "You need to hang up the phone, Dr. Lahanier. I'm going to need your undivided attention."

As soon as she was seated on the Paris-London train, Avery went to work determining the location marked on the map revealed by the Brazen Head. The first thing she did was send a message request to Jimmy Letson, asking for his assistance. Although she was a crack researcher, Jimmy had a lot more computing power at his disposal, and would have much better luck pinpointing the location based on the scant evidence available. But she also knew that there was a seven-hour time difference between Paris and Washington D.C. where Jimmy lived. It wasn't yet noon in Paris, which meant that the sun was not yet up on the East Coast. Even though she imagined Jimmy as a Red Bull-swilling insomniac, she knew he had to sleep too, so when the message did not generate an immediate reply, she started her own search for mountains in Scotland, south of Glasgow.

There were, she quickly discovered, a lot of mountains—hills actually seemed to be the preferred term—in the region known as the Southern Uplands. The uplands were a beautiful but rugged country, sparsely populated, cut through with rivers and valleys, and dotted with lochs. The primitive map didn't match any of the features in a meaningful way, so Avery began looking at each of the distinct hill ranges one by one, hoping to discover some unique and distinctive attribute, relying more on history than geography to help narrow the search.

The region had been the site of some of the bloodiest battles in the wars between Scotland and England, but those had occurred nearly fifty years after Albert Magnus created the Brazen Head. She could find no evidence that he had ever set foot in Scotland, which meant that either the historical record of his travels was incomplete, or he had used the Brazen Head to pass on a bit of knowledge that he had acquired from someone else. Regardless, however, whatever lay at the designated location had to be something accessible to travelers in the Thirteenth Century. Possibly something going back as far as Roman times.

She felt a tingle of excitement when she read about a place in the Lowther Hills known to the locals as "God's Treasure House in Scotland" because of its abundant mineral wealth. The gold found in the hills there was some of the purest on earth.

Could that have been the secret Albert Magnus had sought to preserve for the ages in the Brazen Head? Was there a secret mine? A treasure trove in the Scottish hills?

It didn't feel like the right answer. None of the men associated with the Brazen Head had shown any inclination toward possessing riches. But maybe they would have been interested in less precious metals. Albert had been an alchemist. So had Nostradamus. And Leonardo, a sculptor, had worked extensively with metals.

The area was also known for deposits of lead, which would have been extremely valuable even in ancient times. The Roman conquest of Britannia had been motivated in no small part by its mineral resources—both precious and base metals. They had made extensive use of lead in plumbing—the word "plumbing" actually derived from the Latin word for "lead." Lead and other substances would have been of great interest to men of science on the cusp of the Renaissance.

As she was writing this all down in the notebook, Jimmy responded to her message. After assuring him that she was still safe, she sent him the .jpg image of the map and told him what she was attempting to do.

"Is that all? Give me five minutes."

Three minutes and thirty-two seconds later, he sent another message. *"The most likely location for that spot is on a hill called Hart Fell, in the Moffat Hills Range."*

The Moffat Hills were actually next on Avery's list, located to the east of the Lowther Hills. Before responding to Jimmy's message, she scanned the Wikipedia entry to familiarize herself.

The range comprised several peaks that formed an inverted triangle, about ten miles on each side. The only populated areas in the region were two small towns; Moffat to the south of the range, and the village of Tweedsmuir to the north. There was evidence of occupation going back to the Bronze Age—fully preserved round houses and standing stones—but there was little in the historical record before the 17th Century. The most noteworthy thing about the Moffat Hills seemed to be its reputation as a spa. The naturally sulfurous and saline water bubbling up in Moffet Spa was reputed to have curative powers for various ailments.

"Healing water?" she mused. Was the map pointing the way to a fountain of youth? If so, it seemed to be a poorly kept secret, and hardly worth the effort.

"How sure are you?"

"*As sure as I can be with what you've given me. It's an eighty percent match. Unfortunately, I can't really tell you what exactly lies at that spot.*"

"Hopefully, I'll know it when I see it." She narrowed her search to Hart Fell.

Hart Fell, she discovered, was a moss-covered 2,651-foot high hill, overlooking a depression with the unusual name of Devil's Beef Tub. Novelist Sir Walter Scott had described the hollow as: "A damned deep, black, blackguard-looking abyss of a hole." It had gotten its name because the Johnstone clan, a gang also known as the Border Reivers—called "devils" by their enemies—had used it to hide stolen cattle. William Wallace reputedly used it as a meeting place from which to launch his attacks against the English. *Maybe that's what the roundel symbolizes,* she thought.

Then she read something that made her sit up straight.

Hart Fell had gotten its name because of an association with the Arthurian wizard Merlin, who according to legend, could change himself into a hart—an archaic term for a stag.

It was generally believed that King Arthur, or the historic figure who inspired the legend, had probably been a 5th or 6th Century war leader, possibly a Roman or Briton, living in Wales and fighting against Saxon invaders. The earliest mention of Arthur was in a 9th Century manuscript that listed the battles of King Arthur, including one where he personally killed nearly a thousand men. Most modern retellings of the legend moved Arthur and his court at Camelot forward in time, to the Age of Chivalry, which not only added anachronistic trappings, like full suits of plate armor, but also conflicted with actual recorded history. Avery had a unique perspective on Arthurian lore as a result of her work with her brother on the Buccaneer investigations, but rather than give her insight into the real history of Arthur, what she had discovered was that the legend of Arthur was much bigger than just one man. Everyone, it seemed, laid claim to a piece of the legend, and in a way, it was probably true. Folklore from all over the British Isles had been woven together to form the tapestry of King Arthur.

The Scottish laid claim to Merlin, or as he was originally known, Myrrdin.

Myrddin first appeared in a Welsh poem from the 6th Century where he was described as the bard to Gwenddoleu, the king of the Welsh-speaking territories of southern Scotland and northern England. When Gwenddoleu was killed in battle, Myrrdin fled to the forests of southern Scotland, which seemed to mark his transformation from bard to seer and wizard.

According to one medieval source, Myrddin met often with Kentigern, a Christian cleric later canonized as Saint Mungo, the founder and patron saint of Glasgow, to discuss his baffling visions of the future, including a premonition of his own death.

While the Scottish tradition of Merlin was different in many respects from the classical version, Avery could not help but notice the common thread that linked Myrddin to the Brazen Head, Nostradamus, and even Rudolph Hess.

Prophecy.

Yet, there was an even more remarkable connection. In the legend, the place where Myrddin sought refuge following the death of King Gwenddoleu was Hart Fell, and specifically a small recess just below the ridge known as Merlin's Cave.

"That's it," she whispered. "That has to be it."

TWENTY-FIVE

Moffat Hills, Scotland

It was early evening when Avery arrived at her destination, Newton Farms, a rustic holiday retreat in the Moffat Hills. She had reserved one of the cottages, paid for online using the Paypal account Jimmy had established for her, but with sunset still a few hours off, there was no reason to delay. The rest of the cottages were vacant, and as near as she could tell, there wasn't another living soul in a five-mile radius, which was fine with her. She had spent the better part of ten hours cooped up, surrounded by people and on the move; high-speed train from Paris to London, another train to Lockerbie, followed by another Uber ride to the cottage located just a few miles north of Moffat. Now, she was as eager to simply get moving again as she was to find Merlin's Cave.

She was certain that the cave was the secret Albert Magnus had preserved with his ingenious map. The Brazen Head did not literally answer questions about the future. Instead, for those with the wisdom to read its message, it pointed the way to a place imbued with the power of prophecy. Merlin's Cave. Leonardo's cave.

She understood now why the Immortal wanted to possess it.

According to the hiking guides she had downloaded, the cave was situated in an outcropping of red sandstone, just off the trail. The fact that the location was on a well-traveled hiking route concerned her. Although remote, thousands of trekkers and tourists must have visited the cave over the centuries, and to the best of her knowledge, none had reported prophetic visions or any other remarkable phenomena. There had to be more to the mystery, some critical piece of information that would unlock the power to see into the future. Still, it was a place to start.

She hiked up the dirt road to a cattle-crossing bridge and then took the unmarked spur trail that led to the wooded bluff where the cave was located. Along the way she passed through a cloud of what she thought were harmless gnats, but after a few seconds, she felt the first of many needle-like pricks on the bare skin of her arms and neck, and realized that she had just encountered the scourge with the seemingly innocuous name of "midges." She began swatting at the bites, trying to shoo away the bloodthirsty no-see-ums, and quickened her step, hoping that distance would bring some relief. She was moving so fast that she almost walked right past the cave entrance.

The near miss was understandable. Merlin's Cave wasn't much to look at. Partially hidden behind overhanging foliage, the entry was an irregularly-shaped fissure, wider at the top than at the bottom, rising just above the level of her waist. She knelt down before it and shone her burner phone's built-in flashlight into the opening.

What lay beyond was even less impressive. Instead of an elaborate labyrinth of passages honeycombing the ancient hills, Merlin's Cave looked more like a cavity in the world's biggest molar; a fissure just big enough to shelter one person, or possibly two if they were in a deeply committed relationship. While there was nothing visually arresting about the cave, the smell was incredible in the most literal sense.

"They got it wrong," she murmured, pulling back and trying to draw a clear breath. "Should have been Merlin's Outhouse."

The odor was like a cross between rotten eggs and congealing blood. Sulfur with a hint of iron. Drawing a deep breath of relatively fresh air, and stifling her disappointment, Avery crawled inside. As she did, her body filled the opening, blocking out the trace of daylight that managed to filter into the interior though her phone's light continued to illuminate the gloomy little recess.

A quick glance only confirmed her first impression. The cave was only a few feet deep. The back wall was visibly damp and covered in what looked like white moss. The floor sloped away from the entrance, disappearing into a pool of stagnant water which was no doubt the source of the disgusting smell.

Avery recalled that the nearby town of Moffat had grown up around the reputed efficacy of the mineral rich water drawn from the well located just to the south of her present position. That water in the cave was probably of a similar composition, maybe even more concentrated than that which permeated through the soil and strata to supply the famous well. Was that water the secret of Merlin's Cave?

That answer seemed too simple, but there was only one way to know for sure.

She frowned, staring at the murky water, dreading the next step and thinking about all the potential consequences. Without thinking, she let out the breath she had been holding and drew another. The stench immediately made her gag, and it took all her willpower to remain where she was.

Just do it, she told herself. Merlin did it. Leonardo did it. You can do it, too.

It was probably faulty logic, but she was desperate to get out of the horrible environment, and she wasn't about to leave until she tested her hypothesis.

Avery cupped her hands together and dipped them into the pool. She had to break through a layer of slime on the surface to get to the water beneath and that nearly made her jerk her hands back in a reflex of disgust. The water was bitterly cold and thick, but she persisted long enough to ladle up a double handful of the substance. She raised it to her lips and took a tentative sip.

The taste was just about as disgusting as she expected. She tried to swallow, but somewhere between intention and execution, her body rebelled. Her stomach seemed to flip upside down. She retched, spattering the wall of the cave with the unswallowed mouthful, along with the partially digested remnants of her last meal, but the voiding brought no relief.

Oh, God. What have I done?

Her body went numb, the world around her dissolving into a haze. She tried to turn, tried to flee, but couldn't tell if she was actually moving at all. She threw her hands out to steady herself, but even though she could feel the rough damp stone against her palms, she was still falling.

The sensation passed after what felt like just a few seconds, but it took a few more for her to become fully aware. She had blacked out—that much was obvious—and was now lying flat on her back, which probably explained why she had come to so quickly. With her body more or less level, the blood was flowing to her brain again. She couldn't see the cave opening, which was strange, but her phone, which lay beside her, was still shining its light up at the low ceiling. By some miracle, it hadn't landed in the pool.

Nor had she, come to think of it. If she had fallen the other way, she might have drowned.

The taste of the foul water was still in her mouth, but not enough to make her gag again. The stench seemed less oppressive too, though that was probably because she had gone nose-blind to it. Even so, she was eager to get some fresh air.

She sat up slowly, retrieved the light, and shone it around until she located the exit, but daylight no longer seeped in through it. She glanced at the clock on the phone and realized that it was nearly ten p.m. She had been unconscious, not for a few seconds, but for a few hours.

Crap, she thought, but then realized that things could have been a lot worse. She was still alive, after all.

She crawled through the opening and out into the cool night. That fresh air was amazing. She leaned back against the sandstone wall and greedily drew it in until her head felt clear again.

Drinking the water had been a huge mistake, but that didn't mean it wasn't somehow connected to the mystery. Maybe there was another way to tap into its properties, perhaps by bathing in it as spa visitors had done for at least a couple centuries. Maybe the water had to be heated in order to….

And then it hit her.

Vapors.

Ingesting the water was clearly impossible—possibly fatal—but prolonged exposure to the vapors might produce a trance state, not unlike Nostradamus breathing nutmeg-laden steam from his scrying bowl.

The cave would act as a natural evaporation chamber and sleeping in it, as Myrddin supposedly had, would have the same effect. There wouldn't even have to be anything particularly special about the chemical composition of the resulting gaseous mixture; if the amount of oxygen in the air dropped below a certain threshold, brain activity would be impaired, producing vivid dreams and possibly even waking hallucinations. And if there was something in the water, some naturally occurring psychotropic substance, the effect would be even more profound.

There was nothing supernatural about it; just wild hallucinations, mistaken for prophecy.

In her mind's eye, she saw Myrddin, not the Tolkien-esque wizard with a flowing beard and star-spangled robes, but a half-naked painted Pictish shaman, roaming the boreal forests, communing with the animals, and retreating to the shelter of the cave at night where the vapors from the pool filled his brain with visions of parallel lives unlived and futures that might never come to pass.

Five hundred years later, Albert of Cologne, inspired by romantic poems of the tales of Arthur and his court, traveled to Glasgow to see the cave of Merlin, and discovered the same magnificent secret, which he preserved in his marvelous talking automaton.

It would be more than two hundred years before the young Florentine genius, Leonardo di ser Piero da Vinci, would unlock Albert's riddle and follow it to the cave to receive his own vision of the future that would someday come to be. Fifty years after that, Michele Nostradame...

No, she realized, Nostradamus had not come here.

The connections were coming almost too fast for her to process, and with each one, her brain seemed to light up.

Nostradamus had not traveled to Scotland to visit the Merlin's Cave. Instead, the cave had gone to him, or more accurately, some of its unusual water carried in a unique receptacle.

The Brazen Head.

Albert's automaton was more than just a map to the cave.

It was a vaporizer.

In another flash of intuition, she realized the story of Nostradamus' scrying bowl was only partially true. The seer had not been breathing from a bowl, at least not at first, but rather had inhaled hallucinogenic steam issuing from the Brazen Head. He had probably replenished it with fresh water, and when he noticed the potency of the visions diminishing, had added other substances—like nutmeg—which he knew would produce a similar effect.

Hess had figured it out as well. His true motive for flying to Scotland had been to reach Merlin's Cave in order to refill the Brazen Head and unlock its full potential.

Almost before she knew what she was doing, she was back inside the little cave, crawling forward on hands and knees to the murky pool where she set her phone down, letting its light shine up at the ceiling. The atrocious smell barely registered as she unzipped the backpack and brought out the Brazen Head. The bright brass caught the light from the phone, casting weird patterns on the walls of the cave.

"Welcome home, old boy," she murmured, and then proceeded to plunge the head into the pool.

A series of faint pops were audible. Bubbles of air, displaced from the reservoir inside the artifact by water rushing in, were rising up and breaking the surface. She kept it submerged until the bubbles stopped, and then drew it out, turning it right side up to let the excess run back out. After a few seconds, the dribbles stopped. It was noticeably heavier now, about a kilogram—two pounds—which meant the reservoir held about a liter of the water.

She tilted it back and forth, but nothing came out. Albert had probably designed it with a one-way gate valve to make it easier to transport.

Now all she needed was a heat source.

She stuffed the head into the backpack, retrieved her phone and headed back out into the night. In the distance, she could make out the lights of Newton Farms, less than a mile away.

Only that wasn't what she was actually seeing. The cabins were dark, a barely discernible silhouette against the starlit sky. These lights were closer, floating in the foreground and moving toward her. Three tiny points of illumination bobbing and flickering like fireflies or fairies…

Or flashlights.

Somebody was coming up the trail.

There was probably a reasonable explanation for what she was seeing—a visiting tourist out for a late evening stroll, a local shepherd trying to track down a stray member of his flock—but Avery's instincts told her that it would be better not to wait around and find out.

She shut off the light on her phone and was immediately plunged into darkness. The flashlights were definitely moving in her direction and getting closer with each passing second. She considered ducking back into the cave but discarded that idea. The cave wasn't exactly a well-kept secret; it was the first place they would look.

She turned away, staring into the near total darkness of the woods around her. Strangely, she had no trouble at all visualizing her immediate surroundings.

Her mind's eye had just gone blind. Her recollection of the terrain she had traversed to reach the cave was startlingly detailed, but it was just that—a recollection. She had not gone past the cave, so that was where her memory map ended.

Voices became audible. Avery couldn't distinguish what was being said, just fragmented sounds carried on the breeze, but growing louder.

A man's voice. A woman's...

She cocked her head sideways for a moment, listening intently and then breathed a sigh of relief. She switched on her phone and held it over her head. "Tam! Billy! I'm here."

TWENTY-SIX

Tamara Broderick was not by any stretch of the imagination a touchy-feely sort of person, but when Avery ran up and embraced her, she returned the hug in the spirit in which it was given. After everything they had gone through in the last few days, it just felt right.

"Hey, save some of that for the rest of us," Sievers said.

"You just wait your turn," Tam shot back with a grin.

Avery gave Tam another squeeze for good measure. "How did you guys find me?" she asked.

"Weren't nothin'," the Texan replied as he swept Avery into a bear hug. "Not with bloodhound Stone sniffin' out your trail."

"Speaking of sniffing," Tam said, wrinkling her nose. "I hate to be impolite, but Avery honey... you reek."

"Sorry. I'll explain... Wait, Stone? You found him?"

"I didn't realize I was lost," Stone said, stepping out from behind Sievers.

Avery hugged him, too.

As they made their way back toward the cottages, Tam briefly recounted how Stone had tracked Avery to Paris using the police surveillance camera network. They had almost caught up to her at Lahanier's laboratory, missing her by only a few minutes. Once they had convinced the radiologist that they were Avery's friends, he had given them the map of Scotland, but it had taken a little while to figure out where it was leading.

"What about Kasey and Greg?" Avery spoke hesitantly, as if she knew the answer and dreaded hearing it.

"A little worse for wear," Tam said, trying to sound upbeat. "But they're both alive."

Tears were welling up in Avery's eyes, glistening like

diamonds as they reflected the flashlight beams. "Kasey was…"

Tam decided to give her another hug. "Avery. They're alive. And so are you. You did good."

Avery nodded, then let go and held Tam at arm's length. "Thom is the Immortal, isn't he?"

Tam made no effort to hide her surprise. "That's right. But how did you figure it out?"

Avery's eyebrows drew together in a frown of consternation. "I'm not sure really. I just sort of…" She shrugged. "What does he want?"

"The Brazen Head," Stone said. He paused a beat before adding. "You figured out its secret, didn't you?"

Avery nodded slowly. "I think so. The Brazen Head is just a vessel."

"A vessel?" Tam asked. "For what?"

Avery pointed back in the direction from which they had just come. "There's a cave back there. Merlin's Cave."

"Merlin as in King Arthur?"

Avery nodded. "According to local folklore, Merlin lived in that cave. I don't know if it's true, but the water in the cave has some pretty unusual properties."

"Ah, of course," Stone said, sounding unusually sarcastic. "Now it makes sense."

"Not to me," Tam admitted. "Does it really tell you the future?"

Avery shook her head. "Not really. More like it opens your mind up to crazy possibilities."

"The water is probably infused with naturally occurring alkaloid compounds." Stone said.

"Alkaloids?" Tam glanced over at him. "You mean narcotics?"

"Probably something fungal," Stone replied. "Psilocybin. Or possibly ergoline. Given the local flora and environmental conditions, it could be either one. That's just a guess, but a chemical analysis of the water will probably confirm it."

Sievers asked the question that was on the tip of

Tam's tongue. "You're saying the water around here will get you high?"

"As the proverbial kite," Stone said. "Psilocybin is the compound found in magic mushrooms, and ergoline is produced by a fungus that grows in rye crops. It's a naturally occurring version of lysergic acid. LSD."

"Actually," Avery said. "Drinking the water will just make you puke your guts out. You have to inhale it. That's the other secret of the Brazen Head. You heat it up, and it breathes out the vapors." She nodded down the long row of empty cabins, just a few steps away. "I'll show you when we get inside."

Stone regarded her with a slightly amused expression. "Hallucinogens and psychotropics work by stimulating every part of the brain simultaneously. Basically, processing faster than your nerves can deliver the data, so it fills in the gaps with psychedelic imagery. Most people today use substances like this recreationally, but originally, they had a powerful spiritual component."

"So it's basically nitro for the brain?" Sievers said.

"Pretty much. There may also be some cognitive enhancement effects as well. There's a whole class of substances called 'nootropics'—smart drugs—that we're only just beginning to understand."

"Like in that show, *Limitless*."

Stone shrugged, clearly not grasping the reference.

Tam shook her head in confusion. "I don't understand. If that's all it is, why was it so important to the Immortal?"

"Maybe he thought it was something more than that," Sievers suggested. "Real magic."

Stone's only answer was a thoughtful nod. No one else spoke as Avery led them to the porch of a dark cabin.

"Anyway it's over now," she said as she twisted the door handle. "We stopped him, right?"

"We stopped his attack on Mystic," Tam replied. "And you kept him from getting his hands on the Brazen Head. If he's smart, he'll probably lay low. Shack up with Furst in

Switzerland or somewhere."

"We haven't seen the last of him," Stone said, almost absently. "He *is* smart. Not as smart as he thinks he is, but smart enough to have a contingency plan."

Before Avery could cross the threshold, a familiar voice issued from the dark interior. "Smarter than *you* think, Stone."

Tam reacted immediately, whipping out her Makarov. Sievers drew his pistol as well, but as fast as they were, it was already too late. The air around them was suddenly crisscrossed with blazing shafts of intense light. Even though she couldn't see past the painfully brilliant illumination, Tam knew that the lights were almost certainly attached to guns that were, just like the lights, pointed right at them.

TWENTY-SEVEN

As she raised a hand to shade her eyes, Avery saw a pair of men in black combat fatigues, faces hidden behind matching balaclavas, step forward to relieve Tam and Sievers of their weapons. The latter pair were roughly put in a prone position and thoroughly searched for additional weapons before having their wrists zip-tied together. Stone and Avery must have seemed less of a threat because the two men ignored them. The figure standing in the doorway, however, did not.

The man Avery knew only as Thom Martiel stepped out onto the porch, approached her and extended an open hand. Avery resisted the urge to spit in it, and instead slid the backpack off her shoulder and dropped it on the ground at his feet.

If the gesture of defiance irritated Martiel, he did not show it. Instead, he knelt and unzipped the backpack, then took his prize out, cradling it in both hands. A satisfied smile lit up his face.

"Let me guess," Stone said. "You're pissed off about what happened in New Jersey with Mystic. There's a simple explanation, really. You're batshit crazy, and we had to stop you."

"Swear jar," Tam muttered.

"We beat you there," Stone continued. "And Avery solved the mystery of the Brazen Head all on her own. You're no genius. You're a fraud. No wonder you needed somebody else to figure it all out. You're hopeless."

"In hindsight," Martiel said, rising to his full height again, "I probably should have assigned a higher priority to acquiring this. If I made a mistake, it was in thinking that it would be an irresistible mystery for you, Gavin, but it seems to have worked out nonetheless." He continued to regard Avery with what might have passed for admiration.

"Your protégé evidently possesses a sense of wonder that you have lost."

"How did you find me?" Avery asked. She was curious since she had been careful to avoid detection, but mostly she just wanted to prove, if only to herself, that she was as fearless as Tam and Stone.

"Actually, we didn't," replied one of the men still hiding in the shadows. His next words told Avery that he was probably the same man who had tried to kill them outside the Nostradamus museum. "I waited for you to come to the hospital, but you never did. Instead, your friends showed up. I followed them instead."

"Once we realized they were heading to Scotland," Martiel said, "it wasn't too difficult to figure out that Miss Halsey had solved the mystery of the Brazen Head. All that remained was following them here."

"My hat's off to you gents," Sievers said, raising his head and peering in the direction of the voice. "I never once suspected we'd picked up a tail. One professional to another, that was a job well done. Let me guess, ARD-10, right?"

The silence seemed answer enough.

"Thought so," he went on. "Are you running this on the side, or does this go all the way to the top of the Swiss government?"

Martiel laughed. "The Swiss government is utterly beholden to the bankers. There are many brave patriots like Lieutenant Colonel LeMans in every nation who share my vision of a world where those chains are cast off forever.

"To answer your earlier question," he went on, "I did know exactly what the Brazen Head was for. Rudolph Hess kept extensive notes regarding his experiments with it which I found in the course of my research. Actually, that is how Peter and I became acquainted. He managed to acquire Hess's diaries, which were smuggled out of Spandau prison. Our mutual interest in Hess brought us together.

"Hess figured out the Brazen Head's function as vapor delivery system and knew he would need to visit the well in Scotland to recharge it. It would have saved a lot of trouble if he had recorded a copy of the map or named the precise destination, but *c'est la vie*."

"Why am I not surprised that you're right there with the Nazi connection?" Stone muttered.

Martiel glanced over at him. "My interest was purely academic at first. Like you, Gavin, I'm fascinated by human behavior. Why do we do the things we do? Hess' decision to leave Germany and fly into enemy territory has always intrigued me, and when I started looking into the mystery, I began to realize that the conventional thinking falls short of explaining the behavior of this remarkable man."

Tam, still face down, let out a snort of derision.

Martiel ignored her. "My research, as well as my acquaintance with Peter, opened my eyes to the reality of the world we live in, a world controlled by greedy usurers. Everything I've told you is the absolute truth, Gavin. The bankers—the money lenders—own everything and everyone. We are all enslaved, and the chain that holds us captive is this credit-based monetary system.

"Hess *was* remarkable. The only one of Hitler's inner circle to survive into our lifetime. The only witness to what really happened. He knew that what Hitler really wanted was to break the stranglehold of the Rothschilds' global banking monopoly."

"The Rothschilds?" Avery shook her head in disbelief. "Next you'll tell me it's all a Zionist conspiracy. You've been spending too much time online."

"Just because it's paranoid doesn't mean it's not true," Martiel replied. "And you're not wrong. The banks control the world, and the secret order that controls the banks has a distinctively Semitic composition.

"Hess realized what was happening. That was the message he planned to deliver directly to the royal family, once his primary mission to refill the Brazen Head from the well was complete. Churchill was a Rothschild stooge, but the royals—they were as eager to throw off the chains of the bankers as Hitler. This was the secret that Hess kept for forty years. And it's why he could not be allowed to leave Spandau Prison alive. In 1987, there was a movement afoot to commute his sentence in order to spend his last remaining days with his family, but the secret order couldn't take the chance that he would tell the world the truth, so they engineered his suicide to hide the truth."

"Speaking of Nazis, where is your buddy, Pete?" Stone asked. "I thought he'd want to be here, at the tip of the spear."

"Peter is making our final travel arrangements. He's so much better at managing the logistical details. Which reminds me..." He took out a phone, tapped out a quick text message, and then put it away.

"Travel arrangements? Where you headed now? Going to take the battle straight to Illuminati Headquarters at the Denver airport?"

Martiel smiled. "You're closer than you realize. But I think I'll save that for a surprise."

"Oh, come on," Stone pressed. "What are you afraid of? That I'll beat you again? Oh, maybe you are. That would explain why you need the performance enhancers."

Martiel, not looking the least bit embarrassed, turned the Brazen Head so that the robotic visage was looking up at him. "In that respect, I am no different than those who went before me. Albert of Cologne. Leonardo da Vinci. Even Hess. When a man of true genius awakens the full potential of his brain, what do you call him if not a god?"

Sievers let out a derisive chuckle. "Buddy, sounds like you already started hitting the vapors."

Martiel, however, cocked his head sideways as if listening to something. A moment later, Avery heard it, too; the distinctive roar of a jet engine and the rhythmic thump-thump of rotor blades beating the air.

"Our transportation has arrived," Martiel said. "All your questions will be answered in due course." He turned back to Stone. "You'll be coming with me, Gavin. And you, Miss Halsey. There's so much I want to tell you. Things were rushed in New Jersey, and I apologize for that. It was never my intention for this to be an adversarial relationship."

"You're kidding, right?" Stone said, shaking his head. "You want to beat me so bad I can smell it coming off you. Your self-esteem must be in the toilet."

"It would be satisfying to prove my intellectual superiority," Martiel admitted. "But ours should have been a friendly rivalry. Two chess grandmasters, sharpening each other through competition in order to realize our full potential. Imagine what we could accomplish with our combined genius, unlocked by the Brazen Head? And I'm not discounting your contribution, Miss Halsey. You're much more clever than I think even Gavin realizes."

"Cut the crap," Stone said. "You're only bringing her along as leverage." He then quickly added. "And you're wrong. I *do* realize how smart she is."

"Thanks," Avery said, grinning a little in spite of the situation. "I think. And it's *Doctor* Halsey, actually."

Martiel shrugged. "I believe that when you understand what I am trying to accomplish, you will freely choose the path of cooperation."

"What about Tam and Billy? Are you going to kill them?"

Martiel glanced down at the two trussed-up figures. "Once the three of us are safely on our way, they will be released unharmed. I'm not the villain you think I am."

The beat of the rotor blades grew louder, making further conversation at anything below a shout impossible. Avery spotted the lights of the aircraft, coming in from the north—probably from Glasgow—and followed its approach. Just a few minutes later, it passed overhead, so close that she could feel the wind of its passage, and then circled around to touch down about a hundred yards away, not far from the trail she had followed earlier.

Martiel faced Stone and, cupping his hands around his

mouth to amplify his voice, shouted, "Let's go."

Stone did not immediately move, but instead glanced down at Tam who was looking back at him intently.

Tam's strong voice cut through the noise. "Look out for each other."

Stone nodded then turned to Avery. He held out his hand, and she took it, and then together they followed Martiel toward the idling helicopter.

When the din of turbines and rotor blades finally began to subside, diminishing away to nothing as the departing aircraft headed north with its two unwilling passengers, Tam finally raised her head and peered into the surrounding darkness.

Their captors—Swiss Army Special Forces if Sievers had judged correctly—had remained concealed in shadow, all except for the two men who had ventured out to search and restrain the two of them, but based on the number of flashlights, she knew there were at least six of them.

Six against two was bad enough, but six armed men against her and Sievers, with no weapons and their hands tied behind their backs?

"Lieutenant Colonel LeMans," she said. "Did I get that right?"

"*Oberstleutnant*," corrected an irritated voice from the shadows. "He should not have told you that."

"That was you that hit my people in Provence, wasn't it?"

"It was necessary. Nothing personal, you understand."

Oh, it's personal, Tam thought.

"One professional to another," Sievers said. "You were never going to cut us loose, were you?"

One of the lights was extinguished, and then from that spot, a masked figure stepped forward into the zone of illumination. As he did, he allowed his Heckler & Koch MP5S with its attached MagLite tactical flashlight, to hang from its sling across his chest, and took Tam's Makarov from his belt. The compact pistol looked like a toy in his gloved hands. He covered the top of the pistol with his left hand and drew back the slide halfway, visually checking to see if there was a round in the chamber. There was, of course; Tam always kept the weapon chambered and ready to fire.

"One professional to another," LeMans said, as he released the slide on the pistol, letting the buffer spring shove the assembly forward with an audible rasp and click. He knelt beside Sievers. "What do you think?"

TWENTY-EIGHT

Although she could not see the men behind the high-intensity tactical flashlights, Tam knew that, to a man, they had each removed their fingers from the triggers of their machine pistols. They would not want to take the chance of accidentally loosing a round with their leader so close to one of the prisoners.

She wouldn't get a better chance.

Tam lifted her bound hands a few inches above her back. It was an awkward position, and she could feel the strain of it in her shoulders, but she put the pain out of her mind, focusing on what would happen next. Her timing would have to be perfect. As LeMans lowered the Makarov, preparing to shoot Sievers in the back of the head, Tam moved like a striking rattlesnake, flexing her body in the middle and snapping her forearms against her backside.

She felt the briefest sensation of pain as the zip-tie dug into her skin, but then the forcefulness of the blow ripped the plastic teeth past the metal ratchet stay. Had the Swiss commandos used tactical flexicuffs, which consisted of two conjoined heavy duty zip-tie collars, designed to mimic actual handcuffs, the maneuver probably would have been unsuccessful, but the simple hardware store cable ties weren't designed to withstand a sudden forceful blow, and just like that, Tam's hands were loose.

In the same motion, she brought them down to the ground and pushed hard, springing off the ground high enough that she was able to slide her right leg forward, bringing her knee up until it touched her chest. She planted her foot beneath her, and sprang forward like a sprinter exploding off the starting blocks, aiming herself straight at the kneeling LeMans.

Taken completely by surprise, LeMans tried to raise

the Makarov, but was a fraction of a second too slow. Tam swung her left knee forward, connecting solidly with his head, and then kept going, plowing through him like he wasn't even there.

She expected at any moment to feel hot lead plucking at her body, but her escape bid had evidently caught LeMans' men off guard as well. Tam knew better than to stop and give them a stationary target, however. She kept moving, pivoting away from the cabins and the unseen commandos with their flashlights and guns, sprinting toward the uncertain refuge of the dark trail leading into the hills.

LeMans shouted something in German and abruptly the air around her was crisscrossed with flashlight beams. She veered left for a few steps, then cut back to the right, weaving to stay ahead of the searching spotlights. Over the pounding of her heart and the thump of her footfalls, she could distinctly hear the sound of bullets whooshing past her, far too close for comfort. There were no accompanying reports—the commandos were carrying suppressed weapons, making it impossible to judge just how far away they were, but ultimately that mattered little. She was still in their range, and all they would need was one lucky shot, and she would be done for.

Less than fifty yards behind her, Billy Sievers was dealing with a different set of problems. He had been hoping that Tam would make a move—counting on it actually—and when she had launched into motion, he had done his best to capitalize on the commotion to make his own escape attempt. The results had been a mixed bag.

As Tam bowled LeMans over, Sievers rolled onto his side, trying to get his feet under him. Before he could do this, one of the Swiss commandos rushed from the shadows beside the cabin and swung his machine pistol like a cudgel, so Sievers instead flipped onto his back and spun his body around so that his feet were between himself and the commando. As the man's rush brought him closer, Sievers drew his legs up and then struck out with both feet, smashing his heels into the man's knee. The commando uttered a harsh cry and toppled forward, crashing down on top of Sievers. The impact knocked the wind out of Sievers. Worse, the combined weight of both men crushed painfully against his still-bound hands.

As he gasped for the air to cry out in agony, he could hear the cough of suppressed reports, machine pistols huffing bursts of fully automatic fire. He could also hear LeMans shouting, ordering his men to stop shooting, to chase after Tam. Through the haze of pain, he saw several black-clad figures do just that, racing off into the darkness with their lights bobbing and flashing as they ran.

But not all of them. The commando who had just flattened him was still there, cursing in German as he rolled off Sievers and scrambled back to his feet—or foot rather, since his left leg seemed unable to bear any weight. With a final snarl, he leveled his MP5S at Sievers and curled his finger around the trigger.

"Stop!" shouted LeMans. He had stayed behind, too.

The injured commando's finger uncurled but the business end of the weapon remained trained on Sievers, who could only gape at the man, mouth open and working like a beached fish as he struggled to draw breath.

LeMans picked himself up, retrieved the fallen Makarov, and stood over Sievers. In some dim corner of his mind, Sievers thought he understood why LeMans had stopped his subordinate from taking the shot. He wanted to use Tam's pistol, thereby leaving behind a little bit less in the way of incriminating forensic evidence. But the commando leader seemed to have a different motive for the brief reprieve.

"You work for her, no?" LeMans said, shaking his head in mock sympathy. "I almost feel sorry for you."

Sievers' breath finally returned. Through clenched teeth, he said, "I was going to say the same thing to you."

A smile twitched across the other man's lips. "Your display of bravado is admirable. One professional to another. But she left you to die, this woman you work for. She is a coward, interested in saving her own skin."

"Guess you don't know her like I do."

LeMans continued smiling as he aimed the Makarov at Sievers. "I think I do."

Tam hit the dirt as bullets sizzled through the air around her, but she did not stop moving. Instead, she began high crawling over the soft grassy terrain, scrambling on all fours as she searched for cover.

She needed to lose her pursuers, if only for a few seconds. Just long enough to force them to split up and spread out to search for her. Unarmed, she couldn't hope to take on a group of gunmen, but in a one-on-one encounter, she just might have a chance.

The sound of bullets slicing through the air ceased as the men stopped firing, but she could still hear the men shouting to each other as the lights continued to search the landscape around her. She froze, pressed herself flat lest any movement betray her location, and waited to see what would happen next. The men were still more or less clustered together, moving in a staggered formation toward the trail that she and the others had followed back to the cabins. They were about twenty yards behind her, and if they kept moving in a straight line, they would pass within about fifteen feet of where she lay.

Too close.

Then she spotted something that gave her hope. As the lights roved back and forth, they briefly illuminated a cattle bridge that crossed over a small creek and continued on to the main trail. Merlin's Cave was on the near side of the creek, further to the east, so they had not crossed the bridge earlier, but she remembered seeing it. The bridge did not interest her; it was a choke point, and she would never make it across without being seen, but the creek was another matter.

She watched the lights sweep back and forth a few more times, waiting for the moment when all of the beams were pointed away from where she wanted to go, and when it arrived, she bounded to her feet and took off running in the direction of the bridge.

Another shout, and the lights swung toward her. She zigzagged a couple times but tried to maintain her visualization of the unseen landscape. If she veered off course by a degree or two or misjudged the location of the creek by even a few steps, instead of providing her with a place to hide, she might very well end up with broken bones or miss the creek altogether.

Now, she thought as she threw herself flat again and continued the rest of the way at a fast crawl. Her estimation was nearly perfect. After crawling just a few feet, the ground fell away beneath her, and she pitched headfirst down a steep embankment. She slid about ten feet, striking half-buried roots and stones before splashing into a shallow rivulet of chilly water.

The cold nearly took her breath away, but she forced herself to lie completely still, lifting her head out of the water just high enough to clear her nostrils. The lights continued to sweep back and forth, but she heard nothing to indicate that the men knew where she had gone.

She waited, counting the seconds with short breaths, fighting to keep her teeth from chattering. The lights grew brighter, closer. One of the men ventured onto the bridge and shone his light down into the creek. The circle of light it cast passed within inches of where Tam lay, but kept moving, giving no indication that she had been spotted. After a few more seconds, the man continued over the bridge and darkness returned.

Moving slowly, careful not to make any noise, she reached down and began untying her shoes. She would need a weapon, and since the Swiss commandos had taken everything else, she would have to improvise. Her fingers were getting stiff and numb, and she fumbled with the knots for nearly a minute before finally succeeding. Then, gripping the laces in her right hand, she began crawling back up the embankment but froze again as LeMans' voice reached out across the still landscape.

"Agent Broderick. I know you can hear me."

He was close, maybe within fifty feet of the bridge.

"I have your friend with me. Agent Sievers. He thinks you are going to come to his rescue. That would be a foolish thing to do. You cannot save his life, but if you surrender now, I can promise that you will rescue him from a great deal of unnecessary pain and suffering."

Tam could see what LeMans was building up to and knew that she didn't have much time left. Despite the risk of exposure, she started moving again, slithering up to the top of the embankment.

She could see several pinpoints of light scattered across the open landscape. As expected, the searching commandos had indeed split up, spreading out to cover more terrain. But which one was LeMans?

"A demonstration then."

The voice had come, not from one of the lights but from the darkness. She stared in the general direction, orienting on the sound until she thought she could make out an irregular silhouette against the night sky.

Lord Jesus, she prayed, *let that be them.* Then she started moving.

"In sixty seconds, I will put a bullet through his right foot. Then I will begin counting. Sixty seconds after that, I will shoot his left foot. I will keep doing this. Feet, knees, hands, elbows, every sixty seconds, until you surrender yourself to my men. I can make your friend's last few minutes on earth last a very long time, Agent Broderick. It's up to you. Tick tock."

He paused, and Tam froze again. As long as he was talking, she could count on his voice covering up the faint rustle of her body moving through the grass. She waited a few seconds more, hoping that he would resume his taunts, but when he did not, she started moving again. The clock was running down, and she couldn't afford to wait any longer.

Tick, tock.

"Time's up, Agent Broderick. The next sound you hear will be your friend screaming."

A light flashed on, partially revealing the prone form of Billy Sievers. The illuminated area shrank to just a small circle around his feet as LeMans brought his machine pistol closer to his target.

In that instant, Tam knew, LeMans would be blind to everything happening outside that circumference of brilliance. In the time he had given her, she had managed to creep past him and was now about ten yards behind him. His silhouette was unmistakable. Throwing the last of her caution to the wind, she sprang to her stockinged feet, covered the remaining ten yards or so in three quick bounds, and dropped her field-expedient shoestring garrote over the killer's head, pulling it taut with such force she could feel it all the way up to her elbows.

LeMans immediately let go of his weapon and began clawing frantically at his throat, but any chance he might have had to slip a finger in between the strangling cord and his neck had already passed. Before he could change tactics, Tam rammed her knee into his back, which not only dug the string in deeper but bore the Swiss commando forward, slamming him face down onto the ground alongside Billy Sievers.

LeMans thrashed desperately for a few more seconds, then went rigid as oxygen deprivation took its final toll. Tam just kept pulling tighter, barely even noticing when his struggles ceased altogether.

"Tam," Sievers hissed. "Cut me loose."

The urgency in his voice brought her back to the moment. Further away, the shouts of other commandos were audible. They knew something was wrong and it was only a matter of time before they came to investigate.

She released the makeshift garrote, allowing LeMans' lifeless body to slump on the grass, and quickly patted him down. She felt an oblong shape in one pocket that could only be a folding pocket knife and drew it out, fumbling to get her fingernail on the edge of the largest blade. In the ambient illumination cast by the tactical flashlight on the discarded machine pistol, she could see the knife's red plastic body marked with a distinctive shield and cross.

A Swiss army knife.

Naturally, Tam thought.

The stainless-steel blade finally swung out and clicked into place. She bent over Sievers and, working more by feel than sight, found the zip-tie holding his wrists together. A quick snick of the blade cut them apart, after which she closed the blade and slipped it into her pocket.

Sievers shook his arms a few times to restore his circulation then scooped up the MP5S. He immediately switched off the tactical flashlight, plunging them once more into darkness but also hiding their location from the other commandos. The nearest man was a good fifty yards away but moving cautiously back in their direction. Sievers aimed his weapon at the approaching figure but did not pull the trigger. If the situation escalated into a firefight, the odds were still against him and Tam.

"I think we can make it back to the car," he whispered. "But there's one straggler between us and it. Better gun up, just in case. I think your Makarov is on his belt."

Tam nodded and resumed searching the dead man until she located her pistol and two spare magazines for the machine pistol which she passed up to Sievers. She also found a key ring with a single plastic sheathed automobile key.

As she stood up again, she glanced down at the dark, motionless lump one last time and muttered, "That was for Kasey, you son of a bitch."

She was about to add another mental IOU to the swear jar but then thought better of it. Instead, she simply added, "You can keep the shoelaces."

Sievers looked down at LeMans as well. "Tried to warn you."

TWENTY-NINE

The noise of the helicopter's engines made conversation impossible during the short flight over the Moffat Hills to Glasgow. After boarding, Martiel had donned a pair of headphones with an attached microphone, which allowed him to converse with the aircraft's pilot and the sole passenger, an older man whom Avery could only assume was Peter Furst. No headsets were offered to her or Stone, which was fine with Avery. She wasn't particularly interested in talking to her captors, but it would have been nice to talk to Stone. He could be a real jerk sometimes, but he wasn't the least bit intimidated by Martiel. She really could have used a bit of his confidence.

The flight lasted about twenty minutes, at which point the helicopter landed on the airport tarmac, well away from the main runways. While the rotors were still spinning overhead, Furst and Martiel climbed out, the latter indicating that Avery and Stone should follow. They moved a short distance away and were met by a van which carried them to a different but no less remote corner of the airport where a small business jet was waiting. As they stepped out of the van, Avery could hear the whine of the idling jet engines. The aircraft was evidently ready for takeoff.

Martiel ushered them up the steps and back into the luxuriously appointed forward cabin. "Make yourselves at home."

Stone plopped down into the nearest chair—it looked more like a La-z-Boy recliner than an airplane seat—and stretched his legs out as if planning to take a nap. "Got any puzzle books?"

Avery was less eager to get comfortable. "Where are we going?"

Martiel regarded her with a look of amusement for a

moment, then glanced over at Stone. "You want a puzzle? Let's see if you can figure—"

"Spokane," Stone said, and then stifled a yawn. "I'll need something more challenging than that. It's going to be... what, twelve hours flying time?"

A nerve near Martiel's right eye twitched. "Closer to eight in this plane." Then he stalked past the seating area and disappeared into the next partitioned cabin.

Behind them, a crewman pulled the door shut, sealing them inside the plane. Avery felt a mild throbbing in her inner ear as the plane was pressurized and realized only then that Furst had not accompanied them aboard the plane. She, Stone and Martiel seemed to be the only passengers.

The whine of the engines was a barely audible hum now, but Avery detected a slight change in pitch as they began spinning faster. A moment later, the plane rocked gently and started moving. Martiel wasn't wasting any time moving to the next phase of his plan, whatever that was.

A subdued male voice came over the public-address system, warning them that take-off was imminent and advising them to take their seats and buckle up.

Avery took a seat opposite Stone. "Spokane, Washington," she said, in a low whisper. "Where the Mystic server facility is located?"

Stone nodded. "Our host is a regular Johnny One-note." Unlike Avery, he spoke in a loud voice, so that Martiel could not help but overhear. "He thinks Mystic is the key to everything. He can't see past it. For all his bragging, he really isn't very clever at all."

Martiel took the bait. "Mystic *is* the key to everything," he said as he stepped back into view. He haughtily strode forward and sat down in the chair across the aisle from Avery. Outside, the lights of the taxiway were visible, passing slowly by as the jet maneuvered toward the runway.

Stone continued addressing Avery. "His original plan to crash the economy through the user terminals would have only accomplished so much. The only way to make the damage permanent would be to corrupt the operating system, and the only way to do that is from the master terminal at the server farm. To pull off a hack like that, he knew he would need an edge, something to ramp his brain up to 110%. That's why he was so insistent that Furst get him the Brazen Head before setting the wheels in motion."

"The two-part attack I originally envisioned would have achieved optimal results," Martiel said. "But once I take control of Mystic, I will be able to effect nearly the same outcome."

"I see Peter decided to sit this one out."

"As I said, he's better at handling the logistical piece. He can do a lot more from his headquarters in Switzerland."

"And he probably knows that even his highly-placed friends won't be able to protect him this time."

Martiel spread his hands in a gesture of acknowledgment. "Discretion and valor, et cetera. But when the dust settles, the politicians and business leaders will look to him as their savior."

Stone uttered a noncommittal grunt.

"Honestly, Gavin, I'm surprised that you are still so resistant to this. You know what Mystic really is. It represents everything you detest."

Avery glanced over at Stone. "What's he mean by that?"

Martiel was ready with an answer. "Do you know what Mystic is, Dr. Halsey?"

"Sure. It's a trading platform that employs artificial intelligence to predict how world events will affect the economy and manage risk accordingly."

Martiel shook his head. "Is that what the Wikipedia entry said? I promise you, it's so much more than that. You're familiar with the term 'data mining'? Mystic is the mill that takes that data, grinds it to powder, and from that dust, creates a virtual universe. You've probably heard stories about primitive tribes who believe that taking someone's photograph steals their soul, giving the person who takes the picture power over the subject. That's exactly what Mystic and our Big Data surveillance state is doing. Taking away our power, controlling us with targeted advertising, propaganda, manipulation, and reaping enormous profits on the backs of our desperation. Gavin has quite a reputation for opposing the Big Data surveillance state. Has he told you about the algorithm he created?"

"I know about it," Avery said, a little too quickly.

The algorithm Martiel was referring to was a piece of machine code—a predictive tool that employed massive amounts of personal data to accurately forecast the behavior of groups and even individuals. Long before Avery had first met him, Stone had gotten in hot water for stealing the algorithm. In fact, a primary reason that the ordinarily solitary Stone had chosen to work with Tam and the Myrmidons was as a way to avoid the dire consequences of that action. However, Stone had never once indicated that the algorithm was his own creation.

Stone must have sensed the unasked question. "Created is a bit of an exaggeration," he explained dismissively. "I was part of the development team. We parted company after a disagreement about intellectual property."

Martiel chuckled. "And yet after you disappeared with it, no one was ever able to reproduce your work. Mystic is a poor imitation, but it serves the same basic purpose. It is a tool for controlling us all. They watch us all constantly, monitor our Google searches, what we shop for, what we look at, and use it to control us. They know what we want before we do. It has to stop. Surely you see that, Gavin."

"Oh, please," Stone said with a snort of disgust. "Save the heroic speeches for your Nazi fanboys on the Immortal forum. That's the difference between us, you know. I know what you really want, and it doesn't have anything to do with championing privacy or stopping Jewish bankers. You're an open book to me, but you have no idea what makes me tick."

Avery managed to hide her smile. Martiel had seriously misjudged his rival. Stone wasn't a bad guy, but neither was he an altruistic privacy crusader, fighting the intrusiveness of Big Data or the NSA or anyone else. His interest in the algorithm was motivated solely by his desire to understand the seemingly chaotic nature of human behavior, and in so doing, unlock what he called "the source code of the universe."

Martiel seemed taken aback. "Is that a fact? And what is it you think I really want?"

"To be the smartest guy in the room. But you never will be. Not while I'm in the room with you."

The air between the men seemed to crackle with tension. Stone was intentionally provoking Martiel, and from what Avery could tell, he was hitting all the right pressure points. But they were still Martiel's captives, and she couldn't see how taunting the man would improve their situation at all.

As if to underscore their helplessness, Avery felt something like an invisible hand press her back in her seat as the plane accelerated down the runway and leaped into the sky. She cleared her throat. "You said you would cut Tam and Billy loose once we were on our way."

Martiel glanced over at her, his eyes burning with barely contained ire. He shook his head. "A small deception, I'm afraid. I'll need to keep them under wraps a while longer, both to ensure that they don't interfere and to keep the two of you from misbehaving."

Avery knew that Tam would expect them to do exactly that—misbehave—but until they were on terra firma, there wasn't a lot she and Stone could do. Maybe when they were back on American soil, they would be able to slip away or at the very least, scream for help.

"There is one thing I'm curious about," Stone said, seeming to ignore the none-too-subtle threat. "I get that you think the Brazen Head is going to super-charge your brain so that you'll be able to hack into Mystic. That might actually work. But the Mystic server farm is probably the most secure non-governmental data storage facility on earth. Do you really think you're just going to waltz into Mystic and do as you please?

An anticipatory gleam replaced some of the anger in Martiel's eyes. "Oh, it won't be a waltz, but it will definitely be a dance."

THIRTY

Tam did not know with any certainty where the helicopter had gone, but Glasgow was the closest destination of any consequence and represented their best chance of picking up the trail. Her instincts told her that Martiel would not stay in Scotland, and if he intended to fly out, Glasgow was the likeliest jumping off point for international travel, but there were dozens of cities across the United Kingdom within easy reach of the helicopter. Figuring out where it went, and where its occupants had subsequently gone, would take old fashioned leg work and Tam, unfortunately, had left her shoes in the creek at Newton Farms.

The car's heater had saved her from hypothermia following her dip in the creek, but she was still soaked through and filthy, so upon reaching Glasgow, they booked a room at a hotel near the airport. Tam headed straight for the shower, while Sievers went out to find her some dry clothes and shoes.

Her hands were bruised and raw where she had gripped the shoestring garrote, and the abraded skin stung at first, but she scrubbed them thoroughly, and after a few seconds, the pain subsided. The muscles in her arms and shoulders were aching, too—another consequence of that brief but violent exertion—but the steady stream of hot water brought a measure of relief. As tempting as it would have been to luxuriate in the shower until the water ran cold, the thought of Stone and Avery in danger made relaxation impossible, so after what seemed like only a few minutes, she grudgingly shut it off and got out. As she toweled off, she began composing a list of phone calls she would have to make.

Her first call would be to the CIA's chief of station in London to let him know that she was in his area of operations and that things had gone sideways. He would probably give her an earful for leaving a corpse in a cow pasture in Scotland, but she doubted it would even come up. LeMans' men were professionals. They would have removed his body and sanitized the site before leaving, so as far as the locals were concerned, nothing had happened at Newton Farms.

The COS would also be able to supply her with the necessary law enforcement credentials to get regional air traffic control to cooperate so she could begin tracing Martiel's movements, but even with full cooperation, it would be a tedious process. Helicopters didn't have to file flight plans, and only had to check in with ATC when entering restricted airspace. Furthermore, since she didn't have a tail number, or even the make and model of the bird that had carried her friends away, she would have to review all the radio traffic logged by the controllers to get tail numbers for each helicopter that had come and gone from the airspace, identify the operator and pilot of each, and then start conducting in-person interviews.

Having both Stone and Avery on the team had spoiled her. Between them, they usually had the answer to any question, sometimes before Tam even finished asking. She didn't have Stone's computer savvy or his ability to make intuitive leaps, and she didn't have Avery's ability to know exactly where to look for answers.

No shortcuts this time, she thought ruefully as she wrapped the towel around her torso, and reached for the door knob.

When she opened the door, she found a large plastic bag waiting for her.

Maybe I was in there longer than I realized, she thought.

"That was fast," she sang out. Inside the bag was a T-shirt emblazoned with the Scottish flag, a pair of gray sweatpants, and a pair of flip-flops. Not exactly her first choice of attire for pounding the pavement and running down leads, but probably the best she could hope for given the hour. First thing in the morning, she would have to hit a department store.

"Hurry up," Sievers called back from the main room. "You need to see this."

Hearing the urgency in his tone, Tam decided to forgo getting dressed and simply ventured out as is. The towel covered up the essentials, though only just, but Sievers didn't even look her way; his attention was riveted to the television.

The set was tuned to a satellite news channel. The screen was displaying a live feed; a male reporter stood on what appeared to be a rural farm road. Behind him several pickup trucks were parked diagonally across the lane, blocking all access. Milling around the vehicles were at least a dozen men attired in Carhartt duck coats and Army surplus field jackets, wearing ball caps sporting a variety of instantly recognizable logos—ranging from a popular brand of chewing tobacco to the Gadsden flag. Some had taken the added measure of concealing their faces with scarves and sunglasses. All were armed—Tam saw quite a few AR15s, as well as hunting rifles, shotguns, and holstered pistols—but it was obvious, even without the accompanying commentary from the reporter, that they were not there for a hunting trip.

Although she was joining the unfolding story in midstream, she was quickly able to piece together what was happening. Just a glance at the text graphic in the bottom left corner of the screen was enough to explain Sievers' urgent request for her attention. It read: STANDOFF IN SPOKANE.

She did some mental math. Spokane was eight hours behind Glasgow time. It would be mid-afternoon there. "This is live?"

Sievers nodded.

The live feed ended with the field reporter handing off to the anchor in the studio. *"If you're just joining us, breaking news from eastern Washington State, just north of Spokane. In a scene that's eerily reminiscent of last year's standoff at the Malheur wildlife refuge in Oregon, a group of armed protestors—estimates put the number anywhere from fifty to a hundred and fifty—have shut down this road leading to a data facility operated by Iron River Asset Management, a New York-based investment firm. The protestors are calling themselves 'privacy advocates,' and say they're only trying to draw attention to what they call the illegal collection of personal information by Iron River and other companies, which can be used by the government in violation of the Fourth Amendment of the Constitution, information they say is being stored at the data center."*

Sievers thumbed the volume down. "That's the Mystic server farm," he said. He turned to her, did a double-take when he realized what she wasn't wearing, then shook his head and looked her in the eye. "This can't be a coincidence."

Tam pretended not to notice him noticing. "Agreed. Stone said it was about Mystic from the get go. These guys are all anti-government conspiracy nuts. Martiel created the Immortal Mysteries forum to recruit them to be his foot soldiers. This was always the plan." She sighed, crossing her arms over her chest in consternation. "But what *is* the actual plan? Send these yokels in to burn the place down?"

Sievers' eyebrows drew together in a frown. "They'd never even get close. Fifteen percent of the national economy is managed in that facility. FBI and Treasury are probably already playing Rochambeau to decide who's got jurisdiction. This will be over before you know it. Makes me wonder if it's not just another distraction."

"I'm not so sure about that," Tam countered. "Remember what happened with that group in Oregon last year? Or I should say, what didn't happen?"

In January of 2016, a group of about thirty anti-government militants took over the headquarters of the Malheur National Wildlife Refuge in a remote corner of Oregon. The men claimed to be protesting the arrest and conviction of two men accused of setting fires on public lands, but the real goal of their illegal occupation was to rally more support for their opposition to the federal government, and in particular, federal ownership and management of public lands through the Department of the Interior and National Forest Service. The leaders of the uprising were cattle ranchers with a long history of grazing their herds on public rangelands without paying the required fees or federal income tax—essentially getting a free ride at the taxpayer's expense. With the government building a case against them, their solution had been to cast themselves as David, fighting the oppressive Goliath of big government, and they had rallied fellow "sovereign citizens" to the cause, not once but twice. In 2014, they had staged a very public blockade to prevent federal agents from confiscating the cattle. That standoff lasted a few weeks before rising public sympathy for the ranchers and fear of a violent escalation prompted the government to back down. Similarly, during the wildlife refuge incident, government officials had been reluctant to use force against the occupiers, choosing instead to wait them out. The siege had dragged on for forty days before dwindling supplies and freezing temperatures prompted most of the militants to leave whereupon all were arrested, except for one who was killed while resisting arrest.

That, however, wasn't the end of the story.

"Half the guys who pulled that stunt were acquitted," Tam said. "Every one of the guys out there knows it. Martiel knows it, too."

"This isn't some backwater ranger station," Sievers countered. "Valero doesn't just have Paul Blart minimum-wage mall cop guarding the place. Believe me, I know the guys who end up working gigs like that. And I guarantee the feds will send in tactical teams to back them up."

"How will they get inside?" Tam said. "Run the roadblock? Helicopter? That turns it into a shooting war. They won't do that as long as they think there's a non-violent alternative. Especially not with the media and the world watching, thinking this is all a political protest. Nobody wants to see this turn into the next Waco or Ruby Ridge. The FBI playbook for this kind of thing is wait-and-see, just like last time. And don't forget the new guy in the

White House. He's not going to authorize any kind of action against them. They're his voting base, and he knows it. He's probably rooting for them."

Sievers checked his phone and grunted. "Nothing on Twitter yet." He looked up, saw Tam shaking her head, and gave a guilty shrugged. "What? I follow him."

"We're gonna have to talk about that when all this is over."

He grinned and put his phone away. "So the protestors hold the perimeter and keep law enforcement out, while Martiel takes a strike team inside to deal with internal security. That's going to get ugly. And if he takes Avery and Stone in with him…" He shook his head, leaving the rest unsaid. "We have to tell someone what's really going on."

"Who? I'm not sure who would believe us, and even if they do, they're not going to act fast enough. Besides," she added, "I'm running out of people who owe me favors."

"How 'bout Valero? He's probably already shi… ah, dropping bricks. I'm sure he'd appreciate the head's up."

"He's going to need a lot more than that, but it's a start. I'll give him a call. Nice save, by the way."

"I took a pay cut when I came to work for you and your swear jar's cutting into my beer fund." He regarded her for a moment. "You know we need to get inside that place."

"Same problem. How?"

"I've got an idea, but you're not going to…" He broke off suddenly and smacked his forehead with an open palm. "What am I saying? You're going to love it."

THIRTY-ONE

Spokane, Washington

Exhausted after days of travel and being on the run, Avery slept through most of the trans-continental flight, stretched out on one of the plush couches in the rear mid-cabin. She awoke to the pilot's announcement that they were on final approach to Spokane and that local time was 11:47 p.m. Pacific Daylight Time. As Martiel had promised, the flight from Glasgow to Spokane International Airport had lasted about eight hours, which was exactly the time difference between the two cities, so instead of waking up to a new dawn, Avery found herself at the tail end of the same fateful day that had started with her visit to the Louvre and her discovery of the secret of the Brazen Head.

It was as if time had stood still.

She roused herself, splashed some water on her face and tried to straighten her rumpled clothing before heading up into the forward cabin where Stone and Martiel were seated in the same chairs they had occupied at the flight's start. The latter was staring at the screen of a laptop computer, occasionally typing in messages. After a quick glance, which revealed that he was browsing the Immortal Mysteries Forum, Avery took the seat across from Stone.

"What did I miss?" she asked in a low, conspiratorial whisper.

"A lot of grandiose monologuing and fiendish cackling," Stone said with an indifferent shrug. "You're lucky you slept through it."

Martiel uttered a short, humorless, but not particularly fiendish laugh, and then snapped his laptop shut. "Don't think I don't know what you're trying to do. You won't provoke me with schoolyard taunts."

"Is that what I'm doing?" Stone replied, shooting

Avery a wink. "He really does like the sound of his own voice. I spent eight months at that black site in Romania undergoing 'enhanced interrogation techniques,' but I swear, eight hours of listening to him go on about Big Data and the Zionist banking conspiracy…that's torture."

Avery knew Stone well enough to grasp the significance of the comment. Stone had survived those long months of imprisonment by studying the behavior of the men guarding and interrogating him, so that, when the opportunity for escape finally presented itself, he had known exactly which weaknesses to exploit, which buttons to push. By referencing his earlier captivity, Stone was telling her that he had spent the last eight hours learning Martiel's patterns of behavior, studying his microexpressions, his tells, judging his reactions, learning what made him tick and what absolutely set him off.

Even without Stone's astute powers of observation, Avery knew that Martiel's repeated assertions of intellectual superiority indicated just the opposite—a textbook inferiority complex. It was the only explanation for why he had brought Stone and herself along, even though doing so might jeopardize his plan. He couldn't help himself. He was like Marty McFly in the *Back to the Future* movies—pathologically driven to prove himself, even when doing so played right into the hands of his opponent. Stone, a master at social engineering, would be able to play Martiel like a fiddle.

And yet, Stone had completely misjudged the significance of the Brazen Head in Martiel's grand scheme. What if the Immortal really was as smart as he claimed to be?

Nothing more was said as the jet finished its descent, touching down a few minutes later and taxiing to a private hanger away from the small terminal. When they finally received permission to unbuckle their seat belts, Martiel's demeanor became cold and ruthless.

"I've treated you as my guests up to this point," he said, "but I'm afraid that will change now. When we disembark, we will be met by a group of men who have sworn themselves to the success of this mission. They are military veterans with combat experience. I would strongly suggest that you refrain from provoking them, or for that matter, interacting with them in any way. Suffice it to say, any attempt to escape or draw attention to yourselves would be met with an immediate and disproportionate response. Do I make myself clear?"

Avery, suddenly feeling a little less confident, nodded. Stone didn't respond at all.

"Then let's be on our way, shall we?" Martiel rose, slung the backpack containing the Brazen Head over one shoulder, and started for the door. "If you stay close to me," he added without looking back, "you just might survive to see the sunrise."

Stone reached out and took Avery's hand, giving it a squeeze. "Stay close to *me*," he said. "Everything will be okay."

Martiel's goons were waiting just outside, and they were exactly as advertised.

The men, half-a-dozen of them in all, reminded her a lot of Billy Sievers, though more in the way they carried themselves than in their overall appearance. All were Caucasian though that seemed to be their only common trait. They sported a variety of grooming styles ranging from barely kempt to clean-shaven and bald as a cue-ball, but they all looked poised for action, eyes constantly moving, looking around for any potential threat or target.

A white van with the logo of a popular television news channel was parked behind them near the open door of the hangar, and as Martiel started toward it, the six men collapsed around him, none-too-subtly sending an unspoken message to Avery and Stone that they should keep up with him. Martiel climbed into the back of the van which, despite its outward appearance, contained no broadcast equipment. The rear passenger seats had been removed to create a large cargo area, which was mostly empty aside from a row of black plastic Pelican cases stacked up in the middle.

"Make yourselves comfortable," Martiel said, clearly speaking only to Avery and Stone. "It's about forty minutes to where we're going. Unfortunately, we're done riding in style."

Avery got in after him and followed his example by sitting on the floor with her back against the sidewall, knees drawn up and toes just touching the cases. Once Stone was inside, two of the men got in the front seats while the rest boarded through the rear door, the last one pulling the door shut behind him. Although there were windows front and back, Avery's line of sight was completely blocked. It felt like being sealed in a tomb.

The van pulled away and began the journey to what Avery assumed was the Mystic server farm. The ride seemed to take a lot longer than forty minutes. The precarious seating arrangement amplified every turn and every bump in the road. The van possessed little or no insulation against road noise, making conversation at any volume below a shout impossible, but none of the occupants seemed interested in conversing. Yet, as bad as it was, Avery was dreading what would happen when the van reached its destination.

When the van slowed and then came to a full stop, she thought the moment of truth had arrived, but it soon became immediately apparent that this was only a temporary halt.

Martiel leaned close to her and whispered. "Not a word. Understand?"

Avery nodded. She didn't know what she would be able to accomplish with just one word, given the circumstances, but then she became aware of the flashing blue and red lights that were just visible in the narrow sliver of the windshield that she could see.

Police cars, she realized. For a fleeting instant, she felt a surge of hope before realizing that this was what Martiel had been talking about.

The driver rolled his window down and spoke to

someone outside. "Evening, deputy."

Avery could just make out the voice of a man—presumably a law enforcement official. "Road's closed, fellas. Haven't you heard?"

Martiel got up suddenly and came forward, leaning over the driver's shoulder to speak to the deputy. "We're here to interview the leader of the protest."

"They aren't giving interviews. Even if they were, we're not letting anyone inside the perimeter."

"We've made special arrangements. Check with your superiors. Tell them Thom Martiel is here."

The deputy paused. "Of course. We've been expecting you. It's an honor to meet you, sir."

Avery's heart fell, though she shouldn't have been surprised that Martiel had followers working inside law enforcement. The Myrmidons' investigation into the Dominion had revealed a concerted effort, both by that group and other anti-government and white supremacist organizations, to infiltrate state and local police agencies, particularly in rural areas.

"Thank you," Martiel said. "Your loyalty will not be forgotten."

As the van started forward, Avery thought she could hear shouts of dismay, probably other reporters—actual journalists—who had been turned back at the barricade. Martiel remained where he was as the van rolled ahead slowly, only to stop again a few seconds later.

Another unfamiliar voice came through the open window. "How'd you guys get past the cops?"

"We had a special press pass. The name is Thom Martiel."

"Mr. Martiel. It's an honor to finally meet you in person."

"He's a regular alt-right rock star," Stone muttered, which earned him an angry hiss from one of the other men in the back seat.

"What do you need us to do?" asked the man outside.

"Just let us through and keep doing what you're doing.

This will all be over soon. When the sun rises tomorrow, it will shine on a new world."

"Amen to that, brother." A few moments of silence followed before Martiel clapped the driver on the shoulder and the van began moving again.

Avery wasn't really sure exactly what was going on in the world outside the van, but she could feel the tension inside increasing by degrees. There was an eagerness for what was coming, but also anxiety. The men, as Martiel had pointed out, were veterans of combat; they knew, in ways that Martiel himself could only imagine, all the things that could happen to them once the bullets started flying.

Martiel half-turned to face them all. Avery thought he was going to make some kind of inspirational speech, but all he said was, "Phase one."

One of the men reacted immediately by popping open the nearest Pelican case and taking out a battered old Betamax video camera. It was a relic, probably not even functional, but Avery guessed that didn't matter.

The van stopped again, and this time Martiel moved to the side door, popped it open, and stepped out with the ersatz cameraman right behind him.

As soon as they were outside, a male voice, electronically amplified, probably with a bullhorn, said. "Stop right there, or we will open fire."

"We're journalists," Martiel shouted. "We're here to interview Mr. Spaulding about the protests."

"Don't come any closer," warned the voice. "We will open fire."

Martiel stuck his head through the door again. His face was a mask of barely contained rage. "Somebody tipped them," he snarled, and then his gaze fell upon Avery. "And I think I know who."

Tam! Avery thought, feeling a measure of satisfaction. *He's talking about Tam. She figured out what he was planning and warned the people at Mystic.*

"I guess we're going to have to do this the hard way. Phase two, now."

"They've got the numbers on us," cautioned the driver before anyone else could move. "And we don't have the element of surprise anymore. They're giving us an out. Maybe we should take it."

"Absolutely not," Martiel shot back. But then he seemed to pause. His eyes returned to Avery. "I've got an idea. Watch for my signal."

Then, before she could even yelp in protest, he reached out and snared her wrist, yanking her across the van and out the door. She would have fallen face first on the pavement if Martiel had not maintained his grip on her arm. He pulled her up and then wrapped his left arm around her midsection, holding her against his body. She could feel something hard and cold pressing into the side of her neck as he stepped away from the van, using her as a human shield.

Her first look at the outside world was a shock to the system. The van had stopped about fifty yards from a gate that blocked the road. The road led to an enormous building—only two or three stories high, but longer than several city blocks—which Avery assumed had to be the Mystic server farm, or at least part of it, but the gate was not the only thing standing between Martiel and his destination. Several concrete K-rail barriers had been dragged across the road just behind the gate, and hunkered down behind them were at least a dozen men wearing dark military-style uniforms and brandishing assault rifles.

Martiel started advancing.

"Stop, or we will open fire," the voice repeated, the words tinged with a barely perceptible quaver of fear.

"Put down your weapons, or I'll kill her," Martiel shouted, practically screaming, right next to Avery's ear.

For the first time since France, she felt truly terrified.

The man with the bullhorn kept repeating his warning, his voice growing more strained with each step forward. "We know what you want. We are not going to let you come in here. We will open fire."

"Then you'll kill her, too!" Martiel screamed back. "Is

that what you want?"

"Don't come any—"

Before the disembodied voice could complete the warning, Martiel suddenly threw himself flat on the ground, pulling Avery down with him. As he dropped, he shouted, "Now!"

And then everything went to hell.

THIRTY-TWO

Billy Sievers wasn't wrong. Tam did love his plan for getting them into the Mystic server farm, but there were two serious problems with it.

The first was mathematical. Although she didn't know exactly what kind of odds they would be facing, she doubted very much that the two of them would stand a chance against Martiel's killers.

They would need reinforcements, and since this would be an unsanctioned operation, those reinforcements would have to be recruited through unofficial channels. Fortunately, she knew just who to call.

The first call she made was to Wayne Valero, advising him that the protest outside the server farm was really just a smokescreen to cover what was essentially a heist. She had also offered to help end the threat permanently. Valero, who was already en route to Spokane, thanked her for the head's up and promised to advise his on-site security team, which as Sievers had suggested, was composed largely of former SWAT officers and men with special operations backgrounds, but he nevertheless chartered a private jet—a Global 8000—to get her and Sievers to Spokane at Mach 0.95, and agreed to provide logistical support in assembling and equipping her ad hoc strike team.

They were all waiting for her in the hangar at the airport when they arrived, just six hours after taking off from Glasgow.

The first man to greet her was Pete "Professor" Chapman. The lanky sandy-haired former Navy SEAL was actually already one of the Myrmidons, though his current ongoing assignment—safeguarding archaeologist and trouble-magnet Jade Ihara—usually kept him otherwise occupied. He simply acknowledged her with a nod, but the man behind him was more effusive with his greeting.

"Girl, when I told you to hit me up, this wasn't what I had in mind."

The deep voice belonged to one of Professor's old SEAL teammates—she was told they preferred the term "swim buddies"—Willis Sanders. Willis was, Tam had to admit, a fine-looking specimen—tall, with a sculpted physique and a smile to die for—but his carefree attitude made him somewhat less than ideal relationship material. He knew, for instance, that she hated being called "girl," and was just saying it to get a rise out of her. She decided not to take a swing at the obvious slow pitch; this wasn't a social gathering, and there wasn't time for banter.

Standing alongside Willis was a slightly shorter man, with a medium build and dark brown hair, named Matt Barnaby. The two men were close friends, and had both joined the Myrmidons during the Atlantis crisis a few years earlier, along with their boss, Avery's brother Dane Maddock, and his partner-in-crime Uriah "Bones" Bonebrake, though all had since returned to their civilian professions.

Maddock and Bones were there as well, and neither of them looked pleased to see Tam. She braced herself for one of Bones' signature off-color juvenile quips, but to her astonishment, the normally reserved Maddock spoke first.

"Damn it, Tam. I can't believe you put Avery at risk like this."

Tam understood his anger, even if it was misplaced. She squared her shoulders and faced him. "Your sister is a grown woman, Maddock, and she can take care of herself."

"Obviously," Bones snorted. "I guess we can go home then."

Sievers spoke up. "I know this is going to be hard for you to hear, Maddock, but right now, Avery is the least of our worries."

Tam winced as Maddock's gaze swung toward the Texan. Maddock was not typically given to chest-thumping displays of manhood, but this situation involved family. Sievers was relatively new to the team. He had never worked with Maddock, and certainly didn't know him the way Tam did.

The air between the two men seemed to go a few degrees cooler. Sievers, however didn't back down. "She's safe. For the moment, at least. Martiel won't kill her until he gets what he's after. We have to focus on stopping him. Period."

Maddock's stormy blue eyes regarded Sievers for several long seconds, and then he turned back to Tam. "Okay, you called, we came. What's the plan?"

Tam turned to the remaining person in the room. "Mr. Valero, can you give us the virtual tour?"

Wayne Valero, who had been standing off to the side, chatting with Maddock's other crewman, Corey Dean, motioned for the rest of them to gather around in a horseshoe. Corey held up an oversized tablet computer, screen facing and displaying a satellite image of the facility, which consisted of three large rectangular buildings. Tam didn't get a sense of scale until Valero zoomed in and showed the cars parked out front.

Bones let out a low whistle. "Whoa. That place is bigger than my—"

"Bones!" Tam just managed to silence him before he embarrassed himself with an impossible comparison.

"Hey," he said, feigning innocence. "I was going to say Caesar's Palace."

The buildings were beyond enormous. The largest was probably as big as three or four football stadiums laid side-by-side.

"This is the administration building," Valero said, pointing to the smallest of the three. He moved his finger to the second and largest building. "The servers are in here, and this—" He indicated a slightly smaller building at the top of the screen, "is the facilities plant. It houses the power plant and coolant systems, which as you can imagine are critical to our operation. If they wanted to destroy Mystic, the facilities plant would be the area of greatest vulnerability."

"I don't think he wants to destroy it," Tam said. "I think he wants to hack it."

Valero frowned. "He'd have an easier time sabotaging it. As I told you earlier, the only way to change the operating system is from the master terminal in the center of the server complex. And it's a secure terminal. He won't be able to just walk up to it and log on."

"Secure how?" asked Corey Dean.

"Swipe card and biometric just to get in the room. Then you need a sysadmin account and password to log on."

"There's always an exploit."

"Not with Mystic."

Corey just shrugged. The only member of Maddock's crew without military experience, Corey earned his keep as the resident tech whiz, and while he was nowhere near as proficient with computer systems as Stone, Tam was inclined to believe him. No system was completely bombproof, and with the Brazen Head in his possession, Martiel had an edge.

Sievers was quick to point out the obvious. "What's to stop him from just grabbing one of your techs and putting a gun to his head?"

"Uh, well… That's why I have an internal security force. There's also a duress protocol. It's an alternate login password that will notify security of an attempted breach without immediately blocking access."

Sievers nodded slowly. "You trust your people to think straight under that kind of stress?"

Valero's head sank a little. "Even if he gets past that, there's another layer of security. A rotating cipher that changes every minute. The sysadmin has to request it from HQ in New York. It's sent by text message."

"Automated?"

"As a rule, yes. But under the circumstances—"

"Under the circumstances, if Martiel threatens to start

killing people, are you going to give him the keys to save their lives?"

Rather than explore that rabbit hole, Tam broke in. "We're not going to let him get that far, but for argument's sake, let's assume that's what he's going to attempt. How do we stop him?"

"Well, the only way into the server farm is through underground tunnels leading from the admin building."

"There aren't any other entrances? Emergency exits? Windows?"

"There are one-way fire exits in the admin building, but not in the server farm or the facilities building."

"How'd you clear that with OSHA?" Bones wondered aloud.

"So that's our objective," Tam said, ignoring the question. "We're going to secure the admin building, stash the civilians somewhere they'll be safe, then pull your security forces back inside and set a trap for Martiel. Can we get a look at the interior layout?"

Corey turned the screen away for a few seconds, then displayed it again, this time showing the floor plan of the admin building.

"We can set an ambush in the lobby," Tam continued. "Let them get inside, and then take them down."

Maddock crossed his arms over his chest. "You're forgetting about the hostages. If this Martiel guy is using Avery as a human shield, we're screwed. And so is she."

"About that," Tam said with a sigh. Maddock's question had indirectly brought her to the second problem with Sievers' original plan, and she knew the men standing around her weren't going to like her solution. "We're going to be using less lethal weapons for the takedown. No guns."

The declaration was received about as well as she had anticipated.

"You're freaking kidding me," Bones said.

Tam shook her head. "Even if we didn't have to consider the hostages, we would have to do it this way. I don't have the authority to conduct a law enforcement operation on American soil."

"Screw authority. It's private property. They're trespassing."

Tam shook her head. "Mr. Valero's security team might get a pass, but technically the rest of us are vigilantes, and if we start killing people, the law won't be on our side. Especially not out here in the boonies."

Maddock raised his hands. "Bones, let's hear her out. I'm not saying I like the idea, but at least it ensures that Avery and Stone won't take friendly fire." He faced Tam. "What do you mean by less-lethal?"

Tam turned to Valero who took the cue. "I was able to acquire most of what you asked for. A dozen Taser X2 Defender stun guns, six cartridges for each. Three Mossberg 500 pump action shotguns and a case of Hammer bean bag rounds to go in them."

"Did you boys bring along any shotguns?" Tam asked.

Maddock shook his head.

"We'll have to flip for them then. Just remember, less-lethal can still be lethal, and that's what we're trying to avoid." She looked to Valero again. "What about the PHaSR rifle?"

Bones let out a guffaw, probably recalling the first time he and Maddock had met Tam in the jungles of Brazil. She had been working undercover for the FBI then, and armed with one of the futuristic dazzle guns. Despite the name—an homage to *Star Trek*, no doubt—the PHaSR, or Personal Halting and Stimulation Response rifle was a real device, which employed intense light and laser energy to blind and disorient someone, theoretically taking them out of the fight. The PHaSR had been developed for the military, but never really caught on.

Valero shook his head. "Couldn't find any at short notice, but I did pick up some Streamlight Tactical Flashlights. My security team uses them."

Tam shrugged off her disappointment. In terms of bang-for-buck, the tac-lights were probably a better choice, achieving the same effect—temporarily blinding a hostile—without the added bulk. "The goal here is to lure them in and then strike decisively. Lights and Tasers first, bean bag rounds if anyone is still standing. The Tasers will incapacitate for five to ten seconds, so we'll have to move in quick to disarm and restrain. Any questions?"

"How many bad guys are we talking about?" Willis asked.

"That I can't tell you. The news reports put the number of protestors at around a hundred and fifty, but to pull this off, Martiel will need to keep most of them right where they are. He'll probably take a dozen or so with him to take the facility. Any more than that—"

As Tam was trying to finish her assessment, a mobile phone ringtone sounded, distracting her. The phone belonged to Valero, and he turned away to answer the call. Tam had the uneasy feeling that it wasn't good news, and she was right.

Valero's head sagged in defeat as he put the phone away. "We're too late."

"What happened?"

"That was the site manager, Ray Spaulding. It's started. They came in posing as a news crew. When the security force tried to stop them, they used one of the hostages as a human shield and then opened up with automatic weapons. My security team was decimated. They've fallen back to the admin building, but they won't be able to hold out for long."

Maddock stiffened. "We have to go. Now."

Valero shook his head. "Thank you for trying, but it seems our window of opportunity has already closed."

Tam stepped forward and put a hand on his shoulder. "Tell your people inside to barricade the door. Hold them off until we can get there."

"I can't ask them to throw their lives away," Valero said.

"If we don't stop Martiel," Sievers said, "A lot more innocent people are gonna suffer and die."

"They don't have to fight," Tam said, hoping that it would be true. "They just need to buy us some time. Fifteen minutes."

Valero looked unsure but took out his phone. As he made the call, Tam turned back to the others. "Corey, you're going to be our eyes and ears. Coordinate with Valero and his people on the inside. They have to slow Martiel down but tell them not take any crazy chances. Everyone else…" She paused a beat and grinned remembering the part of Sievers' plan she was actually looking forward to. "Grab your gear. It's time to go jump out of a perfectly good airplane."

THIRTY-THREE

Avery averted her eyes as Martiel pushed her ahead of him, through the impromptu maze of bullet-pocked and blood-spattered K-rails. Her ears were still ringing from the tumult and the air stank of burnt gunpowder. In her peripheral vision, she could make out the unmoving shapes of the security guards who had been cut down in the onslaught.

While their attention had had been on her and Martiel, the rest of the men in the van had broken out automatic rifles and tactical gear from the Pelican cases and then slipped out the back to await the signal. When that signal had come, they had acted without mercy, gunning down at least four of the guards before any of them could return fire. Only one of Martiel's men had been injured, sustaining a flesh wound to the thigh that had slowed him down but not taken him out of the fight. The van, however, had been riddled with bullets. The windshield was a spiderweb of fracture lines, and the radiator was venting steam from several holes. But even if it had remained intact, they still would have been forced to proceed on foot because of the barricades.

Martiel continued to hide behind her, gun pressed to the side of her neck, even though there had been no return fire since the initial exchange. They were at the rear of the formation, along with Stone and the limping wounded man, while the five able-bodied shooters moved in a tight knot, weapons at the high ready. Avery had overheard one of them reporting that at least some of the security guards had retreated to the main building, but even if that was true, there was little the survivors could hope to accomplish. Martiel's deceptive and cowardly use of Avery as his human shield had allowed his smaller force to score a decisive victory. Now the odds were firmly in their favor.

Once past the barricades, they proceeded down the paved road to the rather plain looking entrance to the nearest building in the complex. There was just a single unmarked door with a large pull handle and lock plate equipped with an alphanumeric keypad. One of the men ran forward and tried the door, then looked back and shook his head. "Locked!"

"Blow it," Martiel said.

Another man carrying a small duffel bag ran up, knelt down before the door and took out a small packet which he taped in place next to the latch plate. He then took out a spool of what looked like speaker wire, attached an end of it to the packet, and then returned to the group, gesturing for the rest of them to move back and get down. When they were about fifty yards away, he dropped to a prone position and, after shouting a final warning, squeezed the detonator trigger.

A bright flash and a puff of smoke. The noise wasn't much louder than the reports of the assault rifles, but Avery felt the shock wave reverberate through her body. As the smoke cleared, she saw the door still mostly intact, swinging gently away on its hinges. The gunmen waited a few seconds to see if anyone inside was going to start shooting, and when that didn't happen, they began moving forward. Martiel pulled Avery to her feet and propelled her toward the entrance. When he got within about twenty yards, he put the gun away and cupped a hand to his mouth.

"Attention in the building!"

As the echoes of his shout died away, one of his men produced the bullhorn they had taken from a dead security guard at the front gate, and handed it to Martiel. He held it up to his mouth and depressed the trigger, which resulted in a loud squawk, right in Avery's ear. "Attention in the building. Mr. Spaulding, if you can hear me, I want to discuss a peaceful resolution."

A shout came from the entry. "What do you want?"

"Am I speaking to Mr. Ray Spaulding?"

"Yes. Who are you?"

"That's not important, Mr. Spaulding. What is important is that you listen carefully and follow my instructions without delay or deviation. If you do, I promise no further harm will come to anyone. I think there's been enough violence already, don't you?"

"What do you want?" Spaulding asked again.

"First, I need all your remaining security men to come outside, one at a time, with their weapons held over their heads. Once outside, they will be disarmed and restrained. Do you understand?"

"You promise not to shoot them?"

Avery felt Martiel grow tense with impatience. "I promise only that if you do not follow my instructions, everyone will suffer the consequences."

A momentary pause, then, "Okay. We're coming out now."

A figure wearing a black tactical uniform emerged from the doorway, his automatic rifle held high above his head with one hand. His other arm was bandaged across his chest with a makeshift sling, and a crude, blood-soaked bandage was wrapped around his biceps.

Martiel instructed the man to continue forward several more steps, and then to throw down his weapon and assume a kneeling position, after which he signaled for the next man to come out.

Only four men from the security detail had survived the attack at the gate, and of them, only three were ambulatory, but Spaulding gave his word that all the weapons had been removed from the building. Once the security team was dealt with, Martiel announced that he and his men would be coming in, and instructed everyone inside to gather in the lobby. Then, he handed off the bullhorn and drew his pistol, once again holding it to Avery's neck as he moved toward the building.

There were only about a dozen people in the lobby, including the critically wounded security guard who lay sprawled out on a table. Someone had cut away his uniform and begun basic first aid—bandaging his wounds and even starting an intravenous drip. The others were all face down on the floor, as instructed.

Martiel's men marched the zip-tied guards inside and forced them to kneel with others.

"Who's Spaulding?" Martiel barked.

"I am." A stout man wearing a short-sleeved dress shirt and Coke bottle spectacles looked up. Even though the air-conditioned lobby was uncomfortably cool, beads of perspiration were visible on his bald pate.

"Do you actually expect me to believe that this is everyone?"

"People are scared. A lot of them are hiding."

"I warned you what would happen if you didn't follow my instructions." Martiel regarded him with a skeptical eye for a moment. "But I'm not interested in hurting people, and I don't have time for recriminations. But I warn you, if any of those scared people cowering under their desks try anything, everyone in this room will pay the price."

"Understood."

"Excellent," Martiel said with a grin. "Now, if you would be so good as to show me to your cafeteria."

Spaulding might not have understood the unusual request, but Avery immediately grasped Martiel's intent. So, evidently, did Stone. "Snack time, right? A little brain food?'

Martiel answered with a knowing wink.

The cafeteria was only a short walk from the lobby. Martiel had brought along one of his men, leaving the others to watch over the hostages, and while he maintained his grip on Avery's arm, his manner was less aggressive than it had been outside. His ultimate victory was in sight, and he knew it. As they entered the fully-equipped institutional kitchen, he headed straight for the four-burner gas stove, barely able to contain his eagerness.

He let go of her arm and used both hands to unzip the backpack and take out the Brazen Head. He held it up, giving it a shake like a child trying to guess the contents of a wrapped Christmas gift, and then looked over at Avery. "You got it to work before, didn't you?"

"In Paris. But only with distilled water."

"I was tempted to try it out on the plane, but I didn't want to waste the gift, especially since I don't know how long the effects will last."

Stone chuckled. "It would be pretty embarrassing if you reverted to stupid before carrying out your diabolical plan."

Martiel ignored the jibe, and instead placed the Brazen Head on one of the burners. He glanced at Avery again. "Like this, right? Hess' notes were a bit vague."

She nodded. "It will take a few minutes to heat up, just like a tea kettle."

Even though she was afraid and a little angry at being forced to help him, she was also curious to see what would happen when the Brazen Head began exhaling its mind-altering vapors.

He turned the knob, and heard a faint whooshing sound as a circle of blue flames appeared under the flat base of the brass automaton. An uncomprehending Spaulding hung back a few steps, as did Martiel's gunman but Stone, despite himself, took a step closer.

After just a few seconds, the Brazen Head began ticking like an old radiator, the metal heating and expanding, the water inside making rushing sounds as the pressure built. Even before the first wisps of steam became visible, a foul odor filled the air.

Spaulding shuddered. "What is that smell? It's disgusting."

There was a softer clicking noise as clockwork gears began turning inside the artifact. Its eyes opened, flickering with barely visible light. and then its mouth opened too, issuing the cryptic haunting refrain that Avery had almost forgotten about.

"*Memento mori. Memento mori.*"

"Remember you are mortal," Martiel whispered.

Stone laughed again. "I think it's trying to tell you

something."

Avery laughed, too, unable to help herself. Her sense of terror was slipping away by degrees, replaced by a strange calm.

Memento mori, she thought. *Remember you will die. Everyone dies. Rich man, poor man, beggarman, thief. There was no escaping it. Nobody was immortal.*

It didn't matter if Martiel succeeded because eventually, he would die too.

Maybe Stone was right. Maybe everything—finding the Brazen Head, solving the mystery of its purpose and function, and ultimately, losing it to Martiel—maybe all of that was inevitable. Maybe everything happened the way it did because it couldn't happen any other way, and if that was true, nothing really mattered at all.

The shiny brass head looked vaguely angelic as it floated above the flames, white steam began rushing from its mouth and nostrils, chanting its solemn wisdom.

"Oh my, God," she whispered, giggling a little. "I'm totally tripping."

Martiel leaned in close, sucking greedily at the vapors. "This is amazing," he said, his voice dream-like, full of awe, though that might simply have been caused by Avery's own hallucinatory experience.

"Memento mori. Memento mori."

The words carried her out of her body. The kitchen walls seemed to shift and stretch like taffy. Thom Martiel, hunched over the Brazen Head, looked both silly and demonic—like something from a cheap carnival house of horrors.

The familiar crack of automatic gunfire in the distance snapped her back to reality.

Martiel looked up abruptly. "Sounds like someone decided to play hero," he remarked. "I warned them what would—"

He was cut off by the sound of another report, but this one was louder and deeper, like the boom of a cannon. A moment later, there was another just like it, and then all was quiet save for the mechanical voice of the Brazen Head.

"Memento mori. Memento mori."

A look of sober worry flitted across Martiel's face. He turned to the gunman. "Find out what's going on." As the man started from the room, Martiel called out again. "Wait. Take these two with you." He drew his pistol, pointed it at Avery and Stone. Then he grabbed Spaulding's arm. "Take me to the master terminal."

"I can't—"

"Don't test me," Martiel warned. "You can and you will. I don't need you alive to get past through the biometrics on the door. I'll drag your corpse if I have to."

Avery lost sight of both men as Martiel's goon stepped between her and them, jabbing the barrel of his automatic rifle at her. "Move."

She complied, still feeling a little numb and dislocated from the mind-altering effects of the steam cloud. As they moved down the connecting hallway, she thought she could hear shouts, not just one person, but many voices jumbled together in an atonal buzz of crowd noise. Underpinning it were bursts of a strange crackling sound, much louder than the clockwork ticking of the Brazen Head. For some reason, it reminded Avery of a party, and the thought almost made her giggle again.

The gunman, however, appeared much more alarmed by the tumult. "What the hell?" he muttered, pushing past Avery and Stone.

As he did, Stone leaned close to Avery, and in an urgent whisper, said, "Keep him busy."

She let out a snort of laughter, and turned to ask for an explanation, but Stone was already gone, sprinting back the way they had come. The gunman didn't even glance back, but continued forward at a jog.

Avery laughed again. "Party pooper," she said, and then headed after the gunman, wondering what exactly she was supposed to do to keep the man occupied, especially since he was already thoroughly distracted.

She was about twenty steps behind the man when he reached the door to the lobby. He paused there for a moment, then pressed his back to the wall beside the door and, with his weapon still raised to his shoulder, cautiously reached down with his left hand and gave the panic bar a push. As the door swung open, he brought his left hand back up to steady the rifle and then swung around the corner....

And was knocked back as if he'd been hit by a charging bull. The unfired rifle flew from his suddenly nerveless grip. Simultaneously, another cannon-like boom rolled, deafeningly loud in the close confines of the hallway.

The gunman writhed on the floor, curling like a worm on a fishhook, clutching his abdomen, though there didn't appear to be any blood. That surprised Avery; judging by the decibel level of the shot that had felled him, she expected him to be blown in half.

An imposing figure filled the doorway, the smoking weapon held to his shoulder and still trained on the fallen man. Avery let out a squeal of delight as she recognized him.

"Bones! What are you doing here?"

Uriah "Bones" Bonebrake looked back at her and grinned. "Yo, chica. I was just in the neighborhood and thought I'd drop by and see if you want to party."

She threw her arms around him, squeezing him as if afraid that he might evaporate if she let go.

Bones chuckled. "I guess that's a 'yes.'"

THIRTY-FOUR

Tam rushed the already stunned gunman and jammed the business end of the Taser X2 Defender into his thigh, depressing the trigger a second time. The device sent another sustained pulse of current through the wires trailing from the barbed probes, as well as into the leads at the end of the Taser, creating a massive full-body muscle seizure. The Taser crackled for exactly five seconds, and then the pulse ended, leaving the gunman a quivering mass on the floor. Tam kicked his assault rifle out of reach and stuffed his hands into a ready pair of flexicuffs, cinching them tight.

The operation had gone well so far, aside from one minor setback. Matt Barnaby's main chute lines had gotten tangled, forcing him to cut away and use his reserve chute, which in turn resulted in him missing the drop zone by a few hundred yards and getting hung up in a tree, but there had been no "dirt darts," as Bones had put it, and that meant they were ahead of the curve. Matt had managed to extricate himself, but it would take him a good five minutes to link up with the others. Since every second was critical, Tam had made the decision not to wait, but instead instructed Matt to establish an overwatch position.

They had made it to the administration building without being noticed. Martiel's men, trusting the security of the perimeter established by the protestors, had not even bothered to shut the door to the lobby, giving Tam's team the element of surprise. They had made a tactical entry, taking down the gunmen in a matter of seconds. One of the men had gotten off a few wild shots before Sievers nailed him with a bean bag round, but none of the bullets had found a flesh and blood target. But Tam wasn't ready to breathe easy just yet. That would happen only after Avery and Stone were safe, and Thom Martiel was in custody.

As if to underscore the fact that things could still go wrong, another shotgun blast thundered through the lobby as someone took down a sixth gunman who had shown up late to the party. The report silenced the growing restless murmur from the hostages, tacitly reminding them to stay flat and quiet until someone gave the all clear.

Tam wheeled in the direction of the sound, and saw Bones grinning at her from a side door. He wasn't alone. "Hey, my date showed up," Bones chortled. "Now we can get this party started."

Maddock, who had just finished securing another of the gunmen, shot to his feet and bounded across the room to embrace his half-sister. Tam was just a few steps behind him, but instead of a joyous reunion, she was interested only in getting answers.

"Where are they?" she asked. "Stone and Martiel?"

Avery looked back, her eyes unfocused as if still in the process of waking up from a dream. "What?"

"I think she's a little buzzed," Bones said.

"Avery!" Tam said, taking a sharper tone. "Don't make me cuss at you, girl. Snap out of it."

To her credit, Avery managed to open her eyes a little wider. "Stone. He left. I don't know where he went." Bones was right; she sounded drunk. "Back to the kitchen, maybe?"

"The kitchen?"

"That's where we left the Brazen Head."

"Is Martiel there?"

Avery shook her head. "No. He wanted Mr. Spaulding to take him to the master terminal."

Tam bit back a blistering curse and half turned away, and took out her phone. Rather than procure additional communications equipment, they had opted for the simpler solution of using a walkie-talkie style app on their mobile devices. "Corey, are you there?"

Corey Dean's voice came back immediately. "Read you loud and clear, over."

"Martiel is headed for the server farm. I need you to talk me in, over."

"Roger, wait one."

A couple seconds passed, and then a different voice issued from the phone. "Break, break, this is Matt. Tam, I've got a whole bunch of civilian vehicles coming your way on the main road. I think you're about to have company. Over."

Tam growled softly as she processed this news. She didn't know if someone had leaked the news of their covert assault to the protestors or if this had been their plan all along, but she knew one thing for sure. They wouldn't be able to hold off four carloads of good ol' boys intent on exercising their Second Amendment rights in defense of their Fourth. Not with Tasers, flashlights and three shotguns loaded with bean bag rounds.

"Corey, did Mr. Valero copy that?"

Wayne Valero's voice came over the line. "I did."

"I need you to contact the sheriff's department. Let them know what's happening in here. Stick to the script, but tell them that if they don't find a way to get these protestors under control, we will defend ourselves. With lethal force, if necessary."

The "script" to which she was referring was a hasty cover story in which Tam's team was a group of private security contractors hired to evacuate Iron River personnel from the facility. That story would hold up as long as they didn't leave a trail of dead American civilians in their wake, which was the reason for taking the less-lethal route, but if the situation continued to escalate, she would have no choice but to take the gloves off.

As one of her weapons instructors had been fond of saying, "Better to be judged by twelve than carried by six."

"I'll do what I can," Valero promised. "But it might take some time to get things moving."

"Understood. Tam, out." She put the phone away and turned to the others. "Guys, we're going to have company."

She picked out one of the recently liberated security guards. "I'm putting you in charge of the civilians. If there's a way to get them out of here safely, do it. Otherwise, find a hole to hide them in. Avery, you go to the kitchen and see if you can find Stone. The rest of you, start collecting weapons and magazines. I'm going after Martiel."

"Are you sure that's a good idea?" Bones said. "If it's as bad as it sounds, we're going to need every gun on the line if we're gonna make it out of here alive."

"If Thom Martiel reaches the master terminal, surviving tonight will be the least of our worries."

THIRTY-FIVE

As he moved through the corridors of the administration building, Gavin Stone felt like a passenger in his own body. He navigated the maze-like environs like a drop of water sliding down a windshield, following an invisible yet inevitable path that could not help but take him to his destination. He did not pause at each junction to consider which way to go; he simply knew, on an unconscious level, which direction would take him where he needed to go.

There was a logic to the layout of the complex, a mathematical pattern woven into the architecture of the place. It defied his ability to describe with words, and yet was so basic, so obvious, that he followed it with the certainty of a migrating bird winging south for the winter.

Though he had mocked Martiel for seeking the artificial enhancement of the nootropic steam from the Brazen Head, he could not argue that it was potent, particularly for someone with a highly-ordered brain.

Someone like himself.

He came to a set of unmarked double doors and knew instinctively that what he sought lay behind them, but when he pulled on the handle, the doors did not open for him.

Locked. Access denied.

Stone glanced down at the numeric keypad beside the door, taking note of the manufacturer and model. It was a commonly used brand, not the absolute best but adequate for internal security. The system utilized a proximity badge reader to automatically release the door for anyone with an RFID chip enabled employee ID card—like the kind Ray Spaulding had worn from a lanyard around his neck—but if for any reason the system could not read the card, the person could manually enter a unique code—typically four digits—to get through. There was also, Stone knew, a thirteen-digit setup code used by the manufacturer for reprogramming and installing firmware updates.

He effortlessly recalled the code for this particular system, keyed it in, and heard the satisfying click of the latch releasing.

The doors opened into a wide hallway that immediately began a gradual downward slope. A cool breeze wafted from the sunken corridor, and a barely perceptible energy seemed to flow through the air, which to Stone's heightened senses felt like the buzzing of a swarm of mosquitoes. The hum grew louder with each step he took, confirming what he already knew to be true; he had found the underground passage connecting the administration building to the server building.

He quickened his pace, almost to a run.

Another set of double doors blocked access to the far end of the passage, but there were no security measures to overcome. He threw them wide and stepped into a vast enclosure that was as cold as the inside of a refrigerator.

Directly in front of him was an aisle, lined on either side with two-story high racks of computer hardware festooned with blinking LEDs. The aisle seemed to go on forever, stretching out to the vanishing point. A wide transverse aisle offered two other choices—left and right—but he knew that either direction would only mean more of the same, row after row after row of nearly identical computer servers, lined up like bookshelves in the world's biggest library. Thick cables snaked up from the server banks, joining together on suspended metal racks overhead. Above that, mirroring the symmetry of the servers, were the pipes and ducts that constantly refreshed the coolant system without which the entire facility would overheat or worse, catch on fire. The white epoxy-coated floors reflected and distributed some of the light shining down from the high ceiling, but the interior was so enormous, so cavernous, as to convey the impression of gloom, and when combined with the chilly temperature, the effect was funereal, but the facility had not been designed with human comfort in mind. This was a world built for machines, and on a scale that made humans seem like ants standing beside a freeway.

And yet, it was an open book to Stone.

He gazed up at the suspended wiring, seeing it not simply as a way to transmit power and data, but as a nervous system—metal and fiber optic neurons connecting the individual cells of Mystic's digital hive mind. The servers stored and indexed the data that not only managed investor assets but also informed the massive simulated reality where every conceivable outcome was examined. The decisions about what to do with that data, however, were handled elsewhere, and all of it was controlled by the operating system—Mystic's brain.

He knew that some data facilities provided bicycles or motorized Segway scooters for maintenance technicians to reach far-flung destinations within the complex, but he did not see anything like that near the entrance and did not have the time to go looking. Besides, if he was right—and he knew he was—the master terminal was only about a quarter of a mile away. He did not need to follow the cables visually. A glance was enough to reveal the underlying mathematical pattern of the design. Guided by his internal GPS wayfinder, Stone took off again, running down the long aisle.

The master terminal was housed inside a glass cube. roughly forty feet on each side. The top of the enclosure was open, and high above it, the data lines came together in a thick tree trunk-like cluster that ran down to a bank of side-by-side processors, each the size of a household refrigerator. Alongside the processors was what appeared to be a simple computer workstation. Atop a utilitarian white desk. were dual flat screen monitors, one of which was filled with monochrome green text—computer code. The other displayed the all too familiar header of the Immortal Mysteries Forum. Hunched over the desk, furiously typing on the ergonomic keyboard, was the Immortal himself.

As Stone crossed the remaining few yards to the cube, he spotted a figure crumpled on the floor behind Martiel. It was Ray Spaulding, lying facedown in a small pool of blood.

Stone was momentarily taken aback. He had not expected Martiel to make good on his threat to kill the man. Despite his aggressiveness in leading the attack on the facility, he had not shown himself to be a killer of the up-close-and-personal variety. Had he misjudged his foe yet again?

After a moment or two, however, he saw the slight rise and fall of Spaulding's chest. He was alive after all, bleeding from a scalp wound. Martiel had probably pistol-whipped him once he had what he wanted: access to the Mystic operating system.

Stone ran up to the glass door and grasped the pull handle. Locked, as expected. The keypad mounted beside it was different, not only a higher-quality unit but also equipped with a handprint scanner. He knew better than to try a bypass code; this system didn't come with backdoors. Instead, he pounded his fists against the inch-thick glass and shouted.

Martiel's head came up, and he glanced over his shoulder. His face registered surprise, but only for a fleeting moment, after which he grinned in triumph. He walked over to the door a pressed a button on the security panel. A crackle of static, and then his voice issued from a small speaker. "Too late, Gavin. You lose."

"I don't think so," Stone retorted. "You're out of time. If you leave now, you just might be able to escape."

"Escape? Why on earth would I want to do that?" Martiel shook his head, still grinning. "That's not how this is going to end, Stone. My people are coming to retake control of the facility. Your friends failed. The cavalry isn't coming. The authorities aren't going to let anyone else in until it's too late. Besides, I'm almost done. It's amazing what you can accomplish with a little boost, isn't it? But I'm glad you're here. It makes my victory that much sweeter."

Stone started to hurl another impotent rejoinder at the glass, but Martiel had already turned away. Stone kicked the glass, but if the other man heard, he gave no indication.

Stone was close enough now to read the lines of computer code on the master terminal display screen. Mystic was a Unix-like system, which even under normal circumstances, he could read almost as effortlessly as plain English. With his brain still energized by the Brazen Head's psychedelic vapors, he didn't even have to think about what he was seeing. He simply knew.

Martiel was changing the security of the operating system, removing the restrictions that had necessitated the invasion of the facility, and doing so in such a way that his actions could not be easily reversed. It would take Valero's technicians days, perhaps even weeks to figure out what he had done and restore it to its original configuration, allowing Martiel and Furst plenty of time to wreck the world's monetary system and usher in their new world order.

The other screen revealed how Martiel was using the Immortal Mysteries Forum to communicate with his network of followers, not only coordinating his human assets in the financial sector, but also the armed protesters laying siege to the Iron River facility.

The latter were closing in on the complex.

Stone pounded the glass again, this time paying attention to the way it vibrated under his fist. He glanced around, looking for a tool, a fire axe or something to either smash the glass or force the lock, but there was nothing with which to even improvise a battering ram, and even if there had been something like that, he knew it would be a futile effort. It would take considerably more force than he could supply to break it.

Think. He told himself. *Can't beat the lock. Can't break through the glass. What's left?*

He looked around again, considering whether it might

be possible to climb the cables, shinny over and then slide down the trunk into cube. Tam or Billy Sievers probably could have made the climb, but he didn't have their strength or stamina, and even if he somehow succeeded, Martiel had a gun and would shoot him as soon as he cleared the wall.

Or would he?

Stone knew he had misjudged Martiel in the past, but he had spent the last nine hours studying the man's behavior. Martiel had no compunction about ordering his acolytes to slaughter the innocent, but taking a life by his own hand might give him pause, particularly if the life in question was his sworn nemesis. Killing Stone would deprive Martiel of his greatest victory.

No, he wouldn't pull the trigger. Stone was certain of that.

Stone still doubted that he could ascend forty-odd feet of insulated cable, but now he realized there was another way to stop Martiel's mad plan. He had learned something else about the man; Martiel, for all his grandiose posturing, was a coward.

Stone backtracked to the nearest bank of servers, and without a moment's hesitation, began climbing the rack like it was a ladder. The shelves bent and flexed as he climbed, circuit boards and panels crunching underfoot, but the racks bore his weight.

Martiel's voice, barely audible over the persistent hum of the server farm, issued from the speaker again. "I understand that a place like this is a playground to men like you and me, but seriously, you're torturing the metaphor."

Stone didn't acknowledge him, didn't even look his way. Another step up brought him high enough to clamber onto the top of the server assembly. He crawled forward until he was over the narrow gap between the back-to-back server stacks, and then rose to his feet.

"Seriously, Gavin," Martiel said, "what are you up to? What can you possibly hope to accomplish up there?"

By way of an answer, Stone flexed his knees and

wrapped his hands around the cables, gripping them like the stalk of a weed he intended to pull up by the roots, and then, with a heave, he wrenched them loose. A flash of blue light briefly illuminated the dark gap between the servers as the electrical supply tried to arc across the broken circuit, then all the lights in the stacked servers under him blinked out simultaneously.

"There are over ten thousand servers in here," Martiel said. "Are you going to pull every plug?"

Stone cautiously held up the frayed wires, inspecting the ends and began peeling away the data transfer lines one by one until he was left with just two thick power cables, each wrapped in heavy duty insulation. He separated them, holding one in each hand, and gingerly brought them together. A loud snap and a flash of bright light. For just an instant, Stone could smell the sharp, clean odor of ozone, but the brisk circulation of cooled air whisked it away just as quickly.

Satisfied with the results, he at last turned and looked down at Martiel. "No, this should do the trick. I'm going to start a fire."

"A fire?" Martiel scoffed. "In here? All that will do is trip the automated fire protection system."

Stone nodded. "Exactly."

Careful to avoid crossing the hot wires, Stone took the cables in his left hand and with his right, pulled his shirt up and over his head. The frigid air immediately raised gooseflesh all over his body and started his teeth chattering. He did his best to ignore the discomfort, knowing it would be only momentary, and instead knelt down and stuffed the shirt into the gap between the server stacks.

"You'll flood this whole section of the building with heptafluoropropane gas," Martiel said, his voice no longer as confident as it had been a few moments before.

"That's right." Stone took the cables in both hands again and brought them down close to the wadded-up piece of cotton-polyester blend fabric, hoping it would be flammable enough to ignite and trigger the fire suppression system.

"You'll suffocate," Martiel said.

"So will you. You might want to leave now."

"Spaulding is in here with me." A palpable measure of panic sounded in Martiel's voice. "You'll kill him."

"Maybe," Stone said, not looking up. "But that's on you, not me."

"You're bluffing. I know you, Stone. You don't want to die."

"You don't know anything about me," Stone said, and brought the cables together again, triggering another brilliant display and a fresh whiff of ozone. With a faint whooshing noise, the shirt burst into flames. "Time to find out if you really are Immortal."

THIRTY-SIX

Tam was just about to ask Corey to remotely release the doors to the server building when a loud claxon alarm sounded. She keyed the push-to-talk button on her phone and shouted to be heard over the din. "Corey, what's happening?"

"The fire suppression system in the server building has been activated," Corey replied.

"And what does that mean? Is there a fire?"

Was this Martiel's plan, she wondered, to destroy the Mystic server farm if he could not take control of it?

"I'm not sure, but you can't go in there. The air in there is filled with a halocarbon gas compound that displaces oxygen."

"I need to know what's going on in there. Are there any cameras you can tap into? And while you're at it, can you shut that alarm off?"

The claxons ceased abruptly, supplying an answer to the latter request, but that was where her luck ended. "Most of our video surveillance is outside," Valero said, over the comm-link. "There aren't any cameras in the server building."

Tam clenched her fists in frustration, but before she could put what she was feeling into words, another voice came over the line. "Tam, it's me." Avery still sounded a little out of it. "I've got the Brazen Head. I mean, I'm here with it. It's still cooling down. I'm trying to find some oven mitts to—"

"Avery, what about Stone? Is he there?"

"No. I don't know where he is."

Tam did know. "He's in the server building. He must have pulled the fire alarm to stop Martiel. I need to get in there, Corey."

"There's nothing you can do for him. Not until the gas

cycles out."

"How long will that take?"

She was halfway through the question when the latch mechanism clicked.

"The release is localized, so the concentration will be higher the closer you get to the source," Valero said. "The suppressant isn't toxic at concentrations of less than nine percent. I still think you should wait a bit, but you should be okay as long as you get in and out quick." Then he added, "Provided there isn't an actual fire."

"I don't know if you'll get reception in there," Corey said. "I'm going to text you the floor plan of the server building."

"Got it." Tam opened the door and started down the long passage to the server building at a fast jog. When she opened the second set of doors, she half expected to find a charred stinking ruin beyond, but instead saw only endless aisles of computer servers. There was no sign that any disturbance had occurred, and not even a hint of smoke in the air. Given the immensity of the place, that was hardly a surprise; the server building made the Superdome feel like a broom closet.

She opened the message with the layout schematic, orienting it in the same direction she was facing and plotted the most direct route to the master terminal, which thankfully was almost a straight shot. As she progressed, she noticed a distinctly pungent odor in the air and fainter still, the smell of burnt plastic and ozone. She knew she should probably slow down and take only shallow breaths, but the knowledge that Stone might be unconscious and suffocating compelled her to move even faster, breathing in more of the potentially tainted air.

Her heart skipped a beat when she spied a misshapen lump on the floor directly ahead. It was definitely a body, but a closer look revealed the face of a stranger—almost certainly the site manager, Ray Spaulding. He was alive and breathing but unconscious, though Tam guessed this had more to do with the still bleeding head wound than exposure to the fire suppressant gas. A long smear of blood continuing up the aisle suggested that someone had dragged him away from the gas-saturated area.

"Stone," Tam muttered, hopeful. But where was he?

She stepped around Spaulding and kept going, following the blood trail to the glass enclosure where the master terminal was located. The room was empty, the door wide open.

The sharp smell was even stronger here, stinging Tam's eyes. She buried her mouth and nose in the curve of her shoulder, hoping that the fabric of her shirt would give her at least a little protection from the gas, and went in.

On the workstation desk, the dual-screen display was still displaying the last activity. One screen was blank except for two words in glowing green monochrome.

CHANGES SAVED

A knot of dread twisted Tam's gut.
I'm too late, she thought.
The other screen was showing the Immortal Mysteries Forum, and in one corner, a private message pop-up window displayed a text conversation between the Immortal and one of his supporters. Tam's gaze flashed to the last transmitted message, and then she spun on her heel and raced from the room.

Billy Sievers watched as a silver Ford F150 pickup, outfitted with a six-inch suspension lift kit, rolled past the gatehouse at the entry point to the compound and then slowly but relentlessly advanced toward the first of the K-rails blocking the road. When the reinforced front bumper kissed the corner of the barrier, the driver put on the brakes. Sievers didn't need to be in the cab to know that the man was shifting the four-wheel-drive gear box to low range. A moment later, the truck began inching forward again, and this time the concrete barrier moved as well, scraping across the pavement and opening a gap wide enough for the vehicle to pass through, at which point the truck moved out of the field of view of the security camera supplying the live feed to the monitor Sievers was viewing at the security station in the lobby. With the big Ford out of the way, Sievers could see the long line of vehicles waiting behind it, many of them also pickups, their beds fully loaded with armed men wearing Carhartts and camouflage.

"The sheep of America will rest easy tonight," said "Bones" Bonebrake, who was standing behind Sievers. Bones was looking over his shoulder which posed no difficulty for the towering Cherokee Indian and former Navy SEAL.

"How's that?"

"All the rednecks are here," growled Bones.

"Bones hates rednecks," explained Willis Sanders. "I ain't got much love for them, neither."

"Good for the sheep," Sievers said, with a nod, "bad for us."

"We might be outnumbered," Maddock said, "but there's only one way in here, and that door is only wide enough to let in one or two in at a time. It's a chokepoint. That takes away their biggest advantage."

"Just like the Battle of Thermopylae," someone else suggested.

Bones shook his head. "Well, aren't you just a ray of sunshine, Professor?"

Pete Chapman shrugged. "You know me, always looking for that silver lining."

Despite the dire circumstances, Sievers allowed himself a grin. It felt good to be surrounded by fellow warriors, especially in the face of such overwhelming odds. He imagined the three hundred Spartans at Thermopylae had drawn strength from a similar camaraderie.

Right before they all got slaughtered.

And yet, part of him could not help but identify with the men outside. He didn't agree with their narrow xenophobic and downright ignorant worldview, but he knew where it came from because he came from a similar place, culturally speaking. He also understood why Tam had looked for an alternative to simply going in with guns blazing. He would have preferred a less-lethal solution to this problem as well, but if the local authorities didn't intervene soon, there would be bloodshed. Theirs and his.

Sievers squeezed the pistol grip of the AR-15 he had taken from one of Martiel's assault team. They were past the point of using stun guns and beanbag rounds. Whatever happened now would be a clear-cut case of self-defense, though he doubted any of them would survive to defend that decision.

"Here they come," Professor announced.

Sievers brought his gaze back to the monitor. The big Ford must have cleared the last of the K-rails because now a procession of vehicles moved through the surveillance camera's field of view.

Maddock switched to a different camera—one mounted in the parking area right outside the building—which showed the approaching army, about two dozen vehicles, and possibly as many as eighty men, all loaded for bear and spoiling for a fight.

"Looks like we're on our own," Maddock said, taking a knee at one corner of the desk and raising his captured rifle to his shoulder.

"Always wondered what it felt like to be at the Alamo," Sievers muttered, assuming a similar stance at the opposite corner.

He could still see the display screen in the corner of his eye. The procession of vehicles was flowing down the road, and the lead trucks turning toward the solitary entrance and then going right past it, making room for those behind it or possibly trying to establish perimeter security.

Sievers placed the butt of the assault rifle against his shoulder, lined the front sight post up with the door, and flipped the fire selector from "safe" to "single."

And waited.

"Any day now," Bones muttered.

Sievers checked the monitor again. The cars and trucks were all stopped now, spaced out at intervals of forty or fifty feet, and armed men were piling out, their weapons at the ready, but they did not appear to be organizing for an assault. Instead, they simply remained where they were, in a defensive posture.

And then, for no apparent reason, they lowered their weapons and climbed back into the waiting vehicles, and then as swiftly as it had arrived, the procession snaked away, heading back down the narrow road out of the complex.

"What the hell?" Bones said. "Maddock, did you forget to put on deodorant this morning?"

Sievers ignored the banter, safed his rifle and rose to his feet, not quite able to believe what he was seeing. He kept watching until the last vehicle disappeared from view.

"Thinks it's some kind of trick?" he asked, looking over at Maddock. "A staged retreat to draw us out?"

"I don't know about you guys," Bones said, "but I'm fine right here."

Maddock took out his phone. "Matt, what's happening out there?"

"They're hightailing," Barnaby replied. "Maybe somebody warned them off."

"We're never that lucky," Maddock said.

As if to offer confirmation, an out of breath Tam Broderick burst from the door behind them. "Stop them!" she panted.

Bones snorted. "You're kidding, right?"

"Tam," Sievers said, "It's over. They're bugging out."

But Tam shook her head and then, as if it explained everything, said. "They've got Stone."

EPILOGUE—GO!

Landstuhl, Germany—Three days later

"You really think this will work?" Tam asked.

"I do," Avery said. It was not the first time Tam had asked, and Avery knew that, more than anything else, what the leader of the Myrmidons was looking for was simple reassurance. After losing so much in their battle with the Immortal, Tam was understandably reluctant to allow herself to hope, particularly when what Avery was asking her to believe verged on the miraculous.

She opened her backpack and took out the Brazen Head, placing it on the bedside table. "I've been doing a lot of reading up on this," she said. "And there's a lot of research to back it up. Hallucinogenic compounds like LSD have been shown to stimulate brain activity and even restore damaged synaptic pathways. That's how Ray Spaulding was able to survive exposure to the fire suppressant. And he only got a small dose of the vapors."

Spaulding had actually made a remarkable recovery not only from his exposure to the fire extinguishing halocarbons but also from the head injury he had received from the butt of Martiel's pistol, which bore further testimony to the efficacy of the vapors.

Avery did not add that the same physical process had enabled Thom Martiel to escape suffocation in the cloud of heptafluoropropane gas released after Stone's electrical fire. Stone had survived as well, though whether he was still alive was one of many unanswered questions about what had happened that night in Spokane.

What they knew for certain was that, following the alarm and the activation of the fire suppression system, someone—presumably Martiel—had dragged Ray Spaulding out of the master terminal enclosure and away from the suffocating cloud, after which that same person had made as-yet-unknown alterations to the Mystic source code before using the Immortal Mysteries Forum to arrange a pick-up at one of the fire exits on the side of the admin building. While Tam had been cautiously making her way down the aisle to the master terminal, Martiel had taken a circuitous route to reach the exit behind her. A review of the feed from the security camera monitoring that door showed two men—Martiel and Stone, though their faces were never turned to the camera—leaving the building and getting in one of the protestor's vehicles. The owner of the truck had covered his license plate with silver tape, making an identification impossible.

Immediately following the pick-up, the protestors had picked up and left en masse, overwhelming the abilities of on-scene law enforcement agencies to maintain control. The sheriff's department, not realizing that the protestors were at least partly complicit in the murder of several Iron River security guards, had simply removed their barricades and allowed the vehicles to depart. The subsequent investigation had identified several of the protestors—some had come from as far away as Tennessee—but none of them admitted to knowledge of the clandestine assault on the data facility, or any personal knowledge of Martiel's current whereabouts. The trail had gone cold.

It was also unclear what Martiel's plan for Mystic had actually been, or if he had succeeded. Wayne Valero had a team of software engineers going through the code with a fine-toothed comb, but so far they had not found any changes to the operating system. Since shutting Mystic down would have been disastrous, everyone was holding their collective breath, waiting for Martiel's data bomb to go off. But when the next day dawned, and the financial markets opened, it was mostly business as usual, and with each passing hour, the likelihood of an attack seemed to diminish. The only unusual activity reported in the markets were a number of unscheduled and sizable payments to the IMF and World Bank loan accounts of several developing nations in Africa and Asia. Funding for the loan payments had come from Nutria Mills Inc. and from the personal accounts of Nutria Mills' chairman Peter Furst, but neither Furst nor anyone from his company were commenting on the profoundly charitable gesture. The unexpected transactions caused a slight but only temporary dip in the currency markets.

Tam had recognized this activity as the opening move in Martiel's plan to crash the currency system, but there had been no subsequent market manipulations. After three days, it seemed evident that someone had pulled the plug on the scheme. The misstep, if that was indeed what it was, had put a dent in Nutria Mills finances, and while the company would almost certainly recover in time, there was no immediate danger of Furst using his fortune as seed money to finance an economic apocalypse.

It was a victory, but both bittersweet and incomplete. Peter Furst had, for the time being at least, escaped justice for his part in the criminal conspiracy. The Immortal, aka Thom Martiel—if that was his real name—remained at large, and even though the Immortal Mysteries Forum had been shut down, the rabid sentiments that had fueled it remained every bit as potent. Worst of all, Gavin Stone was either a hostage or dead.

The Myrmidons would be very busy for the foreseeable future.

Greg Johns and Kasey Kim had both been relocated to the Landstuhl Regional Medical Facility, the primary medical care facility for the US military outside of the United States. Greg would make a full recovery, but the outlook for Kasey was less uncertain. She had been extubated and was breathing on her own, without supplemental oxygen, which was a hopeful sign, but she had not yet regained consciousness and was only partly responsive to stimulus which was why Tam and Avery had made the decision to stop in on their way to Zurich, where they would return the Brazen Head to Maxim Loew.

Avery reached into her backpack again and, after a quick check to make sure that none of the staff were looking, removed a portable single-burner hot plate. She found an electrical outlet, plugged it in and then placed the Brazen Head on the burner. After a few minutes, she heard the familiar ticking and stirring sounds as the water began heating up.

"Once this gets going," Avery said, "we'll probably want to clear out for a few minutes."

Tam looked over at Greg who nodded, and then they both turned and stepped through the door. Avery followed on their heels, closing the door to the private room behind her.

"You sure that stuff is safe?" Tam said. "I mean, you were pretty loopy back at Iron River. And don't even get me started on what happened to you in Scotland."

"I'm fine," Avery said. "I actually feel great. Energized."

"What about acid flashbacks?" Greg said. "I've heard those can happen months, even years later."

Avery frowned at him. "Not helpful." She put a reassuring hand on Tam's shoulder. "Kasey will be fine."

"Yeah, but will she be able to pass a drug test?"

Avery could only shrug.

Just then, they heard a voice from behind the door, the voice of the automaton, chanting its weird mechanical message.

"*Memento mori. Memento mori.*"

"What on earth?" Tam said, looking alarmed as she reached for the doorknob.

Avery winced. "Oops. Forgot about that."

"Does it have a mute button?"

Before Avery could answer, the nurse—a large African-American woman who could have passed for Tam's bigger, slightly meaner twin sister—stepped out of the next room down the hall. She immediately noticed the three of them loitering outside Kasey's room, put her hands on her hips and glared at them accusingly "What's all that commotion?"

"Sorry," Avery said guiltily. "It's the TV. We thought

maybe...uh, you know. Stimulation."

"Y'all are stimulating the entire floor."

"I'll turn it down." Avery didn't know how she was going to make good on the promise, but she figured she had to do something to placate the nurse, so she reached for the door handle. When she opened the door, a cloud of foul-smelling steam rolled out into the corridor.

"Oh, my," cried the nurse, starting toward them. "What is going on in there?"

"It's aromatherapy," Tam said quickly.

"That's right," Greg echoed. He took a step forward, trying to block the woman's path. "She's Korean. That's kimchee you're smelling. It's her favorite—"

"I know what kimchee is," the nurse shot back, "and that ain't it."

Avery grabbed a quick breath of mostly fresh air and then hurried into the room. The air was thick with sulfurous vapors, but she plowed through the haze to the table where the automaton kept chattering away.

"Memento mori."

She switched off the hotplate. It would take a few minutes for the air to clear, but she knew that if she could rapidly cool the Brazen Head, maybe running cold water over it in the sink, it would stop talking, so she ducked into the bathroom and grabbed a towel to protect her hands before grabbing ahold of the hot metal.

That was when she heard someone coughing.

She hurried out of the bathroom and found Kasey, head raised, one hand covering her mouth and nose. Her bleary eyes met Avery's and then she turned her head toward the doorway where Tam, Greg and the nurse were all trying to crowd through.

She stared at them for a moment, her expression a mixture of confusion and revulsion, and then lowered her hand and rolled her eyes. "Really, Greg? Kimchee?"

Unknown location

The man who called himself the Immortal—and sometimes Thom Martiel—placed both his fists on the tabletop, palms facing downward, and raised his eyes to look at Gavin Stone. "Choose."

A wry smile tugged at the corners of Stone's mouth. "We could make a game out of just this," he said. "Do I know enough about you to decide which hand holds the black, and which holds the white? Or even better, can I guess which you think I will choose?"

Martiel frowned. "I didn't make a deliberate choice," he said. "I mixed them up without looking. I don't know which is which. That's the whole point. Randomization."

"Nothing is truly random," Stone said, with a dismissive wave of his hand. "Even though you didn't realize it, you moved the pebbles in a very specific way. Like this…" He reached out with both hands, taking a smooth perfectly round pebble about the diameter of a nickel from each of the two bowls beside the game board, just as Martiel had done a moment before, and held them up—a white pebble in his left hand, a black pebble in his right. "This is the starting configuration."

He brought his hands together, cupping both pebbles between them, and then proceeded to shake them, like a high roller getting ready to shoot craps in Las Vegas. After a few seconds of this, he separated his hands, careful not to drop the pebbles or reveal them to either himself or Martiel. "Which hand holds the black now? Do you know?"

Martiel sighed. "Your right."

Stone shook his head. "You're just guessing. You were supposed to be paying attention. If you had watched my hands, you wouldn't have to guess."

"There's still too much uncertainty in the system," Martiel said. "Do the pebbles change place each time you shake them? There's no way for me to know."

"But there is," Stone insisted. "If you're paying attention. That's your problem. You don't pay attention. You believe there's such a thing as an unimportant detail.

That's why I always beat you."

"Not unimportant. Just unknowable. It's simple chaos theory. Some variables behave in ways that are too complex to be predicted. And I would hardly say that you 'always' beat me."

Stone laughed and then opened his right hand to reveal a black pebble. "Touché," he said, and dropped both pebbles back into their respective bowls. He then reached out with his right hand and tapped Martiel's left fist. "That one."

Martiel uncurled both hands to reveal the pebbles he was holding; the black pebble was in the hand Stone had indicated. Martiel dropped his pebbles into the bowls as well and then drew the bowl with the white pebbles closer to him.

"This is a perfect example of what I mean," Martiel went on, tapping the game board in the center of the table. It was a simple affair—a square of light-colored lacquered wood, about eighteen inches on any side, crisscrossed with a grid pattern of lines—nineteen by nineteen. "It is one of the oldest games in history. A simple game. Simple rules. Much easier to learn than chess or even checkers. The game tokens all have the same value. They don't move. There are no dice to roll. No randomness at all. Just two players taking turns placing their pebbles on the board to claim territory. And yet, from such simple beginnings, there are more possible outcomes than there are atoms in the universe. It's impossible to see all the variations from the beginning of the game."

"I love the name," Stone deadpanned. "*Go*. It's like a reminder to quit stalling."

Martiel chuckled. "I can never tell when you're being serious."

"I'm always serious about the details."

"Is that how you knew we would survive when you triggered the fire suppression system? You observed all those details that everyone else disregarded, did the math in your head, and realized the vapors from the Brazen

Head would keep our brains alive without oxygen?"

Stone stared back at him for a moment. He disliked answering questions, particularly from men like this so-called Immortal, for the same reason he was content to let Martiel ramble on about the ancient Chinese board game. When people talked, they revealed themselves to the world. Sometimes they revealed information through an off-hand comment or a Freudian slip, but more often—and to Stone's way of thinking, more importantly—they exhibited behaviors and habits that could be used for everything from determining truth or falsehood to social engineering. What Avery would call "Jedi mind tricks."

He wondered absently if he would ever see Avery again, then banished the thought. That wasn't important right now.

"I didn't know," he admitted. "I thought we were both going to die."

Martiel blinked, clearly trying to hide his incredulity. "You were willing to sacrifice your own life to stop me? I owe you an apology, Gavin. You were right. I really don't understand the first thing about you."

Good, Stone thought, but he did not say it aloud. "Then let's play."

Martiel picked up a white pebble, held it between a thumb and forefinger. "Tell me this, then. Why did you—"

"No," Stone said. "No more freebies. If you want to learn at my feet, you're going to have to earn it."

"This intrigues me. What sort of arrangement do you have in mind?"

"We play." Stone pointed at the Go board. "Winner gets to ask his question."

Martiel affected a look of surprise. "You? Need to ask me something? What was it you said? I'm an open book to you?"

"There are still one or two things I haven't figured out. I'm sure I'll get it in time, but playing for it gives me added incentive to win."

Martiel considered this for a moment. "And what

question would you ask of me?"

"I'm torn between asking your real name, or why you call yourself 'the Immortal.' I'm more interested in the latter, but I'm really afraid the answer is going to disappoint me."

Martiel chuckled. "Oh, I think you'll like that story. If you win, of course."

"Of course. And just so I know the stakes I'm playing for, what's your question?"

Martiel's smile remained, but his eyes were cold, calculating now. "I'm sure you already know. The same question I've asked you since I woke up. Why? Why didn't you turn me over to your friends? Or leave me there to die? Why did you drag me out of there, impersonate me—tell my followers that you were the Immortal and that I was you?"

He raised his hands high enough to remove most of the slack from the heavy chain attached to both his wrist and ankle manacles and shook them for emphasis. "And why are you keeping me a prisoner here?"

"I guess I should have established some rules about compound questions," Stone said. "But as it happens, there's a single answer to all of those. Not that I'll ever tell you."

"Reneging already?"

"No. I just know that I'm going to win."

Martiel held his stare a moment longer. "Black always starts. It's your move."

End

About the Authors

David Wood is the author of the popular action-adventure series, The Dane Maddock Adventures, and many other works. Under his David Debord pen name he is the author of the Absent Gods fantasy series. When not writing, he co-hosts the Authorcast podcast. David and his family live in Santa Fe, New Mexico. Visit him online at http://www.davidwoodweb.com.

Sean Ellis has authored and co-authored more than 20 action-adventure novels, including the Nick Kismet adventures, the Jack Sigler/Chess Team series with Jeremy Robinson, and the Jade Ihara adventures with David Wood. He served with the Army National Guard in Afghanistan, and has a Bachelor of Science degree in Natural Resources Policy from Oregon State University. Sean is also a member of the International Thriller Writers organization. He currently resides in Arizona, where he divides his time between writing, adventure sports, and trying to figure out how to save the world.

Made in the USA
San Bernardino, CA
30 April 2017